Missing Werecat

P. G. Allison

Cover design 2015 by Cormar Covers
www.cormarcovers.com

Missy the Werecat

Missy_the_Werecat@verizon.net

To be notified when P. G. Allison's next novel is released, go to: http://eepurl.com/bCtlh5 and sign up for the Missy the Werecat Newsletter. Your email address will never be shared and you may unsubscribe at any time.

Missy the Werecat

Table of Contents

Prologue

Imagine a world where werecats at one time did indeed exist, but became extinct eons ago. Then, because their recessive genes managed to survive and get passed on -- thanks to some rare unions with humans -- DNA with these special werecat genes continued down through the ages, further evolving and being inherited by a very small number of descendants. And finally, imagine that two of these very unique individuals -- each one in a billion -- would meet, fall in love and become parents. While three of their four children would be normal humans, one -- their daughter Missy -- would be very special. She would be a werecat.

And thus, Missy the werecat was born in today's era. She's not exactly the same as those ancestor werecats, but she does have many special abilities -- not the least of which is being able to transform, with a great shimmer of light and burst of energy, into another form. She can Change from being fully human in one instant to being a cat animal in the next. In her cat form, she has the same body mass as in her human form and fully retains her human intellect and memory. And, in either form, she has all the instincts and abilities of a wild, predatory mountain lion.

Eventually, she will learn how to Change forms back and forth, and how to manage and control her special abilities. Her genetic anomaly, combined with some evolution along the way, brings her cat endowments into her human form: speed, strength, agility, and enhanced senses of smell, hearing, taste and sight. She is also gifted with rapid healing and is immune to disease. As Missy will gradually learn about herself, she will go from being a girl with great skills to a grown woman with truly fantastic powers.

Chapter One
Jul 2013

In the middle of her last night at soccer camp, Missy awakened with a strong desire to get up and go outside. She just knew this was something she had to do, and right away. So, slipping out of bed and quietly making her way down from her dormitory room, she did go out. Although there was a full moon, it was cloudy and very dark outside, with no streetlights or anything else to illuminate the landscape. However, the darkness did not bother her at all. She could feel something pulling at her, drawing her away from the dorm. And, she also noticed her ability to see in the dark was somehow much greater than ever before.

She had always been able to see, hear and smell things to an extent far greater than those around her, but tonight it was even more so. She knew she had other special abilities as well. She had gradually come to realize that others were not able to do all the things which she could do. She had accepted that she was just different. She had shown an athletic ability which was quite advanced, excelling in little league and youth soccer programs, as well as at karate practice and during any gymnastic events. She easily had won all the competitive races at school and in her local community. All of that had lead to her attending soccer camp every summer.

Soccer camp was in Keene, NH and near Monadnock Mountain. It was now late July, a month after her 13th birthday, and Missy had really been enjoying her time back at this wonderful camp once again. It was so beautiful there! A whole week away from home, where she was getting some elite training in a sport where, as a junior high school player, she had already been noted as being really special. Her mom was keeping all the news articles written about her in a special scrapbook along with several photos.

As this week at camp had been coming to a close, she'd been getting more and more excited about the fall season coming up. This would be her last year in junior high and she just knew her soccer team would go on to win the state championship this year and get to compete in the nationals. Then, the following year, she would finally be competing at the high school level. Her older brother and sister had both been telling her all about the fun activities they were experiencing in high school, and she could hardly wait to get there.

At night, she typically found herself anticipating and dreaming vividly about many of these things and had no trouble sleeping soundly all night long. That's why waking up with this sudden need to go outside in the middle of the night came as such a complete surprise. *What made her wake up and why did she feel this compulsion so strongly?* She could not understand what was happening. Her entire body was experiencing something new and strange, something she had never felt before. Her heart was pounding and her blood was racing! *And, just why was she having all these tingly feelings?*

Once outside, she was drawn towards the nearby trees which marked the edge of the deeper forest and she quickly walked over to them, crossing the courtyard and the small parking lot. The full moon suddenly came out from behind the clouds, shining down brightly. She glanced backwards just once, looking back the way she had come at the dormitory building she was leaving behind. She was thinking, "*What am I doing? Why am I out here?*" But, then she turned and walked deeper into the woods. She just knew this was something urgent and absolutely necessary.

Further and further she went, all the while continuing to experience all kinds of new feelings, with her senses hyper alert and more aware of sights and sounds and smells than ever before. Since she still had not had her first period, she began to wonder if that might be what this was all about. Puberty! Yes, she had been anxiously waiting for this as most of her girlfriends had already had their first period and had started growing hair on their legs, under their arms, etc. Shaving had been a big topic amongst the girls! And, boobs! And boys!

Missy was somewhat of a late bloomer and had not yet really developed. She'd not had her first period yet, in spite of various signs that things would be happening for her very soon. She had experienced some swelling of her breasts and tenderness of her nipples but was concerned she still looked very flat compared to most of the other girls. Although she now did have some hair growing in new places, she had not yet shaved under her arms ... *when would she finally be getting her period anyway!?!*

But all the talks she'd had with her mother and her sister about this important subject had not really suggested anything like what she was feeling right now.

Not only was she physically reacting to something, she was also getting so many thoughts and emotional signals. Whatever was happening was compelling her to be out here ... *something irresistible was forcing her.* Nothing had prepared her for this. And yet, remarkably, she was not at all afraid. Somehow, she just knew ...

And then ... *it happened!* Her body just collapsed and her mind was overwhelmed, going to a quiet place deep within itself. She didn't lose consciousness but felt as though she was in a dream state. She had no control. She knew there was some sort of Change happening to her and then there was a shimmer of light and a burst of energy. She could feel this was coming from within, from *somewhere* deep inside and from *something* that was a part of her. There was no pain or discomfort during this Change. Then, in the next moment, everything was suddenly new and different. *Very different!*

She was a cat. Her form was no longer human but that of a large animal, very much like a mountain lion. She had no idea of that, at least at first. She did notice a huge difference in the sounds and smells around her, which now were even more noticeable. And when she looked out at her surroundings, she could see much more clearly, but without all the color. Since it was dark, there wasn't much awareness of that just yet. Instead, she was noticing more the way things felt to her body. Her arms and legs were very different and were covered with fur. So was the rest of her body, even her face. Her hands and feet were now paws -- paws with claws which could extend and retract.

Missy got up from where she was lying, but now it was on all fours. As she took a few steps, the reality of her new form gradually seeped in. She still weighed the same. But, as she moved, *everything was different.* New and strange at first. Yet, somehow, in this form, she seemed to have an instinct for just what to do. She did not stumble or fall. She wanted to explore, to get a sense for her surroundings. She also wanted to shimmy out of the clothes she was still wearing which were loose yet still restrictive. As she rubbed against some bushes to help remove these bedtime garments, her thoughts began to race. She tried to mentally cope with what had happened, with her new animal form, even as her body processed all the ways she was now experiencing everything so differently.

Once free from her clothing, she knew she needed to move on and get away, to head out through the trees and go onward to find somewhere she could be safe. This need was not a conscious thought, but something instinctive … something part of the awareness she now had in her new form. Slowly at first, but then with an easy pace, she began to follow the paths leading off through the dense underbrush. She knew there was a mountain nearby and she headed in that direction.

Once she had travelled a while and was far enough out so the sounds of civilization had all faded away, she began to really notice the scents of various other animals. She somehow knew that nighttime was when she must hunt, when she must find prey, in order to satisfy the hunger which was now raging inside. It did not take long before she sensed a raccoon up ahead. With almost no thought other than how she needed to do this, she followed the scent until she was able to surprise the animal and leap onto its back, quickly crushing its neck with her jaws. She had made her first kill. She had found food.

While she was eating, her human thoughts returned and she realized her thinking had become compartmentalized. For a while, *her human thoughts had been set aside*, deep within, in order to free her basic instincts which were needed to hunt and feed. And, another of those survival instincts was now telling her to find safety in an area of deep undergrowth and cover. Then, maybe she could think better, try to understand what had happened and consider what to do. She wanted to calmly gather her wits about her now that she was over the initial shock of being in this new form.

She knew she must eventually continue onward, up into the mountain where it would truly be safe. She was concerned about not only her own safety, but the safety of others as well. She wasn't at all sure what amount of control she even had in her new form. But, for now, having fed and escaped all immediate threats, she needed to stop and rest. As the dawn approached, she allowed her ignorance and concern about what had happened to subside and gave in to the desire and need for sleep. Her first Change had not only made her ravenous but had also made her exhausted. So, she settled down and quickly drifted into as deep a sleep as cats are able to manage, while all her senses remained on alert should any actions be needed.

Missy thus began the process which would meld her dual nature into one. This would take some time, with several learning stages to yet go through before full acceptance and understanding would be reached. But, life's experiences would be her teacher and achieving a balance between her human side and her cat form would indeed take place. She would evolve and she would grow into her full werecat potential.

Back at soccer camp, Missy had disappeared. When she didn't show up for breakfast or that day's scheduled activities, the staff members began a search. After a few hours, they realized she really could not be found and phone calls were made. Her family was contacted. The police were called in. An investigation was started and the search quickly expanded with all possible resources being pulled in. Since no one could believe she would go off on her own and none of her belongings were missing from her room, there was great concern that she'd been kidnapped. The FBI was then called in.

Her family members were all quickly eliminated as suspects due to the distance of the soccer camp away from their home in Salem, Massachusetts and they all had various alibis, easily corroborated by their neighbors and co-workers.

After a few days, her discarded pajamas were found in the nearby woods. As this was days later and out in some dry, heavily wooded terrain, no sign remained of any large animal tracks which she might have left behind. The worry she'd been grabbed by someone was thus only further reinforced. The media spent many days covering the story of the missing girl from soccer camp, speculating all about her being a kidnapping victim with various possible scenarios including murder by some sexual predator.

Missy was gone!

Chapter Two
Aug 2013 -- Jul 2015

And so, while her family and friends desperately sought for answers, while the investigators explored every possible explanation and while the media gave wider and wider coverage for Missy's mysterious disappearance, time went on. And Missy? She went up into the mountains which was the only thing she believed she could do. First, she spent a few weeks exploring Monadnock Mountain, making that her territory. In time, as the months went by, she traveled all through the White Mountains of New Hampshire. She endured the bitter cold of winter, coping with various trials and tribulations but managing to survive.

She also tried to cope with what had happened to her, in spite of having no way of knowing how or why. While becoming a predatory cat animal which must hunt and kill other animals was not something easy to understand or adjust to, Missy nonetheless did eventually grow to accept herself and she learned to just keep going forward. She now experienced life in her cat form, while continuing to think with her human intellect. She simply adapted to this dual nature. When she looked at her reflection in any pool of water, she saw her large mountain lion appearance with a tawny, reddish color coat. She saw she had a very long tail. And whiskers. Her eyes were still green but now also had a somewhat golden appearance. Fortunately, she could recall and review all her childhood memories from before, when she was human. And so she lived each day, one day at a time -- as a cat.

Her cat instincts helped her quickly learn all she needed for surviving on her own. Things like finding food and water and how to stalk and ambush her prey and knowing how to cover her meals to hide and protect them from other animals. She learned to defend her kills from wolves and bears but tried to avoid such conflicts when she could. Her survival instincts also make her avoid humans, staying in dense forests and unpopulated mountains. These same instincts convinced her she must not return to civilization. The fear of the unknown was much too great whenever any thoughts of doing that arose. No, she accepted she was now a large cat and, since she had no idea how to reverse that, how to Change back to human form, she avoided all threat of being found. Only in isolation did she feel sure of being safe.

But, even in the mountains she wasn't always safe. She was attacked and badly wounded by a black bear the next spring. The bear was hungry, after hibernating all winter, and challenged her for a deer she had killed. She let her cat instincts to fight and defend her food control her actions. Although she actually won that conflict and chased the bear away, she was badly mauled on her left shoulder and back during the fierce fighting. That healed up well enough over the next few days but did leave some permanent scars. From this, she learned to not always allow her cat's nature to be in control of things, which was a valuable lesson.

Then, she received another permanent scar along her upper right thigh from a hunter's bullet.

Somehow, he'd gotten within range without her noticing him. The bullet only creased her leg, without damaging any bone or internal organs, so she did consider herself lucky. And, healing was again very rapid. But, it was the surprise encounter with that hunter which caused her to migrate south, leaving the White Mountains. She traveled down through the Appalachian and Adirondack Mountain Regions and ended up a year later in the Blue Ridge Mountains of Virginia.

Meanwhile, the search for Missy continued, in spite of there being absolutely no clues and her case gradually growing colder and colder. Her family never gave up hope and exhausted all possible avenues in their search. Her mom and dad were frantic at first but then grew more and more determined as the weeks and months went by. Since her family was somewhat affluent, although not rich by any means, they were able to keep the pressure on and influence the community. Efforts to find Missy remained constant. Every few weeks, a renewal of those efforts was made, with various rally events and fund raising endeavors to continue the search, raise awareness and hold the public's attention.

The TV and media coverage was extensive, with the story of her disappearance brought up again and again. Pictures of her were everywhere. While the speculation was mostly about whether some sexual predator had grabbed her and then, had either murdered her or was keeping her as a slave, this did keep the story going. While her family was not very happy with what these stories were saying, they were hopeful that all the attention might somehow lead to someone coming forward with information.

The FBI assigned Robert Ulrey to the case. He was their top investigator from the Boston office and he kept in constant touch with the family and local authorities. He also utilized all the resources available to the FBI to the fullest. But, all to no avail. With no leads to follow, there really was not much he could do.

With eighteen years in the Bureau, his background in investigations was broad and extensive and in recent years, he had worked several high profile kidnapping cases. He looked like a cop, probably because of his military background. He had served as a Military Police officer in the Army for eight years, after graduating from college where he had received an ROTC scholarship. He still kept his hair neatly cropped close to his head and now that it was somewhat grey, that only added to his official look. He was six feet tall and kept in shape, working out at the gym and running on weekends.

He had been married for fifteen years but was now divorced for the past seven years. They had not had any children and he often wondered if that would have made a difference. His wife had never been happy with what he had become and how the job had changed him over the years.

The kidnapping cases he'd worked had usually involved either high ransom demands or else, as he suspected had happened to Missy, the kidnapper had abducted the person for sex. Whether the victim was then murdered, released or continued being held would depend on all sorts of things and these cases were always difficult. He knew it had affected him, ruined his marriage, working these kidnappings; but he also knew it was important for someone with his background and experience to be the one taking the lead in order to give these victims their best chance for rescue.

For Missy's investigation, it soon became apparent that ransom was not being asked for. And, she had not run away. With all he'd learned about her that scenario simply did not seem possible. She was not at all depressed or unhappy or acting strange or showing any signals to suggest that; just the opposite. And, after going through everything on her smart phone and iPad, there was no evidence she had been lured away or been in contact with anyone who might be a suspect. They cleared all possible people whom she might have had any relationship with, including the various relatives of those people. There was no evidence of anyone having targeted her. Whoever might have grabbed her had left no clues, no trace, nothing they could find to go on.

Since her pajamas were found in the nearby woods and nothing was missing from her belongings, it really looked as though she'd been grabbed by someone. The FBI's lab went over her clothes thoroughly and had samples of her DNA which her family had provided. The discarded pajamas did not have human DNA from anyone else other than Missy. There was no blood. There were some animal hairs but since the pajamas had been in the woods for several days, finding those didn't seem very significant. There simply was nothing to go on. Everything had been checked and checked again but that had all led nowhere and the case was truly cold.

Even so, Robert kept the file open and it was always on his desk. After all the hours he'd invested, all the time he'd spent learning about Missy, interviewing family, friends, doctors, teachers and coaches, he felt as though he knew her. He really wanted this one to end well. Often, he would review his notes, trying to find some new direction for this case. He had summarized all the key information he'd obtained, with highlights and references entered on the first page in her file:

- *Missy McCrea was born in Salem, Massachusetts exactly at midnight on the summer solstice in the year 2000. Since "the stroke of midnight" was considered to be the next day, her birthday was recorded as June 22.*

- *Her father Philip McCrea was forty-one and her mother Julia was thirty-nine. Philip was partner in the industrial law firm of McCrea-Winslow, Inc. He had both a bachelor's degree and a master's degree in engineering and also a law degree. Julia McCrea was a human resources manager. Missy was the third of four children: she had a sister, Heather, seventeen; a brother John, fifteen; a brother Patrick, ten. They lived at 29 Walnut Street, Salem, Massachusetts. (See family history and photos in separate file.)*

- *At thirteen, Missy was five feet six inches and her weight was about 100 pounds. She was tall and thin but very strong and physically fit. (Her athletic accomplishments, even at this early age, were very impressive. See separate file with copy of mother's scrapbook.)*

- *Her doctor and dentist expressed amazement concerning her perfect health and teeth. She never got sick, quickly healed after any injury and hadn't needed any dental work. No scars or birthmarks. (See medical records and doctor interviews in separate file.)*

- *She was very bright and had done well at school. She was a natural leader, setting the example while drawing others to strive towards her goals. They got included in her accomplishments and achievements, "basking in the glow" of shared victories. She managed to somehow avoid the jealous envy of her peers, instead drawing their admiration and respect. From all accounts, she was very protective, always standing up to any bully for those unable to do so. The trust and loyalty which that brought, along with her being so athletic plus her way of "making things fun", all combined to make her a very popular girl with everyone wanting to be her friend. (See teacher and coach interviews in separate file.)*

- *Soccer camp. No incidents, no visitors, no indication Missy was upset, unhappy, or might go off alone. She was getting along great with all the other kids there. Nothing was missing from her belongings. Pajamas were found in the nearby woods. Camp staff members were all cleared. (See separate file on soccer camp.)*

From all the photos, she was a really pretty girl, with dark red hair and deep green eyes, a very nice proportional nose plus a beautiful smile with vertical crease lines in her cheeks like dimples. She had a fair complexion which her Mother explained would tan rather than burn out in the sunlight. Her facial features and bone structure were classic and what everyone found very attractive. She did have a somewhat "feline" look which only added to his impression that, when she grew up, she would indeed be stunning. If she grew up. Her innocent, attractive appearance was what perhaps had made her a target. He dreaded the day he might learn her body had been found, when his case would then become a murder investigation.

Of course, the thought of her being held by a kidnapper did not reduce his anxiety and concern by much. The various ways that might play out did not offer much hope for a happy resolution.

Chapter Three
Aug 2015

After migrating south to the Blue Ridge Mountains, Missy continued living day to day, relying on her instincts and managing to survive well enough as a mountain lion. Her favorite prey were deer but she used various animals in the wild as a food source, such as elk, moose, sheep, coyotes, hogs, mice, squirrels, rabbits and even porcupines. She did not hunt any domestic cattle, sheep, horses or other animals not out in the wild since she knew it was necessary to avoid humans and didn't want to attract any attention. On many occasions she had eaten fish, birds and reptiles. She had managed to avoid having any further conflicts with bears, although she often still was the one to chase them away. If that strategy did not work, she would then be the one to leave as she didn't want to risk fighting like that again. Once was enough!

She also managed to avoid the occasional male mountain lion which would appear and get very interested whenever she came into heat. That had not been a problem during the first year when she was in the White Mountains, but after she fully matured, filling out and gaining weight to her full size, her cat went into heat regularly. She learned this would last for seven or eight days out of every twenty three to twenty four days. After six of these cycles she would stop but two months later, these cycles would be repeated. Since she was still able to think as a human, and definitely did not want to allow her cat's basic nature to have its way during these cycles, this was one instinct she did not give in to. She had learned how to balance between her human side and her cat form.

She also avoided hunters. She avoided any situation which might attract human attention. This isolation lifestyle was very difficult for Missy and she still missed terribly being with her family and friends, competing in sports and learning in school. But, she had adapted, survived and done what she'd needed to do while still dreaming about those days. Her memories sustained her and she continued to have hopes and dreams, while prowling throughout the territory she had established for herself up in the mountains.

And, it was there, just over two years from her first Shift into cat form when, finally, she managed to Shift again. She discovered she could actually Shift back to her human form. She had often stretched out and dreamed of doing this, without success. At first, it had been too early for her werecat nature which had forced itself upon her. Later, she simply had not quite managed to trigger a Shift correctly. But eventually, she did find the right combination, going back into that quiet place in her mind and making a really determined exercise of her will. And so, on this particular day, when she did both of these things just right, once again there was a shimmer of light and burst of energy from within and, in the next moment, she was lying there naked, in human form. Wow!

She had grown, being two years older. She discovered her body had now fully developed. She was bigger and taller; she would later learn just how much she had grown. She was five feet eight inches tall, 130 pounds, solid and very well toned. She also was very curvy with lovely breasts and wide hips. She was no longer that skinny, flat chested little girl. Her hair had grown out more than a foot longer than before and was now well past her shoulders. Those shoulders were also wide and her back was straight and strong, but her waist was small. More important than noticing any of these physical attributes, she was ecstatic to be in human form again! Her hands and feet were no longer paws and she reached up and touched her face, feeling the smooth skin.

Since the day was warm and sunny, she was able to go out and enjoy being able to walk around on two feet. She marveled at now experiencing everything as a human, with a zillion thoughts and feelings all at once. Life was good! She was flooded with emotions as various thoughts crowded in, competing with one another. It was overwhelming but in a way which was really nice, making her so happy!

After enjoying several hours of this euphoric bliss, she gradually realized she was alone in the wilderness, hungry and that evening was coming, bringing with it much cooler temperatures. In human form, this would be somewhat of a problem. But, she just knew with a deep inner certainty that she could now Change back and forth. With a sense of great excitement, she focused with all her might on what it was like to be in cat form, let her mind go where she knew it needed to go, drew upon her tremendous will and was easily able to experience the Change. Just as she knew she would!

Back in cat form, she returned to where she had hidden the remains of the last deer she had killed and she satisfied her raging appetite. She realized those energy bursts associated with her Changing forms did require that she eat lots of food in order to make up for all the calories which were burned. Feeling a great sense of satisfaction and peace, she settled down and went into a deep sleep for the rest of the night.

The next day, she once again Shifted back to human form and ran out into a meadow where she could really just enjoy being alive, once again able to run and jump and sense things the way she had before, before she had Changed that first time. She was thrilled. While still not understanding how or why she was the way she was, she now could at least find some way to return to a life which was not so alone, so isolated. She was convinced she could once again live back with humans.

But, Missy knew she first needed to make sure she really could always be in control. She never wanted to have the Change forced on her the way it had happened that first time. The safety of her family, friends and everyone around her would depend on that. So, for several days she allowed herself to experience being human, up in the mountains where she was safe. She would only Change back into her cat form when she was either too hungry or too cold. Now that she had finally learned how, she found she could easily do this, and she practiced her control. She learned she could trigger the Change either way, but that once she Changed it was necessary to wait at least three hours before she could Change back. And, she would always be very hungry from doing this.

She also was able to figure out a few other things about herself. Apparently, when she had lived as a cat for those many months, her body had continued to grow and develop. She had known she was getting bigger and stronger while still in cat form, but now that she could Change back to human form, she was able to see and appreciate all the changes. And, since her hair had grown out by the same amount as if she had remained human for all those months, she guessed all her physical changes were probably like that. These changes were merely what would have normally happened to her human form over that same time period. But in addition, her life as a cat had required staying in top form, continuously exercising and that was reflected in how strong and well developed her human form had become. There was some carryover from how she was in one form to how she was in the other.

She did see that she now had some scars. Although faded, there were scars on her back and left shoulder area, from where that black bear had mauled her so badly, and also high on her right thigh from being grazed by that bullet. So, again, obviously some things carried over. But, what really showed her how things worked, best of all, was the way she got a sunburn during those first few days. When she'd first Changed back, her skin was very white. Being exposed to the sun as a cat had not carried over to her human skin getting a tan. But then, after several days out in the sun in human form, she was now getting brown all over and this stayed with her as she continued to Change back and forth. She suspected if she were to cut her hair, the new shorter length would likewise stay with her, only growing back at the normal rate.

She spent three weeks getting comfortable in her own skin, learning all about herself, her dual nature and what being back in human form was like. During this time, she also began to plan what steps she could take to finally return home, back to her family and to the life she hoped she could now make for herself. Yes, now that she was able to control which form she could take and stay in full control while in either form, she hoped she could make all her dreams come true. But first, she needed to leave the mountains. And, to do that, she needed to find some clothes.

Chapter Four
Late evening Aug 25 & early morning Aug 26

Missy knew various locations where campers were scattered throughout the region and it was not at all difficult to sneak down to the lower elevations and into one such camp site during the night. She avoided camps where there were any dogs since even just her scent had always made them start barking furiously. That used to bother her before she'd learned about her cat form but now she could understand it.

She found a pair of blue jean shorts and a purple colored sweater which had been left outside on a clothesline. She Changed into human form and tried on these items. They were a few sizes too big but that was not really a problem. The sweater, which was two years old, had faded lettering for the Baltimore Ravens, Superbowl XLVII Champions. For the shorts, she was able to tie together some of the belt loops, drawing them tight enough using a short piece of plastic rope which was lying nearby.

Silently, she slipped back out and headed on down the road.

The next day, there were others also destined to be on the same road as Missy. That morning a man named Bill Stratton called out to his wife Mary, "We're all checked out of our room so make a last look around and let's go." He had just finished strapping their five year old daughter Emily into her car seat and had turned on the little DVD player hanging from the back of the rental car's front passenger seat. It was now playing one of her favorite Disney movies and that would keep her happy and content for a little while.

Several minutes later, Mary returned from the hotel room they'd been staying at and replied, "We're good. I just had to make sure none of Emily's toys were anywhere back there. You know how cranky she gets when she loses any of her favorite toys. I know once we're on the road to our cabin, you won't want to come back here looking for anything, right?"

"Right. Thanks!" Bill closed the car door and walked behind the car. Mary handed him Emily's little suitcase along with one of her own and he slid them into the trunk, on top of all their other bags. Mary got into the car and turned around to check on Emily while he closed the trunk lid and walked around to get behind the wheel on the driver's side. Once he had the car started, he backed out of the parking space and headed through the hotel's parking lot. "We're on our way! Vacation at last, honey!"

They'd been staying at a hotel in Roanoke, Virginia after flying in two days earlier. Bill had met with some of his investors and business associates to discuss the new luxury hotel they were planning for this region but now he was done with work and they were starting their week's vacation. After many visits to this area, they'd finally bought a cabin two years earlier located on a beautiful lake up in the Blue Ridge Mountains. Their close friend Senator Ed Maxwell was going to join them; he'd be driving over from Washington D.C. the next day.

Bill and the senator had been fraternity brothers while attending college and had continued their friendship in the years ever since then. Conveniently, the Stratton home was very near to the senator's Washington D.C. residence.

The senator was driving over rather than flying and was bringing Bill's golf clubs with him. He was always flying from place to place and enjoyed any opportunity to go by car instead. When he and Bill had finished playing their weekly round of golf that past weekend and the senator had been putting Bill's clubs into the back of his own car, he'd said to Bill, "I'm glad to save us both the extra baggage fees the airlines charge now for golf clubs. That's a good enough excuse for my driving, right?"

Laughing, Bill had assured him, "Absolutely! And, I do appreciate it. I've got enough stuff already with everything Mary is bringing. Plus we have Emily's car seat. I've rented a full size car but I doubt there would be any room for my clubs. We're really glad you can join us this time, Ed." In addition to golfing, they planned on doing some fishing. Bill had plenty of fishing equipment already at the cabin, along with a small boat they could take out on the lake.

Now, leaving the hotel parking lot, the Stratton family was on its way up to the mountains. They would be taking the Blue Ridge Parkway once they left Roanoke, and should be arriving at their cabin just before noon. However, theirs was not the only vehicle which would be travelling on the parkway that morning.

Tim looked over at Rich, driving next to him, and then into the back seat once again. The two girls sitting back there were the reason he and Rich were only now finally headed up into the mountains to join their other friends instead of already being up at the campsite. Denise couldn't get away until this morning and Gail wanted to wait for her friend. So, they'd missed the big first night party up there but it was worth it. These girls were fun and incredibly hot. He and Gail had been dating all summer and this weekend was one of their last before he'd be leaving for his first semester away at college. Rich was laughing and said, "Don't worry, guys! I'll have us up there in no time. The parkway is just up ahead and ..."

"Yeah," said Tim. "And it's all uphill from there!"

"Oh, but Rich loves these mountain roads," said Denise. "Last weekend, he drove me up there, just the two of us. It was so romantic! Of course, I had my eyes closed half the time while he was going up and down that parkway, since my stomach just does flip flops going around those curves. But, we got up there and back, no problem."

Their car then turned onto the parkway and Rich accelerated, picking up speed. He intended to get them up there as quickly as possible so they'd not miss out on any more than they'd already missed. He knew his friends were not going to wait around for them and he wanted to get there before they left for the afternoon's activities.

Meanwhile, heading down out of the mountains, Jim and his co-worker, also named Jim, were enjoying the great views. Their boss called them Jimmy One and Jimmy Two. Jimmy One was driving the company's Mack truck, loaded with large appliances headed for a warehouse in Georgia, and he said, "Whenever you can spare the extra time and can get the chance to drive through these mountains, it's really worth it. So much of our regular route is just one monotonous mile after the other."

"I see what you mean," said the other Jim. "And you're so right about how boring most of these road trips can be. I'm glad this trip worked out this way. Stopping for the night up at that campsite and waking up this morning, looking at the mountains reflected in the lake … I'll definitely want to arrange my schedule so I can do this a few more times."

"Yep! There's just no way that any crappy motel room can compare with that," agreed the Jim who was driving as he approached a bend in the road and applied the brakes. Once back onto a straight section, he released the brakes and coasted along for a while until they got to the next curve, when he once again applied the brakes. They were not in any hurry as they'd arrive in Atlanta that afternoon in plenty of time to drop off their appliances and pick up their next load.

As the dawn was breaking, Missy found herself walking along the Blue Ridge Parkway which led down out of the mountains and into the city of Roanoke. She continued her descent for a couple of hours with only the occasional vehicle going by, either going up into the mountains or, like herself, headed down out of them. A large Mack truck was one of the vehicles coming down out of the mountains but when it drove past Missy at a leisurely pace, she didn't pay much attention to it. She was thinking about home.

Suddenly, not too far ahead but still out of sight from where she was, she could hear the screech of tires followed by a loud crunch. This was quickly followed by the sound of a car crashing down the side of a cliff. She ran toward this commotion, racing at top speed and as she came around the final bend she could see two vehicles which had pulled over, a car and a very large truck ... the same Mack truck which had just passed her. There were several people out standing along one side of the road. They were all looking down the embankment which showed signs of a car having gone over the edge.

As she ran up, she could hear snatches of conversations. It quickly became clear from the comments and from where the two vehicles had stopped, just what had happened to a third car. One car had been trying to pass the other when, from the opposite direction around the bend, the large Mack truck had suddenly appeared. The vehicles had all scrambled, attempting to avoid head on collisions, but when the car which had attempted passing had pulled back over, out of the path of the oncoming truck, it had cut off the other car. That car was then forced off the road after smashing into the rear quarter panel of the passing car, making the loud crunching sound which Missy had heard.

While the onlookers continued to mill around, she noticed the distinct smell of gasoline rising up from below. She realized whoever was in that car needed to get out and away before their car exploded into flames. Without any further thought, she started down the cliff taking advantage of her physical skills combined with her enhanced abilities. These enabled her to practically rappel down the side of the steep cliff, which was quite a shear drop, and she quickly reached the car where it had ended up on its passenger side, more than a hundred feet below.

At the car, she could see where fuel was leaking out and she knew she had to move fast. Grabbing a large rock, she smashed the driver's side rear window and crawled into the car. Broken glass shards cut into her arms, legs and back but ignoring that she quickly grabbed the man who was in the driver's seat by the back of his shirt. She saw he had managed to unbuckle his seat belt but was still somewhat in shock, gazing over to his right and mumbling to the woman in the passenger seat. But, she was not responding. Missy yanked the man right out of his seat and pushed him up and through the smashed window. She then reached down and unbuckled the woman's seat belt and yanked her out as well. The woman slowly began to regain consciousness and moaned but made no resistance.

Missy quickly backed her way out through the window, pushing the man ahead of her and pulling the woman behind her. Once out, she dragged the two of them away from the car and up towards some cover afforded by an outcropping of rocks several feet away. She positioned them both behind these rocks and then hurried right back to the car since there was a small child, a little girl, still trapped in there. Missy had noticed the girl when she'd first climbed in, wedged in the back and buckled into a car seat.

Under the car, flames suddenly appeared, along with a whooshing sound just as Missy was diving back through the car window. She now needed to move really fast and all of a sudden, added strength and speed from her cat form just flowed into her. This happened without her having to Change. This was a new experience for Missy, being able to draw on her cat while still human. Apparently, when it was a life or death situation, this ability was possible for her.

With no time to deal with all the buckles and straps holding the child into the car seat, she just yanked them out using her superhuman strength, thanks to her unique werecat inheritance. (This incredible feat would not be discovered by the investigators later, since the evidence would simply get destroyed in the fire.) Backing out through the window once again but with the car now engulfed in flames, Missy started to move away clutching the child tightly to her chest. After taking only a few steps, however, she was violently knocked off her feet when the car finally exploded. She went flying but somehow managed to cradle the little girl within herself, protecting her from any injury by moving into a fetal position with her body, arms and legs all completely surrounding the child.

Missy was knocked unconscious when her head banged onto a large rock. Luckily, she continued to roll further down the hill, away from the burning car. In spite of blacking out, she never let go of the little girl, keeping her tucked closely within her protective embrace. And, that's how they both would be found, still clutched together, more than an hour later when the rescue team finally arrived on the scene.

Meanwhile, Bill and Mary Stratton, the man and woman she had rescued, were both okay but didn't realize Missy and their child Emily had managed to escape. In the aftermath of the huge explosion, their first concern was for their little girl. They were slowly starting to recover their senses but were still dazed, somewhat numb and in shock from their ordeal. First, from their car having gone off the road and crashing onto the rocks at the bottom of a steep cliff. And then, from somehow being miraculously dragged to safety. Even so, they tried to approach the burning car, but the intense heat from the flames was too great. Horrified, they could only stand there, watching helplessly while grief and despair overwhelmed them.

Only when the rescue team came down to assist was it discovered that, by some miracle, no one was inside the car. Quickly, a search of the area was performed and Missy's crumpled body was found, quite a distance away, where she had landed and rolled after being blown up in the explosion. Her sweater and shorts were scorched, she had some burns, she was bleeding from numerous cuts and scratches, and she was out cold. At first glance, they thought she was dead. But, when one member of the rescue team made his way down to where she was lying, he found she was still alive and was holding onto the little girl, who had not received any injuries at all. Not a scratch. It was truly a miracle!

Chapter Five

Late morning Aug 26

Things up on the road at the scene of the accident had gone from very hectic to a controlled chaos which eventually did settle down. There had been two men in the truck and the driver had used his cell phone to call 911 right away after he had pulled over and stopped. They both had gotten out and walked over to see where the car had gone off the road. Four teenagers had emerged from the other car and had joined them. The teenagers had all started arguing with one another about what had happened and then were apologizing to the men from the truck. They had all been trying to see over the edge of the road, looking for the third car, when Missy had come running up and without even stopping, she had gone right over the edge and down the cliff.

No one had been able to see anything since the cliff face was so steep, but they all had heard when Missy smashed the window, not even a minute later. And then, shortly after that, there had been the huge explosion followed by flames and smoke rising up from the fire. At first, they all had assumed anyone down there had to be dead. But then, they'd heard the anguished cries from the man and woman below. It seemed impossible but somehow, there had been survivors! They'd called down with assurances that help was on the way. And, the truck driver had dialed 911 again to explain there were some survivors who needed help.

The police and a rescue team did arrive, forty minutes later, coming up from the city of Roanoke which was closest. But it then took another fifteen minutes before the team was able to get down to the car below and put out the fire. There was a news helicopter circling the area, taking film shots for the evening news. They actually managed getting there in time to film the fire, just before the rescue team put it out. They also filmed all the rescue activities which followed.

The couple being rescued was too distraught about losing their little girl and would not leave the burned out car. Then, when it was determined there were no dead bodies inside, a search led to Missy being found further down the cliff. And, when it was learned she had managed to save the little girl who was not injured in any way, there were shouts and screams of joy from the couple. Soon the three Stratton family members were all hoisted up to the road above, where an ambulance waited to take them to the hospital.

More police and firemen arrived plus another ambulance. The stretcher went down for Missy and she was carefully hoisted up and put into the second ambulance. Once both ambulances were gone, the firemen went down to look at what was left of the car, assisted by the rescue team, while the police took charge of everything up above. Interviews were done, statements were recorded, photos and measurements were taken and the investigation at the scene was completed. Temporary railings along the edge of the road were erected, with police tape and markers. Gradually, everyone dispersed and one of the police cars was the last to finally leave.

Outside the William Osborne Memorial Hospital in Roanoke, it had been real busy for a while, with two ambulances pulling in along with a police car. Two news teams had already been waiting, one from the newspaper and the other from the local TV station. The word had spread about the miracle rescue, with a little girl being saved along with her parents. The evening news on TV would be showing the car fire being put out as well as where it had crashed down the side of a steep cliff from the road above. And, there would be all the rescue team actions plus the police and fire men at the scene.

No one yet had any details about what Missy had done, but enough of the story had leaked out to raise speculation about the mystery girl who was somehow involved with this miracle. Thus, when the ambulances arrived at the hospital, these received a lot of attention, as everyone wanted to get all the details for what clearly was a very big story.

When the rescued family members emerged from the first ambulance, they were each on a stretcher which was rushed inside. The news teams did get film and photo coverage but there were no statements given out. Then, when Missy was taken from the second ambulance, this was repeated. And, once inside, only doctors and nurses were allowed beyond the emergency room, so it was another hour of waiting before any news was given out. Then, it was announced the little girl was unharmed and her parents were also okay, with the mild concussion for the mother being the most severe injury. They would all be kept overnight for observation but it was expected they would be released the next day.

As for Missy, no one knew who she was or anything about where she had come from. Her condition was critical and she was in the ICU. The extent of her injuries was still being evaluated but she had definitely suffered a severe blow to the head and had not regained consciousness. It was announced no further information would be available for at least a day or two.

The news teams then focused on the police and firemen, the witnesses and the rescue team. The police were able to provide identities for the Stratton family and were conducting a search hoping to learn who the mystery girl was and how she had happened to be there. Missy had simply appeared out of nowhere and, without a word, had gone over the edge and dropped out of sight. Details were learned how she had somehow managed to get down to the car, smash the window and pull all three people out. The truck driver had provided his account and one of the rescue workers had also been telling his story.

That rescue worker had talked to the little girl's parents at the scene down below when he'd first arrived and while they'd been frantically worrying about their daughter. All they'd known was someone had pulled them to safety and then had gone back but suddenly there'd been the big explosion. This rescue worker had also been the one to find Missy and the little girl after the fire had been put out. It had truly been a miracle the way the girl had been held safely by Missy in spite of the explosion and fire and the obvious injuries Missy had received.

The identity of the Stratton family added to the newsworthiness of the story, as Bill Stratton was a well known real estate developer from Washington D.C. who owned a chain of luxury hotels. He also was a close friend of Ed Maxwell, the junior senator from Massachusetts. It was learned Senator Maxwell was already on his way and would arrive later that evening. Evidently, the Stratton family had been vacationing in the Blue Ridge Mountains area for years. They had left Roanoke that morning on their way up to their lakeside cabin. The senator had planned on joining them, driving over from his place in the capital. Now, of course, the senator would be visiting them at the hospital.

Meanwhile, Missy's initial examination at the hospital had been completed. After determining Missy was stable, a CT scan had been performed. This showed there were no broken bones or internal injuries. Because of the serious head injury, Doctor Walker was assigned to her case and had requested an MRI in order to better understand whether any brain damage had occurred. The nurses had removed her sweater and blue jean shorts, treating several deep slashes from the car window glass as well as her burns, cuts, scrapes, and bruises from the explosion and fire.

Nurse Gladys, the lead nurse, had some comments for the doctor. "There are certainly a lot of very strange things about this patient, Doctor Walker, and nothing which really helps us identify who she might be. When she arrived, after we peeled away her clothes, we checked them for any possessions which might provide a clue, but she had nothing. Nothing in her pockets, no purse, no shoes ... why, she didn't even have any bra or panties! What teenage girl today will go around like that?"

"That's indeed very unusual," the doctor agreed.

Gladys went on to say, "Oh, that's not all. Her shorts were much too big, with only a piece of rope instead of a belt, and her sweater was also much too large. Since she has no tan lines and is tanned pretty much the same all over, it doesn't look like she actually wears clothes all that much when she's outside. She also doesn't shave her legs or under her arms. And, she has no jewelry. Her ears used to have holes for pierced earrings but those healed up a long time ago. Maybe she's a naturalist from some strange commune or some other weird group, some sort of a nudist colony."

Doctor Walker observed, "Well, I did notice she has almost no body fat and is in really amazing physical shape. I think that helped save her from more serious injuries during the explosion. She must be some sort of an athlete which maybe would explain some things."

Gladys said, "Yes, her pulse was only in the fifties, which we thought was too low and so we double checked it. It was fifty-six both times. But, steady and strong, with really good blood pressure. We do see this for athletes having exceptionally good aerobic conditioning such as long distance runners, for example. That would explain the low body fat, right?"

Doctor Walker replied, "Yes, it would. Only, she has a lot more muscle mass than a runner would. Maybe that helps explain the incredible rescue they say she managed to perform up there on that mountain, yanking those three people out of that car just before the explosion."

"No one can understand how she could have done that or even how she managed getting down to the car," said Gladys. "I hear it's a huge drop down the side of a cliff. The rescue team only got down there by using lots of equipment. And, those three people she saved are all doing just fine now. The woman had a mild concussion but, other than bruises from their seatbelts and minor scratches from broken glass, they all came out of the crash in good shape. It looks like this girl smashed out a window, but she seems to be the only one who got any bad cuts. She was slashed in several places going in and getting them all out."

"Well, those cuts will heal okay and shouldn't leave any scars. But, what about those scars which I saw she already has? Gladys, can't those scars help identify her?"

"That's another part of what's so strange! She has a long six inch crease on her thigh which looks like it could only have been caused by a bullet wound. It's not very recent though and has healed up okay. It was deep enough so she should have had stitches, but she didn't have any. Then, there are all the scars on her shoulder and back. Those are also old and faded and although they healed up okay, there were no stitches for those either. They look like she was mauled by claws from some kind of a wild animal."

"Yeah, that's what those looked like to me ..."

"We've checked with all the hospital databases and no patient has ever been recorded having scars like hers," Gladys continued. "Of course, since there were no stitches, that might explain why she's not in any database. It seems really negligent for a girl like that to not get any medical attention after such serious injuries. All the more reason to think she's from some strange group up in those mountains, right?"

"Well, she's only a teenager and we really need to reach next of kin. We don't yet know what treatment she'll need but we'll want either a parent or guardian to sign a consent form. Have you asked the police for help?"

"Yes, Doctor Walker, we called them again just an hour ago. They have interviewed all the witnesses from where that car went off the road, but they all say this girl just appeared out of nowhere, racing down from the direction of the mountain. She's definitely not from around here. The police are checking now with each of the camping areas up there but there are a lot of campers. No one has reported her missing, but of course it's still early. Hopefully, someone will call in about a missing girl."

"Okay, Gladys. For now, just keep her sedated in the ICU and keep all the monitors hooked up. We'll see how she makes it through the night. Hopefully, the MRI and those other tests I've asked for will show us how we can best help her."

Chapter Six

Early afternoon Aug 27

In the middle of the second day at the hospital, Missy gradually came to in the ICU but was so heavily drugged from the sedatives she'd been given she was unable to fully wake up. She was lying in a bed, constraints attached to her arms and legs with several tubes and wires all connected to various parts of her, including a urinary catheter for her bladder. This was all because Doctor Walker was very concerned about possible brain trauma, based on how badly smashed the side of her head appeared to be. In order to avoid any secondary brain injury, the doctor wanted to keep her unconscious for the first few days, monitoring all her vital signs, plus all the fluids that went in and came out. Various tests had been conducted and were still being evaluated to determine what might be the best treatment and, possibly, whether any neurological surgery might be necessary.

Any normal human would have remained out cold but Missy, of course, was different. Her metabolism and ability to heal allowed her system to revive and come back to some level of awareness, in spite of all the drugs. Although not fully conscious, she was able to hear Doctor Walker and Nurse Gladys talking. They had just looked in on her and happened to be nearby. She was also aware of being constrained in the bed, with machines all around her.

Missy managed to listen to some of the conversation, but she could not really understand very much. It seemed they were talking about her; who she might be and where she might have come from. So, she made an effort and tried to speak to them. She wanted to get their attention and provide some explanation. She said, "I was coming out of the mountains ... I wanted to go home ... please ..." but her words were mumbled.

Upon hearing this, Doctor Walker rushed to her side, very surprised Missy was awake and very concerned about her condition and any possible injuries she might do to herself. Turning to Gladys, she asked, "Why has the sedative worn off so soon? Hasn't she been getting the dosage which I prescribed?"

Gladys answered, "Why definitely, doctor! Here, see for yourself! And, it's been going in through this IV tube right here. Look, you can see the bag is not yet empty so it's not time yet for another dose. This girl must have an unusual resistance to drugs if she's able to wake up."

Doctor Walker checked to verify the bag did have the medication which she had specified, and that it was indeed dripping properly into one of the tubes running into Missy's arm. She then ordered a syringe with another sedative and the nurse rushed off to get it. Turning back to Missy, the doctor said, "Hello, I'm Doctor Walker. You're in the hospital. Please don't try to move; you really need to rest and you shouldn't be awake right now."

But, Missy struggled to sit up and repeated herself, saying in a louder, stronger voice, "I was coming out of the mountains so I could go home." Then, she added, "I never got to say goodbye ... please let me up ...

what are all these tubes and things? Please take these off me!"

"No, no!" Doctor Walker said, pushing her back down. "Don't try to move. It's important for you to lie still and not get excited." But, she was very encouraged by the fact Missy seemed coherent, so she then asked her, "Can you tell me your name?"

Missy was still very drowsy but she struggled to explain. "I was at soccer camp and I had to leave ... couldn't say goodbye ... please ... tell my mom ..."

The doctor interrupted again to ask her, "Can you tell me your name? And, can I call your mom for you? Where does she live?"

Missy was then able to say, "My name is Missy McCrea and my mom lives in Salem, Massachusetts. On Walnut Street. Tell her how sorry I am ... but, please, let me get up!"

Just then Nurse Gladys returned and the doctor administered the sedative from the syringe, directly into one of the IV tubes. She told the nurse, "I hope her trauma is not affected by her waking up. Although she sounds okay, there are many possible problems and complications which we want to avoid if possible. This should knock her out. And, increase the dosage of that sedative in her medication by 30%; that should keep her out. We really want to wait at least another day before we attempt bringing her back. She probably was able to overcome the first dosage due to being so exceptionally healthy and fit."

Missy dropped back into a deep sleep and didn't hear any of the conversation after that. Gladys remarked, "I hear that Stratton family she rescued is really good friends with Senator Maxwell and that he arrived here last night to visit them. Then, all three of them were released just a little while ago and there was a big news conference outside. The senator sure had some nice things to say about our mystery girl here."

Doctor Walker said, "This could have been a real tragedy but it looks like no one other than Missy here is hurt. We'll have to wait and see what happens, but I'm sure everyone will want to thank her for being such a hero."

"Oh, is that her name? Missy?" asked Gladys. "Did she say anything else?"

"Yes, she did. She mentioned she had gone up into the mountains from soccer camp and that her home is in Massachusetts. We can call her family up there and we should also try to contact whichever soccer camp she was at down here, so they'll know she's been found. We can check the phone company for listings in Salem, Mass on Walnut Street with the name McCrea. I'll go try to call them now while you let the police know about checking for soccer camps."

"Massachusetts, huh?" said Gladys. "Maybe that's why our database search didn't find anyone having those scars … we just didn't check far enough away. And, I guess her being at soccer camp makes sense, since she's so athletic. I'll let the police know. They'll sure be glad the mystery girl's identity has been established."

Chapter Seven
Late afternoon Aug 27

An hour later, after getting the phone number from information, the doctor placed the call to Missy's home. When the phone was answered by a woman, the doctor started to explain, "Hello? Is this Mrs. McCrea? I'm Doctor Stephanie Walker and I'm at the William Osborne Memorial Hospital in Roanoke, Virginia. We have your daughter Missy, who was injured down here and is being treated in our hospital."

Missy's mother was shocked to hear any news about Missy. She glanced at her photos of Missy, two on the living room mantel and another on a nearby bookshelf. She had looked at these photos so many times during the past two years, while trying to hope for the best and not despair for the worst. She exclaimed, "Doctor, are you sure it's really our daughter Missy? And, is she okay?"

Doctor Walker answered, "Well, she was able to give us her name and your address. She's in the ICU because she was found unconscious after her head hit a rock. We are monitoring her very closely and it's too soon to give you much of a prognosis. Can either you or a responsible family member possibly come down here, in case we need authorization signatures for any treatment or procedures?"

"But, this is incredible! And, you're certain it's our Missy?" her mother asked again.

"Well, she says that's who she is. She mentioned leaving soccer camp but not saying goodbye. Can you tell us which camp, so we can notify them that we have her?"

Missy's mother now said, "If it's really our Missy, we'll all be so happy! But, doctor … our Missy has been missing for over two years now!"

Now it was Doctor Walker's turn to be shocked. "We had no idea about any of that," she explained.

"Virginia is so far away. I'm sure you can understand why we want to be very certain the girl you have down there is really her," Missy's mother explained. "We think she was kidnapped from soccer camp in Keene, New Hampshire and no one has heard anything about her in all this time. Do you think that's the soccer camp this girl was talking about?"

The doctor could only say, "Missy only mentioned leaving soccer camp without saying goodbye, but she's heavily sedated and I can't say for sure just what she meant by that. I was lucky she could give me her name and tell me where you are living."

Missy's mother then remarked, "We really should get the FBI into this; they've been searching and their investigation is still open. If she has escaped from her kidnapper … maybe she's still in danger …"

Doctor Walker said, "Certainly, we'll take precautions. If there is any risk that anyone might be after this girl … we'll contact our local police to arrange for protection in our hospital immediately. Go ahead and have the FBI call me and have them also contact our police chief directly. We will help in any way we can. And, if she really is your Missy, I can only say we are doing everything we possibly can to help her make a full recovery. It's too soon to make any promises, but the fact she was able to respond, give us her name and address, and is apparently so strong and healthy, these are all very positive signs."

"Really?" exclaimed Missy's mother. "If only this could be true! It would be such a miracle if she is really our Missy and if she can really be okay. I don't care what she has been through; we can deal with anything and everything if she can just really be alive and able to come back home to us."

After getting off the phone, Doctor Walker called the police and explained how Missy's mother was concerned about a possible kidnapper and that the FBI was now coming. She advised them to expect to hear from the FBI right away since the investigation was still open and this case was now looking as though there may have been some sort of a crime. She then went looking for Gladys, since she knew it was important to preserve any evidence.

When she found the nurse, she explained what she had learned and how there was an ongoing investigation. They both went into the staff lounge nearby and using the computer there, they entered Missy's name on Google's search page. Sure enough, there actually were all sorts of stories in the news from two years ago, all about the girl who had gone missing from soccer camp. Looking at the news photos, they could see a definite resemblance to the girl they had in the ICU. The photos showed a girl that was smaller and younger, but the face was very similar and the dark red hair and green eyes were the same.

"I can't believe this," exclaimed Gladys. "What has been happening to this girl for the past two years? She obviously has been through some very rough experiences ... those scars from both a bullet and from some sort of animal attack ... was she actually staying up in the mountains? How did she manage to get all the way down here, hundreds of miles from where she disappeared two years ago? And, how was she able to merely be walking down the road ..."

Doctor Walker said, "Now that we are aware she may be a victim, we need to gather all possible evidence for the authorities. They'll want to know everything for their investigation. They'll probably even ask us whether she's been sexually assaulted ..."

Right away, Gladys interrupted her to say, "Well, at least we can tell them there's no evidence of that. When we inserted that catheter we had to take extra care ... you know ... so we wouldn't tear her hymen, which is still quite intact and less than an inch lower. She's definitely still a virgin! So, whatever happened to her, at least she seems to have been spared from any of that. Nothing sexual, no molestation ..."

"Amazing, but thank goodness for that," exclaimed Doctor Walker. "This Missy is quite the mystery girl but it's good to know whatever trauma she may have been through during these past two years ..."

Just then, there was a knock on the door which interrupted them and Officer Williams from the Roanoke police force came in and introduced himself. He'd been sent to help watch over Missy's room and make sure she wouldn't have any unwanted visitors.

Chapter Eight
Evening Aug 27

Just a couple hours after her first time awake, Missy once again woke up, still constrained in her hospital bed. She knew the doctor had told her not to move but she also knew, even in her drugged state, that she needed to Shift. Her instincts made her aware that doing so would help speed her recovery and healing. And, she had been surviving on her instincts for two years now.

Slowly, she forced herself to really wake up and take stock of her surroundings. As her awareness of everything increased, she realized her arms and legs were being restrained in addition to all those pesky wires and tubes that were now bothering her more and more. Her right arm was being held at the wrist by some sort of collar held together by Velcro, but she exerted some pressure and was able to enlarge that enough so she could yank her arm back through and out. Once free, she quickly reached each of the other Velcro collars and removed them.

The tubes sticking out from her were next. She especially disliked the catheter tube for her bladder and carefully pulled that one out first. That was followed by each of the others. These were attached to needles, which she also removed. And, then there were all the wires connected to sticky things on her which ran to machines at the side of her bed. Once she had everything off, she crawled out of bed and slowly stood up. She found she was wearing some sort of hospital gown which was open in the back.

At first she felt woozy and dizzy but as she forced herself to move, her head gradually cleared and she moved to the door of her room. She parsed all the various scents over her tongue and across the roof of her mouth as well as with her nose. Doing that, she could clearly detect her surroundings and, when she knew there was no one nearby, she went out into the hallway.

Glancing right and left, she spotted EXIT signs and made her way to a stairway. Once through the door and onto the stairs, she stopped to again check for scents and then headed up the stairs. Up she went and after three flights of stairs, she reached level six, the top level. From there, she was able to ascend even further to climb out a doorway that opened onto the roof.

She patrolled the entire roof area and found a section where several air conditioners were bolted down, with a maze of various ducts running in and out. She knew she had found as good a hiding area as she could get and, removing her gown, she focused on her cat and Shifted. Back in cat form, she immediately began to feel much better! Gone were the various minor aches and pains, along with that really bad headache. She could think clearly again, no longer groggy from medication. Her system was able to purge whatever residue remained and she padded around for several minutes, feeling the exhilaration of being whole once again. Herself, albeit as a cat. So be it. Then, feeling able to think clearly, she settled down to ponder all that had happened and consider what she should do next, going forward. She realized she had asked that Doctor Walker to call her mom and so she hoped her return back home was finally going to happen, sometime soon!

Doctor Walker and Nurse Gladys were still talking to Officer Williams in the staff lounge when their beepers both went off. They each quickly checked in and learned Missy was not in her room. She was gone! All the tubes and wires had been removed and she was simply missing. There had been some beeping at the nurse's station alerting them the monitors were no longer properly connected but when they checked in on Missy to fix that, they found she'd vanished. She should have been practically in a coma due to all the medication she was getting, not to mention her severe head injury. Everyone was concerned someone had to have grabbed her and wheeled her out on a gurney or in a wheelchair. But, no one could recall seeing either of those.

The hospital went on full alert with Officer Williams working with the hospital security personnel. All entrances and exits were immediately blocked off and all video surveillance footage of these areas and the parking areas was examined. More local policemen arrived and a thorough search was begun. Floor by floor, every area was carefully searched. But, no one really thought to give the roof a thorough check. One policeman did actually step out and give the roof area a cursory look. But, he did not see Missy, nestled down in the maze of ductwork, taking a nap. They were all looking more for a bed or wheelchair or something which a body might be hidden within, as well as for some stranger who might have kidnapped her. They weren't really checking just for her all by herself.

After several frustrating hours with no clues and no Missy, the police had to give up the search although they continued to monitor and keep watch on all entrances and exits. Officer Williams with a couple of other officers remained at the hospital to oversee this activity, but little hope remained that she would be found. They believed she'd somehow been abducted. Doctor Walker and Gladys were very upset but could not really blame any of the nurses or other hospital staff members who were on duty at the time. Another mystery, added to the already long list of strange things they had come to learn about Missy.

Then, the Stratton family whom Missy had saved, along with their close friend Senator Maxwell, chose that evening to pay a visit and ask about her. They were not expecting to actually see or visit her, as they knew she was in the ICU. But, they did want to hear an update and were hoping to learn when an actual visit might be possible, so they could thank her for what she had done. It didn't take them long, with the Senator right there with them, to learn all about Missy. First, that she was now missing and then how she was this girl who had apparently been kidnapped while at soccer camp in New Hampshire two years earlier. How, because of that suspected kidnapping, the FBI investigators were on their way to the hospital and would surely be taking over once they arrived.

Senator Maxwell remembered hearing all about that case and was astonished to learn she had turned up down here, in such a strange way. Missy's case had been a big story in Massachusetts back then and was probably going to be an even bigger story now. He wanted to be updated on any news concerning the hospital's search for her and to be alerted when the FBI arrived.

Chapter Nine

Early morning, pre-dawn Aug 28

Meanwhile, Missy stretched and got up, once again padding across the roof top. She had noticed the policeman who had earlier walked out and looked around, but since he had quickly gone back inside, she had not bothered to move. She had been enjoying herself, thinking about finally going home, back to her family and back to her life as a human. And, she had napped. Now, she felt she needed to get up and get going. And, she was ravenous! It was time to find some food, before she could consider any other actions.

She Changed back to human form and put the hospital gown back on, since she had nothing else to wear. Tying the ties, she then went back inside and looked down the stairwell. She could tell by the smell of food which had been cooked that the kitchen was down on the lowest level, and she quietly made her way down the stairs. At each floor, she stopped to let her senses tell her what was happening and whether any others were about to come out into the stairwell. But, it was now late at night and no one seemed interested in taking the stairs. She was able to reach the bottom level and find her way to the kitchen, without meeting anyone.

Once in the kitchen, she went to the refrigerator and found where a whole chicken had been cooked and then put away for the next day. This was exactly what she needed, and she brought the chicken over to a nearby table and sat down to enjoy her meal. This was actually her first meal in human form in more than two years! She was starved and the cooked chicken was delicious!

No feeding tubes for Missy! She actually smiled at the thought and knew she would probably be finding a few hospital folks who would be angry with her. But, she had to survive as she knew best, relying on her own instincts for what was needed. She really had not figured out yet just what she would be able to say to everyone. She knew she absolutely could not explain about being able to Shift into her cat form. That would definitely cause her many problems, all unknown, and her instincts were very strong about fearing the unknown.

At the same time, she realized how her having helped rescue that family from their car would probably mean folks would not get too angry with her. She was actually looking forward to seeing that little girl again. She wanted to assure herself the girl was really all right and didn't experience anything which was too traumatic. First the car crash and then the explosion. The little girl surely would have been very scared while all those things had been happening.

As luck would have it, Missy was just finishing her meal when she noticed someone else was coming towards the kitchen. Oh, well! She knew she shouldn't keep herself hidden away any longer; she needed to finally start talking to people. So, she made no attempt to sneak away but just sat there as a woman walked into the kitchen and turned on the light. Missy hadn't bothered with the light earlier since she could see in the dark just fine.

When the woman noticed Missy, calmly sitting there at the table with a plate full of chicken bones in front of her, she screamed! It was just so unexpected. But, she quickly realized Missy might be the missing girl the entire hospital had been searching for all night. She said, "Oh, I'm so sorry but you startled me! The light wasn't on and I had no idea anyone was in here. Why are you down here anyway? Aren't you the girl everyone is looking for? I think I heard her name was Missy."

"Well, my name is Missy. But, I didn't know anyone was looking for me. I was hungry and came in here to get something to eat."

The woman introduced herself saying, "I'm Helena and I work in Maternity. But I know they've been searching for you. Weren't you in the ICU? That's the Intensive Care Unit on level three, for folks who are really sick or injured."

Missy replied, "I don't know what my room was called but it was on the third floor. I guess I can go back up there, now that I've finished eating."

Helena knew it was best to have folks come down to the kitchen rather than letting Missy go wandering off anywhere. She had never seen such an intensive search effort at the hospital before and, without knowing any details about this girl, she knew to have her stay right where she was. Waving at Missy to just stay seated, she walked over to a nearby wall phone and called the main office. Quickly, she explained about finding a girl named Missy there in the kitchen and was told to just stay right there and not let Missy make a move.

Not long after that several people all crowded into the kitchen at once. There were even a couple of policemen. Missy recognized Doctor Walker along with that nurse she'd seen in her room earlier; they both came up to her before any of the others. The nurse turned to wave everyone else back so the doctor could sit down with Missy alone. Doctor Walker looked at her closely and asked, "Are you really okay, Missy? You're not supposed to be out of bed. What are you doing down here? Are you all alone or did anyone else come down here with you?"

Missy answered, "I was starving and had to get something to eat. I came down here by myself and I'm sorry if I wasn't supposed to raid the refrigerator like this, but I was so hungry! Yesterday, when I asked you to let me get up, you wouldn't help me and instead you gave me that shot to make me sleepy. I really hated all those tubes and wires and being tied up in bed the way I was."

Doctor Walker was of course very concerned about her patient -- even though it was a huge relief to see Missy sitting there, apparently safe -- so she wanted to make sure Missy's head injury wouldn't suddenly cause some secondary trauma. Brain damage was tricky and it was still very possible things could quickly take a turn for the worse. She then noticed the plate in front of Missy and asked, "What have you had to eat, there,

Missy? Was there some leftover chicken? How much have you had? It's best to go slow at first ..."

Missy interrupted, "Yes, there was this chicken in the refrigerator and I ate it. It was really good, too! I'm sorry if I wasn't supposed to." She wanted to admit what she'd done and take full responsibility.

"How much chicken was there?"

"Err ... I guess it was, you know, a chicken." Missy pointed to all the bones on the plate in front of her.

"Are you saying you ate a *whole* chicken? Not just a couple pieces, but the whole entire chicken?" Doctor Walker asked, looking at all the bones with a shocked expression. But she quickly recovered and went on to explain, "We try to keep track of what our patients are eating, so it's important that you tell me how many pieces you had, Missy."

"Um, yes, I have to say it was the whole chicken. But, that did fill me up. Mostly. I'm not hungry anymore." Missy then gave her a big smile.

Doctor Walker really didn't know what to think about this astonishing news but it had been a long day and an even longer night, filled with far more than she'd wanted to cope with. So, not wanting to play detective, she didn't ask where Missy had been for the past several hours or how she'd managed to eat an entire chicken. Instead, she decided to just get Missy settled back into a room. She chatted with her for a little while longer, just making conversation, and was really amazed at how alert and fully awake Missy was now.

It was pretty obvious Missy didn't belong in the ICU anymore. But, the doctor couldn't understand how Missy had made such a remarkable recovery. She examined the side of Missy's head, where her injury had been, and there now was much less swelling. And, Missy really seemed quite coherent. So, she turned around to the others standing there and she started giving everyone directions.

Missy was to be given a private room and there would be a policeman staying outside in the hallway. This should be just a normal room since there wouldn't be any machines or IV tubes or anything else like that. Oh, and be sure it had a nice TV! Missy was going to stay for observation for at least another couple of days. Also, there were some FBI folks who were coming to talk to her later. And, of course, Missy's mother was expected sometime soon. So, once they got Missy settled, everyone was to get back to their normal routine.

Chapter Ten
Morning Aug 28

Things did settle down after that. Missy went to her new room, where things were nicely set up for her and which included a TV with a remote. As she hadn't watched any TV in over two years, this was fascinating and she promised she would stay right there. She did circle everything on the menu for each of her meals. Doctor Walker had approved her now having whatever she wanted to eat and she wanted to take full advantage of that. So, she settled in, played with the remote, watched some TV and enjoyed a delicious breakfast once the morning finally came. After eating everything which was brought in, she then went right to sleep.

Outside her room, a policeman kept watch and made certain the only ones going into her room were the assigned nurses. Everyone else had to be cleared by either Officer Williams or Doctor Walker. Officer Williams had coordinated all procedures with the hospital staff and with Doctor Walker. He had stayed on at the hospital, as did both Doctor Walker and Nurse Gladys, who each did finally manage to take a nap and get a little sleep themselves.

Because of all the activity when the exits had been blocked and every room had been searched, there were a lot of doctors and nurses who now wanted to hear what all the fuss had been about. Word had leaked out and there were some reporters outside the hospital who were also asking questions. Therefore, an internal memo was issued that explained there had been a mix-up which resulted in the alert, but everything was now fine and under control. There would continue to be a police detail providing added security, but this was only expected to be for a day or two. Since it was well known that Senator Maxwell was visiting, due to the press conference he'd given the day before, this arrangement seemed normal and routine.

For the general public, a general statement was issued explaining that Missy had finally been identified and that she was now conscious, out of the ICU and resting comfortably. Because she was only fifteen, her name was being withheld and no further details were being shared. Her mother was expected to arrive later that day, so perhaps more details would be released then. Thus, finally, things really did settle down.

Then, just before noon, Robert Ulrey arrived with Susan Donavan, another agent from the FBI. Susan had not worked on Missy's case before but had worked for several years in the Special Victims Unit and was very experienced. She was fifty-two and looked more like a school teacher than an FBI agent. She was out of the Washington D.C. office and had just been assigned as an added resource the night before, right after there'd been some communication to the FBI headquarters from Senator Maxwell's office.

Missy's mother Julia had been the one to call Robert the day before, once she'd learned Missy was supposedly in some hospital down in Virginia. Could he go down there and make sure she was really safe?

He had assured her he would drop everything and rush right down there. Then he'd called the hospital and had his office call ahead to the Roanoke police. A security detail at the hospital was requested, to watch Missy's room until he could get there. He also had asked his office to send him whatever local news reports there might be about the accident on Blue Ridge Parkway. He'd download these to his laptop to read the articles and watch the videos later. He then went home to pack, bringing Missy's file with him.

Later, he received the call from the hospital about the ongoing search for Missy who had disappeared from her room. This was very disturbing news! Shortly after that, his boss called and explained about the contact from Senator Maxwell's office. And, since the airlines had no direct flights into Roanoke, he was booked on a flight to Washington D.C. He was to stay in a hotel there at the airport that night and meet up with Special Agent Donavan who was going with him. He was going to need her help, with the added responsibility from these new developments combined with the high visibility this case was now getting. The two of them were booked on the first flight out the next morning and they should be able to get to the hospital by noon.

After flying down and checking into his hotel, he had called and briefed Susan Donavan with all that he'd learned about the case. She had read the files and already knew most of it by the time he'd called; they both were then anxious to meet Missy, if only she could be found. They had discussed various items they hoped she could tell them about: what had she been through, was there a kidnapper, was there more than one person involved, how had she escaped, was she traumatized, would she be willing to testify, were there other victims, what could they learn about any other criminal activity and many other questions they hoped to find answers to.

When the good news was delivered early the next day that Missy was actually okay, it came as a great relief. They learned she'd been located in the kitchen without any kidnapper involved or anything else suspicious going on and there now was a police detail watching her room as well as all the hospital entrances.

Robert called Missy's mother right away to make sure she knew. She had gone through a sleepless night and was overjoyed to learn Missy was not only safe, but was now awake and no longer in the ICU. She was scheduled to arrive mid afternoon and would see him then.

The flight into Roanoke was very pleasant, as it seemed the long lost Missy was really going to be going home to her family. During the flight, Robert and Susan also got to watch the news coverage and read all the stories about the rescue which had resulted in Missy being brought to the hospital. They naturally had some questions about all of that but since the accident on the parkway was not an FBI matter they wouldn't really have to investigate any of those details. Finally, they reviewed the need to keep Senator Maxwell in the loop. They had both worked other cases over the years where it was necessary to provide briefings to various high ranking officials and politicians, so this was merely business as usual for them.

Thus, they were pretty well prepared when they arrived at the hospital and were glad to find both Officer Williams and Doctor Walker waiting for them. They were given an office to work out of plus a dedicated conference room they could use. As first priority, they reviewed all the security arrangements and were pleased that Officer Williams would stay on as liaison. While they would now be taking charge of things, the cooperation from the local police was needed and appreciated. Their main concern was making sure no one who might be after Missy could get to her.

The hours she'd gone missing during the night had been a real scare for everyone. If Missy had escaped from someone, that person would be desperate to prevent Missy from identifying whoever that person might be. And, after all the publicity with her arrival at the hospital, that person would now know where she was. It had already been announced she was no longer in the ICU but was now conscious, right? That news had been impossible to suppress, considering the alert and search activity during the night. And, even though her identity had been withheld, how much longer would that last?

Next, after being satisfied with Missy's security situation, they wanted to interview Doctor Walker privately. First, they wanted to understand Missy's current condition and medical situation. They were hoping to interview Missy once her mother arrived and wanted to know if Missy would be up for that. Then, they also wanted any information about Missy's physical condition which might reveal what she'd been through the past two years. And, of course, was there any evidence they could use. What could they get from

Missy's belongings, what was she wearing when she arrived, etc.

Doctor Walker could only say how shocked she was that Missy was not still out from the heavy sedation. She explained, "Based on my initial examination, Missy's head injury appeared so severe that brain damage was very likely, if not already present. That's why we wanted her sedated and we had no intention that she be awake this soon. Only after enough time for healing, perhaps with some surgery ... but, we hadn't even finished all the testing or even evaluated her MRI. That, by the way, shows several areas of real concern. We certainly would have been recommending some treatment. The fact that Missy got up, wandered around until ending up in our kitchen, and then was able to not just eat something. Why, she completely devoured an entire chicken! And, when I examined her there, her injury was so much less apparent. All the earlier bruising and swelling was looking so much better! And, she was up and talking to me as though nothing had ever happened! I cannot explain that and I've already requested another MRI for her later this evening."

"That's remarkable, doctor. You're saying she's able to actually talk now?"

"I really can't explain the way Missy appears to be so coherent," she continued. "But, she is! So, yes, you can probably have your interview and she should be able to handle that. You will see for yourselves just how aware and fully conscious she is now. Whether a miracle or merely a mystery, this girl will definitely amaze you."

Robert acknowledged, "This is certainly good news, doctor. But, are we sure it's really our missing teenager from two years ago? Could there be some sort of mistake or mix-up …?"

"Oh, it's her all right," said Doctor Walker. "Nurse Gladys and I looked at all the news clippings available on the internet, which included plenty of photos. This girl is older but the resemblance is too close. Her hair and her eyes … you'll see. And, of course, she gave us her name and address."

"Well, her mother will be here to identify her. I'm sure you're right, but there won't be any doubt after that. Now, what else can you tell us?" Robert asked.

Susan then added her questions. "Yes, doctor. What can you tell us about this girl, aside from her recent injuries? From what we read on the way in, she was injured from a car explosion? We don't yet know why she was there, do we?"

Doctor Walker explained, "Not really, no. She apparently was coming down from the mountains. It seems she was just walking along the parkway but then ran up to where the accident happened. The media doesn't have the full story yet, but this girl is quite the hero. She went down the side of that cliff and rescued that family from their car. No one can explain how she managed that, but the witnesses up on the road saw her plunge right over the edge and then heard her smash the car window. This all happened so quickly, too! No one else dared to climb down there, as the drop is down a steep cliff with nothing to hold onto, no pathway down. It took the rescue team several minutes with all their equipment. Yet, according to the witnesses at the scene, she managed getting down there almost like she just dropped straight down."

Susan said, "Yes, I read in one of the accounts that she appeared out of nowhere and did exactly that, without saying anything ... just coming up to the edge where everyone was standing and then going right over. There was also an interview with one of the rescue workers who quoted what the parents had to say. They told him this girl really pulled them both out of their car and then, after dragging them to safety, she went back for their little girl. They thought for sure that both she and their daughter were in that car when it exploded. They were so overjoyed when their girl was found later, safe and unhurt. They said it all happened so fast ..."

Robert asked, "Could this girl really even do any of that, doctor? How could she have the strength to pull these two adults out of the car? I can see maybe smashing the window and helping, but ...?"

"Oh, she did it, they both attest to that. They have been telling our staff here in the hospital the same thing. And this girl Missy is really strong ... quite the athlete in fact," explained Doctor Walker. "That's why we think she's been able to recover so quickly and resist all the sedatives we gave her. At least, we think that's the logical explanation."

Robert said, "She was an exceptional athlete two years ago, but still -- how does a one hundred pound girl ...?" He looked at the doctor and then at Susan, with a real questioning expression on his face.

"Well, you'll see she's grown a lot since then, and while I agree it's an incredible feat, this girl is now probably thirty pounds heavier and has almost no body fat -- she has a very low pulse rate, typical of long distance runners, but she also has some real solid muscle. Way more than any runner. She's obviously been working out, wherever she's been, in order to get herself into such excellent physical condition."

Susan asked, "But, being a long distance runner? Working out? That's not consistent with her being locked in a room or sitting around in any sort of confinement, is it? We assumed she'd escaped from something exactly like that! How else could she have disappeared so completely until now, without any trace, unless she was being held by someone?"

"This girl has many strange things about her," said the doctor. "Nurse Gladys and I tried to sort through some of them, but we just couldn't make sense of them all."

"Well, now you have my attention, doctor!" exclaimed Robert. "Please explain." He and Susan both looked at her with interest and concern.

Doctor Walker went on to say, "Okay. This girl is not only in the best physical condition that I've ever seen for anyone, but she also seems to be some sort of a naturalist. She has not shaved her legs, under her arms, or anywhere. She was wearing only blue jeans shorts and a sweater, both much too large for her. And, no underwear. No bra, no panties. Barefoot. And it's obvious from her tan that she's been running around naked. No tan lines at all."

"Really?" said Susan. "That actually does suggest she was being held by someone. Maybe not confined, but not free to leave because of some other reason. Kinky! Maybe he forced her to exercise. Naked. I'm almost afraid to ask about what sexual abuse this poor child must have experienced."

"Well, that's just part of all the mystery, then," said Doctor Walker. "Missy is still a virgin. No matter what else she may have gone through, she was never molested or touched in any physical way."

"Is that possible?" exclaimed Robert. "She's a virgin?" He and Susan had concluded that a sexual motive was the most likely one. This had been true for most of the cases they'd worked where a little girl had disappeared and where the motive was not money. The only exceptions were when some relative was involved, as often happened during custody disputes. Either that, or else the girl had been a runaway, which didn't seem at all likely for Missy's case. It was because of the high probability Missy had been grabbed by some predator that Susan had been assigned to the case.

"Oh, yes," said the doctor. "Untouched. Definitely still a virgin. Nurse Gladys assured me of that. We had anticipated your investigation was going to need any evidence of abuse once we learned from her mother that she'd been missing and that the FBI would be coming here. But the nurses noticed this about her when they inserted the catheter tube for her bladder. It meant they had to take extra care, so they wouldn't … you know …damage her down there. At the time, they just thought this was normal for a fifteen year old girl. Now that we know she's been missing for more than two years, which can only be explained if she was grabbed by someone …"

"Wow!" said Susan. "I think I see why you said she's either a miracle or a mystery! Maybe this guy was someone who only wanted to watch …" She allowed her thoughts to continue along that line, with several deviant criminal types coming to mind, each with various sick reasons for not actually touching … maybe he was waiting, she thought. She looked at Robert and could tell he was having similar considerations.

"And, did I mention her scars?" asked the doctor.

"What scars?" said both Robert and Susan at the same time.

"Yes. I knew you'd be interested in those. First, the one on her right thigh. That was a bullet, but no stitches. If I had to guess, it was a rifle bullet since the caliber was large … she really should have had stitches. But, it doesn't look as though she received any medical care. However, it seems to have healed well enough."

"Wow!" said Susan. "This indeed is consistent with her being abused. Someone must have been holding her … right, Robert?"

He replied, "The fact that she had no stitches suggests this person obviously was trying to keep her hidden. He couldn't risk any questions about her getting shot so he never brought her in for treatment. I sure hope we can get her to tell us about this person, whoever it was."

The doctor then remarked, "Oh, but that's the least of it. She also has some scars on her shoulder which had to have been from some wild animal. Those were much worse, but she never got stitches or medical care for those either. It's really surprising how those all managed to heal up okay without causing her some problems. At first, when we learned she was from the New England area, we thought we just had not checked hospital databases far enough away. But, we've now verified this girl is not in any databases either here in the U.S. or in Canada. And, scars like that would definitely have been recorded if she'd ever been treated in any hospital."

"Really?" said Susan. "What a monster, to allow that to happen to a little girl. Poor Missy!"

On that note, the discussion ended and Doctor Walker excused herself so she could go check on her patients. Robert and Susan went down and examined Missy's clothing but, as had already been explained, there really was nothing there to provide any clue; nothing for any follow on investigation. Missy had arrived with only the two items, shorts and a sweatshirt, which not only were not her size but they doubted Missy was a Baltimore Ravens fan, coming from Massachusetts. They'd ask her, of course, but they doubted this was going to lead them anywhere.

Chapter Eleven
Mid afternoon Aug 28

At three thirty, Missy's mother Julia arrived at the hospital. She was still afraid to believe this was really happening and her daughter was alive and well. She'd only be convinced of that when she was able to actually see Missy, hold her in her arms and have Missy hugging her right back. She asked for Doctor Walker as soon as she arrived and found the doctor was already there waiting for her when she came in.

Missy had been told Julia was coming and was really excited. She couldn't wait. After being alone for so many months, not sure if she would ever see her family again, this was making her the happiest girl alive! She now just wanted to go home.

Earlier, when waking up from her nice nap, Missy had enjoyed her lunch, once again eating everything they'd brought up and astonishing all the nurses with how much she could eat. Doctor Walker had visited and when Missy asked her when she could leave, she was told it would be soon … maybe the next day, depending on various things. The doctor did say that Missy's recovery seemed to be miraculous. Not only was her head injury looking so much better, but the burns and cuts they'd treated her for now all looked like that had been more than a week ago, rather than barely forty eight hours. Everything was healing nicely and it definitely didn't look like anything would be leaving any new scars. When Doctor Walker mentioned that, Missy acted a little embarrassed and touched her left shoulder, but didn't say anything. She could see the doctor wanted to ask her about her old scars but she hoped to avoid that subject, for now.

Then, Nurse Gladys came in, bringing a fresh gown for Missy to wear, as well as some toiletries she could use. She even helped Missy comb out her hair. She and Doctor Walker both seemed really pleased with how Missy looked now. After they left, Missy had a chance to look at herself in the mirror. She studied her reflection which was much clearer than when she'd looked at herself up in the mountains, with only pools of water to glance into. She was still trying to get used to being in human form again. This of course made her think of her mother coming and she got more and more excited.

So then, when Doctor Walker returned, bringing Julia into Missy's room with her, the emotions were overwhelming. Julia rushed over to Missy and the tears of joy from each of them would just not stop for several minutes. They hugged each other and cried and hugged some more. Julia pushed back so she could look at Missy, marveling at how grown up she was, only to grab her and squeeze that much tighter. Missy kept telling her mother how much she loved her and how happy she was.

Finally, Missy asked about her dad and everyone else. Julia explained they all wanted to come but that it had been decided they could wait for Julia to bring Missy home with her, provided they got to see her on their home computer. Julia then brought an iPad out so they could make a Skype video call. The hospital's wireless connection was working well enough in Missy's room and they soon were connected, with more crying and screams of joy as Missy got to see them all and they were able to see and talk to Missy.

Everyone was talking at once, of course, and it didn't really matter what was being said. They were all just so happy to see it was really Missy and she was ecstatic to finally experience each of them once again. After forty minutes of this, Julia finally asked that everyone finish up and say goodbye. She assured them she'd be bringing Missy home soon. After ending the Skype call, she then sat back to talk to Missy all to herself. They both were emotionally drained by that time, but really happy and filled with joy. They alternated between crying, laughing and just hugging each other again and again. There were almost no words that either of them could use to express all the feelings they shared.

But, finally, Julia explained she was meeting with Doctor Walker. "Missy, I need to have the doctor tell me all about your condition. And, when you can go home. I came straight here from the airport and have no idea how many days this might be. I'm sure you understand, right?"

Missy said, "Sure, Mom. Go ahead. Doctor Walker has been really good to me and I know you probably have lots to talk about. Grown up stuff, right?" Laughing, she added, "It's just so wonderful to see you again!"

Julia agreed, laughing right with her. She then left Missy to go to Doctor Walker's office, where the doctor was waiting for her. She wanted to learn all she could about how Missy came to be in the hospital, after being gone for more than two years. Since she also was concerned about Missy's safety, she wanted to talk to Robert Ulrey as well. She had talked to him many times since Missy first had gone missing two years earlier and she knew he was very committed to Missy's case. If there were any risk someone might be after Missy, she knew he would do everything to protect her and find whoever might be out there.

The doctor fully briefed her about everything as best she could, explaining how another MRI was scheduled for Missy that evening and how she wanted to review that before saying when Missy could be released. She showed Julia what the initial MRI revealed, explaining how serious the injury to Missy's head really had been. Brain damage was often experienced in such cases. She admitted it was not possible to explain how Missy had managed to recover so quickly, heal so quickly and apparently be in such wonderful condition now, after what she'd been through and with the injury it appeared she'd received. Julia could understand why the doctor was being so cautious and agreed no one wanted to take any risks for possible brain damage or any other problems Missy might yet experience from all this.

Doctor Walker also told her everything she had shared with the FBI about Missy. Julia was truly relieved to hear that Missy was still a virgin, as that had been almost too much to hope for. But, she was shocked to learn about Missy's scars and how she not only had been injured like that but then, since there were not any stitches, how it was not clear what medical treatment, if any, Missy might have received.

She agreed to meet with the Stratton family and Senator Maxwell, who knew she was there and had asked to see her. They really wanted to thank Missy in person once that could be arranged. And, the senator knew all about Missy having disappeared from soccer camp two years ago. He could appreciate there was still a lot to learn about all of this and that Missy might still need protection. He had been very alarmed the night before when they all thought someone had grabbed her again. It was agreed to continue withholding her identity, as this was likely to be a very big story if all the details leaked out. Since Missy was only fifteen, they hoped they could avoid that. Julia suggested they check the next morning to see if Missy might be up to having them visit.

Julia then sat down with Robert in the FBI's conference room. She was introduced to Susan Donavan and they discussed Missy's situation at great length. She learned all the details about the rescue Missy had performed and watched the news clips which had been recorded. She was totally amazed to see the car, the fire, the steep cliff, and even watched how Missy was brought up on a stretcher. It seemed unbelievable that Missy was responsible for getting that family out of their car before the explosion. Especially amazing was how she'd saved the little girl from any injury, in spite of being knocked out herself. And, why was she even there? How did it happen that she came along, out of nowhere? The more they discussed everything about the incredible rescue plus what little they knew about Missy's whereabouts during the past two years, the more it was obvious that only by talking to her would they ever be able to understand any of these things. Only then might they determine if there was someone still out there they needed to be worried about.

Julia agreed that later in the evening, after Missy had received her MRI, they could try to all sit down with her to see what she would have to say.

Chapter Twelve

Early evening Aug 28

Julia went back to Missy's room and joined her for dinner. She explained about the FBI being there and that, in order to assure everyone that Missy was really safe now, it was necessary for them all to talk about things. Maybe after the MRI procedure? Missy said she understood, but inside she was very nervous. She really still had no idea just what she could tell everyone. She was able to see how people were all thinking she had to have been kidnapped. How else could she explain being forced to leave, forced to stay away for over two years? She didn't want to tell any lies but she also knew she couldn't explain what had really happened.

Julia also explained how the Stratton family she'd rescued along with Senator Maxwell all wanted to express their thanks. Missy did want to see the little girl and was fine with seeing them all the next morning. Missy told her mother she would be okay to this meeting but that she wouldn't feel comfortable sitting in bed in a hospital gown, even if wearing a robe, for an interview with the senator being there. She looked at the suitcase which Julia had brought into her room when she'd first arrived. Could her mother get her any clothes? And, could the meeting be in another room, perhaps?

Julia understood this and agreed to help, but quickly determined Missy had grown so much that none of her own clothes would fit. Missy was now much too big. Julia was only five-six and nowhere near as broad in the shoulders or wide in the hips. As Julia studied her daughter, she was taken aback by just how much she really had filled out and grown up. Since Missy was going soon for her MRI, Julia said she'd use that time to run out to a nearby store and get her a few things.

When she then tried to discuss sizes, Missy looked at her directly and said, "There are some things I'm not going to be able to talk about, Mom. Maybe later. Can you maybe just guess what I am and bring what you think might be right for me?" She simply had no idea what to share with her mother about the past two years. Two years during which she'd not been wearing any clothes! During which she knew she'd changed a great deal, getting taller and heavier and developing these nice boobs she now had! She was still trying to adjust to those and to how differently she was now experiencing certain sensations and feelings. Her sensitive nipples were especially disconcerting!

Julia then said, "Well, okay, but I will need to bring back two or three sizes to see what fits best. Do you know your bra size, Missy?"

"No, Mom, I don't." And, Missy just stared at her. She'd just been thinking about those sensitive nipples and now was totally at a loss. There was no way she could discuss any of this with her mom.

"Oh," said Julia, and as she looked into her daughter's eyes she realized she was seeing someone much, much older than the little girl who had disappeared from soccer camp. Missy had an unfathomable expression which was suddenly way too mature and grown up. It made Julia realize she still had no idea just what Missy had gone through, what experiences she wasn't able to talk about. "Okay. Stand up for me. I'll guess at things the best I can, Missy".

"Thanks, Mom. I really appreciate that." With great relief, Missy got up and let her mother make some comparisons. Julia managed this by going into her suitcase and using her own clothing items which she held up against Missy in order to estimate what sizes might be appropriate for her.

Julia grabbed her purse and was about to leave when Missy said, "Oh, and Mom? I think I'm getting my period soon. Can you bring me back some pads for that?" Missy knew it was now twenty five days since her first Shift back to human form and it hadn't happened yet, so it should be any time now. Her first period! She wanted to be ready but this was just one more subject which she didn't want to discuss with anyone else.

When Missy came back to her room, after her MRI procedure, she knew it would soon be time to finally explain things ... her mom and the FBI agents were going to want some answers. She felt about as ready as she'd ever be. She hoped they'd all be satisfied with what she planned to tell them. She knew there was a lot she simply couldn't explain. So, when her mother returned from shopping a little while later, they all got together down in the conference room which was being used by the FBI agents. Prior to going down there, Missy put on a nice bathrobe her mom had just purchased for her.

Doctor Walker was invited, but had not arrived yet since she was taking a quick look at Missy's latest MRI. Julia introduced Robert and Susan, explaining how the FBI had worked very closely with the family. Missy studied each of them, feeling much more secure now that she was able to pull her robe around herself. She wanted to appear more grown up and being in the robe helped with that, somehow. Even so, she was still nervous.

Robert said, "It's such a pleasure to meet you, Missy! Your family never gave up hope that you'd return and neither did we at the Bureau. When we heard the wonderful news that you were here at this hospital … even though at first it wasn't clear how badly injured you might be … well, all I can say is we were very pleased and excited."

Susan added, "We're also just that much more excited you've recovered so quickly. That explosion had to have been pretty bad for you. We understand you were knocked unconscious for a couple of days. We were really impressed by how you helped that family get out of their car. That was such a brave thing to do, Missy!"

"Oh," said Missy. "Thank you. It's nice to meet you folks, too. My mom has explained how you wanted to talk to me … you know … about stuff." She was very careful to pick and choose her words. She continued to look back and forth at the two of them. This was only small talk and she knew it. She didn't want to open up about anything yet, so she ignored the nice words of praise from Susan.

Julia suggested, "Let's wait another minute for the doctor. I think she's coming now." She knew how nervous her daughter was and wanted to give her just a little more time to fully compose herself.

Doctor Walker came in and her expression was a happy one. "Well," she said, "the MRI shows very little injury now, which is very good news. I can't understand it, Missy, and can only say this is a small miracle. Maybe even a big miracle!" Everyone laughed.

Missy said, "I really do feel pretty good now, doctor! I hope I haven't been a lot of trouble for everyone. You've all been very nice to me ... well, after that first time ... when you gave me that shot which made me go back to sleep, even though I tried to tell you I wanted to get up ..." She sort of ran out of anything more to say, so paused right there and looked at everyone again.

Robert took that opening to ask, "Where did you go that night, Missy? Everyone was really so worried ... we thought someone had maybe grabbed you. When they told us you were okay and were only getting something to eat in the kitchen, that was a big relief. But, that wasn't until much later, right? The hospital spent a few hours searching everywhere ..."

"I know, I know, I'm sorry!" Missy said. "I snuck out of my room and went up to the roof. That stuff Doctor Walker gave me was making me feel very woozy and I just had to get some fresh air. I had to get away from all those tubes and wires and machines and things. I may have napped up there for a while ... my head did still hurt ... then I was so, so hungry! I do need to eat a lot ... you know ... to keep my strength up and everything." She let all these words spill out in a rush, hoping to gloss over the details for that night.

"Hmmm, that's very interesting," said Susan. "I understand you really are a big eater, Missy. The nurses here have been telling us what a big appetite you have. Have you always been like that?" She looked over at Julia, to see if she might have any comment but Julia was staring at her daughter and didn't notice.

Missy then looked at each one of them. Slowly and carefully she said, "Okay. I know you really all want to ask me about my being gone. About why I'm now down here in Virginia, right?" She knew the adults really wanted to discuss her being missing for the past two years and not what a big appetite she might have or even what a great rescue job that had been up on the parkway two days ago.

Robert said, "Well, Missy, when you disappeared from soccer camp we never believed that you just ran away. And, then when we found your pajamas out in the woods ...?" He left that hanging there as a question, waiting to see her reaction and what she might offer as an explanation. He wanted to go very slowly and carefully, as there were so many possible ways this interview might evolve and he wasn't sure yet just how willing Missy really was to talk about all this.

Missy said, "I was forced to Change. And, I had no choice ... I had to go up into the mountains. That's where I've been all this time. In the mountains. But, there are things I can't explain." This was all the truth, of course, but Missy knew they couldn't understand what she really meant when she told them she was "forced to Change".

Julia then asked, "Can you tell us about that, Missy? Was there someone making you do that, forcing you to do things?" She knew this was the question which everyone wanted to ask about and she herself had certainly been tortured enough these past months with all the terrible worries, all the nightmares. Who had grabbed her daughter and what had they done!

"Mom, I can't really talk about a lot of this. All I can say is it wouldn't have been *safe* for you and Dad and everyone else ... if I hadn't gone up into those mountains, I just knew *bad things would happen*. I couldn't let those things happen. I'm so sorry!"

Tears were beginning to come down from Missy's eyes. She had really emphasized the word *safe*. And, the way she'd said *bad things would happen* made Julia realize that her daughter had really believed that. She'd believed that in a way which had left her no choice. It was somehow worse than merely being physically forced to go away. Her mother gave her some tissues. Missy wiped her face and then blew her nose.

Susan said, "All right, Missy. But, it's safe now, right? You can tell us now, right?" She was beginning to understand why a locked room may not have been necessary. Missy had clearly been threatened. She'd been terrified her family would be attacked and made to suffer the consequences if she didn't go along with whatever she was being forced to do.

"Well, there are so many things I can't explain," Missy replied. "This was a very difficult experience for me and I don't think anyone else can really understand. It's also that a lot of stuff has happened to me that I don't want to tell anyone about …"

Robert asked, "We don't want to embarrass you, Missy, but we do need to be sure you're safe now. And, that others are safe. You can see that, right?"

"Yes, I guess so."

"Can you tell us about those scars you have, Missy?" asked Susan. "That's a bullet wound on your leg, isn't it?" She thought maybe getting Missy to talk about something specific which had happened might get her to open up more.

"Yes." And, that was all Missy intended to say. The silence after she said that one word just hung there, but she didn't let that bother her. She patiently sat back and just looked at everyone.

Susan finally broke the silence by asking, "Can you explain how that happened?"

"Nope." Again, the silence was almost palpable. Missy looked at her mother, and took strength from the compassion she could see shining in Julia's eyes.

"What about on your shoulder? You have what looks like claw marks there. Did some wild animal do that?" Susan again looked for some way to get Missy to open up. She hoped asking about an animal attack would be better than trying to push Missy for information about how she'd been shot.

"Yep. That was a bear. A black bear. I was … I …" Missy paused. She really was not able to explain that and had no idea how she could continue. This was a story she knew she could never tell.

"Oh, Missy!" exclaimed Julia, breaking down at last. "You poor girl! What happened to you?" Now tears were coming from her eyes and she grabbed the tissues.

"Did you get any medical care for those injuries, Missy?" asked Doctor Walker. "There don't seem to be any stitches, but it appears they did heal up okay." She had understood what the two FBI agents were trying to do and thought maybe a different line of questioning might give Missy an easier way to open up and talk to them.

"No. No stitches. But, I healed up quickly. Just like now. But, these are just things I can't explain. Please don't ask me to talk about them. I just can't. I told you there was a lot of stuff that happened to me. I told you there was a lot that I couldn't talk about. Please. Why do you have to know this stuff, anyway?" Missy was starting to feel frustrated, knowing she wasn't able to tell anyone what she'd been through.

Robert then said, "Missy, we really need to protect you. If there's someone out there doing things, we need to get that person. You understand that, right?"

"Yes. Yes, I do," said Missy. Now she took a deep breath and looked at Robert. Then at Susan. Then, back again at Robert. She said, very slowly and with careful deliberation, "And, I can tell you this. There isn't anyone that you need to go get. It's safe now." She finally had something she knew she could talk about. She could say there was no one they needed to get. She could say it was safe now. It was over. Maybe they'd just leave her alone if she could make them believe that.

At this revelation, Robert and Susan looked at one another. Various possibilities for just what it might mean were going through their minds. In a very quiet voice, Susan asked, "How did you get down here, Missy? Why Virginia? When did you leave New Hampshire?"

Missy didn't really want to talk about other subjects. She wanted to further emphasize the fact that it was now safe. That there was no one they needed to go and get. So, giving them the short version, she explained, "After almost a year in the White Mountains, I came south. It was after the black bear mauled my shoulder. And after I was shot in the leg. It was time to leave that area." Again, she just paused, not wanting to add any more details.

"Did you come down in a car, Missy?" asked Robert. He was hoping to get some lead they could follow; anything that might lead to whoever had been keeping Missy in those mountains. He also kept hoping she'd begin to open up. He could see she was holding back on explaining things and he was looking for some way to keep the conversation going.

"No. No car. I walked."

"All the way here, from New Hampshire? You walked?" Robert wanted to pry information out of her but she was simply not giving him anything. And this just seemed incredible.

"Yes. It took a few months but I've been in the mountains around here for most of the last year. I saw some signs … these are called the Blue Ridge Mountains, right?" Missy asked. She avoided giving them any details and hoped she could continue doing that, avoiding things but being honest and truthful at the same time.

"And, you couldn't escape until just recently?" asked Susan.

Missy explained, "It still wasn't safe. I couldn't leave the mountains. I just couldn't. I didn't want anything bad to happen."

"But, what about now?" asked Susan. She and Robert exchanged glances. The discussion had gone full circle and they both knew it. They were back talking about why it was now safe, after all this time.

Missy knew what they were asking. She looked at them both and said, "There are things I can't tell you about. Please don't keep asking me. All I can say is that it's safe now. And there is no one that you need to get. *No one.*" She really emphasized these last two words.

After a very long pause, Robert suddenly said, "I think we're done here. Missy, thank you for talking to us. We really appreciate this."

Missy looked at her mother and gave a big sigh of relief, obviously happy the interview was over. "Can I go back to my room now? I'm feeling a bit tired. Thanks for being a friend to my family and helping look for me and everything. Mom told me about that."

Julia stood up and said, "Yes, this has been a lot for Missy. And, tomorrow's going to be a full day. We are meeting with that Stratton family Missy saved and with Senator Maxwell. And, maybe the hospital will release Missy, right? Doctor Walker?"

Doctor Walker could only acknowledge that indeed things looked very good and there really wasn't any reason not to release her after one more night of observation, assuming Missy was still feeling well the next day. Missy and her mom then left the conference room and returned to Missy's room. They were talking about trying on the new clothes which Julia had purchased.

Chapter Thirteen
Evening Aug 28 & Aug 29

Once Missy and her mom had left the conference room, Robert turned to Susan and Doctor Walker and said, "What do you think? She was so positive about how safe it is now and kept telling us there's no one to go after. And, it was obvious she wasn't going to say anything else. I believed her. And, she knows we can't find anything without her telling us where to look. Could this fifteen year old girl have really killed whoever was holding her? Or, could something else have happened, but now they're all dead ... whoever he or she or they might be?'

Doctor Walker exclaimed, "Is that why you said you were done? I was really surprised when you said that."

Susan said, "I was reaching the same conclusion as you, Robert. And, this girl has shown just how strong and capable she really is, rescuing that family, right?" She looked at each of them and went on to say, "We are not going to ever get anywhere trying to accuse a fifteen year old girl, a hero in fact, of having committed any crime. If she killed anyone, after whatever hell she was put through these past two years, it was certainly justified."

Robert said, "Exactly. There is no crime for us now. We certainly will never charge Missy with anything. There isn't much point in demanding she provide details. She obviously isn't willing to do that and we have no way of forcing her. She's been living with fear, forced to accept circumstances and conditions we'll never know about in order to protect her family. We'll never know since she's never going to tell us. And, she's no longer afraid. We certainly can't threaten her with anything. Nothing could possibly compare. As much as I'd like to dig up any bodies which might be up there in those mountains ..."

Doctor Walker now understood. "Closing the case is really okay, isn't it? She was very clear about there not being anyone to go and get. It doesn't sound like there are other victims to be concerned about ... there just wasn't that kind of vibe in anything discussed here was there?"

"No, doctor, not at all," said Robert. "While we sure would love to know all the answers, the important thing -- at the end of the day -- is whether or not there's any criminal activity to be concerned about. The way Missy looked at me, both times she said there was no one to get, it's pretty definite. She was very clear. Case closed. If she refuses to tell us anything, all we have is her walking down out of the mountains. We have no clue where in those mountains we might find anything. And, I'm pretty sure from the way Missy was acting, there won't be anything turning up. If it does, we can always reopen the case, but for now? We're done."

Susan added, "Yes, I was really sensing so many emotions and other things from this girl. She's only fifteen, but when she looks at you with those deep green eyes like that, eyes that have seen and experienced so much during these past two years. It really shows. She is definitely not a little kid any more. I know I wasn't working on this case until just two days ago, Robert, but the conviction which I've gotten from sitting here with her, listening to her talk. And also listening to her *not* talk. She was really amazing. It was those things, the things she said she couldn't tell us about as well as the way she said she couldn't talk about them, which really made shivers go up and down my back."

"Yes," Robert said, turning to look at Doctor Walker, "and it was you who said she was either a mystery or a miracle. I guess I'm not sure which, but there certainly are a lot of things deep inside of that girl. I agree with Susan here: she's amazing. The way she looked at us and quietly admitted to being shot, being mauled by a black bear. Those things were no big deal. But, about it not being safe for her family and other folks if she did not ...whatever! We'll never know. *That* was the really big deal for her. I really hope she can go home and somehow have a normal life now. If that's possible."

"Doctor, we're going to want the hospital to continue keeping a lid on all of this," Susan explained. "Since she's only fifteen, you really don't have to give out her identity, do you? We'll talk to that Stratton family she saved and Senator Maxwell. And, the police ... I know they'll all agree to cooperate. Can you explain the situation to the hospital staff?"

"Yes, I can see that's for the best," agreed the doctor. "If word gets out about her being found, after two years, the media will turn this whole rescue story into a circus. They won't leave the poor girl and her family alone, will they? They'll insist on getting answers about what happened up in those mountains."

"Answers, and maybe they'll want to dig up whatever bodies might be buried up there as well," Robert pointed out. "Just look at some of the articles which were written about her when she disappeared two years ago. There was so much speculation about sexual abuse, her maybe being held as a sex slave by some predator. We know she somehow got through this without being physically molested, but we really have no idea what she actually did go through. Just imagine what the media spin will be. She'll be described as the victim and when she refuses to talk, that will only feed into the story all the more."

Susan pointed out, "All that talk about it not being safe for others down here if she didn't stay up in those mountains. Robert, you are definitely right. She was totally convinced about that. She was forced into the role of being a martyr, along with whatever other roles she had to play in order to survive. There's no point in allowing the media to feast on any of this stuff. And, the sex slave stigma? How could she ever live that down? Let her and her family try to go forward now, without being bothered with any of that."

So, it was all agreed. The hospital would keep Missy's identity a secret, saying the family was very concerned. Since she was only a minor and not a public figure, she was entitled to her privacy. The dramatic rescue story would run out after a day or so, with all the focus being on the Strattons who were rescued and the visit from their good friend, Senator Maxwell. That should be enough news to satisfy everyone.

The senator fully understood and was happy to take the lead, and the spotlight. He scheduled another news conference for the next day, away from the hospital. He also agreed to work with Robert on how they could break the news story up north about Missy turning up, returning home after two years. Even without anyone knowing about her turning up in Virginia and her role in this rescue down here, there still would be a big news story in Massachusetts once she showed up back home.

The security detail was no longer needed, so Officer Williams and the other policemen all left the hospital that night. No one other than Officer Williams had ever really been told who Missy was. They only knew there'd been some concern about the mystery girl which the FBI agents had somehow managed to resolve. Robert and Susan paid a visit to the Roanoke police office and made sure everyone there was willing to protect Missy's secret. Most had only known about Doctor Walker and the FBI office requesting a security detail over at the hospital. Nothing had been confirmed at that time about exactly who Missy was; only that she'd been identified and that her family had some concerns. And, now everything was resolved.

Other than Nurse Gladys and a few other staff members, Doctor Walker didn't have anyone else she needed to explain things to at the hospital. Things had settled down and while there'd been a great deal of interest in the mystery girl, due to all the media reporting about the accident and rescue, followed by the hospital alert and search activity the previous night, that was now just old news. There had been that memo earlier in the day, explaining about there being a mix-up. Then, the mystery girl's mother had arrived. Now that the security detail was gone, the Strattons had been released and Missy was no longer in the ICU, everyone's focus shifted to all the other high priority activities the hospital had to deal with.

Missy and her mom spent a quiet evening together. After Missy tried on several of her new things, they sorted out just which sizes would fit her best now. She learned her bra size was 34C. And, there was a green dress they both really loved. When Missy saw the way she looked in that, she really began to cry. Her mother just had no idea what she was experiencing now, being a human once again. Seeing herself in a dress. Missy even asked Julia about help shaving her legs and under her arms. She ignored all the looks her mother gave her about that, refusing to explain anything and just pleaded for help.

Julia was so happy to be reunited with Missy that she chose not to push her about anything. All of the things she'd heard during the interview with the FBI were still whirling around inside her head. And then, she was so moved by the way her daughter completely broke down when standing in that dress in front of the mirror. She went over to her and just hugged her, holding on tight until Missy was finally able to regain some control. It was the first time Missy had lost her composure and it was heartbreaking. The questions about shaving, which it was obvious Missy had never done before, just somehow reinforced the fact that her daughter really had things she probably was never going to tell her about. Yet, none of that mattered any more. Her Missy was back!

The next day was very busy. First, of course, Missy had to eat her breakfast. Then, she wanted Julia's help getting dressed for their meeting with Senator Maxwell and the Strattons. She even let her mom apply a little bit of makeup and lipstick. She knew she looked pretty spectacular in her new green dress which matched her eyes, with her long red hair all combed out really nice. She was seeing the reactions from everyone else and it was a bit overwhelming. After having lived the way she'd been forced to live during these past two years -- a wild, predatory cat animal -- not knowing if she'd really ever be human again, this was almost all too much for her now.

They all gathered in one of the hospital conference rooms and it really was very festive. Doctor Walker and Nurse Gladys were there, along with some of Missy's other doctors and nurses as well as two members from the hospital public relations staff. Everyone understood about keeping Missy's secret, so she could go home and release whatever story would bring her the least amount of notoriety. There would be no connection with the recent events down here. Senator Maxwell and the Stratton family would be giving the hospital lots of good publicity, which was more than enough. Leaking anything about Missy would only result in losing this goodwill from the senator and his friends. So, this was truly just a "feel good" meeting and decorations had been brought in as well as some refreshments. They even had a cake, all in honor of Missy and what she had done.

Bill and Mary Stratton were there with Emily, who was really excited about getting to see Missy. Senator Maxwell had brought in two members of his staff. They'd flown in and were helping with various arrangements, including all the hospital publicity and his news conferences with the local media. Then, the senator still planned to join the Strattons up at their cabin for several days. Their vacations had been delayed but starting today, they intended to make the best of it. They all had a lot to be thankful for and were definitely looking forward to getting away, now more than ever.

Robert Ulrey and Susan Donavan had both come, as they really wanted to wish Missy all the best. They didn't often have a case that ended well, like this one had. And Missy had really impressed them. So, when Julia walked in with Missy, right away the celebration got going. She was the reason the Strattons were all alive and able to now continue on their vacation and everyone there wanted to acknowledge that. They also wanted to celebrate Missy's recovery, which was truly remarkable. It was less than seventy-two hours since Missy had arrived on that stretcher, unconscious, barely alive. Now she was radiant, with no hint of having experienced any injuries.

All dressed up with her long hair combed out and wearing the makeup and lipstick her mom had applied, Missy was absolutely stunning. Her natural beauty was breathtaking and she immediately captured everyone's attention. She was tall and the three inch heels on the shoes she now was wearing just made her height all the more apparent. She moved with a smooth grace but also exuded strength and power, somehow giving an impression of greatness in spite of her only being a teenage girl. Julia recognized the subtle changes which the past two years had made in her daughter.

And, also, there were the not so subtle changes. She stepped back and watched how everyone there was now so obviously affected by Missy. By this Missy, entering the room in full command of herself, alert and aware. Fearless. With depths which could not be penetrated. This Missy was not at all a victim, in any way, and that gave Julia a moment's pause. She really no longer knew her daughter and found herself in awe, just as those around her seemed to be.

Everyone kept taking turns in congratulating Missy, who in turn was very gracious. She thanked each of them but made little of what she had done, as though anyone would have done this. Robert was reminded of the comments he'd heard over and over from her teachers and coaches. In particular, how they had described Missy as being such a leader to others: *They get included in her accomplishments and achievements, "basking in the glow" of shared victories.* She was doing it now. Even the senator was being swept up by her charm and ... yes ... there was definitely some glowing. Incredible.

Emily suddenly stole the show by rushing into Missy's arms and being swept up, with squeals of happiness interrupting everyone else's attempts at conversation. Missy was genuinely touched and hugged her tightly, taking the time to really focus on the little girl. Her concern about the ordeal which Emily had been through was touching and everyone responded to that. Missy kept asking if Emily was okay now and if everything was good. Then, she held Emily at arm's length and looked right into her eyes as she told her, "Please call me if you ever, *ever* have anything you want to talk about or if I can help in any way, Emily. Promise me!" This made Emily just melt, as she promised she would definitely call Missy and everyone around was able to see there was a real connection there. Emily and Missy were now bonded, almost like sisters.

Cake and ice cream was enjoyed and the party gradually wound down as each person said their goodbye to Missy, wishing her luck and all the best. The senator pulled Julia aside to offer his assistance with any public statement she and her husband would want to make about Missy's return. He then turned to Missy to thank her for saving the lives of his close friends, assuring her of just how important that was to him. If he could provide her any help in the future, she was to be sure and let him know. He went on to explain, "Missy, I have instructed everyone on my staff that any time you should call my office, about anything … anything at all … they are to give you immediate access to me, wherever I am. If I can somehow repay you for the heroic actions you performed, I will be really happy to do that. Especially because this heroism is being kept a secret, due to the circumstances surrounding your safe return home, two years after being forced to disappear from that soccer camp."

Missy and Julia were deeply moved by everyone's assurances and good wishes, and especially by Senator Maxwell's sincere offer to help. They thanked everyone and said their goodbyes and finally managed to leave the hospital. Julia had booked a hotel room for that night, with flights home the next day. She wanted to take Missy shopping and so that's what they did for the rest of the day. By the time they settled into their suite, with room service sending up dinner ... a huge steak for Missy and a salad with a glass of wine for Julia ... they had managed to buy Missy enough clothes and accessories to fill two large suitcases. They were both extremely happy and kept laughing about how much fun the whole experience had been, with Missy trying on dozens of outfits at the various department stores, which she then paraded around in as though she were a model on the runway in Paris. For both of them, this day was truly one of the happiest days of their lives.

Chapter Fourteen
Aug 30 & later

Their flights home after checking out the next morning went well and they arrived at Logan airport mid afternoon, after a short layover in Atlanta. When they entered the terminal, heading for the baggage claim area, Missy's dad was of course waiting there with Heather and John and Patrick. Once again, the emotions escalated and the hugging seemed to go on forever. Then they finally collected all the bags, piled into the family car and went home. Missy actually broke down and could not control her sobs of happiness when she entered her home. There were balloons and banners everywhere and she thought her heart would burst with all the love she was feeling. Much later, when she went up to her room and found that it was exactly as she had left it, two years earlier, she again was overcome with emotion. Her family had truly never given up searching for her and hoping for her safe return.

The next day, the rest of Missy's family all came over. Grandparents, aunts, uncles, cousins and distant relatives she'd never even met before. It was a huge party, another McCrea family event like so many in the past, only this time it was all about her. She was able to enjoy the big reunion without getting overwhelmed too much, but it was indeed difficult. The way everyone was so thrilled about her safe return was so special and, the fact that she had dreamed of this for so many months, living in her cat form without really knowing if it would ever be possible, made it all that much more significant and meaningful. Her heart was truly bursting. Her tears would not stop flowing and it seemed this was contagious, as so many of her family all seemed to be having the same problem.

Julia had explained things to her husband, who had then called everyone in the family ahead of time. They all understood it was too soon for Missy to share anything at all about her experiences during the past two years. And, it was especially too soon to ask her for any details about why she had been forced to disappear and live up in the mountains and not call anyone for help. Only the closest family members were even told about Missy actually turning up in Virginia. Her parents wanted to find the right story they could give the public which would minimize the difficulty Missy was going to have. She, in turn, was really grateful everyone was being so understanding about her situation. She did have a few awkward moments when someone would ask her something specific or when she'd overhear various comments being made, which was more often the case. With her enhanced hearing, she was able to listen in on many of their conversations and knew they were all very curious about "Missy's secrets". But, she managed getting through it all and she really did appreciate all the love and good wishes.

As for her immediate plans, she was able to tell everyone that for the next year she would be studying with a few tutors whom her parents were arranging for. She had missed two years of school and would be missing one more while she worked with these tutors. This home schooling was going to require a real effort, as it meant doing three years worth of schoolwork in order to pass all the exams and qualify for entrance to her junior year at high school. But, she was determined to do all this in one year and get back on track with her life. She received a lot of encouragement from everyone and was assured they would help in any way they could. She knew, of course, there really wasn't much anyone else could do. It would all be up to her to do the work and demonstrate proficiency in each of her subjects. She had a full year ahead of her.

Granddad McCrea reminded her how he'd had to play catch-up, years ago. "After spending three years in two colleges, getting only one year's worth of credits, I went into the Army. When I came home from Vietnam, I was a sophomore my first year back in school but the next year I was a senior; I actually graduated in October rather than June. They mailed my degree in October after that one last class I took at night school during the summer to finish up. I'd already been hired full time as an engineer in June, of course. Cramming three years worth of engineering courses into just two had sure been a lot of work, especially since your uncle was born the end of the first year," he told her, laughing. She had heard the story before, but laughed with him. She really enjoyed listening to all his old stories.

"Yes, I know I have your great example, Granddad," she told him. "That will keep me going, for sure!" Her dad really looked up to his father, who had served as an artillery officer in Vietnam, and then had continued in the Army Reserve for the extra income while raising the family. He was still working part time as a retiree, while drawing pensions from two companies plus one from the Army. After staying in the Reserves for more than twenty years, he'd retired with the rank of Major. His Army retirement benefits had started once he'd turned sixty several years ago. "Can I count on you to come over and help with my math homework? You know my dad's always too busy, right? And, now that you're retired and all …?" she asked him. They both broke out laughing, and it really felt so good for Missy to be back home again.

She did ask her family to support her in other ways, in addition to arranging for her tutors. She knew she absolutely needed to be active physically. This, just like the huge appetite she had for lots of meat, was part of her dual nature. She got up each morning and ran five miles before breakfast, but that was not enough. Since she would not be enrolled in high school for another year yet, she couldn't participate on any school athletic teams. And, she had outgrown all of the youth sports programs which were available in her local community. But, she could participate in certain things, such as continuing with karate and taking various martial arts courses, such as kickboxing and jiu-jitsu. There were even competitions. She was eventually able to schedule two hours each Monday, Wednesday and Friday afternoon with additional events and meets on the weekends. Plus, she worked out at the gym on Tuesday, Thursday and Saturday, when she would do weight training.

But, before Missy started any of these activities, her family first wanted to announce her return to the news media. They waited a few days, while they all privately enjoyed having Missy back, and then Julia called Robert Ulrey for help. Would he be supportive for their story and announcement about Missy's return? Some of their friends and neighbors were already asking about her and it was important to issue a news release right away. Robert agreed and together they discussed the best approach for doing that, which included some of the suggestions from Senator Maxwell's office. The strategy they decided on was to first have Missy speaking for herself and to then have Robert come forward. He would have representatives be there from the local police as well. They'd invite the press to the McCrea home where Missy could read a statement. Since she was only fifteen, it was more than likely that any difficult, penetrating questions could either be deflected or avoided. Robert and the police would answer all the follow on questions, including whether the case was now closed or was there still any ongoing investigation.

The next afternoon, there was a large turnout by both the newspapers and local TV stations. Robert had talked to the police in Salem and Boston and they had helped alert the media about the breaking story. Both police departments had several members present there. A member from Senator Maxwell's staff was also there; he had been at Missy's celebration party that last day at the hospital and he had helped with some of the arrangements for this meeting. Having the senator's office involved had definitely added strong support and increased the turnout. A podium was set up outside Missy's house, with several microphones. She and her family came out and greeted everyone. Since this included many of her relatives, they made quite a large group. Her dad then started things off explaining their daughter Missy had returned home and, after a few short remarks, he introduced her so they could see her for themselves.

Then Missy stepped forward to read her statement. She was again looking spectacular, with one of her new outfits on and with her long red hair cascading past her shoulders. She was wearing just the slightest application of lipstick and makeup. This outfit was a casual ensemble consisting of khaki pleated pants, a white top and a dark yellow and gold blazer. Her smart sandals only had one inch heels so her height was not as much a factor; she was surrounded by several adults who were much taller. The intent was to have her looking very much like the young teenager she really was, rather than someone all grown up. Her appearance was definitely doing exactly that, giving her a fresh innocent schoolgirl look.

She gave everyone a huge smile and then said "Hi and thank you all for coming today." Looking at her prepared statement, she continued, "My family wanted everyone to know that I have returned, safe and sound, and the long ordeal of my being gone has ended. They also wanted me to say that all the support they have received during my absence has been greatly appreciated." Missy looked up and was able to continue speaking in a clear voice, only glancing down occasionally at the words she was reading. She made eye contact with each person in the audience as she told them, "I was forced to leave soccer camp two years ago due to some very unique circumstances and this has been a shocking experience."

She paused for just a moment, and then continued, "I know the story about my disappearance was in the news and that both an intensive search and a huge investigation were done, all in my behalf. This was a very difficult time for my family and I am so happy to finally be reunited with them once again." At this, she turned to smile at them all gathered around behind her and received many smiles in return. She looked back out at the crowd in front, glanced down at her statement, and added, "I was not able to communicate with anyone or free to leave until now. There are many things concerning my case which I still am not able to discuss. But, I am back now and look forward to returning to a normal life, catching up with all my school work and making up for lost time." She paused there for just a moment, looking out at her audience. Missy then glanced down once more at her statement after which she closed by saying, "Again, my family is ever so grateful for all the assistance and cooperation they have received from everyone. This was a terrible situation. But, it is over and I am home. Thank you all for coming."

Immediately, a dozen hands were raised and several voices called out asking questions. Most of these were some variation of "Missy, where were you?" or "Did someone kidnap you?" or "How did you escape?" or "Did the police rescue you?" Her dad stepped forward and held up both arms, saying, "Please, everyone. My daughter is not able to discuss many details and aspects of her case. The circumstances were very unique but the authorities have been extremely helpful. We have a representative here from the FBI who will talk to you. This is Robert Ulrey, the lead investigator in charge of Missy's case who has been helping us since the very beginning." With that, he turned to Robert who stepped up so Missy was now standing between the two of them. All three were at the podium in a united front which made for an excellent photo opportunity. Everyone in the audience with a camera took full advantage of this and many photos along with film footage were immediately taken, capturing the moment for broadcast on the news that night as well as for stories which would appear in newspapers and on the internet.

Robert then pointed to specific individuals who had their hands raised and fielded their questions one by one. No, his office was not at liberty to reveal exactly where Missy had been during the past two years. As a general answer, she had been up in the mountains. No, they were not ready to disclose any information about kidnappers or possible suspects. There had not been any arrests or confrontations. And, no, there was no one currently being held in custody or pending any charges. Also, what was important to note, there were not any suspects now at large. No, there weren't any other victims. Yes, Missy was safe now. No, the details and circumstances concerning her ordeal would not be shared. Full disclosure was, in this instance, not considered to be in the public's best interest. On and on it went with occasional comments from the police. Robert really handled the whole interview very well, with Missy and her entire family only needing to be seen there, all together now. As a final comment, Robert asked that the family be allowed some privacy and reminded everyone that Missy was, after all, only fifteen.

The press conference now over, the crowd slowly dispersed and those remaining were only looking to offer the family their congratulations and good wishes, rather than seeking any further information. Several friends and neighbors came up to express their joy and happiness about Missy's return. They complimented her on her statement, which she'd been able to give without appearing too nervous. She, in turn, was very gracious and expressed her thanks to everyone. Her "fifteen minutes of fame" now over, she hoped her public appearance would be enough to satisfy all the inquiring minds, and that she could now stay below the radar and keep a low profile. She was very aware that a lot of folks were still really curious, wanting to learn "what really happened to Missy" but she hoped all the attention would gradually go away. Having the FBI officially close the case while explaining the details were being withheld from the public for reasons which could not be shared really took the focus away from her. Let everyone go chase the government for answers.

She was very appreciative of what Robert Ulrey had just done for her and her family. His being there, answering all the questions in such an official manner while deflecting anything which might cause her any embarrassment was really huge. Everyone in her family fully understood how important his role had been and how well he had performed. His assistance and cooperation really helped and she could not thank him enough. He acknowledged her thanks and only asked that she put in a nice word for him with her good friend, Senator Maxwell. They both laughed at this, and Missy assured him that she would certainly do that.

Chapter Fifteen
Sep 2015 -- Nov 2015

Days went by, then weeks, then months. Missy worked very hard with her tutors and applied herself to her studies. At first, the task she had set for herself seemed overwhelming. How could she possibly accomplish three years of schoolwork in just one? But, she refused to get discouraged and continued working hard in each of her subjects. Some, like English and History, she really enjoyed and had no problem with. Other courses, like Math and Science, she found a bit of a struggle but she liked problem solving and was interested in these subjects, so making an effort was not that difficult. She especially wanted to take Biology but had to wait a bit, as that would come later. She first needed to complete her eighth and ninth grade courses.

Eventually, she would learn Spanish and find she enjoyed that. But, there were other things she would really have to work hard at. She did not like anything which required pure memorization, preferring things she could apply logic and reasoning to in order to get the correct answers. She was doing lots and lots of reading for all her various classes and the only way she avoided going completely stir crazy while doing that was by also spending several hours each afternoon performing some rigorous physical activity. Either working out at the gym or expending lots of energy during her various martial arts classes. She quickly moved up to brown belt in karate and knew she wanted to get her black belt over the next year or so. Her Sensei was very encouraging and provided her with an excellent training program, allowing her to advance at an accelerated pace.

Everyone who she would spar with, whether in karate or kickboxing or jiu-jitsu, would quickly complain that she was way beyond their level. She was just so fast. Her speed and agility, combined with her strength and fitness, always had them at a great disadvantage. She was also tough and resilient so she didn't seem to get bothered very much, even when she received blows which others might find debilitating. Of course, she was only trying to maintain her conditioning and had learned how to manage this with her dual nature without revealing just how enhanced her abilities and skills really were. She only entered competitive events in order to continue advancing in rank, without looking to win a lot of trophies. Even so, she kept winning the first place trophy every time she would participate at any tournament and she soon had the reputation as the competitor whom no one could beat.

She also reconnected with each member of her family. She learned about all of the various things which had happened during her absence, in addition to how big an effort had been made in searching for her. Her sister Heather had graduated from high school and was now starting her second year studying engineering at a university in Boston. Both their dad and Granddad McCrea had engineering degrees, so this was not any big surprise. She was living in Boston but early next year she'd begin her first co-op job, which meant she would be back living at home again for six months. Her university was noted for its Cooperative Education Program where students would alternate school and work sessions. It took one year longer to get a bachelor's degree but graduates then had accumulated about two years of practical experience working in whatever field their degree was in, which really helped their early careers when starting out.

Her brother John was now a senior at high school and she really enjoyed hearing about all the crazy things he and his buddies were involved in. He was the one who always made her laugh and the stories about his many escapades and how he managed to escape punishment were hilarious. He always got caught but then somehow came out blameless for all the mischief, in spite of really being quite guilty of having instigated everything. She knew who to go to if she ever needed any good excuses. His creativity was truly amazing. And, he did very well in all his subjects in school. Unlike Heather, he wanted to be a business major rather than becoming an engineer. He soon began visiting various colleges with their parents while he tried to decide where he wanted to apply. He also was very active at school, being treasurer on the student council that year as well as participating in several other extra-curricular activities. These would all look good on his college applications. Since he hadn't been much of an athlete, he thought these would be necessary and make up for that.

No one, other than Missy, had demonstrated anything special on the playing field. While Heather and John had both been on little league and youth soccer teams and had also participated on various school teams when they were younger, they did not continue in any sports programs once they got into high school. Even Patrick, who was in the seventh grade that year, was clearly not going to be any star athlete. Nor did he have any enhanced senses or other special abilities. While he was doing just great in school and was obviously just as bright and gifted as Heather and John, he had not inherited werecat abilities the way she had. And, Missy had been really watching Patrick very closely, as she'd wondered if he might. As he entered puberty, would he experience the Change and Shift? Missy believed her dual nature had to be genetic, which was partly why she was anxious to study Biology.

When she'd been in seventh grade, just a few months before that fateful day at soccer camp when she had her first Change, she'd done a science project all about Mendel's pea plant experiments. She had put together some simple charts showing how one in four pea plants would have purebred dominant traits, two in four would have hybrid traits and one in four would have purebred recessive traits. Thus, three out of four pea plants might be tall while one out of four might be short. Her charts used that to explain how two parents who both had brown eyes might have a blue eyed child. Brown was dominant and blue was recessive. While this was a rather simple explanation of genetics and heredity, she'd often thought about all this during the two years she'd lived in her cat form. She'd kept thinking what had happened to her must somehow have been caused by genes she'd inherited. Even before that first Change, she'd known she was different, with special abilities, and that others were not able to do all the things which she could do.

So now, she'd been watching Patrick. And, she was pretty much convinced that he, like Heather and John, was normal and had not inherited whatever it was that made her the way she was and what she was. A werecat. Someday soon she wanted to reveal this to her family, explaining how she had this dual nature. She knew she'd have to actually show them, since otherwise it wasn't likely anyone would ever believe her. But, her siblings needed to understand that if they someday had any children, there was a possibility one or more of their children could also be like her. It was only fair. No one else should ever have to experience the pain and terror, being completely ignorant of what was happening to them, which Missy had endured.

While other family members were probably not as much at risk, Missy still looked very closely at each of her cousins who hadn't yet reached puberty. So far, no one was showing any special abilities the way she had. It was knowing she really had been unique before that first Shift which, in hindsight, was helping her understand many things about herself now. Her Change had been forced on her at puberty, but being a werecat had not started then. She had always been a dual natured werecat. Then, she'd grown and matured, experienced the Change and all her powers and abilities had increased accordingly.

She now had blended her two natures, melding them into one. She'd learned to compartmentalize her thoughts and instincts. She could control herself and be either way in either form. And, she had all these enhanced senses and abilities with a great deal of carryover. While she might not see in the dark as well in her human form as she did in her cat form, her nocturnal vision was way more than that of any other human. It had been more even before her first Shift but now, it was way more. This was true for all her senses and abilities. And, as she'd learned when rescuing the

Stratton family, at times of great stress she could draw on her cat form while still human and gain even greater power, if and when needed.

Her first two months back home hadn't provided any opportunities to Shift back into her cat form. And, she'd wanted to test herself and see if prolonged periods as a human would cause her any problems. She'd managed okay but had definitely been feeling a need, a pull, to Change. After that, she found ways to be alone for time periods longer than the three hour minimum she needed. And, she found places where she could be a mountain lion without risk of discovery. She could strip down, hide her clothes, Shift and allow herself to again experience being a cat. This always brought her great joy and fulfillment. Since she knew she could later Shift back, get dressed and return to her human life, these hours when her "beast within" could roam free were all the more exhilarating. To be complete, every once in a while she had to be a cat.

Chapter Sixteen

Sep 2015 -- Nov 2015

Her old friends all came to see her but she only reconnected with a few of them. It was very difficult at first, as she wouldn't discuss details of her time away and, unlike her family who understood this, her friends did not. They couldn't help pushing and probing for more. And, so much had happened for them, it was almost like they were total strangers. Without being in school, there weren't the shared experiences and it was difficult finding things in common. She hadn't even watched TV for two years. And, now that she was working so hard with her tutors, she just had so little time. Few of her old friends were going to the gym and none were in any of her martial arts classes. After several weeks, the novelty of her return was gone and most of her friends began saying how things would be better next year. Next year, when she was finally back in school with them.

But then, she found herself making some new friends, girls from those martial arts classes and also from the gym. Most were older than she was, but that was okay. Her social life was so limited by the schedule she was on, it didn't matter. She would relax and have fun with whoever was available during those few times each day when she had the chance. After the isolation she'd lived through in the mountains, this was more than enough. That, and the fact she really was very shy about relationships with boys. She wasn't at all ready to begin dating yet. She was feeling a lot of things in ways which were so different now. Now that she'd returned and now that she was coping with all those raging hormones! Before, she really hadn't experienced sexual desires the way she was having them now.

Oh, sure, she'd noticed some things when she was twelve. And, at thirteen, the talk was always about boys and sex but, it was only talk. No one was doing anything and she was quite happy to merely listen to all the talk and laugh at all the silly stuff. Boys hadn't really been all that interested in the girls back then. It had been more what all the girls were saying and they were definitely the ones taking the lead. Since Missy had been such a late bloomer, she'd stayed in the background. With all her other activities, it had been easy to ignore a lot of the whole boy-girl drama and being ignored didn't matter much either. Then, after she Changed, matured as a mountain lion and began cycle after cycle of being in heat, sex had a whole new meaning for her. Things had then gotten serious and she had to not only control her own animal nature and instincts but also deal with several male mountain lions. Sex was just not going to happen with any of them and that required some real effort. Effort to ignore her own body's cravings and more effort to escape into the wilderness without being followed.

Now, at fifteen and once again a human girl, Missy was learning about sex all over again. There were all the ways her body was reacting and she needed to find ways to control those feelings. Thank goodness for bras since her naughty nipples would often stand up and take notice, and these would then act like control knobs for how things would tingle and feel down below. She wore comfortable bras which didn't betray how things might be happening for her. And, she always wore her karate gi or judo gi at the gym as well as during all her martial arts classes. This loose fitting uniform kept her well covered up, so all her curves were not so noticeable. This was important since she could see that now, boys were very interested. Interested in sex and very interested in her. She knew she was attractive and because of the way her body had now filled out, with nice long legs, curvy hips, narrow waist and a very visible bust line … well, even all covered up she was constantly getting attention. Lots and lots of it.

With her enhanced hearing, she could hear many of the male conversations and from the remarks being made about her, she knew just how much she affected them. Even all covered up, she apparently "had a great ass" and "wonderful tits" which they were still able to notice. And, wishing they could see more of. This was a subject they seemed to constantly talk about amongst themselves, endlessly making comparisons and speculating about just how "hot" she was. Of course, from many of them, she also heard all their theories about her having been a sex slave and how she was now "damaged goods". Ugh! Thank goodness there were several boys who refused to believe any of that and spoke up on her behalf. She took notice and knew who they were as well as who all the others were.

What was more disconcerting, however, was how much the "awareness" of the opposite sex could sometimes affect her. Just the musky, male scent from some handsome, hunky guy could catch her attention and then cause her immediate arousal; this often was quite difficult to ignore. Missy was a very physical, sensual person and her body was now fully awakened to sexual desires. Everything was enhanced for all her senses and feelings. While not ready to allow herself to have any sex, just as when her cat form had been in heat, her body's hungers and needs were easily triggered and she often would experience those familiar throbbing, pulsating sensations. In the words she kept hearing the guys all use, she often was feeling very "horny". But for Missy, as with every other aspect of her life, losing control was not an option. She learned to control herself in this with the same determination and will she used for all her other efforts and activities.

Since her experience with relationships was lagging far behind her physical senses and abilities, and living alone for two years had certainly not helped with that, Missy continued being very shy with boys. She just didn't know what to say or do. And, she didn't have time for relationships anyway. She was much too focused on balancing everything else going on in her life. First, there was adjusting and reconnecting, just being back home again with family and friends. Then she had all the homeschooling work so she could return to school combined with the physical activities which were so essential to her well being. Finding opportunities to Change every once in a while and enjoy a few hours as a cat were far more important than investing any time in relationships with boys. That would just have to wait until later.

Of course, later was only a few short months away. While she still wouldn't exactly be having relationships or changing how she was spending her time, she would overcome her shyness and become quite comfortable dealing with the opposite sex.

Perhaps be even more comfortable than when being with the girls.

While her karate training could continue very nicely as she made steady progress toward earning her black belt, this was not the case for kickboxing and jiu-jitsu. Even second degree and third degree black belt ranks would be possible in karate, still with her same instructors. But the girls taking kickboxing and jiu-jitsu were nowhere near as serious and dedicated as Missy and so the instructors available locally weren't that good; they really couldn't help her advance very far. There hadn't been the demand, so there just wasn't that high a level of teaching available in the Salem area. Or, even in Boston. The sessions were merely workouts where she was getting some exercise but after a few months, when everyone refused to spar with her anymore, even that benefit went away. She really couldn't complain. She knew, even though she was holding back, her opponents were all getting completely overwhelmed and she didn't blame them. She just needed to move on to something else.

Most of these local classes were co-ed with the competitions separate for girls and boys, but there was one mixed martial arts class with only male students. The instructors for that class were excellent. After a long discussion with the Sensei, who by then had heard all about "the girl whom no one could beat" in any tournament competition, she was allowed to enroll. She wouldn't actually compete in any local tournaments as there were no female competitors. So, unless she was willing to travel to some distant cities, which she really didn't have the time for, she'd have to be okay with that.

She was the only female and, at first, she wasn't even able to spar with the others. After two weeks, she began to insist. She assured everyone she didn't care about tournaments or trophies, but that she deserved the opportunity to spar. That way, even though she wouldn't be earning any official recognition for advancing in levels, she knew she'd be getting the actual training she wanted as well as the extreme exercise she needed so badly.

She was starting out at an intermediate level, due to what she'd already demonstrated in her other martial arts courses. And, there were some guys who had only been training a year or two, whom she was matched up with. That was okay for a few weeks, but soon Missy wanted more. Sparring with these intermediate level guys was no longer a challenge. The other guys, however, were very advanced and they all wanted to ignore her. Not only did they have so much more training, but many of them were very big guys. Some were several inches taller who weighed eighty to a hundred pounds more than Missy did. One guy was more than double her weight, and it was all solid muscle. Plus, she wasn't even sixteen yet. They insisted they couldn't spar with her because she'd be injured, for sure, and they didn't want to be responsible for that. Unlike her karate and her other courses, the sparring in this course was full on contact.

Missy asked her dad to help, since he was a lawyer. She wanted legal waiver forms she and her parents could sign so she then could compete with any of them. After all, it wasn't official. This sparring wasn't in any tournament. She wouldn't even be getting credit towards any belt. She just wanted to spar once a week during the regular classes. Eventually, she was able to get her way. When the intermediate level guys no longer wanted to spar with her, because she was just too good and too fast, that definitely helped.

She was slowly earning everyone's respect for her natural abilities without damaging any of their fragile egos. She'd been very careful not to do that, and had been very willing to allow many of their blows to land in the process. Getting pummeled was okay since she was able to avoid any serious damage or injury to herself, and she healed up so quickly, it didn't matter. Her opponents weren't losing face, even though she was much faster and able to place her kicks and strikes on them with obvious skill. They stopped worrying about hurting her and actually took some satisfaction in at least scoring some decent points against her, even if they were often the one losing the contest.

Her resilience was amazing. This became a reason for the guys to constantly strive harder. No matter what they did, no matter how hard they might hit her, she never seemed to really get hurt. She always just bounced right back up again, and they all just sort of got used to that. Without really thinking about it, they accepted it. Missy was no longer "a girl" but just "another guy" when they were sparring. Of course, she gave as good as she got, and they learned never to underestimate her. Once they were sparring, they quickly learned not to be distracted by her obvious female assets. She was so fast and her blows were very powerful, even though she weighed so much less than they did. One by one, each of the bigger, stronger, more experienced guys would get in the ring and spar with her. Not quite at the no holds barred level, but the more they sparred with Missy, the more they would go all out. Missy was finally getting the extreme exercise she wanted. And, she was able to be more and more relaxed being around guys. Her shyness just gradually went away without her giving that much thought to it.

She did not, however, encourage any relationships. They all kidded her about never dating. Their attitude towards her was greatly influenced by her skills and abilities combined with her good natured willingness to accept whatever they could dish out in the ring. The ring actually was an octagon cage with walls. They'd toss, throw or kick her up against one of those walls again and again, only to have her bounce back and sweep them off their feet. As week after week of this went by, Missy managed being accepted as a person without being seen as a sex object.

She continued to only wear karate or judo gi uniforms and always had a protective sports bra underneath. This helped to blur many of her female curves. She didn't change before or after class, but came in that way and went home that way. Her long hair was always in braids or tightly tucked into a bun. She didn't wear any makeup and avoided looking glamorous. They all still considered her very attractive anyway. Outside of the ring, they considered her sexy and hot as hell. But, they just didn't think of her as a possible girlfriend.

Chapter Seventeen
Nov 2015

At home, she was also getting more relaxed whenever John's friends were around. She'd known most of these guys for years but things now were different. No longer was she the pesky little sister who they all wanted to ignore. Now, she had grown up and was definitely attracting their attention. She was turning them on just by being in the same room with them. Or, by being in the next room. Even had she not gone missing for two years, returning with secrets they naturally all wanted to find out about, this would have been true. She was so attractive and her sexuality was now such an obvious part of her presence, regardless of whether she dressed up or not, they all practically tripped over themselves whenever they came around.

Her martial arts reputation wasn't that much a factor with them, one way or the other, since they'd all known her for years. The mystery with "Missy's secrets" only added to their wanting to know her better. John kept them in line, of course, but they all enjoyed teasing her any time they got the chance.

Weekends, when they'd be there and see her eating any of her meals, they'd always make comments. "Look how much food she's devouring!" and, "That's surely going to affect her girlish figure!" She always had lots of meat, typically cooked quite rare, at every meal: morning, noon and night. Her family had accepted this and because she exercised so much, running every morning and working out every afternoon, her huge appetite no longer surprised them. John's friends all knew how active she was but they grabbed at any excuse to talk about her figure.

It wasn't just how curvy and sensuous she appeared, but also the way she moved. She had such grace and style, gliding smoothly, effortlessly. At times, she'd sneak up on them without their even knowing she was there. Missy definitely got their blood racing whenever she was around and they loved the way she always would react, laughing and being very much a fun person. She also knew all their girlfriends and who was dating whom and who had broken up, so that just added to the banter as she'd threaten to tell on them.

They trusted her, though, because she never would tell tales or betray any confidences and they all knew it. They often would tell her things without realizing just how revealing that was. Things they wouldn't share with John or any of their other friends but they'd end up discussing them openly with her. And, that was how Missy learned about Alice having some sort of a problem, from one of these private discussions with Mark.

Alice Morris was a really pretty blond, blue eyes, five-five with a nice figure and was supposedly Mark's girlfriend; they'd been going out, off and on, for years. She was now a junior, a year older than Missy, and while never a close friend they still had all grown up together and knew one another pretty well. But, Missy was learning things with Alice had somehow changed. Mark told her, "She just really gets so uptight whenever we try to make out. Anything more than a little kissing and she freezes. She says she really cares about me but she just can't let herself relax and ... well ... whenever I touch her, it's no good."

Missy asked, "Are you sure you're not moving too fast, Mark?"

"No, not at all. She's not just sending me signals, she actually tells me she wants me to do stuff. But, if I touch her breast or start getting physical in any way, she turns into a cold statue. She actually will let me do whatever I want but I know she's not feeling good about it, which pretty much kills it for me. Can you talk to her, Missy? See if you can get her to tell you anything? I know there's no one else that she's seeing or has any interest in seeing. This has just been the way she always reacts. It didn't matter that much at first but we're older now and I sort of thought we'd be taking things to new levels, you know?"

"What about other girls for you, Mark? Are you really sure you're into Alice this much?" Missy knew he'd been out with a few other girls, and he was a very good looking guy, popular at school.

"That's just it, Missy," said Mark. "I've dated other girls and even ... well, we never went all the way or anything but ... let's just say I know when a girl is actually enjoying the way I ... you know. Stuff. Hot and heavy. I could have done lots more with a couple girls, but they weren't Alice. And, it's always been Alice, for me, you know? I want to see where things might be going for her and I, especially since this is my last year in high school. Next year, when I'm away at college, will I be coming back to see her or will I be moving on? It's

way too soon for any big commitments but, you know …
right?"

"Okay, Mark. I'll go see her. I won't tell her
about your feelings for her, as that's for you to do. And,
I won't mention your concern about how she freezes up
like that. But, I know I can find out if there's some
problem, one way or another, and I'll get back to you.
Promise." And, Missy kissed Mark on his cheek, just as
she would her brother.

He left, greatly relieved, and Missy found an
excuse the next day to drop by Alice's house to pay her a
visit. She told Alice she was doing a project for one of
her home school classes and was interviewing random
students in each grade about the five things they liked
and the five things they didn't like at the high school.
For her assignment, she was then going to analyze all
the data, summarize the results and provide some
recommendations. She was assuring everyone that
their participation was completely anonymous, so they
could be honest and say whatever they really wanted.
Maybe her report would be submitted to the school
paper; she wasn't sure about that yet.

Alice invited her in and they spent a half hour
talking about various things. She wanted to help.
Everyone knew how hard Missy was working to catch up
with her subjects. And, they shared a lot of the same
friends so there was plenty to talk about. What Alice
didn't realize, however, was that Missy was able to scent
a man's smell on her. And, to Missy's sensitive nose, it
was obvious that Alice had very definitely been having
sex with that man. Missy noticed this right away, as
soon as she came in and sat down with Alice. She could

also scent this man was living there. So, after chatting about everything and getting Alice's answers for her survey questions, Missy then asked about Alice's mom. How were things going? She learned that Alice had a stepfather, Tony Gonzales, who had married her mother three years ago.

Her father had never been in the picture, having divorced her mom when Alice was only three. He'd moved away and never checked on them. He'd avoided paying any child support and was not interested in them at all. Her mom had always worked to support the two of them and getting married again was supposed to be making things so much better. Financially. Tony owned three restaurants. Now they lived in this nice house rather than that crappy third floor walkup. As Alice explained things, Missy could see there was some real tension whenever she was talking about Tony. It became obvious Alice wanted to avoid talking about him at all. She kept changing the subject and saying how hard it still was for her mom, who worked nights at Walmart. Second shift paid more. And, Tony wasn't all that generous with his money.

Missy was pretty sure she understood the situation well enough. Alice didn't want to hurt her mother, who had sacrificed everything working as a single mom and then, finally, had ended up with a husband who was supporting them. The fact this guy had managed to molest and abuse Alice, probably starting when she was only thirteen, and had forced her to keep that a secret? Not such a big surprise. Missy had read about situations like this but had no idea how to deal with it. She could remember seeing TV shows, from back when she used to watch TV, which showed how things like this could happen. And, how the victims could feel so trapped, afraid to reveal anything. Afraid they'd be blamed, afraid their mother would be hurt, and all sorts of other fears. Fears that made them keep silent.

She told Alice she had to get going and thanked her for helping with her assignment. She wanted to go home and sort through what she'd learned and try to find some way to help Alice. And, she didn't think talking to Mark was going to accomplish anything good. Alice would have to eventually do that, but only when she was ready. Missy was going to have to figure this one out on her own. Before she left, she looked directly at Alice and said, "You know, if you ever need a friend, Alice … someone you can tell stuff to and who can keep a secret? I know how it is, when you have to keep stuff secret. And, I've had to deal with some pretty terrible things … I might be able to relate to stuff, you know? You can call me. Anytime." Missy stopped and just looked at Alice.

Alice suddenly had tears welling up in her eyes. It looked like she wanted to say something, but then she held back. She stopped herself and looked away. However, she finally did look back and said, "Missy, that's really so nice of you. You're a special person. I'll think about that …"

Missy stepped up and gave Alice a hug. It was all she knew how to do, for the moment. It was obvious Alice would need more time. She'd been keeping a terrible secret for a long time and wasn't ready to tell Missy anything. But, Missy felt they'd shared a connection, and hoped Alice might realize that if anyone could relate, that person was Missy. While she'd not really been a victim, she knew what everyone else thought, so she was hoping to use that now. She hoped Alice's thinking Missy had been grabbed by someone would help convince her to talk to Missy about her stepfather. But, she knew this would not happen all at once and so she said goodbye and left.

Once back home, she decided to do some research about Tony. She learned he'd been married before and had a daughter named Roseanne who was now twenty-five. His first wife had died tragically six years earlier from a hit and run accident when she was walking home from the corner store. The driver was never found. Tony was at one of his restaurants when the accident happened. Missy was able to learn these things by finding the wife's obituary on the internet along with some of the news stories about the tragic accident, but she didn't really know how to find out anything else. Then, that night, she got a call from Alice.

Alice had been very moved by her meeting with Missy and, as Missy suspected, she did believe Missy probably had been molested and abused. She had watched Missy's press conference on TV and was surprised that no details were being given out. But then, she'd thought to herself that really was a good thing; the public didn't really need to know. She'd wished right then her problem could somehow be solved that way. So, now she called Missy back. Hesitating, she asked, "Did you really mean that today, Missy? About keeping secrets?" From the emotion in her voice, Missy just knew what Alice wanted to tell her. And, that she was ready to do that.

Missy assured her, "Oh, yes! Alice, you can tell me stuff. Really, you can. I'll help and I won't tell anyone else unless you want me to." Pausing, she waited several seconds. Then she added, "I think I already know anyway. It's your stepfather, right? He's … doing stuff to you and won't stop. And, you can't tell your mom?"

"Oh, Missy," cried Alice. "How did you know that? Please don't tell anyone! If he even suspected anyone else knew, I don't know what he might do to me! Please promise. Please?" Missy heard all the fear but she also could hear some relief in Alice's voice.

"Alice, I promise. And, you can talk to me. Tell me everything. You need to tell someone about stuff like this. Let's try to find out what can be done." Missy wanted to reassure Alice and maybe together they might find a way to deal with it.

"Can you come back over here, Missy? My mom's at work and Tony's actually out of town on a business trip. I can't do this on the phone." Alice felt as though a huge weight was being lifted off her shoulders, even though she didn't really expect Missy could help solve things. But, if Missy could just keep her secret? The way she'd been keeping her own secrets? She thought that might make some difference if she were able to tell Missy her secret about Tony without fear of anyone else finding out.

"I'm on my way right now," Missy told her. "Be right there!"

An hour later, Alice had ended up telling Missy everything. Once she'd started talking and had admitted how her stepfather had come into her bedroom that first time, not long after he'd married her mom, the rest of the story had all come out. Missy was shocked at many of the details but then again, not so shocked. She really could understand why Alice had felt so trapped and helpless. This kind of sexual molestation happened all the time and there were no simple, easy solutions. Even now, Alice was horrified to think how hurt her mother would be to find out. Would she even believe it? And, if she did, would she believe Alice was the one at fault? Tony had her convinced that no one would ever believe he was the bad guy here. And, now that she was over sixteen, the laws were not as strict; she'd reached the age of consent in Massachusetts. He'd claim she was the one who seduced him and it would be his word against hers. She had no way to prove anything had ever happened before she'd turned sixteen. She had no way to prove anything now.

Missy told Alice not to panic and that she'd definitely help her. They talked for a long time and Missy even wondered about Tony's daughter, Roseanne. Did Alice know anything about her? Missy wondered if she might have also been molested. If so, and if she filed a complaint about incest, age of consent wouldn't matter and it was still well below the statute of limitations. Missy's dad was a lawyer so she'd known enough to check this out on the internet. Alice really had never thought about any of this before. And, she actually had met the daughter once. It had been at the wedding three years ago. Then, when they checked in her mom's address book, they found a phone number for her.

Alice said she didn't want to contact or confront Roseanne. She was too afraid of what might happen and not at all sure how things might go, either way. But, she was starting to really feel she could trust Missy. And, Missy kept assuring her it wasn't hopeless. Somehow, they'd find a way. Alice felt so good being able to finally discuss what she'd lived through, knowing she wasn't being judged or blamed. Missy just had a way of making her feel okay about things. Hopeful, even. And, protected. The numbing fear she'd held inside for so long was not there when she talked to Missy.

Missy, meanwhile, knew it was time to take a step back. She'd survived in those mountains for two years as a predatory cat, stalking her prey. There was no rush. She did tell Alice that once her stepfather returned, if he gave her any problems, Missy would rush right over there. She wouldn't confront him about anything but merely show up saying they'd arranged a sleepover. Alice only needed to send her a blank text message and she'd be over there, ringing the doorbell, in less than fifteen minutes. Alice felt confident she could manage and cope knowing that. She'd been living with this monster for three years now and knew how to anticipate what he would do and what demands he would make. She could evade him well enough and, when she knew he was going to want sex, she now could explain Missy was on her way over for a pre-arranged sleepover. If he forced her to call Missy to cancel, that would obviously be a red flag and she knew Missy would then definitely find some excuse to show up.

Chapter Eighteen
Nov 2015

Things went well after that, for more than a week. Missy did go over a few times and was introduced to Tony as Alice's good friend, now back home again. Mark's best friend was John McCrea, remember? And, Missy was John's sister. Alice had talked about all these guys often enough, so it wasn't that strange for Missy to suddenly be showing up, even though she wasn't in Alice's classes. Of course her stepfather had heard about Missy. Who hadn't? She wasn't back in school yet because she was doing all that makeup work with her tutors.

The thing Missy noticed most about Alice's stepfather during all this was how his eyes kept wandering all over her body. It was very obvious he was undressing her in his mind. But, she was able to smile and put on a great act, giving no indication she knew anything about his abuses of Alice.

In addition, Missy tracked down Roseanne. It hadn't been difficult finding her. With a couple of fake phone calls, she'd learned where she worked and by what last name she was going by now. She'd married but was now divorced. Interestingly, she'd kept her married name rather than go back to her maiden name. Missy used internet searches and found some arrest records, once for drug possession and once for prostitution. She hadn't been convicted for either of these but had gone to rehab, paid for by the state. Six months ago, she'd been released from rehab and was now holding a steady job as a waitress over in Lynn. She was still staying at a halfway house, also in Lynn.

Missy had John bring her over to the restaurant where Roseanne worked and they both entered and sat in a booth. Roseanne came up and introduced herself as their waitress. If a different waitress had been assigned, Missy would've asked to move so they'd end up with Roseanne but that hadn't been necessary. She ordered her usual huge meal, which included a large steak which Missy went into great detail talking about, explaining how rare it needed to be cooked. John laughed at her and ordered a fisherman's platter. When her meal came, Missy asked Roseanne to explain several things and then began chatting, just making conversation. These conversations were enough, however. Missy was able to get a pretty good sense about Roseanne.

The good news was she was sober and not taking any drugs. Missy could tell just by her scent she wasn't using anything. The bad news was Roseanne would never make a credible witness. And, she wasn't ever going to the police. She'd never be filing any complaint. Her life had just been too hard and, at only twenty-five, she was all washed up and looked forty. She had a very low sense of self worth and it showed. Missy felt really sorry for her.

At the end of their meal, Missy called Roseanne over and introduced herself, explaining she was good friends with Alice. Talking very fast, so Roseanne had no chance to get a word in, she babbled on and on. Without saying how she knew about it, she just started talking about Alice's stepfather Tony being Roseanne's father. Roseanne was too slow to question this. Missy pretended seeing her there was just a happy coincidence and kept saying things about Alice's stepfather, as though Alice, Tony and Roseanne were all one big happy family. Then she asked in all innocence when Roseanne had last seen Tony. That caused a curtain to drop down and brought fear into Roseanne's eyes. She stared at Missy and said, "I hope I never see that bastard again! Tell your friend to get as far away from him as possible!" With that, she quickly turned around and walked away.

John looked at her and asked, "What was that all about, Missy? And, how do you even know that woman? When did you start hanging out with Alice, anyway?" Missy went right on with her innocent act, as though nothing unusual was going on and changed the subject. She asked him, "When will I be meeting this new girlfriend of yours, John? Are you bringing her over for dinner anytime soon, so she can meet the family?"

This question did successfully distract John, who replied, "Claire has already met everyone, except for you, Missy. And, the way you eat, I certainly don't plan to bring her over to watch that spectacle. She's not really my new *new* girlfriend anyways. She's my new *old* girlfriend, since we went out for a while last year. That's why everyone else already knows her. Maybe some night after dinner, I'll bring her over so you can meet her. We can all watch a movie together or something. Only if you promise not to eat up all the peanuts, popcorn and pretzels though!"

Missy laughed and promised she'd be on her best behavior. John told her he'd love to see that, and they bantered back and forth all the way home. He never did figure out exactly why she'd made him bring her over to that restaurant in Lynn. Meanwhile, Missy had pretty much confirmed her suspicion that Alice's stepfather had sexually abused his own daughter when she was a young girl. She felt certain Roseanne's many problems could most likely be traced back to that. Unfortunately, that wasn't going to help Alice in any way now. Some other strategy was needed. She just wished she had some other ideas for what might help.

Three days later, she got a blank text message from Alice at 9:35 p.m. She grabbed the small suitcase she had prepared earlier, already packed and ready for this situation, and raced out telling her mom she was going over to Alice's. She was able to cut through back yards and get over to Alice's house in twelve minutes. She rang the front doorbell and waited. She could hear muffled cries from upstairs and she rang the bell again. There was no one coming down so after thirty seconds, she ran around back. There was a bulkhead door leading down into the cellar and she forced her way in, applying some extra strength to the wooden door at the bottom so the lock just broke off. Once inside, it was dark but she was able to see where the stairs were and raced up, entering a pantry off the kitchen. That door wasn't locked so she came in, turning on lights and calling out, "Hey, Alice, I'm here now. Where is everyone?"

This brought Alice's stepfather down and he was definitely not happy to see her. "Why are you here, Missy?" he growled at her. "Alice didn't mention anyone coming over tonight." He stood at the bottom of the stairs, blocking the way up. Tony was only two inches taller than Missy but weighed about two hundred pounds.

Missy put on her innocent act and said, "Oh, really? Maybe I got the nights mixed up or something. Can I talk to Alice? She'll know." She was now in the middle of the living room, still holding her little suitcase.

Tony said, "Alice isn't feeling well so she won't be coming down to talk to you. I think you should go home now. I'll have her call you tomorrow." He clearly wanted her to just leave and wasn't going to call up the stairs for Alice to come down.

Missy dropped her suitcase and said, "Oh, I'll just go up and check on her. If she's not feeling well, maybe I can get her something. I'll only be a minute." Without giving him a chance to even object, she raced over and squeezed past him. Before he could stop her, she was up the stairs and walked down to Alice's room. She was, after all, able to move really, really fast when she wanted to. He turned around, shocked and now getting very angry. He yelled at her, "Hey, get the hell out of here! Where do you think you're going, young lady?"

Missy was already in Alice's room and could see poor Alice all curled up in bed in a fetal position. She was naked, under a sheet. And, lying in plain sight on the nearby dresser was a condom, still in its wrapper which had already been torn open. It was very obvious what she was walking in on and had obviously stopped from happening. Just in time. Behind her, Tony came into the room and he was furious. But, Missy looked at him and yelled, "Stop! Stop right there or I'm calling the police on you!"

"You bitch!" he yelled at her. "You don't know anything and you're not calling anyone, you hear?" He tried to move forward but all of a sudden Missy was standing right in front of him. She'd moved so fast he never even saw her. She was just suddenly there. He took a step back and started to raise his right arm but she grabbed his wrist and said, "Really?" She held on with an iron grip and all of a sudden he realized she was an immoveable object, a force he could do nothing to stop. She just stood there, staring at him with eyes which were deep green with some yellow specks showing. He didn't remember seeing those yellow specks before and he didn't like the way she was looking at him now. It wasn't that he was physically intimidated. But, he just suddenly knew. Missy was in total control and he was not going to bully or browbeat her.

Missy looked over at Alice and asked, "Are you okay, Alice? He's not going to do anything. Not ever again, right?" With that, she turned around and stared at him. She let go of his wrist and squared her shoulders. Then she slowly pushed him backwards, out of the room. He was instantly aware that any excuse he might try would not work. No amount of bluster or outraged indignity was going to stand up to what Missy's eyes were showing. He was looking at a wild predator, not a girl, and fear suddenly zinged right through him. He needed to find some way to control this situation. In a panicky voice, he asked her, "What do you want? Let's be reasonable and talk about this, okay? No one has been harmed here. Alice, honey?

Tell her you're okay. Nothing happened. Right? Tell her."

Missy went over to Alice and helped her get up. Slowly, Alice wrapped a blanket around herself and then looked up at Missy. Tears welled up in her eyes. She still couldn't say anything. She sat back down on the bed. But, there was no longer any defeat in her expression; now she looked determined. And, relieved. Missy was there. Things would be okay, now.

Missy walked back out and pointed downstairs. "Move," she commanded. Tony walked over to the stairs and went down, his mind racing through all the possible scenarios for handling this. Missy followed him into the living room and said, "Here's what's going to happen. You are leaving tonight. You will call your wife to tell her you're moving out but you'll say nothing about any of this. Not now, not ever. Do you understand?" When he looked at her, she added, "Tell her your marriage is over. Tell her you're very sorry, but you just can't go on here anymore. Then, tell her you're signing over this house to her and you're setting up a trust fund for Alice. You'll continue paying off the mortgage plus taxes and insurance. They'll both be taken care of financially, from now on, no more worries about that. Tell her things have simply not worked out and this is all for the best. You're making a clean break and starting over. A fresh start. Best for everyone."

He looked at Missy and slowly, he started thinking about his alternatives. What were his options? He said, "But, my wife loves me! She'll never understand my just leaving this way. She'll want me to give her a second chance ..."

Missy said, "Cut the crap. I've seen what your daughter Roseanne's life has turned out like and that's never going to happen here. Not to Alice. Not to her mom, either. Do you want to spend years in prison? For rape, incest, all kinds of charges which you know you truly deserve? Or, will you go quietly, without causing this family any more grief than you already have?"

He still wasn't getting the whole picture. "But …"

Missy didn't let him say anything more. "You can walk out now. Keep your mouth shut and no one will know. No one. Alice will not tell her mom. Or, anyone else. You can come back and pack up your things later. You will make the financial arrangements just as I've explained them. You have those three restaurants, right? So I know you can afford to do all this. And, you then can live your life in freedom, without everyone knowing what a sick bastard you really are."

He wasn't convinced yet. He looked around. He looked back at Missy.

She said, "Did you see the news about me when I came home? Do you know why the FBI has covered everything up? About me? Do you really want to mess with me?"

Suddenly, he got it. Just like that, as though a switch had clicked in his head. He realized he didn't know any details about those two years Missy had been gone. Sure, he'd even salivated at the thought of what it must have been like. How, whoever had grabbed her must have really enjoyed himself for those two years. But, now suddenly, things were coming quickly into focus. Missy was standing there in front of him. And, she didn't really look very much like a victim. The FBI was in on it, whatever the hell had really happened. He'd even heard the senator's office was somehow involved. She and her family had some friends in very high places and what did he have?

Missy saw the look of recognition when the realization washed through him. He had no viable options. Either he went quietly, doing things as she was insisting, or she was going to bring down some real trouble on his head. All those rationalizations he'd lived with, convincing himself he didn't have any worries about getting caught. He'd always been sure no one would believe Alice, just as no one had ever considered Roseanne's claims anything but ridiculous. Those beliefs were now up in smoke. Gone. Missy was standing there and he recognized she held all the cards. It was all in her power and if he didn't play along, he'd be sitting in an interview room down at the police station. With her friends in the background, pulling the strings. Even if a good lawyer could save him from actually being convicted, his life would still be over.

Tony was not a brave or courageous individual. He was all bluster. And, he'd been living a fantasy. He'd be "innocent until proven guilty" and everyone would give him the benefit of the doubt, right? But now he was facing reality. Being dragged through a sordid trial, while Missy's influential friends manipulated everything? He had nothing to go against all of that. Everyone would believe he was guilty and it wouldn't even matter about the trial. His restaurant businesses would all go under. He'd lose all his friends. He'd be left with nothing.

"Okay," he said. "I'll go. I'll do as you say. But, how will I know you won't turn me in later? What do I have ...?"

"Please," Missy told him. "Alice doesn't want anyone to know what you've done to her. She won't even tell her mother. She will, however, be talking to a psychologist that I'll arrange for her to start seeing. And, you're going to pay the bill for that. Someone to help her deal with the horror you've turned her life into these past three years. And, while I won't be telling the police what you've done, I will have some of my good friends checking to make sure you're never anywhere near young girls again. Are we clear?"

He nodded. Thinking better of that, he said aloud, "Yes. Clear. I just don't want any of this to come out. You're right. It wouldn't be good for Alice. Or her mother. My businesses would be ruined. No one needs to get hurt. I can change. I won't ever do this again. As you said earlier ... a fresh start, right?"

Chapter Nineteen
Dec 2015

Drew Martinson had presented his credentials to Nurse Gladys and asked if he could discuss one of her cases with her. He was with the U.S. Government, in charge of their "P" Branch. When she'd learned he wanted to discuss that girl Missy McCrea from last August, she'd suggested he really should speak to Doctor Walker. But, Doctor Walker was away on a week's vacation and he was only following up. He knew all about the two FBI agents. So, she could see no harm in answering one or two questions. For his file. They'd all kept Missy's secrets safe at the hospital and he wasn't going to expose her. He, like those FBI agents, was part of the government, after all.

"Gladys, I really appreciate your taking the time to help me with this." Drew had already showed her many of the documents he'd collected for Missy's file. There were all the local news articles about that car accident up on the mountain. Plus, Senator Maxwell's visit and those press conferences he'd given. And, that nice Stratton family; there were several articles about them as well. "I'm curious about the rescue which took place up there that day. These articles don't really provide much detail. They do mention some teenage girl being involved, but none of the articles actually say it was Missy McCrea. They only mention there being this girl who was later identified. It's reported she eventually recovered and left with her mother who showed up two days after the accident. But, her name was withheld due to her being only fifteen, is that right?"

"Well, that was the official reason, sure." Gladys took a sip from the coffee he'd bought for her and looked around the hospital's cafeteria. "Since she was a minor, the rest of it didn't need to come out. About her being that girl who had gone missing for two years. And, the FBI was satisfied her kidnapper was no longer still out there … you know. Doctor Walker told me how absolutely positive Missy was about that. So, with no one for those FBI agents to chase after, there was no need to tell the press anything. Good riddance, I say!"

"Are you saying Missy might have done something to her kidnapper, Gladys?" Drew looked at her with raised eyebrows. He was a very nice looking man, quiet and easy going, with a warm pleasant demeanor. His manner made most people willing to readily share little tidbits of information and Gladys was quite comfortable talking to him. He continued, "I didn't see any mention of that in Robert Ulrey's report."

"Robert Ulrey, yes. That was one of the FBI agents who came here. I recognize the name. He was very nice and Doctor Walker really liked him." Gladys thought for a moment and then went on, saying, "Whatever happened up in those mountains to poor Missy, she somehow survived all that. Forced to run around naked. Those horrible injuries with no medical treatment … it's amazing how she managed to heal up okay. Of course, she certainly amazed all of us by how quickly she healed up here. Looking back, I don't think we actually did anything that helped her all that much.

We gave her a place to sleep and rest up. And food, of course. That girl could sure eat! But, …"

"You were saying … about her kidnapper?"

"Oh, yes! Well, he obviously was dead. Missy never explained. She only said it now was *safe*." Gladys strongly emphasized the word *safe*. "At least, that's how Doctor Walker explained it to me. They all agreed, she and those FBI agents and even the senator. Since Missy wouldn't give them any details about what happened and yet it was a hundred percent sure that now it was safe, there was no point in trying to force her. That girl had been forced enough! Good grief! If she did kill anyone, he deserved it. No one was going to bring any charges against Missy, a fifteen year old girl. Really!"

"I think I'm seeing it now," said Drew. "And, I can see why exposing something like that would be rather sensational. The media would never have let any details stay hidden. Poor girl. You say she had some old injuries? From before?"

"Yes, Missy had those scars. One on her thigh from a rifle bullet. And, on her shoulder and back? Several claw marks. From some wild animal. She told Doctor Walker it was from a black bear! Can you imagine? A little girl, only thirteen or fourteen, being mauled like that? And, from the way those scars healed up, you could tell she had no stitches. It's a miracle she didn't die from infection."

Drew Martinson wrote this information on his notepad. "And, you said something about her being forced to do things? Run naked? Was she sexually molested?"

"Actually, no," Gladys said. "That's a bit of a mystery … how she managed being held for over two years and was obviously abused, mentally and physically, but still came through it all with her virginity intact. Untouched. Doctor Walker suggested she was forced to do whatever he wanted because of threats to her family. She was able to run around free only she wasn't really free, since she was so afraid. So, maybe he was just waiting before he touched her, you know? Since he thought he owned her? She couldn't escape? He had her. So, he was just saving her for later?"

"An interesting theory." Drew made more notes on his notepad. "Did she actually talk about this?"

"Not a word. But, she came here with clothes which didn't belong to her. No underwear. And, no tan lines. She'd been running around for weeks, stark naked, that was obvious. If she didn't want to talk about that, why try to force her? Doctor Walker says she'd been forced enough. Poor Missy!"

"I see. Very interesting. And, then she somehow did finally escape? So, the threat was gone and she was safe and her family was safe. And, nobody for the FBI to arrest? I see why it's so obvious. Hmmm." He was writing all this on his notepad and kept looking back up at her, noting how she was nodding her head in agreement.

Then he changed subjects and asked, "And, so, she just happened to be walking down the road when the Stratton car went over?" Drew looked at the nurse with raised eyebrows once again.

Gladys said, "Yes, she just appeared out of nowhere. Coming down from those mountains."

"What about the rescue? Did she really help?"

"Oh, absolutely! That girl saved all three of them, pulling them out before their car exploded. No one knows how she managed that. One minute she's up there on the road and the next minute she's pulling them out of the car. You've seen that video which was on the TV, right? That car was down a sheer cliff, at least a hundred foot drop. Yet, she somehow climbed down there … and the Stratton couple, Bill and Mary? Bill was very groggy and Mary was actually knocked out, crashing down that cliff like that. Suddenly, Missy was there and went in through the back window. She just yanked them both right out. As though she had super strength. Just like Supergirl, you know? Then, she went back and got little Emily. Then, boom! Missy was injured pretty badly from that explosion, but Emily? Not a scratch."

"Oh, so Missy's injuries were bad?" asked Drew. "I thought she wasn't hurt that much, since she was released only three days later."

"Ha, just another of Missy's many, many mysteries." Gladys looked directly at Drew, as though she wasn't sure he'd believe everything she had to say. "That girl was definitely hurt pretty bad from that explosion. That first MRI on the day she came in here? For her head injury, where she got knocked unconscious? Doctor Walker is still trying to understand that. It looked like severe brain damage was highly likely. Plus all the cuts she got from the broken car window. And she had burns and bumps and bruises everywhere. But, forty-eight hours later? The second MRI shows everything all healed up, just fine."

"Well, there's nothing in any of the reports which I've read about any of that, Gladys. Are you sure?"

"You can check with Doctor Walker next week. Missy's head injury got all better, her cuts and burns all healed up right away and she walked out of here as though nothing had ever happened. She and her mom, happy as could be. And, I hear she's doing just great back home in Massachusetts."

Drew asked, "Can you explain that? Any theories?"

"Doctor Walker has no clue. Me? I think it's when she disappeared on us that second night. She never should have been able to wake up, with all the sedatives we were giving her. An induced coma, see? We increased the dosage after she woke up earlier. But, that didn't matter. She just got up anyway and disappeared from her room. Gone all night while the hospital got searched from top to bottom. Then? She's eating down in the kitchen. Wide awake, alert as can be. And eat? That girl never stopped eating. She devoured an entire chicken that night and kept eating everything at every meal after that like there was no tomorrow."

"I did read something about the hospital being on alert. So, that was when she disappeared, eh? Very interesting. Did she say where she went?"

"Well, she did say something about going up to the roof. For some fresh air. We searched everywhere, for hours, but I guess no one really thought to look up there. She was supposed to be in a coma, remember? We're looking for a kidnapper maybe pushing her in either a wheelchair or whatever. Then she's down in the kitchen, nice as you please, and looking just great, practically all better? I think something happened that night. We'll just never know. Like I said before, she's got many, many mysteries."

Drew returned to his hotel room and wrote up this latest update from all his notes. Yes, he thought. Missy McCrea was a girl with many, many mysteries. It had taken weeks before various items had found their way to his office and finally captured his attention. It was that rescue. Fortunately, since the Strattons were close friends to Senator Maxwell, their rescue had been widely reported. Otherwise, he might never have spotted anything. In spite of all the software he had searching for such stories. Stories where anything special or "superhuman" might have happened.

But, he now had a very complete file on Missy and would continue to update that file going forward. She was just a young teenage girl. But, if his suspicions proved to be true, she was the first female to show up. Drew Martinson, who headed up the U.S. Government's "P" Branch, was definitely impressed. So far, his team had only found evidence of a few males. This "P" Branch which he headed up was the designation for Paranormal Branch but only those in a need to know actually knew that. And, there were very damn few who ever had any need to know.

Chapter Twenty
May 2016

Missy's sister Heather was fixing her hair, putting it up high in a complicated weave which included four tiny braids, all held in place with pins and clips which glittered. Their mother Julia called from downstairs and said, "Missy, Jeff is here now and John called. He has Claire and will be back soon. He says Mark and Alice are on their way here also. We have to get photos of everyone before you all leave in the limo."

"Okay, Mom. Is the limo here yet?" She looked at herself in the mirror as Heather stepped back. Her red prom gown had large puffy sleeves over her shoulders, hiding her scars; only the ones on her back were visible and those were mostly covered. The gown was cut low in front, revealing quite a bit of her breasts and deep cleavage. With her pushup bra, the effect was stunning. She wasn't used to looking so glamorous and had to admit she was enjoying this. She was also glad she had a shawl, so she wouldn't be quite so exposed the entire evening. She could wrap that around herself, covering up whenever she wanted.

She headed out, with Heather following her, and went down the stairs. When she walked into the living room, Julia and Jeff both told her how fantastic she looked, while her dad and Patrick looked on from the kitchen. Patrick made funny faces and swooning gestures, which cracked her up. "I'll get you for this," she told her brother. "Just wait and see what I do to you! My revenge will be so awesome!"

Just then Mark and Alice came in and everyone ooh'ed and aah'ed over the two of them, making appropriate comments about how great they looked. Jeff came up and helped her slip a lovely corsage onto her wrist. He was six-two, with broad shoulders and a very nice smile. She preened at what he'd brought her. His eyes were sparkling and his attention was now focused only on her. "You're the most beautiful girl on the planet, Missy," he whispered in her ear. This really made her blush and she kissed him on the cheek. They had sort of been dating over the past couple of months, ever since she'd agreed to go to the senior prom with him. He wasn't an athlete and could be a bit of a nerd. But, like Mark Mathews, Jeff Johnson was one of John's best friends and she'd known him all her life.

Outside, a sleek black limo pulled up in front of their house. A moment later, John's car pulled into their driveway. John and Claire got out and everyone went outside to join them. Julia got dozens of photos, as they all posed for her during the next ten minutes. Then John announced it was time to go, so they all climbed into the limo. After a few more photos were taken, they finally were headed off to the hotel ballroom where their prom was being held that night.

Claire McKenna, like Alice, was a junior and had only been dating John a couple of years. She was a vivacious and bubbly girl, very sexy and outgoing, with dark brown hair and brown eyes. They had been pretty much exclusive for the past six months during which Missy got to know her pretty well. Claire had moved to Salem from New York three years earlier, right before Missy went missing, so they'd never actually met until John brought her over last November. Since then, they'd become close friends and it was Claire who had convinced Missy to accept Jeff's invitation. She giggled as she whispered in Missy's ear, "Look how handsome Jeff looks in his tux, Missy! The two of you make such a great couple. And, he really has the hots for you. I heard him telling the other guys how bad he's had them ever since you returned. He hasn't been able to hardly look at any other girls."

"Oh, I know, I know! John's been telling me the same thing. And, it's been fun going out with him. I just don't want to get serious with anyone, you know?"

"Yeah, I know. But, you can give the poor guy a little, right?" Claire laughed at the way Missy blushed. Then, she leaned over to snuggle up to John, grabbing his head and pulling it down while meeting his lips with her own in a long, leisurely kiss. This dragged on for several seconds and John finally came up for air, laughing, "Mmmmm! What did I do right to deserve that, honey? I want to know so I can keep doing it, whatever it is!"

They all laughed and Claire squeezed closer to him and said, "Oh, just you being you, John! I'm only making sure you know who you're bringing to this dance. Just in case your eyes start to wander when you see how nice all the other girls look. I'm sure they'll all be making plays for you studs, so Missy and Alice and I are staking our claims now, before we even get there. Right girls?"

"Oh, absolutely! You better believe it!" Missy and Alice exchanged looks and it made Missy feel really great, knowing how well Alice was doing now. She'd been seeing Dr. Susan Thomas, the psychologist Missy's parents had actually wanted her to meet with when she'd first come home from Virginia. Missy had gone to her twice, in November, but not for herself. The first meeting was to make sure this doctor could help Alice and the second was when she'd brought Alice. This was after that night she'd confronted Tony, getting him to move out. And, since she'd anticipated he might be having some second thoughts, she'd actually gone over to see him two days later at his restaurant. After she'd laid it all out for him, all over again, he'd agreed to everything she'd wanted.

And, so far, Tony was keeping his end of the bargain. He'd met with Thomas Mooney, the lawyer representing Alice's mother, and had signed all the necessary agreements. Missy's dad had recommended this particular lawyer, who was a friend of his, when Missy explained about Alice's parents splitting up. No one knew anything other than that and even Alice's mom was still trying to understand. The fact that Tony was taking care of things financially was still a mystery to her. He'd not been all that generous while they'd been together. She figured he had to be guilty about something but thought it must be related to his restaurant business. She could understand how he'd do anything he thought necessary to protect that.

A month after Tony had left, Alice's mother had admitted to Alice there'd been almost no sex life and she really didn't miss Tony at all. Their marriage had mostly been for the financial security and since that had actually worked out better than she ever would have imagined, she was really very happy now. Alice told Missy, "The part about no sex life was certainly not a surprise to me since the bastard was forcing himself on me all this time instead. If Mom only knew! And, you made me realize he'd done that to his own daughter earlier."

Dr. Thomas had helped Alice a lot and it showed in how comfortable she and Mark were with one another now. Mark still didn't know any details but he knew Missy had somehow worked some miracles. She'd only told him to be patient a little longer with Alice and things would work out. And, they had. All the talking to Dr. Thomas about everything had really helped Alice. That, and having Missy as her friend. She couldn't stop thanking Missy for everything and the two of them had grown really close.

Alice would occasionally ask Missy about the secrets she knew Missy was keeping. Wouldn't that help Missy if she could share any of them? After all, she'd completely bared herself to Missy, right? And, talking had helped so much once she did. She now could tell both Missy and Dr. Thomas anything, sharing all the details about the horrible things she'd experienced, and it had made all the difference. Alice didn't know if she'd ever be able to talk to her mom. But, someday, she hoped she could tell Mark. She was really falling in love with Mark and he seemed equally crazy about her.

Whenever Alice had asked about her secrets, Missy had assured her she was good. Finally, she'd said, "I know you want to help but my secrets are just things I can't explain or talk about. They're all in the past. And, I'm making great progress getting my life back on track, right?" Alice had accepted this; she knew how hard

Missy worked at everything and acknowledged that Missy actually seemed more solid and together than even Dr. Thomas. Was it all the martial arts workouts? Should Alice join her at the gym? They laughed about that. And, Alice actually did join her at the gym.

Chapter Twenty-One
May 2016

The prom was the first time Missy had really gone out in public, all dressed up and looking so spectacular, since her return home. Usually, she was either in jeans or something casual with her hair in a ponytail or braids. Other times, she was in her karate or judo gi. But, tonight, she was in this formal gown wearing four inch heels with her hair and makeup perfect and she looked like a supermodel. The way the gown flowed over her curves, accentuating how fabulous her body was, combined with the way Missy moved? She was a sensation.

A lot of people took notice of her that night. This was no little girl, the way most remembered her being described in all the stories. Here was this tall, elegant, gorgeous young woman. She looked all grown up, even though not yet sixteen. Her presence was dazzling. And, she seemed to be very comfortable out there with a lot of friends all around her, having a wonderful time. For most, any residual thoughts of Missy as a victim were completely banished. All the months which had gone by had helped dampen most of the speculation about her. While they were still very curious, and probably always would be, the fact that nothing further was being published in the news tended to make everything fade away. Missy was home and things were back to normal. End of story. They were pleased to see her there, being so happy.

For some, however, there was jealousy. And, for a few, in addition to envy there was resentment. To those who only knew the negative things they'd heard about her, hearing others say anything good or nice now only made them suspicious. Why was Missy so special? Why should she deserve all the attention? Seeing her appear at the prom that night, looking so fantastic when they believed she was really just damaged goods? It rankled them. Why was she worthy? What really had happened during those two years, anyway? It was probably only human nature for a few to be there, resenting her. Add to that some alcohol and drugs, and not surprisingly, some nasty confrontations were inevitable.

There was plenty of both alcohol and drugs and, being at a hotel, there were rooms which had been booked by many of the attendees. Groups would come and go from the dance, sneaking up to these rooms where they could drink or snort or get a fix. Or, have sex. Some of the girls who went up there had no intention of getting drunk or high. But, after a few times up in these rooms, with enough drinks or perhaps some pills, they'd end up getting really drunk or stoned. And then they'd find themselves having sex. Sex with their date or sometimes, sex with a stranger.

Missy had thoroughly enjoyed herself for the first few hours. Jeff was great and their group of friends had constantly been getting out on the dance floor. They'd get really worked up during a few of the fast dance songs, dancing like crazy, only to return back to their tables and collapse, feigning complete exhaustion. Five minutes later, after a lot of laughter and bantering back and forth, they'd all venture back out all over again. Missy danced with several guys but saved all the slow dances for Jeff. They did, of course, take a lot of breaks when they'd go off to either grab some refreshments or step outside for some fresh air. And, the girls would always head to the ladies room in a group.

It was during one of the visits to the ladies room with just Claire along that Missy overheard several of the other girls talking about room 323. These girls were in a large group of more than a dozen and several had been drinking heavily. Now they were arguing amongst themselves and things were getting very heated. While some were trying to explain what a great time it was, going up to the rooms where all the drinking was, three girls were yelling that someone had to do something about room 323. One of these girls named Janie had barely made it out, after stopping in with her date for a drink. It turned out there were several rooms all together in a large suite at the end of the corridor and 323 was merely the entrance. Once inside, the party was pretty wild with lots of drinking and various other things all going on. There were a lot of guys in there and some looked much older than just high school. And, things in there just weren't right.

Janie had seen right away that her date wanted to get her into one of the bedrooms and she'd bolted. Had she waited to have a drink, she might not have managed escaping. Her date had already been pretty drunk and she was explaining to the group how that probably had saved her since he was so horny and so stupid, he hadn't even waited but had tried to rush things. She didn't know the guy all that well and was quick to get the hell out once she realized he was looking to have sex. It was very obvious, looking at some of the girls in there, that lots of sexual activity was definitely going on. She suspected roofies were being used or else these girls were just so stoned or drunk, they didn't care.

The problem the group was discussing now was because Janie and her two friends knew about two other girls who had already gone up to that same room a half hour ago. Knowing what was happening up there had them very upset but they didn't want to go up there themselves and were arguing with the group what they should do. If they called the cops, would their friends get in trouble just for being in there? But, if they didn't, would their friends get into even more trouble? Maybe even get raped?

Many in the group were yelling back at them and saying if anyone called the cops, there'd be hell to pay. These girls had boyfriends up there that they wanted to protect and since they themselves had been in and out once or twice, they didn't think it was any big deal. Just because Janie's date had turned out to be a pig was no reason to call the cops. Things were escalating on up from there.

This whole discussion had just taken place and Claire wasn't able to hear much of it. But Missy heard every word. She told Claire, "Hey, go back without me; I need to go help out a couple of girls that I know and I'll be gone for a few minutes." She looked over at the other group as she explained this.

"Okay, I guess. I didn't know you knew any of these girls. I think they're mostly seniors or else they go to a different school and so I don't even know any of them." Claire then headed back out.

Missy walked up to the two girls with Janie, pulled the three of them away from the group and asked, "What are the names of your two friends and what are they wearing? I'll go up there but ... can you describe them for me so I'll recognize them?"

Just then, one of the other girls from the group noticed this and she came up and confronted Missy. "Aren't you that Missy McCrea everyone's buzzing about tonight? What do you care? What can you do up there? You're only going to make trouble! Leave us alone." She was one of those who resented Missy and turned to the others and started to really bad mouth her. Right away, more of her friends all crowded around. They joined in with derogatory comments and soon there were jeers and some very vulgar language was being used to describe what a slut Missy really was. The emotions had already been running high and many were also quite drunk, so Missy's offer to help had somehow ignited a firestorm and the big group was quickly getting out of control.

Many of these girls were from a different school, attending the prom as dates to the boys in this school. Since there was already an existing rivalry for these girls with the girls in this school, Missy's interference was just a perfect excuse to raise hell. Marcia Newton, the one bad mouthing Missy, was the leader for these outsiders and she knew just enough about Missy to really stir things up. "Missy doesn't even go to any school, so she's obviously not just a slut who runs away from home, but she's a really stupid slut, right?" She and her friends got more and more abusive.

Finally, ignoring the group, one of the girls Missy had approached turned back to Missy and said, "Our friends are Nancy Bailey and Evelyn Striker. Can you really help us? Nancy has blond hair and her gown is blue, with silver showing where there are pleats. Evelyn has a pink gown. Pink with some white, too. Her hair is a little darker, sort of a dirty blond, you know?" She stared at Missy with very mixed feelings. "You can't be serious about going into that room, though, can you? I mean, did you hear what Janie has been telling us?"

Several of the girls were now gathered in front of Missy and started all talking at once. Some were arguing it was a total waste of time discussing this with Missy while others were asking if she really could do anything to help. A few spoke up saying they'd get their boyfriends to go up there. Others said that was stupid and they'd better get the cops. It seemed these girls wanted the cops to raid the place but not if their two friends would be arrested.

Missy held up her hands and said, "Hey, I'll only be a couple minutes, okay? I'll bring your two friends out and then you can have the cops raid the place. Nancy and Evelyn, right?" She held the hand of one of the girls, pulling her to come with her and motioned to some of the others to follow. "Come up with me but then just wait out in the corridor. Let's go." And, leading the way, Missy walked out and headed for the elevator. Several of the girls followed after her while Marcia and her gang continued to rant and rave with more and more threats. A couple of the girls stayed behind but called out for someone to text them once it was time to send up the cops.

Missy stopped the girls that came up with her when they were several doors away and she went on alone, quickly slipping inside room 323 when the door was opened. Any girl, all alone, was more than welcome to enter, no problem. Once inside, she quickly moved through the crowd and started checking out each of the rooms. She was able to scent what was happening in most of the rooms without even needing to look. And, she was able to see clearly in rooms where the lights were turned down. She was moving very fast and no one was paying that much attention to her until she entered a bedroom in the back. The lights were very low but she saw a girl was struggling with a huge guy over on the bed. Her blue gown was already half off and he was tossing her bra on the floor. He didn't notice Missy come in but he had a friend there who did. The friend was trying to watch the action on the bed but was also guarding the door. He noticed when Missy opened the door and he turned, trying to block her way. Missy could see the girl on the bed had to be Nancy and, slipping easily past the guy at the door, she rushed over and yanked the other guy right off her. He was shocked to find himself being thrown against the wall and had no idea what had even happened. Missy asked the girl, "Where's Evelyn, Nancy? Get up. We're getting you out of here."

She moaned, not able to really talk but at least she started to sit up. Missy spun around to deal with the two guys who were both heading straight at her. She hadn't been taking those martial arts courses these past several months without knowing exactly where she could hit a guy and she wasted no time. Both guys were suddenly lying on the floor, out cold, without ever knowing what hit them. Missy picked up the girl's bra, grabbed her shoes and helped her off the bed. Together, they walked towards the door with Missy yanking one of the blankets from the bed as they went. She wrapped it around the girl and said, "Nancy, can you just wait here a minute? I'm going to find Evelyn and then we'll go, okay?"

Nancy was still in a daze and just stood there, nodding her head. Missy went out and closed the door behind her, quickly pushing her way past two couples who were very drunk, groping at each other's clothes, and a third couple taking turns snorting coke. She could hear sounds coming from another bedroom and knew that had to be Evelyn, sobbing hysterically. She pushed her way inside. Evelyn looked up and said, "My friend Nancy is getting raped. And, I'm next. We couldn't stop them ..."

The guy who had been snorting coke was suddenly blocking the doorway behind her and said, "Welcome to the party, pretty girl with the red dress on! You're going to be ..." His words stopped right there because Missy simply knuckled him with a blow behind the ear and he went down, out cold, just like the first two guys. Missy continued moving very fast and no one was really aware she was doing anything. Towing Evelyn, she went back to where she'd left Nancy, opened that door and pulled her out. Evelyn was still mostly dressed, clutching her purse. Missy asked, "Where's Nancy's purse? Evelyn only shrugged, so Missy pushed the two of them forward toward room 323. While they stumbled their way into that room,

Missy went back and searched both bedrooms. Nancy's purse was lying on the floor in the room where Evelyn had been crying.

There were some others now starting to crowd into these back rooms but Missy was already slipping through them and joined Nancy and Evelyn in room 323. She led them forward and then stopped to confront two guys blocking the way out. One she recognized as the guy who'd let her enter, just a few minutes ago. He was definitely a lot older than these high school kids who were all being so rowdy. Most of them were pretty stoned on something but he was quite sober. She could smell a lot of coke in the room, now that she'd seen it being snorted and knew what it was. There were a few other scents she didn't recognize but knew these were also drugs, since many of these kids were just reeking with them. She reached over and turned off the lights. That stopped everyone and she guided Nancy and Evelyn right around the younger guy at the door. She then cold cocked the older guy, like she had the others, with a quick hit behind the ear. Suddenly they were all standing outside the room. She closed the door and then led the girls down to where their friends were waiting. She'd gone in, silently knocked out four guys, and was back out with the two girls in less than five minutes. She hadn't even messed up her dress.

Since there'd been no noise or commotion, no one quite realized what had just happened. Missy told the group to text their friends to send the cops up and then she had everyone get on the elevator. She stayed behind to wait for the police. Twice the elevator opened and some guys with their dates started to get off. Missy told them the cops were on the way and they probably didn't want to get off at this floor. They all agreed and let the doors close; the elevator went back down with them still inside. When the cops finally came, there were two of them and more would be on the way when these two called for backup. Missy quietly stepped aside and they hardly even glanced at her. She watched them head down the corridor towards room 323. Then she stepped into the elevator they'd just left, hit the button for the lobby and went down to join her friends.

There was a lot written up in the local newspapers about the big drug bust that night, with several high school teens all arrested. There were also some sexual assault complaints by a few girls but no one was willing to actually testify to anything, so those charges were eventually all dropped. The older guy, who had been found unconscious when the police walked in, was identified as a known drug dealer with several prior convictions. He was not released on bail and was going away this time for several years. No one seemed to know anything about why this guy had been unconscious. Or, why three high school guys were also found out cold in the back bedrooms. It had been a wild party which had gotten out of control, so it was assumed there'd merely been rough housing amongst the guys to explain this. When people were faced with things they didn't really understand, they let the only plausible explanations somehow be the ones they ended up believing.

No one arrested ever mentioned Missy being there. A few of them did remember seeing a girl with a red dress, but several girls had been in and out and this wasn't considered significant. None of the guys Missy had knocked out had really gotten a good look at her and hadn't seen what hit them. Even the two cops didn't recall seeing Missy. They'd been focused on getting to room 323 and only vaguely recalled there being anyone in the corridor, waiting for the elevator.

Nancy and Evelyn had both been very drunk and didn't really remember much either. They were not able to explain how Missy had managed getting them out but Evelyn thought she'd seen Missy hit that one guy who had been keeping her in the bedroom. She really hadn't seen what Missy had done but had seen the guy just suddenly collapse. Things had been pretty dark, even before the lights had gone out. Then, they'd found themselves standing outside the room with their friends waiting for them further down the corridor. By some miracle, they both still had their purses, wallets, cell phones, keys and everything else they'd gone in there with. Nancy had been able to go home, fully dressed, with her shoes on and wearing her bra. Her gown had unfortunately been badly torn in a few places. Neither one ever mentioned anything to their parents about having been up to room 323, even though their dates had ended up in jail that night.

Marcia Newton was especially upset since her boyfriend was one of those arrested and her night had been ruined. She and a few of her friends ended up blaming Missy for causing all the trouble. Rumors circulated long afterwards and word of mouth spread a lot of negative things about Missy McCrea.

Missy's friends, meanwhile, didn't really know where she'd disappeared to after she'd asked Claire to go back without her. She'd appeared twenty minutes later, had rejoined their happy group and had never said anything about where she'd been. When word of the big raid by the police began to circulate, she didn't say a thing.

The evening had ended well enough at a little past one in the morning, with the limo then dropping each of them off at their own home. Jeff was a little disappointed he'd not been able to do much more than some kissing and heavy petting with Missy. He wasn't getting past first base with her, but the touching and fondling had gone a lot further than ever before.

It was only when John was approached by a few of the girls in school, three days later, that he learned Missy had gone up to room 323 that night. They wanted him to tell his sister how much they appreciated what she'd done, rescuing their two friends. They didn't know how she'd managed bringing them out like that and neither Nancy nor Evelyn seemed to know much. Evelyn was now saying Missy had to have done something to that one guy, because she'd seen him go down. Was it true what they'd heard that Missy was taking karate? They'd even heard she might be going up for her black belt sometime soon. Was that true?

John assured them he'd let Missy know and, yes, his little sister was indeed going for her black belt next month. She was quite the athlete, wasn't she? When he came home and asked her about it, she admitted she'd gone to help a couple girls that night. Before the police raid. No big deal. Hadn't Claire told him?

Chapter Twenty-Two
Jul 2016

Missy knew it was time. She needed to explain to her family she was a werecat. She had put this off but it really couldn't be postponed any longer. She'd wanted both Heather and John to know by this summer and definitely before they went off to college in the fall. And, she'd wanted to finally tell her parents all her secrets.

Her sixteenth birthday two weeks earlier had been another huge family event, with all the relatives coming over for the big celebration in the back yard. Mom and Heather had done their usual great job, both with decorations and all the food. Hot dogs, hamburgers, chicken and steak tips had all been cooked up on three grills with the guys all taking turns. Cake and ice cream, of course, with everyone cheering and taking photos while she blew out all the candles. She couldn't believe all the presents she got, but everyone kept saying this was making up for the two years she hadn't been there.

Then her dad drove up the driveway in a car, a low mileage 2013 Toyota Corolla, and told her it was hers. White with red interior. A big red bow on the roof. Happy Birthday. Wow, she was so shocked. She was only just now getting her learner's permit with her driver's license still six months away, but her dad wanted her to have her car now. She'd worked so hard this past year with her homeschooling and he said she'd earned it. She still had a lot of work to complete before

September and it was now obvious there were a few subjects which would even take a couple months after that. But the school had already agreed with her tutors that all her tests and papers so far showed she'd be ready. She could enroll as a junior and go back to school. She'd be finished with her tutors before Thanksgiving and would then be all caught up.

Her family was really proud of her and, once again, her heart was bursting from all the emotions she felt inside. It was time she explained things. They deserved to know. She waited until Patrick left; he was staying overnight with one of his friends. He wouldn't be told yet; that could wait a couple more years. But, Heather and John were both home and she told them to go get Mom and Dad. It was early afternoon on a Saturday and they were both home. She had something important to discuss and they all needed to hear this.

Once everyone was seated in the living room, Missy stood up and started her story. "A year ago, I was finally able to leave the mountains. I was finally able to Change and be human again. For two years, I didn't know if that would ever be possible. And I was terrified, worried if I didn't stay up in the mountains, no one here would be safe. Safe from me. I couldn't risk it. I didn't know if I could control myself. You have to understand that because it's why I stayed away."

"But, Missy," said Julia, "you're not making any sense. You have to know we would never judge you. Whatever you had to do …"

"Mom, I know you think I was grabbed by someone. You and everyone else think that. And, you probably believe that person is dead now; maybe even dead because I killed him. I apologize for letting you all believe that. I know it's what Mr. Ulrey at the FBI must be thinking and I know you've talked to him about this." She could see by their facial expressions and body language it was exactly what they believed. "There was no one. My being human again is about my changing back from my other form. In my other form, I'm a cat." There, she'd told them. She stared at each of them.

"What?" "Huh?" "What do you mean?" Everyone was asking at once, looking at her like she was crazy. "Don't be silly!"

"I'm a werecat. I can Change forms, back and forth. Only, when it first happened to me, I didn't know I could Change back. It just happened to me. That night at soccer camp. And, I didn't know what else to do. So, I went into the mountains,"

"Missy, you're not making any sense at all. Please, we can find someone who can help." Her mom was trying to find words but Missy held up her hand.

"Please, everyone, just listen to me! I knew you wouldn't believe me unless I showed you. And, I intend to show you. So, be patient. Give me a chance, okay?"

"You mean you're going to show us how you're a cat?" asked John.

"Yes. Only, I don't want to do it here, in our living room. You have to understand that once I Change ..."

"Why not?" John insisted. He clearly didn't believe her and she didn't think any of the others believed her either.

"Because once I Change, I have to wait at least three hours before I can Change back. And, even though I now know I can control myself, do you really want to have a huge mountain lion in here? What if anyone comes over? I can't take any chances. No one else can know about me. Okay?"

"Wait a minute," said her dad. "Are you serious? This is ridiculous, Missy."

"Oh, I'm perfectly serious, Dad. I'm a werecat. I can Change forms anytime I want, as long as it's been at least three hours. Back and forth. And, when I'm in my cat form, I'm pretty sure that's the best way to describe me. I'm still me but anyone seeing me is going to believe that I'm a mountain lion. Or, a cougar. Or, maybe a puma. A big cat. Much too big not to be inside a cage."

"Does it hurt? When you Change? Like, in those werewolf movies when all your bones ... you know ..." Heather was looking at her and trying to figure out whether or not to believe any of this.

"No, it doesn't. There's a big burst of some kind of energy and I just Change forms. You'll see. You and Mom. I'm going to ask Dad and John to not watch me actually Change since I'm going to be naked when I do it. Bring a blanket you can hold up when I get undressed. Oh, and those steaks I put in the fridge earlier? Those are for me. I get really, really hungry when I do this."

"Where are we going? You really are serious about this, aren't you?" asked her dad. "I can't believe I'm actually letting you talk me into taking you anywhere."

"Can we go to the state forest over in Andover? It's just over a half hour away. I haven't been able to really enjoy myself that much the few times I've been able to Change since last October. I can hide well enough in the Lynn woods or a few places around here, but it's not the same, you know? We can talk more on the ride over."

They continued making various comments and asking her questions but she told them she wanted them to really see with their own eyes so they wouldn't have any further doubts about any of this. Missy already had the blanket ready so they grabbed the steaks and all went out to the family car. Soon, they were on their way. Missy was a little nervous but mostly very excited. She'd dreamed of doing this for a long time.

Once there, Missy walked them into the woods a little ways and stopped at a small clearing. She could scent they were well away from any others and she knew they were out of sight. "You have to keep all of this as our secret. I don't know if I'm the only werecat but I definitely don't want to become any government specimen. My theory is we have something in our genes and, in my case, it came out. Maybe I'm a throwback. I know I was born this way. And, I know none of you or Patrick or any of my cousins are werecats but the genes are in our family. So, it's possible there might be more like me. That's why I want John and Heather to understand all this. Someday, one of your kids might end up like me."

"Oh, now you're really talking crazy," said John. "Are the rest of you really buying into any of this?" He looked at Heather and then at their parents.

Heather had been thinking a lot during the ride out. "This really would explain a lot of things, Missy. The way you can eat so much. And, why you're so good at karate and stuff, right?" She wasn't skeptical anymore. She'd always known Missy had some special abilities no one else seemed to have.

"Oh, you have no idea how much I've always been holding back, hiding what I can do and what I am. I was so afraid. It's such a relief to finally share my secrets with each of you."

Missy's dad asked, "All the martial arts stuff, sparring and everything? Our signing those waivers for you? I thought you needed that because you never wanted to be vulnerable again. You know, to avoid whatever was done to you during those two years, all the stuff you refused to tell us about. Even though you somehow came back still a virgin ..."

"Dad! Please!" Missy looked over at her brother. "Too much information, here! How would you even know anything about that, one way or another?"

Julia said, "My fault, Missy, I'm sorry! But, I did explain to everyone what they told me. The doctors and nurses at the hospital last year. They all knew. No one thought much about that until they found out you'd been missing and probably kidnapped for those two years. Doctor Walker told me. They noticed when you first came in. You were unconscious and ..."

"Okay, okay, I get it! Jeez, can't a girl have anything private?" She watched the way everyone was rolling their eyes and started laughing. "To answer your question, Dad, I needed the martial arts and the sparring because I have all this stuff inside that I need to let out, somehow. I wasn't able to Change very often so getting in the ring helped. And, I held back. I didn't hurt anyone too much. And, I never let them lose face. I was careful about that."

They had all watched her spar, usually coming back early to pick her up after dropping her off earlier. John said, "You were holding back out there? Is that why you were always bouncing off the walls? You were letting them do all that stuff to you?"

"Guilty. Dad, you mentioned those waivers we signed? I kept thinking how it was the guys who should be signing waivers. If only they knew!" She started laughing and soon the rest of them joined in. "Please don't tell on me," she said. That broke them all up laughing even more.

Missy had removed her necklace, rings and earrings and now put all her jewelry into a pocket. "It's Showtime, guys! Once I Change, I won't be able to talk so either ask me something now or wait until I Change back in a few hours. I'll stay here for a few minutes at first and I want you to take some pictures for me, Mom.

I intend to have a couple of them blown up nice and big and hang them in my room."

Julia laughed but did get out her camera. "I still can't believe you're really going to do this, Missy. I guess you're right, though. Unless we actually see it, we just would never believe you."

"After you get those pictures of me, I'm going to run off and explore up here since I have the chance. I really do need this. You just have no idea. But, I'll chow down on those steaks before I go." Missy had one more thought, and she added, "Be sure to only get my good side, Mom. I don't want those scars on my left shoulder to show up in any of the photos. Someone might actually recognize me!"

"You really got those from a black bear?" asked John. "I never got the story since you wouldn't say but Mom said something." He was starting to realize his sister was really about to do this.

"Oh, yes. It was the end of that first winter, when I didn't know any better. He found a deer I'd killed the day before and I was hungry. I guess he was hungry too. When I returned for my meal and found him there … well, I guess I should have let him have the deer. But, we fought and I chased him off. It all happened very fast. I did let him live."

"And, your leg? Was that from some hunter?"

"Yep. I let him live also." With that, Missy giggled. She turned to Julia and Heather and said, "Hold up that blanket. I'm getting undressed now."

While her dad and her brother stood back, giving her privacy behind the blanket her mom and Heather were holding, she undressed and placed all her clothes in a neat pile. "Please have these here for me when I return." She then crouched down and Shifted. She was used to the shimmer of light and burst of energy but Julia and Heather gasped.

"Oh, my God! Missy! Heather, just look at her. Tell me you're seeing this too."

"Oh, yeah! Wow!" Heather dropped the blanket and turned to her dad and then looked at John. "John, what do you think now, huh?" She quickly turned back to study her sister. Her sister, the cat.

Missy stretched first and then slowly moved forward, proudly stepping with her head high. Her tail was straight up and she walked around the clearing so they could all really get a good look. Then she went over to the steaks, lying on the ground with plastic underneath. She looked right into John's eyes and then lowered her mouth, her jaws biting into the meat. She lifted her head, showing her large fangs, and continued to eat. It was very obvious she was quite pleased with herself.

John was truly amazed and looked at his dad. "Did you see that glow and feel the energy when she did that? This is unbelievable. But what's really getting me the most are her eyes. They have a lot of yellow gold in them now but you can really still see that it's Missy, can't you?" He looked at his mom and Heather for their agreement.

Heather walked up to Missy and asked, "Can I touch you? Oh, Missy!" She stroked Missy's head a few times, gently at first and then she reached out with both arms and dropped down beside her sister, wrapping her arms around her. When Missy started purring, very loudly, she began to cry. These were tears of happiness plus all the strong emotions she was feeling. Julia came over and joined them.

"My poor Missy," Julia said. "What you must have suffered when this first happened to you. I'm only now really seeing what a terrifying experience that must have been. How you managed to survive, living this way for two years, I just can't imagine." Heather got up and let her mom kneel down so she could hug Missy.

Everyone got to pet Missy and, after she finished eating the steaks, she posed for photos. Pretty soon, things were getting a bit hilarious as Missy started hamming things up. She rolled around on her back, she invited each of them to embrace her, she extended her claws and showed her fangs, making fierce growling noises and the longer things went on the wilder her antics became. They were laughing themselves silly by the time she finally walked to the edge of the clearing, turned to look at them one last moment, and disappeared. They couldn't even hear her moving away through the underbrush.

They all looked at one another and Julia said, "I feel so much better now, about so many things, but I also feel just terrible about so many other things. Anyone else feeling like that?" Her daughter was a werecat.

Chapter Twenty-Three
Nov 2016

It was Thanksgiving and everyone was home. Heather, from her apartment in Boston near the university campus and John from his college dorm in Easton, an hour away. Patrick was now in the eighth grade and Missy had returned to school in the eleventh grade. Junior year. She'd finished the last of her makeup work with her tutors and was free to begin other activities.

She had earned her black belt in karate and was working towards second degree which would probably happen sometime the next summer. Her goal was to earn her third degree belt a year after that, right before she'd be going away to college. She was playing soccer and lacrosse for her high school varsity teams and intended to play basketball and softball for them later on. And, next year? She'd do it all again. She loved competing in sports, even though she was holding herself back. She didn't take unfair advantage of her skills but used them in a way which most benefited her team. Even so, she was being written up in the local news as quite the star athlete. Julia was adding these to that scrapbook she'd put together years earlier.

While her mixed martial arts workouts were now only once during the week with maybe an event every other weekend, it was here where she was able to really let herself go. She loved the challenge and the extreme exercise. No one could move as fast as she could but she still allowed the guys to pummel her. They'd long since forgotten having any qualms about her sparring with them. She made it fun and somehow never seemed to get hurt. More and more spectators had been showing up each week as the word had gradually gotten out about "that girl" the guys were sparring with. It wasn't a contest for who would win or lose. It was more an exhibition with her holding her own, in spite of all the ways they'd come at her and all the punishment they seemed to be giving her. She kept bobbing right back up and would send them flying. Most now admitted they'd actually improved their own skills a great deal during all of these bouts.

The big discussion at the dinner on Thanksgiving was about the MMA World Expo coming up that weekend in New York City. Missy had finally agreed to actually compete and was entered in the Amateur Women's Middleweight class. It would be her first time competing against women in mixed martial arts. She did this in karate tournaments all the time, which she always won. But those weren't full contact like these MMA bouts would be. The whole family was going down to watch her. Her MMA Sensei had recently re-organized his school into a larger club and she was representing them. Club enrollment had doubled since Missy had joined a year ago. She was still the only female.

The Middleweight class was for over 135 pounds and up to 145 pounds, max. She could easily qualify for the next lower class since her weight usually was 135 or less. But, she wanted to go up against the best of the best, and those women were in this higher weight class. And, she had a plan. She was pretty sure she would easily win but that wasn't her only goal. She wanted to have some fun and put on a show. The notoriety would be great for her club.

During the last couple weeks of the summer, when John had Claire over along with Jeff and Mark and Alice, they'd all watched some movies together. The guys had insisted on a marathon with one of their favorite actors and it was two of those movies which gave her the idea for her current plan. In one, the actor had gained sixty pounds over the course of making the movie, to portray the lead character in his later years. And in the other, he'd spent six months preparing for his role with an intense training program during which he'd really bulked up. He'd worn a lot of fantastic prison tattoos for this movie. And, she'd read he got so much bigger from working out, they'd had to enlarge some of those tattoos.

Missy knew all about incredible body transformations. So, she'd been working out at the gym with some heavier weights and then been washing down all the large meals she was eating with protein shakes. She was now 155 pounds of solid muscle but carrying a bit more body fat than a year earlier. She could easily lose 20 pounds if she were to run as a cat for a week in the mountains, so she wasn't at all concerned. She wanted to see what she could make her body look like for the upcoming competition.

The extra pounds actually filled out her curves, making them appear a lot more rounded. Many of her friends were now kidding her about that, comparing her curvaceous figure to that of Jessica Rabbit, the voluptuous cartoon siren. She thought that was pretty funny, since it reminded her about all the poor rabbits she'd devoured as prey in her mountain lion form. And, she was enjoying the opportunity this MMA bout was giving her to eat even larger portions at each meal. She intended to make an amazing appearance at this event. Her family and everyone at her club were very enthusiastic plus several more friends were coming down from her school. She even had friends from the gym and her karate class all heading to New York City to watch her.

But, this Thanksgiving meal was her last full meal. Patrick didn't know she was a werecat so she didn't discuss her plan until he was out of hearing range. Then she explained it to the others. Over the next forty-eight hours, she intended to Change back and forth several times. She knew what the energy bursts did to her body each time. She was burning calories but not losing muscle. She knew just how much she could eat in between each Change, managing her loss of body fat, so her body would look shredded and ripped by Saturday when she entered that ring in New York. She would have twelve-pack abs rather than six-pack abs. Her arm and leg muscles would look like steel cables. Her family needed to help, since she intended to stay hidden in her room during the cycles when she was in her cat form.

Ever since she'd revealed to them what she was, they'd been taking turns bringing her back and forth to the state forest where she'd been able to run free for hours at a time. As a cat. Missy had never felt so complete and these past few months had been wonderful. And, these opportunities had allowed her to fully exercise all her enhanced abilities, which she'd carryover from one form to the other.

     That Saturday morning, Heather helped Missy with her final preparations and she was definitely feeling butterflies from all the anticipation. Her long hair was up in a tight bun which included several braids, all woven together. Finally, hearing her name being called, she walked out into the large stadium. There were several MMA cages for the competitors, all on raised platforms, and a huge crowd of spectators were seated all around. Her family and friends began screaming her name out as soon as they saw her. Her club had given her a special cape, a dark red which matched her hair, with large lettering in black and white. She was wearing a lot of bright green eye paint and her eyes were blazing; her lipstick was a deep wine colored red. After parading down the aisles, with Heather trailing behind her, she approached the cage for her first match. Her opponent was already inside, bouncing from one foot to the other. With a theatrical gesture Missy removed her cape, climbed up the few steps and went inside.

     Now, everyone could get a good look at her and many were shocked at what they saw. Most of her friends and even those at her club and her gym had only ever seen her when all covered up in her gi uniform or wearing casual clothes which covered her scars. But, for this event, Missy was wearing only some very small shorts and a little sports bra, both a bright iridescent green, so her body was mostly exposed. Wide hips, narrow waist, long legs, and an upper body which was perfect. Her successive Changes had stripped away all her body fat and her weight had dropped down to just under 145 pounds. She now looked awesome with solid muscles rippling under her silky, shiny skin. Her muscles appeared lean, not bulky, and she had incredible symmetry. The way the light reflected off her body as she moved around just made the definition in her stunning physique more noticeable. Heather had helped her apply oil all over and that actually made her silvery white scars much more obvious.

She definitely had an intimidating "bad girl" look which was exactly what she'd wanted. There were a lot of spectators suddenly taking notice of Missy and going through their program looking for information about her. She was new to the MMA world having never competed before and was a complete unknown. This was the heaviest women's class at the World Expo and all the other women were fairly well known, in spite of this being an amateur event. None were as young as Missy. No one had heard about her club even having any women. It wasn't a large club but it had sent male competitors to some of the past Expo's and its Sensei was well known due to his early career in the sport.

Interest in Missy was soon growing, with a lot of word-of-mouth drawing more and more attention to her. This was helped by her actual performance, since she easily won each bout, and by late afternoon of that first day her reputation as a serious contender had been firmly established. A lot of interested bystanders crowded around to study her. Her movements were really beautiful to watch, fluid and graceful, whether wearing her cape outside in the aisles or walking around inside the cage, waiting for the signal to be given. This feline display was all very deceptive since the way she'd then turn things on for each bout was so explosive. Whether she was blocking kicks or dodging blows or attacking her opponents, her speed was an impossible blur. And, she was so powerful that opponent after opponent would stagger out. Most just didn't know what hit them. Three of her wins were knockouts in less than thirty seconds. Three more wins were by submission holds.

Missy was thrilled at the end of the day and having the time of her life. Back in the hotel with her family, she was glowing with excitement. Six bouts, all wins. Everyone kept saying what a great job she was doing and couldn't get over the way she looked out there and what a great show she was putting on. Her brother Patrick, who still thought she was only normal, couldn't get over her appearance. She looked so different. What had she done to herself and how had she ever done it all so quickly? He'd not really seen her that much since that Thanksgiving dinner. The others all knew and just smiled at one another. Their Missy was really something.

Sunday was just more of the same. The crowd got more and more enthusiastic about her consistent wins and when she stepped into the cage for the final bout, she was clearly their favorite. Missy had pumped herself up, Changing once more during the night so when she Changed back that morning, her rock hard body showed even more definition. The effect, with the oil glistening all over, was truly something to see. Photos were being taken constantly and she played up to the crowd, turning so all the scars on her left shoulder were prominently in view. "Get my good side!" she'd yell, laughing mischievously. Then she'd give them some fierce expressions and pose like a bodybuilder. Hamming things up like that, flexing her arms and arching her back, making a real spectacle of herself was such delicious fun.

But, as she faced her final opponent, she focused solely on the bout itself without letting anything distract her. She'd trained herself for extreme fighting like this and when it was time to fight, nothing else mattered. If neither contestant could win by knockout or by getting their opponent to tap out, indicating submission, then the bout would be evaluated and scored by three judges. Since this was the championship match, there would be five rounds, each of five minutes duration with a one minute rest period between each round. Missy's opponent was a powerful girl named Kalinda Johanat who of course was billed as "Killer Kalinda".

Kalinda was wearing black and she had blond hair. She was an inch shorter than Missy with arms and legs which showed some very big muscles. She didn't have the definition which Missy had and her shoulders and hips were not as wide, so she'd packed more of her weight into those powerful arms and legs. Her appearance just looked beefier and she was clearly a brawler. She had won most of her matches by knockout. She looked at Missy with an expression which clearly showed she was determined to win by knockout this time as well.

Scoring really came down to effective striking and effective grappling. Effective striking would be the total number of legal heavy strikes which were landed while effective grappling would be the amount of legal takedowns and reversals. Control of the fighting area and effective aggressiveness and defense were additional factors considered by the judges but to win, there needed to be some real dominance displayed in the striking and grappling. There were penalties for fouls and prohibited conduct which would cause points to be deducted, so these were to be avoided. Three fouls were cause for disqualification.

At the referee's signal both girls moved forward but Missy quickly darted away and then spun back to deliver a kick. She had moved so fast that Kalinda was caught by surprise and unable to block. Advantage Missy. With a grimace, Kalinda charged and managed to connect with her knee but it was only a glancing blow since Missy was moving away. When she tried to follow that with a kick, Missy suddenly out maneuvered her and executed a takedown which definitely caught her by surprise. She was quick to recover and the girls began exchanging blows, causing the spectators to start making noise. The flurry of activity, with each girl demonstrating her prowess in bursts, was indeed exciting to watch. Often, the movements were just a blur.

As the end of the first five minutes approached, Missy suddenly spun and managed a magnificent takedown, with Kalinda falling hard on her ass. Advantage Missy. She had dominated this round and Kalinda was no longer very confident about any knockout. Missy was just a little too fast, always managing to avoid any serious punishment and showing a resilience and stamina which was truly remarkable. As the round ended and they went to their corners to rest, it was obvious this match would be going the full distance, all five rounds.

Rounds two and three went in similar fashion, with Kalinda beginning to tire out there. But, for round four, Kalinda got her second wind and came at Missy with full force, pummeling her with blow after blow in a ferocious effort which got the crowd really riled up as they watched to see if Missy would fall. Instead, Missy countered with an explosive series of movements which suddenly had Kalinda falling back, her fury spent. Then, once again a takedown by Missy which left no doubt who was in charge. She put Kalinda in a hold which might have forced her to submit had the round not ended. It was the video clip of this round which would later almost go viral on the internet.

Round five was not really that spectacular but it didn't matter. The crowd was now so worked up the level of excitement just continued on. Missy danced around out there and Kalinda never had any serious chance to upset her. When the five minutes ended, Kalinda stopped in the middle of the ring and just stared at Missy. She nodded her head, acknowledging the amazing performance Missy had given and there was a lot of respect in her eyes. Missy had clearly beaten her, fair and square. There had been no fouls and no penalties for either side.

For Missy, winning the MMA Amateur Women's Middleweight trophy was almost anti-climatic after all the playful strutting and preening she'd done all day. The bout had been a good one and Missy had put on a nice show, making sure Kalinda got in some decent strikes and blows, with a lot of grappling. She wasn't trying to make anyone there look bad and so she'd kept things exciting, making it appear close. It's what she'd been doing all year with the guys in her club, after all.

As she'd done for most of her bouts that day, she'd won this one by decision rather than by knockout or submission. It was a unanimous decision by the judges and she was the clear winner. From the crowd's reaction, it was a popular decision as well.

Missy had accomplished her goal and made a real spectacle of herself. She'd brought glory to her club, beating the best of the best. Her Sensei and all the guys were ecstatic. She was approached by a lot of people after that but told them all the same thing. She was now retiring from any further MMA competitions and would only be working out back at her club in the future. She didn't bother mentioning there were no women in her club and only a few articles written about her included that info. Many of the writers didn't bother to research her background all that much since, if she wasn't going to continue competing, they didn't see much value in that. The photos and videos were plenty for the stories they turned in that day. Then, it was on to the next big event.

But there were several writers who did take note. Missy had really impressed them and they believed she was someone pretty special. Coming in and easily dominating all the top competitors that day? And, looking outrageously spectacular as well? They were convinced Missy was indeed someone they'd want to keep tabs on. And, when they did research her background? What they learned only further convinced them of that. They added her as one of the athletes they intended to keep following.

She did keep seeing some of her best photos long afterwards, showing her in all her magnificent splendor. Some were enlarged and prominently displayed in various places. Her club of course put up two life-size pictures, each under glass and in a heavy frame. In one she was holding her first place trophy and someone had positioned her cape in the background, with the club lettering clearly visible. In the other she was giving her most intimidating look, with her eyes blazing and a fierce expression on her face. This photo showed it all: her heavy makeup, her well oiled body, her silvery shoulder scars, her pumped and flexed muscles, a curvy hip thrust forward and it was even angled so her sports bra revealed plenty of cleavage.

Her gym was another place where a full sized photo of her appeared on the wall. She did convince her instructors over at her karate school not to put any pictures up. But there was no stopping all the photos being taped inside many of the lockers at her school. Some were taped up inside lockers at various other schools as well, as word of mouth quickly spread her fame. And, long afterwards, several YouTube video clips were still out there on the internet, where anyone could watch her in action. That fourth round of her final match was especially popular. Missy had thoroughly enjoyed the whole experience and really didn't mind. She'd had fun. And, her club would be famous for years, long after she'd grown up and moved on.

Meanwhile, life went back to normal. And, after three weeks of a regular diet and several planned activities, Missy's weight was down to 135 pounds and she looked pretty much back to normal. Being voluptuous and then being ripped and shredded had all been great fun, but she was much more comfortable with herself the way she'd been before.

There was one disturbing item, however, that upset Missy a great deal. A week before Christmas her brother John called her on the phone. "Hey, did you hear about that waitress? I recognized her picture in the newspaper and the article even mentions that restaurant we went to in Lynn. About a year ago. I'm sure she's the one you talked to. About her dad and Alice and stuff, remember? Roseanne something-or-other. She got upset about something you said and just walked away. You never did tell me how you knew her."

"Sure, Roseanne. Her father is Alice's stepfather, Tony. What about her?"

"Oh, yeah, that's right. Well, she's dead. You may want to tell Alice, then. Drug overdose. The article says she had a history ... they don't know if it was accidental or suicide."

Chapter Twenty-Four
Jan 2017

"Hey, Missy? Heather's on the phone."

Her mother was in the kitchen and Missy was just walking in at the back door. Dinner was almost ready and smelled really, really good. It was Friday the 13th and it had been a busy week, the first full week after the holidays with all five days back in school. She'd had a good workout at the gym and now she was starved, as usual. "I'll get it upstairs, Mom!" she called as she raced by, heading for her room so she could dump her gear and change. She hung up her coat on the way to the stairs, which she took two at a time. Picking up the extension next to her bed, she answered, "Hello, Heather! Miss me already?"

They hadn't talked since just after New Year's when her sister had returned to school. Heather had again lived at home during her co-op assignment at the jet engine factory over in Lynn, only fifteen minutes away. They'd grown pretty close these past few months and Missy had enjoyed having her around. Now Heather was back in Boston where she shared an apartment off campus with Bethany. They'd found this place two semesters earlier and during the months they were away on co-op work assignments, their friends Lisa and Marie stayed there. Many co-op students at the university did this, alternating back and forth, trading places for their work/study cycles. So far, the arrangement had been just perfect.

"You know it, Missy! Everyone back here is so dull and boring. No fun. Not like all the interesting, exciting stuff you're always getting involved in, now that you've finally caught up with all your school work. That first year back? You were way too intense with all that home study stuff. But ever since last August? Much more fun. You know. Ever since you '*let the cat out of the bag*' and spilled all your secrets, right? I can say that, can't I?" Heather started laughing hilariously, once again kidding Missy about being a cat. She delighted in doing that, every chance she could, but only when no one else could possibly learn about Missy's secret. "Actually, about that? It's kinda why I'm calling. I want to check something with you. About what you maybe can do, okay?"

Missy was giggling at her sister's joking around but then she caught something in Heather's voice at the end which sounded a little serious. "Sure, sure! Anything for you, you know that. Always. Now, what's going on?"

"Can you get away? Maybe even come in here tonight? Beth and I found some things. Some cameras, actually. I don't really know if you can, you know … can you help us figure out who might have put them here?"

"Hey, I'll drive in right after dinner. Be there in less than an hour, no problem. I'm sure I can help with whatever it is. But, tell me more about these cameras. What do you mean by *someone put them there*?" Missy emphasized these last words. She was getting a bad feeling about this.

"Well, we got this call today. From Lisa and Marie. They were really upset and told us to check. And, sure enough, just like they thought, there are video cameras. Three so far, but we're still looking. Someone got in here and placed them so they could spy on us. They obviously know girls are always living here."

"Wait a minute, are you saying what I think you're saying?" Missy was getting the picture all right. "Spy cameras? Taking videos? Let me guess. Bathroom and bedrooms, right?"

"Yeah. We found wireless transmitters inside the ductwork along with motion sensors. We want to find where the signals are going ... probably a laptop somewhere in our building. That could then link to the internet so whatever's getting filmed can be downloaded anywhere. Lisa and Marie just found out and ... this is really terrible, Missy!" Heather paused. "There are videos of them on one of those porn sites. Someone recognized them and told them to check and, sure enough, the videos are showing them right here in our apartment."

"Umm, what about you and Beth? Are you saying ..."

"I think we're mostly okay," Heather said, interrupting her obvious question. "We don't think these cameras were here until a few months ago. And, Beth and I don't think anything which may have been filmed since we've been back has been very ... revealing. Or, compromising ... you know. Even the camera in the bathroom ... maybe me naked for a few nano seconds, hopping into the shower? But, I doubt that's enough to interest anyone. Still … gives me the creeps. Such a violation! An invasion of privacy like this can really mess with your head."

"What about Lisa and Marie, then?" asked Missy. "Have they had guys staying over and … you know …"

"Worse than that, Missy. Ahh … you see … they're actually a couple. They're gay. And, a few times … with all the lights on in Lisa's bedroom? They told us they can get pretty uninhibited and …" Heather sighed. "Even when they're alone, they each …it seems there's still lots. Dildos and stuff. You know."

"Were they maybe targeted, then? Do they have any idea who might have done this? Someone planned all this and if there are several cameras and other equipment? Who have they allowed in there? Or, was the place broken into?"

"That's the thing. And, why I was asking if maybe you can help us figure out who might have put them here. They do have a list of possible suspects. Lisa and Marie even included addresses for most of them. But, what can we do? There probably are no fingerprints and tracing the equipment isn't likely to help much."

Missy's thoughts were racing. "Let me help you search. First, let's get all the equipment which is in your apartment. Then, if we can find that laptop you mentioned? Somewhere in the building? Hopefully, from all this stuff I can get a good enough scent. Then, we can check out each of your suspects. I'll know who it is by their scent."

"Really? I wasn't sure, but I was hoping there might be some way … you know, you having *special powers*, right?" Giggling, and greatly relieved, Heather said, "If you can stay the night, we'll see how far we can get with all this by tomorrow afternoon. Lisa and Marie will be here then."

Two hours later, Missy was sifting and sorting through all the stuff the three of them had ended up finding. Five cameras with microphones, three motion sensors, two wireless transmitters and, from an alcove under the stairs going up to the roof, a laptop. This was inside a backpack which Missy found, in spite of it being very well hidden under some old clothes. Now that she had that, she had a very clear scent. One person had done this and the backpack material held that person's scent especially well. She would know who he was once she found his scent.

They were now discussing the list of suspects. Heather was pretending to Bethany that her sister was psychic and able to determine who the guilty guy was merely by touching all these items. And, if they went around to each suspect's address, Missy might "get a vibe". Bethany was looking at the two of them like they were crazy but, at this point, she was desperate and willing to grasp at anything. "Sure, you guys go ahead. I'm going to see what I can learn from this laptop. Maybe I can crack the password." Looking at Missy, Bethany asked Heather, "Can your sister get any vibe which tells her what the damn password might be?"

After staying overnight, sleeping on the living room couch, Missy was up early the next morning and in the kitchen making breakfast. When the others joined her at the table, she served them first and then sat down to her usual huge meal, which was enough to feed a small army. Knowing this was the first time Bethany had ever seen Missy eat, Heather started to explain things. "About all this food, Beth. My sister works out a lot. She does sports at school, goes running every day, does karate and martial arts, plus at the gym …"

Bethany laughed. "Relax. I know all that. When my friends found out that I was sharing an apartment with you, they all started asking me about your famous sister. Thanksgiving weekend? When Missy won that big trophy? Amateur Women's something-or-other in martial arts? It was all over the internet. YouTube videos and all those photos. Wow. Those were really some big, scary photos." Turning to Missy, she said, "You looked a lot bigger, somehow. Have you actually *lost* weight since then? Eat up, girl! Have all you want!" Everyone broke out laughing at that.

Heather and Missy then went out and canvassed the area. Lisa and Marie had provided fifteen names on their list, so far, and were still trying to think if any more should be added. While there were a few workmen, who'd been in once or twice to install or repair something, most were other students they'd invited in for some partying. Evidently, they were very popular girls and their being lesbian lovers didn't matter very much. So, they had a lot of friends and there'd been some wild parties. No drugs but plenty of alcohol. First, they'd made a list of everyone they could remember having ever come to any of their parties. Then, they'd crossed off those they were positive would never have done this. But, if the search through the fifteen names didn't result in anything turning up, they would think again about all those friends and whether to maybe add some names back on the list again. They were standing by, waiting for a progress report.

While it was tedious going around to each of the addresses, it was a really beautiful day in Boston; crisp and cold but very sunny. A recent snowfall had covered all the usual city dirt with an inch of snow, so it was now a winter's wonderland. Heather had wondered if that would affect Missy's being able to scent things, but Missy assured her she'd know when they found the right address. And, just before noon, they did. When they entered the foyer of a large apartment building which was on the list, she knew immediately. The guy they were after had been there. She could tell he'd definitely been inside this building several times.

They waited in the foyer until one of the tenants came out and then slipped past him through the open door, entering inside just as though they lived there. Getting into these old apartment buildings was not very difficult. Just as it probably had not been much of a problem for this guy to get into Heather's apartment while Lisa and Marie were living there. Going door to door on each level, they found the guy's room on the fourth floor. Room 410, in a corner at the rear of the building. The scent was much stronger than in the foyer and hardly anyone else had been going into this room, so it had to be his. Missy got down on her knees to sniff under the door and inhale the air from inside the room. He wasn't home today but he'd been there not that long ago.

His door was very solid and had two locks on it. These locks were not the usual type for such places but instead had been installed special. This guy obviously was concerned about his security. Picking these locks would probably not be possible. There was an outside fire escape which could be accessed through a window at the end of the hall. But, that didn't go anywhere near the windows for his room. It looked like it did go up to the roof, however, which was up a few more levels.

They went back down to check names on the mailboxes. It turned out this guy wasn't even on the list. Jonathan Baxter. Nope, not on the list. But, William Fallon in room 402 was on the list. Perhaps William had brought his friend Jonathan along to one of the parties. He might not even know anything about all the spy cameras which Jonathan later went back and installed. Or, maybe he did. They'd find out.

First, they needed a plan. Knowing Jonathan Baxter had done this was one thing. What to do about that was another. Back at Heather's place, the three of them discussed things for over an hour. Over lunch. Another big feast for Missy which was sent up by the local deli -- a huge chicken Caesar salad with lots of turkey lunchmeat and Swiss cheese on the side. Heather and Bethany each had some fruit, yogurt and a small salad.

As they talked, the mood really lightened up. Since Bethany wasn't too sure about Missy truly being a psychic, she thought at first they were not being serious. Then, as their various plans became more and more outlandish, she was positive. They absolutely couldn't possibly be serious. Could they? They were all getting a little giddy from laughing so much. Missy kept saying how they had to have a Plan A and a Plan B. Heather turned to Bethany and said, "You don't even want to know about her Plan C, Beth. No, no, no. Trust me on this. Please don't ever ask her."

Missy then said, "You know what Granddad McCrea always says, right?"

Heather broke out laughing and said, "Oh, yeah, I know that's where you get all this stuff from. You listen to all his crazy Army stories and then you love to get all military." Looking at Bethany, she said in a deep voice, "Plan your work, then work your plan!" More laughter.

Chapter Twenty-Five
Jan 2017

Lisa and Marie arrived just after three in the afternoon. They were both exceptionally beautiful girls and Missy learned they'd been working as models for a few years now. They'd met while on a photo shoot when back in high school and had ended up together now in college. Lisa was studying criminology and planned to join the police force when she graduated, just as many from her family had done. And, Marie was a computer science major. This creep Jonathan Baxter had definitely messed with the wrong girls.

They were discussing all the spy equipment and how it worked. Marie explained that since the cameras and microphones were only activated when they got a signal from the motion sensors, their battery life was good for several months. The laptop had been plugged into an extension cord which, like the laptop, had been cleverly hidden. It was still powered up even now but they couldn't get past the screensaver password, which Bethany had given up trying to guess at. For internet access, there were dozens of WiFi accounts active in their building. Most were protected by security but the password key was often not that difficult to crack. There was readily available software out there which could easily do it.

"So," Missy asked, "once he managed to get this stuff all set up, he wouldn't need to return for months? And, unless you noticed the equipment, it would all just keep turning on and sending him videos whenever anyone was moving in the bathroom or the bedrooms? Wow. Then, I suppose he edits those films and uploads them to those porn sites. I assume he's getting paid somehow, right?"

Lisa replied, "Yeah, we contacted that site we found ourselves on and they've pulled the films. They claim they pay for all their films and get authorization release forms from the girls in them but when we insisted those forms were forgeries they were quick to back down. They don't want any trouble and agreed to yank down all the stuff showing us right away. I'm betting that happens for a lot of the stuff they get. Anybody challenges them? They just delete the stuff. But, they wouldn't identify their source. That would take a court order or something."

"And, we don't know what other sites he may have sold our stuff to," said Marie. "We really are hoping we can find this guy and somehow access his computer. Only then can we maybe track down what he's done with all the films he has which show either one of us. I'm mostly interested in doing that so we can get everything off all those internet sites. We still do modeling and if the agencies learn about any of this stuff, we're going to be dropped and never get any decent photo shoots again."

Lisa asked, "Yeah, but we also want some revenge. How sure are you about this guy Jonathan Baxter being the one? I mean, he wasn't even on our list. Is Missy really that good a psychic?" She, like Bethany, was clearly somewhat skeptical. "And, Billy Fallon? He's just this wimpy guy in Marie's computer lab who's always asking to come to our parties. He knows we're gay but since our parties are always pretty great, he's always asking to come just so he can impress all his friends. Even though he's on our list, I somehow can't see him ever doing this."

Marie said, "Yeah, but I think he was at that big bash we had, the one just before we went home for that long Thanksgiving weekend. So, maybe ... if he brought any of those friends ..."

"We're actually pretty sure about this," Heather answered. "And, if we can get you inside his place, we're hoping you can find some definite proof. Missy says she can get you inside for a quick look and, if he's not the guy, you can leave without his ever knowing. No harm, no foul, right? Even if he is the guy, you can still leave without his ever knowing. It doesn't look like he's staying there at the moment. He probably went home for the weekend or something. So, let's see if we can do this."

"If I can just get into his computer ..." said Marie, wistfully. "Then we'll know. From what you've told us, he apparently has some really great security locks on his door. So, maybe he doesn't bother with any passwords to access his computer. I'll bet it's just left on all the time, downloading stuff from wherever he has any of these laptops set up to send him videos. He probably thinks he's pretty safe. I'll bet there are no fingerprints or anything incriminating on any of this stuff of his which you have here. But, how the hell can you get inside his place, anyway?"

Missy assured them, "No problem! I'll drop down from the roof and get in through his window. I doubt anyone on the fourth floor bothers to lock their windows, right? Then, I'll buzz you guys up. Once you're done checking his place and leave, I'll lock up and go back out the same way. He'll never even know we were in there."

"Oh, and don't ask her what she'll do if the windows are all locked," said Bethany. "We've been having lots of fun talking about that while we were waiting for you to get here. Missy has her Plan B for that. She even has a Plan C, but Heather assures me that we definitely don't ever want to know about her Plan C." They all broke out laughing at that. But, it was obvious Bethany still didn't believe they were discussing anything they could actually do. For real.

Lisa thought for a minute and then asked, "But, wait … you said the roof was several floors higher up. Do you mean you're going to climb up the fire escape to the roof and then climb down some rope to this guy's window?" She figured Missy and Heather were only kidding about this. "You do realize that it's well below freezing out there today, right? Dangling from some rope up a hundred feet in the air? What if you fall? What if someone sees you? What if …"

"Trust me, guys, please!" Missy looked at them and smiled. "I didn't get to the gym today, so I really need the exercise. This will be fun!"

Heather was the only one who really believed her. The other three were finding it very difficult to believe she was serious. But, they all headed out and went over to Jonathan Baxter's building anyway, with a quick stop at the local hardware store to buy some rope.

They were joking about "giving a guy enough rope to hang himself" and were making several other ridiculous comments about their situation as they approached their destination. They were only humoring the two sisters but since they didn't have anything else they could do, they figured they'd at least come along and look at the building. Maybe they'd see Billy Fallon.

It was now going for five and was quite dark out, which Missy said would help her avoid being seen. Marie said, "Missy, I don't know about that. Your coat is white and that's going to show up against this dark building." The building had a lot of soot which had accumulated over more than a hundred years.

"My blue jeans are dark and so is my New England Patriots sweatshirt," Missy announced. "I'm taking off the coat, which would only be in my way. Trust me. Just wait in the foyer and I'll buzz you in." Then, off she went carrying the rope, in spite of only Heather actually believing her. None of the others believed anything Missy was saying was at all possible. They were convinced this was merely more joking around.

Missy walked around to the fire escape while the others entered the building. She quickly made her way up to the roof and worked her way around to the corner above Baxter's apartment. She secured one end of the rope to the parapet, removed her jacket, hat and gloves and then swung herself over the edge. Yes it was cold, but for Missy's enhanced metabolism that was not a problem; she hardly noticed. She easily lowered herself down the rope, hand under hand, feet walking along the side of the building. This required tremendous strength in her hands and fingers but, again, not a problem for her.

Outside the first window to Baxter's apartment, she could see it was tightly secured and might be difficult. This was due to the storm windows being closed all the way. Working her way sideways over to the next window, she saw she was in luck. Since there was already a two inch opening in the storm window, she was able to easily slide it fully open. There was a screen inside, but she was able to jiggle that open and slide it all the way up. These old buildings with their ancient storm windows were making her job easy. No need for Plan B.

The inside window was not locked, just as she'd guessed, so she was able to open this fully as well. Stepping through, she was in. She found herself in the bedroom and walked, in the dark, over to the entrance to the living room. She turned on the lights and, after a quick look around, she pressed the button to unlock the door at the lobby where the girls were waiting for her. It had only been a few minutes and the total shock and surprise for three of those girls made Heather break out laughing.

When Missy greeted Lisa and Marie at the door to Baxter's apartment, they were still trying to get over their amazement. They were really doing this! By some miracle, Missy had managed actually getting them in there. They stared at the open door with its two sturdy locks and shook their heads. They noticed Missy was not wearing any coat. Still wondering if this was all some trick, they went in. Heather followed behind and gave Missy a warm smile.

Bethany had remained down in the foyer and would call on her cell phone if anyone who might be Baxter showed up. They didn't know what he looked like so they were anticipating several alerts. Hopefully, they'd all be false alerts. Heather had insisted on this, saying it was still Missy's plan to not get caught. For each alert, the girls would get out and wait down the hall. Missy would lock up and go out the window. If it wasn't Baxter, she'd come back inside and open his door for them to return.

So, now that Missy had them in there, they all looked around the place. That did not take long. The two large computer monitors sitting side by side in the middle of the second bedroom were very obvious. And, the computer was on and running. Marie moved the mouse and the screensavers cleared without requiring any password. She squealed in delight, "Gotcha, you bastard! Now, let's see what you've been up to."

Ten minutes later, she turned around and told the others, "This is our guy, all right. Missy, I don't know how you figured it out and I'm not really buying any of that psychic mumbo-jumbo crap. But, who cares? You're just a miracle worker, that's all I know. Look here, Lisa. He has special folders, just for us. And, he has another forty folders, one for each of his other victims. Here's one for Bethany and another for Heather." Turning to look at Heather, she said, "You were right, or maybe just lucky. Those don't seem to have anything much as yet. But, he's been filming some of these other girls for quite a while now. Unbelievable. What a slime ball!"

Marie continued clicking on various folders, while Lisa looked over her shoulder. Suddenly, Marie exclaimed "Ahhhh, but, he's such an *organized* slime ball! That's going to be his downfall! Lisa, look here. He even has a folder for all his passwords. It has several spreadsheet files each containing various login ID's and passwords. And see here? His personal accounts, his college student accounts, his banks ... oh, look! All his porn sites! And, here's his email accounts ... you name it. It's all here." She kept pointing at the screen and getting more and more excited.

Lisa asked, "What about accessing his computer, can we do that?" She looked at Heather and Missy and explained, "Marie was telling me how she can set things up so she can access a computer from anywhere, if she just knows the guy's passwords and codes. Then, once she's in? She can upload her own spy program. After that, she can keep getting back in without his knowing it and he can't block her. Plus, she can do everything just like she's sitting right here. With his passwords, she owns him."

Marie said, "Yes, his identity is forever mine. Look ... here's all of his personal info. Full name, social security number, date of birth, addresses, all so nicely organized. We can keep stealing his identity and messing with him for the rest of his miserable life. I'm soon going to clean out all his bank accounts, get him kicked out of school and fired from any real jobs he ever gets. All in good time. But, first, let's see where else he's sold our videos and who else he's maybe just given them to. He's so super organized, I'm betting we'll have no problem figuring all that out just from his emails."

Heather went down to check with Bethany and let her know the good news. Marie had looked at everything he'd recorded on them both and so far, nothing much. Nothing he'd have uploaded anywhere. Bethany was greatly relieved. And, no one had come in down there yet, so there hadn't been any need to raise an alert. She was slowly becoming a true believer. Not only was her roommate's sister famous for kicking butt in that tournament but Missy was truly a miracle worker.

Meanwhile, Lisa and Marie kept looking at various files on Baxter's computer and Missy prowled through the rest of his apartment. She could see he was mostly a loner, with an undergraduate degree in business. He was now a graduate student, working on his MBA. All the text books were related to business with a few related to computers. And, he loved his porn. Magazines, photo albums and videos. He had a large collection of DVD's and even some old VCR tapes. From the titles, these were all clearly hardcore. It was doubtful he ever entertained anyone else at his place. She definitely couldn't scent anyone female, which was not a surprise.

Once Marie had everything she needed to log back into his computer from her own computer, they got ready to leave. After checking around to be sure they weren't leaving any trace that they'd been there, Lisa and Marie went out and down to join Heather and Marie. Missy locked up the door, just as Baxter had left it, turned off the lights and went back out through the bedroom window. She closed the inside window, then pulled down the screen and finally closed the storm window leaving the same two inch opening at the bottom. He'd never know anyone had been there. Then, hand over hand, she pulled herself back up the rope with her feet again walking on the side of the building. At the top, she hoisted herself onto the roof, coiled up her rope, put on her coat and went down the fire escape. She joined the other girls out front and they all returned to Heather's place.

The girls couldn't stop talking about what Missy had done. Even more impressive was how quickly she'd managed doing it. Both getting in and then getting back out. They wished they'd filmed her doing it. Climbing in and out of the window, dangling from the rope, going up and down the side of the building, all in freezing cold with no coat on ... were these things even humanly possible? Hey? Was there any chance she'd go back and do it all again? Just for them? Lots of laughter.

Missy was impressed by what Marie had explained about remote access and asked her to demonstrate what she could do. Marie showed her how easy it was, getting into Baxter's computer by logging in from Heather's computer, using all the info they'd collected. She explained how she'd turned on file sharing, which made all this possible. Now, they could do this from anywhere, with any computer. And, once logged in, Marie showed her how they could copy all the stuff they wanted and even upload anything they wanted. Like the spy program she had which would allow her to continue having access, even if he turned the file sharing off. Seemed more than fitting, right? A spy program as retributive justice for all the spying he'd been doing.

Of course, Lisa was already talking about the virus they'd eventually infect him with, once they'd done as much damage to his personal accounts as they possibly could. They'd empty out his bank accounts, max out his credit cards and do whatever other mischief and mayhem they could manage. Ruin his life.

Plus, all of his other victims would soon be getting emails informing them about all the porn sites where he'd uploaded his videos of them. These emails would be from him, of course. Lisa thought there'd be enough complaints from these other victims combined with all the evidence these victims could provide so she and Marie could simply stay completely in the background. No reason to get involved.

Then, they'd destroy all his files with Lisa's nasty virus. Once he managed to recover? They'd steal his identity and ruin him all over again. Who knows? Maybe they'd even get Missy to come back and break into his place once more so they could wreak even more havoc. He would not be selling any videos ever again, that was for sure.

Missy stayed over one more night with Bethany and Heather. It was after midnight by the time Lisa and Marie finally left. They'd all thoroughly enjoyed this adventure. While it had started out looking like a real disaster, thanks to Missy, they'd managed to avoid that. Instead, it ended up being a big disaster about to happen for Jonathan Baxter. When she returned home Sunday morning and her mom asked if she'd had a good time with Heather, she told her "You bet, Mom. Absolutely! We had the best time!"

Chapter Twenty-Six
Mar 2017

Tony was finally ready. His revenge was going to be all the more satisfying because he'd taken such special steps to prepare everything. That bitch Missy had messed everything up with her interference and her threats. Friends in high places, so he had no choice, huh? Well, she'd find out. She'd signed her own death warrant. She'd disappeared for those two years, which was what made his plan so great. She'd disappear once again, only this time she'd never be found. Not ever.

And the two guys he'd arranged to grab her? They wouldn't know what happened to her either. Once they had her doped up, out cold in the trunk of their car, they'd leave that car overnight in the parking garage. Then, poof! She'd disappear and they'd never know where she went or who'd paid them for grabbing her. He was the one with friends. And, his friends always came through with the favors he asked for. He took care of laundering all their money and when he needed an occasional favor? No problem. They set everything up and didn't even ask who he was having their "guys on loan" take care of as long as it wasn't anyone associated with the organization.

Tony had grown up in Revere with his good buddy Frank McCarthy. And, Frank was now running things for the criminal organization in East Boston. He'd worked his way up in the organization and when he'd needed someone to launder the organization's money, Tony was the one who knew how to do that. First one, then two, then three restaurants. Then, way more which no one even knew about. All in Tony's name but it was the organization's money from drugs, prostitution, gambling and loan shark activities which had been flushed through and returned to their various legitimate businesses as "clean" money. Tony never got involved with any of the illegal stuff but had no problem asking Frank for help whenever he needed something. Frank knew how to get "loaners" from the New York organization.

And, these "loaner guys" never knew anything. They got their instructions and got their payment, all without knowing who they were being "loaned" out to. Sure, they had to suspect their boss in New York owed a favor to "someone" here in Boston, but things were on a need to know only basis. And, they didn't need to know.

Tony had successfully arranged for his first wife's "car accident" years ago. That hit and run had happened while he was being seen by dozens of witnesses in his restaurant. No problem. Then, he'd recently had his ex-drug addict daughter taken care of. No problem. The cops didn't really care whether she'd OD'd by accident or by suicide. There was never any hint of suspicion tracing back to him for either of those sad, tragic deaths.

And, there wouldn't be any connection now to Missy's disappearance. He'd waited all these months to make sure of that. Alice and her mother wouldn't suspect a thing. And, when enough time had passed, he'd deal with them as well.

It was finally time. He's gone the extra mile for this. Not only would he be getting rid of Missy. That was easy. No, he'd made sure he would have a few "special" days with her first. Days when he could really enjoy himself. Yes, he liked young girls. Roseanne and Alice had been very satisfying, while they'd been young and available. As had the many young girls his buddy Frank had arranged for him to enjoy over the years. But, Missy? She was going to be really special.

He'd been lusting for her since she'd first walked into his home to visit Alice more than a year ago. And, after the way she'd forced him to sign all those papers taking care of Alice and her mom? He'd been watching her very closely ever since. He'd read all the articles in the local news. First, the stories in the archives about her disappearance. Then, the missing teen returns home stories. For the past year, it was all what a great athlete she was on her high school teams. Plus, earning her black belt in karate. Then, that elaborate spectacle she'd made of herself winning the big trophy in martial arts? Some great photos and videos on line after that. Oh, yeah! What a treasure she was! And, she was going to be his to fully enjoy like he'd never experienced any other young girl's "treasures" before.

He'd purchased his little vacation home years ago; a cottage on Plum Island, just under an hour's drive from Salem. Busy in the summer but pretty much deserted in March. And, the entire upstairs was now quite soundproof after the various remodeling improvements he'd had done this past year. Oh, he was going to really enjoy himself while he gave Missy the lessons she so deserved for all the grief she'd caused him. This would be a new chapter for him. Maybe he'd want a few more chapters after he got rid of Missy. Why worry whether some little bitch might somehow find the courage to complain? Why have to deal with the little bitch's mother? This was much less of a risk and he could indulge himself so much more! Such a win-win!

Missy now had her driver's license and really loved going back and forth to school in her Toyota. Getting around afterwards to karate or martial arts or softball or any of her other activities was now so easy. She didn't need anyone else but could get there on her own. Her trips to the state forest could now be made without having to rely on someone else in her family to drop her off and later pick her up. It made such a difference. Things were just so much simpler now.

When she walked towards her car after karate practice, still wearing her gi uniform under a light jacket, she noticed two guys working on a car next to hers in the parking lot. It was just after five on a Friday afternoon and cars were scattered all over, since many had already left for the weekend. Their car was a Chevy and looked a few years old. The hood was up and one guy had his head underneath, looking at the carburetor with a flashlight. The air cleaner was on the ground. The second guy was asking whether it was flooded or was it something else and the first guy was telling him he should have known better. Missy really wasn't concerned or interested in any of this as she headed for her car. She didn't have any reason to be worried as she approached these guys. She was about to learn a lesson, however, and would never blindly trust any situation like this again.

She did notice the unique scent for each guy which she categorized and filed away in her memory, just as she'd been doing with all the other scents she'd experienced ever since her first Change. She didn't consciously think about this; she just did it. And, she never forgot a scent. Her scent memories were even stronger than her visual memories. Her abilities were unique and special, and she didn't think about them all that much anymore. She'd just accepted them as part of what she was.

The first guy with his head bent over the carburetor looked up at her and asked, "Hey, do you have any jumper cables? My buddy here ran the battery down trying to start this damn car, even though it was flooded and I told him to stop." He was dressed in expensive casual attire but the tattoo visible on his neck suggested he was not a member of high society. He looked like a thug and was completely bald.

The other guy said, "Oh, like it's all my fault ..." He turned towards her just as the first guy began backing away from the car, also moving towards her. He too was dressed in expensive clothes but was rather good looking, in a tough guy sort of way. He had long black hair, slicked back, and he wore a diamond earring on his left ear. Suddenly, they both grabbed her and before she could react, the second guy had punctured her neck with a syringe. She immediately exploded into action but was too late. The guy had already pushed down the plunger forcing a knockout drug into her body. She actually sent the two of them flying but then, as the drug coursed through her system, she slowly collapsed. A few moments later, Missy was out cold.

The two guys cursed her as they got back on their feet. They looked around and, luckily for them, no one had noticed any of this. They grabbed Missy, wrapped duct tape around her hands and feet, added a piece of tape across her mouth, wrapped her in a blanket and put her into the trunk of their car. This was all done quickly and efficiently. These guys had done this before and wasted no time. In less than a minute, they were in the car and driving out of the parking lot.

The man with the earring exclaimed, "What a little bitch! She sure was fast! I barely managed to get her with the goddamn syringe when she had me on my ass! What the hell were you doing, Donny?" He was the one driving and he looked over at the guy with the tattoo.

Donny replied, "Glad the damn drug worked. I never expected her to be that strong or that fast. She's only sixteen, right? I know the file on her says something about karate and kung fu crap, but still ... She's a little tiger, isn't she?" He then yelled, "Watch where you're going, Billy! We don't wanna have any accidents now!"

"Oh, relax, I've got this." Billy quickly adjusted the steering wheel while braking and then accelerating as they moved smoothly around a slower car and into the passing lane. "I sure wish we didn't have to leave this little tiger so quickly for that asshole who hired us. Whoever he is. I'd love to play with her a little now that she's out from the drug."

"Yeah, I'm sure you would. But, I'd rather have her when she was awake and able to enjoy it. Doing a girl when she's passed out is no fun. Let's just finish this so we can get paid. Ten grand each isn't a bad day's pay, right? I plan to have myself two lively bimbos at the same time when we get back home. I know this place where the girls will …"

Billy interrupted him to say, "There's the parking garage. Check no one's following us when we drive in there, okay? I'll drive right back out if anyone comes in behind us." He slowed to turn in at the entrance. "As for not doing a girl unless she's awake? When it's someone ugly as you, they only enjoy the money you're paying 'em. And, I don't even wanna know where you're spending all your money at, Donny."

"Billy, Billy, we can't all get 'em free like you do. Roofies and stuff are too risky. Anyway, you probably spend lots more than me, just taking care of everything which happens afterwards." Donny looked around while Billy drove up to the next level, heading for the roof. "No one's behind us. And, I don't see anyone else in here. Almost too easy, huh? We don't even have to dispose of her body. Just come back for this car tomorrow and deliver it to that junkyard in Hartford. She'll be like in that TV show, remember? Without a Trace, right?"

They both laughed at that. When they emerged onto the top level, Billy drove down and parked at the far end. They got out, left the car unlocked so the trunk release was readily available, and walked over to their other car, a late model Ford Mustang. Two minutes later they were back on the street, heading for their motel.

Twenty minutes later, after receiving their call on his throwaway cell phone, Tony drove up in his Honda Civic. He looked around, popped his trunk open, got out and looked around again. Once certain no one was watching, he went over to the Chevy and opened the driver's door so he could reach in and pop open the trunk. He wore gloves so he wasn't leaving any evidence behind. The car would be scrap metal in another day, but why take chances. And, since Missy was wrapped in a blanket, per his instructions, there'd be no DNA trace of her in either car. He'd thought of everything.

An hour later he was parking his car at the back door of his place on Plum Island. No one else was around and only a couple lights showed in any houses; none near his. After carrying Missy on one shoulder up the stairs to his soundproof second floor, he deposited her on the huge bed. He'd already closed the trunk lid after hoisting Missy out but he went downstairs to turn out all the lights and activate his security system. Then, on his way back upstairs, he closed and locked the door behind him. This would be such fun! He'd been dreaming of all the ways he'd be enjoying himself and now it was all coming true. Missy was his!

Missy woke up an hour later. It was an hour or two earlier than for any normal person, drugged as she'd been, but of course she wasn't normal. She was, however, feeling disoriented and groggy as she struggled to clear her mind and all her senses. Right away, she scented Tony. As her memory of being grabbed and drugged came rushing back, she realized he had to have hired those guys. Obviously, Tony planned on killing her and had waited until he felt confident he'd get away with that. She wondered why she wasn't already dead.

Then, she felt the handcuffs tightly binding her wrists and ankles. She was lying on her back, spread-eagled on a bed, and these handcuffs were attached to the four corners with chains. She couldn't move. And, she was completely naked. Now she knew why she was still alive. Tony, being the perverted pedophile that he was, wanted to play first. Then he'd kill her. She shivered as a chill ran through her. That caused her nipples to grow hard. Missy realized things weren't exactly going well for her at the moment. She looked around and, sure enough, there was Tony. Watching her. She could see he was getting pretty excited.

"You're awake so soon? That's great, Missy! I've been really enjoying all this, just watching you. But, now my pleasure will really begin. You have no idea what fun things I've planned for you, you miserable slut. Payback's a bitch, bitch!" With that, Tony started laughing. He was sitting in a chair just a few feet away, on the left side of the bed. "All these months. I've been waiting and waiting. Remember when you asked if I really wanted to mess with you? Well, I sure did! You thought you were such hot stuff with your friends in high places, huh?" More laughter.

"I see you have friends, Tony. Getting those two guys to grab me for you? I suppose I really shouldn't be surprised. You're such a bully and a coward." Missy twisted her head to look at him. "But, aren't you worried they'll talk someday? That you'll be found out? Everyone will know. Not only what a sick bastard you are but what a murdering sick bastard? How are you going to avoid that, Tony?" Missy wanted to get him talking so she could learn as much as possible. He'd hired some help and she wanted to know all about that.

"Watch what you call me, bitch!" He was annoyed she wasn't freaking out more. "And, don't you worry, my good buddy Frank and his organization won't tell anyone. They like the way I take care of washing all their money for them with my restaurants and all my other businesses. We have a real nice arrangement. And, those guys from New York that Frank arranges for? Their boss is only doing him favors, sending them up here each time. They don't know Frank and sure as hell don't know anything about me. Just like when that guy hit my first wife years ago, you know? Hit and run. He had no idea why she needed taking care of. Just a nice clean hit and the police never found anything. Frank always gets these "loaners" to come up here to take care of things. He doesn't even tell me who he deals with down there." He enjoyed bragging to her. She was never going to tell anyone and he wanted her to know just how bad her situation was.

Missy suddenly was seeing Tony in a far more sinister light. If he'd killed his first wife, then ..? "What about Roseanne, Tony?" She felt sickened by his callous treachery.

"Oh, now you're getting smart. Seeing the big picture, right? Sure! I wasn't taking any chances with her blabbing, even though no one was ever gonna listen to her. And, in a year or two? Alice will be taken care of. Now that I've got this special place here, I'll be having girls whenever I want. You're the reason for my going to all this trouble, but it's just working out so well. Girls disappear all the time. It's only a problem if they don't stay disappeared. But, if no body is found? And no evidence ever turns up? Not a problem. And, no one will ever find anything left of you or Alice or any of the other girls I plan to enjoy up here. See what you started, Missy? I really should be thanking you!" Tony started laughing at this. He wanted to see Missy tremble in fear. He waited for her to show some real terror at what he was telling her.

Missy could see how evil and depraved Tony had become, enabled by whoever this Frank was. "So, you take care of Frank's dirty money? And, you trust him? Why wouldn't he turn you in, Tony? Isn't he taking risks doing you favors?" She wanted to know just a little bit more.

Tony wasn't seeing the reaction he wanted yet. He explained, "In Frank's world, everything's a risk but he has this whole risk-reward thing, you know? We grew up together and what we have has always been a win-win deal, with him actually being a big winner. He needs me. He'd never have gotten as high up in the organization without my showing him how to wash their money for them." While saying all this, Tony stood and began running one hand along her thigh. "He likes having me owe him these favors and knowing all my secrets. That way, he knows I can't risk ratting him out to anyone. He's actually more worried about his own organization finding out stuff than he is about the cops. You just have no idea about how things work in the real world, Missy."

He seemed quite fascinated by the scar on her thigh which he began tracing with one finger. "You should never have interfered. That's what's bringing about your loss of innocence and I do mean that *innocence* part in all sorts of interesting ways. Then again, you're such a nasty shameful slut, so maybe you're not so innocent about some things, huh?" Now he had both hands touching her and moving up across her body. He reached up and squeezed her right breast with one hand while his other hand grabbed her left shoulder.

"These are some very interesting scars, Missy!" Tony exclaimed. "They do show up in some of your photos but I wasn't all that sure about them until I had your clothes off and was handcuffing you on the bed here. I can see where you maybe like playing it rough, huh?" At that, he laughed and began rubbing her shoulder with one hand and squeezing her nipple with his other hand. "It's almost a shame I'm gonna have to kill you after I get done playing."

Missy had learned plenty for now. Tony had been touching her long enough. She Shifted. Suddenly, she was no longer a helpless girl restrained by cuffs but after the usual shimmer of light and burst of energy, she was a big cat. There were no longer any restraints, as the cuffs all fell away. She immediately rolled over, standing upright on her four legs, and turned towards Tony. She then let out a long, piercing cougar scream.

Tony was paralyzed, as much by her shrill scream as from his shock at being confronted by a large mountain lion. He stood there and actually wet his pants. Frozen by fear, he was speechless.

Missy jumped off the bed and circled around behind him. Then she leaped back on the bed and stared into his eyes. She watched as the recognition of who she was slowly crept into his facial expression. After a while, his slack jaw twitched. His mouth still hung open but his tongue darted out and back in. Drool dribbled down his chin. She hissed at him, opening her jaws wide and showing her fangs. She reached out with one paw and pushed him back, pressing against his chest and extending her sharp claws. Although these were not ripping into him the way she easily could have done, he could feel them. He fell back onto the chair he'd been sitting in before. Hopping onto the floor, she circled him once again.

He started gulping and gasping, with eyes bulging and in a high voice he managed to squeak, "Missy? But, this isn't possible!" He tried to back away but was immobilized on the chair, with nowhere to go. "How? What …?" Missy quickly moved her head and bared her teeth, forcing him to sit back at any slight movement he made to come forward. Leaping once more onto the bed, she settled down to watch him. He didn't dare make any move and slowly his breathing returned to normal. He sat there and just watched her watching him.

She had three hours to wait and didn't want him getting comfortable so every once in a while, she'd stand up and hiss. Twice she caught him completely off guard by letting out another scream. The second time she did this, he pissed himself all over again. He had no way of knowing what she'd do but he now fully realized this huge cat was indeed Missy. She had total control and he was afraid; he knew he probably was going to die. He could only guess she was merely playing with him, perhaps waiting until he did something. Something that would trigger her tearing into him and just ripping him apart. The eyes were definitely Missy's eyes, only now with more yellow than green. But, how much of her nature might still be human rather than being the wild predator he saw staring at him, he just didn't know.

Missy allowed her cat nature to be dominant, barely restraining the instinct to kill her prey. But, she was also thinking things through with a different part of her mind. Tony was going to tell her who this Frank person was. And, she wanted to find those two guys who'd grabbed her. She pondered all these things while she patiently waited. Then, after almost two hours had passed, Tony decided to take a chance. He suddenly rolled sideways, falling off the chair onto the floor and quickly trying to get up and run. Her scream was the worst thing he'd ever experienced followed immediately by her pouncing on him with her jaws grabbing his neck. She was on his back and just held him in her teeth. Her sharp teeth actually pierced his skin in a few places causing some slow bleeding and a lot of pain. Her mouth was so strong he could do nothing. Reaching one hand up, he touched her jaw. And stopped. Completely helpless. *That* then became the worst thing he'd ever experienced.

Once she saw he wasn't going to make any further moves, she released his neck and stepped off him. He was so frightened, he could barely breathe. She licked at his blood, so it didn't leave any visible stains, and after a few minutes his bleeding stopped. She sat on her haunches and let him lay there. Missy wanted him to think she was licking his neck as though it was her food. The strong ammonia scent from his urine was now permeating the air around him. She got up and made a chuffing noise. Tony didn't move. She took a few steps back and sat down on her haunches again. She waited and Tony just lay flat on his belly, motionless. Ten minutes later, she could see he was sobbing. He'd been completely unnerved by the way her tongue had kept licking at his neck and now he wanted to avoid giving her any excuse to come near him.

She got up and prowled around the room. She found where he'd put her clothes in a plastic bag over in the corner. Obviously, his plan was to eventually kill her and then get rid of her body so she'd never be found. Her clothes and her purse were already bagged, ready for disposal. How long he might have played with her first was anyone's guess. Had she merely been human, the torture he'd have caused her to endure would surely have been unimaginable.

And, he was planning to do this again and again? Eventually even getting Alice? Her mind was made up. Tony was never going to get the chance to hurt anyone ever again. A half hour later, she was able to Change. Tony was still so afraid, he didn't even look up. She walked over and put her clothes on.

Her hair, which had been tied up for karate practice, was now hanging down at full length just as though she'd combed it all out, nice and straight without any tangles. This was how it always came out each time she Changed back. But, her pierced earrings were gone. While loose clothing would remain after Shifting, any jewelry actually attached to her body would always disappear during that burst of energy. She never wore belly button rings or any other pierced jewelry. And, she was annoyed with herself this time for not removing the earrings before karate, the way she had her rings and necklace. She'd rather liked that pair of earrings. Oh, well! Another lesson learned!

Time for some detailed discussion with Tony about his buddy Frank, his restaurant businesses and all his personal affairs along with various other items she was curious about. And, she had very definite plans for the two guys. Walking over to where Tony was lying on the floor, she said, "Get up. But, if you make any funny moves? I won't even bother Changing back. I'll just rip out your throat with my bare hands. Are we clear, Tony?"

Chapter Twenty-Seven
Mar 2017

Missy called home right after she Changed, using her own cell phone. The guys had removed her phone's battery, disabling the GPS, but had left it in her purse along with her phone. She explained to her mom she'd be staying out all night. She'd done that several times before and her mom just figured she needed to be a cat again that night. Since this call wasn't until after eleven, though, her mom had actually been worried. She said, "You should have been home before six, you didn't call and your phone went right to voicemail the three times I tried calling you."

Missy apologized saying she'd forgotten to turn her phone back on after karate and indeed had then Changed; she'd just now Changed back so she could call. She knew her mom realized this would have taken several hours, once she Changed. She also knew her mother didn't worry about her quite as much, ever since she'd revealed herself as a werecat. The rules sometimes needed to be a little different for a werecat daughter!

Then she spent over an hour with Tony, getting him to talk. There'd been a lot more details she'd wanted to get and she'd learned them. When she found out he had a safety deposit box which contained not only all of his important documents but also plenty of evidence about Frank and the East Boston criminal organization, she forced him to give her the key. She also had him write down all the passwords and codes he used for various personal and business accounts. Tony was completely broken. Whatever she asked for, he now was more than willing to give.

When she'd started, he wouldn't say much at first. So she'd threatened to Change back and eat him alive. Slowly. Limb by limb. And, he'd believed her. The way her jaws had gripped his neck had been totally convincing. He didn't understand whether her Changing back and forth was magic or witchcraft or something else again, but he believed she could and would cause him some excruciating pain and suffering and that he had no possible escape. So he talked. Freely. Nothing mattered to him now but placating Missy.

She grilled him all about Frank. Then she had him explain this arrangement for the two guys who had grabbed her. As it turned out, his buddy Frank didn't know anything about Missy being the target; he only knew Tony wanted someone taken care of, once again. And, this was also true for the New York boss who'd sent these two guys up there. Tony had arranged for a folder to be delivered at the motel where these guys were staying. It was an inexpensive motel on Route One in Peabody, not far from a couple of well known strip joints. So, these guys were the only ones who knew about Missy. But, they didn't know Tony and the folder couldn't be traced back to him. And, they didn't know Frank. Interesting!

The instructions in that folder had explained who Missy was, where to leave the kidnap car so Tony could pick her up and what phone number to use for calling Tony. They'd be getting their payment of twenty grand once they'd returned to New York and could show proof the kidnap car they'd used had been disposed of. Nothing could trace back to Tony unless these guys gave up their New York boss who then would have to name Frank. And, no way would these guys ever give up their boss, right? So, Tony had no worries about the kidnapping and only needed to be just as careful when disposing of her body afterwards.

Tony had included in his folder many of the news articles about her, including the ones about her being a black belt in karate and her winning that trophy for mixed martial arts. Just so these guys would be prepared. He'd even told them which knockout drug to use in the syringe. They had no idea why Missy was the target and really didn't care. Twenty grand and they didn't even need to kill her or dispose of her body? There was also a guarantee she'd totally disappear, so they had no worries about ever being caught. They probably wished all their jobs could be this good.

Tony had been very successful arranging the hits on his first wife and then his daughter, using similar arrangements. Frank had known the targets for those hits but wasn't concerned about not knowing this time. Of course, he'd assumed Tony's target would again be killed, not kidnapped. Tony had never gotten his hands dirty before. So, Frank didn't think there was anything to worry about. These simple hits using out of town "loaners" posed zero risk for either Frank or the organization. Right?

Missy packed up Tony's handcuffs and chains so they wouldn't be found at his place. She collected those along with several other interesting items he'd planned to use on her, all sitting in one of the dresser drawers.

Then, she wrapped duct tape around Tony's hands and feet and taped up his mouth, exactly as he'd had those guys do for her. She even used the same blanket, which she wrapped around him and then she carried him out to his car. She had very little difficulty getting his two hundred pounds down the stairs and into the trunk. Werecat strength came in handy for times like this. She went back in, took a last look around to be sure nothing was out of place or could be traced back to her, went out, locked the door and got behind the wheel of Tony's car. It was now well after midnight. Time to pay a visit to those two guys from New York.

The motel in Peabody was one where all the rooms were on one level facing a courtyard, each with a parking space in front of the door. Missy arrived just after one thirty in the morning and found the place very dark and quiet, with mostly vacancies. There were no cars with New York license plates so she strolled slowly in front of each room, using her nose and also parsing the scents over her tongue and across the roof of her mouth. She easily found their two rooms, located at the far end, with no occupied rooms anywhere near them. The tattooed guy's room was on the right. She positioned herself where she couldn't be seen and settled down to wait.

Less than half an hour later, they drove up in their Mustang and parked in front of the room on the left. Missy was able to approach their car without being seen and when the engine was shut off, she could hear them talking inside the car about the girls in the strip joint they'd just left. There seemed to be some debate as to whether all the boobs they'd seen that night were implants. She waited near the driver's door and when it eventually was pushed open, she quickly pulled it wide and slugged the guy at the wheel behind his ear, hitting his carotid artery. Soundlessly, he slumped back in his seat. She bent forward, placing one knee on his lap, and quickly pulled herself inside using the steering wheel. The tattooed guy was halfway out of the car when she yanked him back inside. Then, moments later, he also slumped back in his seat after receiving a knockout blow similar to the one she'd given the driver.

Missy found their room keys and went inside, searched both rooms quickly and came back out. Then, she carried them into the room on the left, one at a time. Using the handcuffs and chains she'd brought from Tony's house, she handcuffed them together on the queen sized bed and chained them so they couldn't get up. She also placed duct tape over each of their mouths. She went out to where she'd left Tony's Honda and drove that up, parking next to the Mustang. Then, she thoroughly searched the Mustang where she not only found Tony's folder with all the instructions for how he wanted her to be kidnapped but his folder for the earlier hit on Roseanne as well. What a coincidence. How convenient.

She then brought in several items from Tony's car and finally went back into the room to deal with Billy Martin and Donny Delgato, whose names and addresses she now knew after going through their wallets. Closing the door, she turned on the lights. She removed her jacket along with her gi uniform top exposing herself in just her sports bra and her gi uniform bottoms. Having Changed twice that night without eating anything since yesterday's lunch, she was starved. Her body was once again showing some excellent definition with no body fat. She pulled her hair back and tied it in a pony tail. Showtime.

There was a fairly new flat screen TV. She was able to connect this up to Tony''s video recorder with an HDMI cable she'd found mixed in amongst all of Tony's recording equipment. Yep, Tony had planned for everything all right, including taping what he did to Missy. She'd already destroyed the tape he'd made showing her being stripped naked and displayed on his bed, along with everything which happened afterward until the two hour tape had run out. She actually got to watch herself Change, which she'd never seen on tape before. Fascinating!

She was thinking how her little brother Patrick would be pleased to see how well she'd managed with all this video equipment. She owed him something special for all those lessons since her return home. Finding the button to toggle the TV's video input over to the recorder's HDMI cable rather than the TV cable, she played the tape in the recorder. The TV only showed a blank tape playing. Then, she stopped and rewound it just a little, so when she hit play this time the TV showed the last part of what she'd recorded at Tony's place. Good. When it reached the end, she stopped the recorder and disconnected the cable. Now it was ready to record from that point forward.

She aimed the recorder at the two guys on the bed and hit the record button. As she taped them, she provided a brief narration identifying them as her kidnappers, to follow up with all the details she'd already recorded at Tony's. She then set the recorder down and moved in front, so she was also being recorded. This tape was for show and tell and she was making a special appearance, just as she had with Tony earlier. She even recorded the two folders, which clearly documented the accusations she'd made in her narration.

She stopped the tape, rewound it back to the beginning, and connected the recorder up to the TV again, ready for showing Billy and Donny just how incriminating all this evidence really was. They'd see Tony spilling all the details about his buddy Frank, about the arrangements for her kidnapping, the hits on Roseanne and her mother, even about the folders. With Missy making an appearance to clearly point the finger at the two of them, this tape was conclusive. Kidnapping and murder. If the cops or FBI ever got this tape, these two were going down for both crimes.

She sat down to wait. This tape was for her Plan B. She wanted even more on it, however, since the security of her entire family was at stake. She needed these guys to not only incriminate themselves, admitting to everything they'd done, but to also name and incriminate their boss. While they might actually risk having the tape go to the authorities, if they only incriminated themselves -- just so they could strike out at her in retaliation or revenge -- she knew they'd never risk that if they incriminated their boss. If it was known they'd named their boss? There was no place on the planet they could hide, no witness protection which would be safe. And, their deaths would be extremely painful. So, she wanted more on this tape. She needed them to name their boss.

After a few minutes, she noticed the ice bucket sitting on the counter. She got up to check the mini-fridge. It had a tray of ice cubes in its freezer which she dumped into the ice bucket. After refilling the tray with water, she placed it back in the freezer. Now she was even better prepared. And, right on cue, Billy was regaining consciousness and starting to stir over there on the bed. It shouldn't be much longer before Donny woke up and she could explain the situation to the two of them.

Chapter Twenty-Eight
Mar 2017

The explanation of her Plans A, B and C went well, up to a point. First Billy roused himself and then Donny did likewise; they each looked around to find her staring at them. When they found themselves restrained and unable to talk, they each went through several stages of outrage and frustration. Disbelief. Then, gradually, their plight became more and more obvious. After struggling against their bindings to no avail, they settled back on the bed and just glared at her. She waited several minutes. She wanted them to sober up. She also knew, since they'd been drinking all night, they probably really needed to relieve themselves very badly about now. She figured the pain and discomfort from their full bladders could only help with hastening their cooperation.

Finally, she spoke to them. "Billy Martin and Donny Delgato, I want you to listen carefully to what I have to say and watch what I have to show you. You'll need to make a decision. About the situation we have here. There are three options: Plan A, Plan B and Plan C." She studied their faces and knew they were mostly focused on how badly they wanted to get her. Hurt her. They weren't at all intimidated by her. Yet.

"Plan A is for the police to come, right now, and pick you up. Actually, since kidnapping is a federal crime, I'll call my good friend at the FBI. Maybe you didn't do enough research ... let me check this folder about me." She pulled out the folder and glanced through the articles. "Here it is. You guys saw this, right? Missing teen Missy McCrea returns home. Missing for two years. Robert Ulrey, lead investigator for the FBI, would not disclose any information about kidnappers or possible suspects … yadda-yadda-yadda. Right?"

Looking at them, she could see they were paying attention. "Yep, I can have the two of you locked up. Tonight. Plan A is pretty simple." As she talked, she walked back and forth at the end of the bed. Their eyes followed her every move and she could see both interest and lust in the way they were staring at her. "Let me help clarify for you just what all the evidence against you guys looks like. I've prepared a little video, just for that purpose. Oh, and as you'll see on this video, a guy named Tony was going to pay you the twenty thousand dollars. Tony has a lot to say about all that. And, about the hits on his first wife years ago and on his daughter Roseanne last November. I don't know about his wife, but since the folder on Roseanne is right here?" She ended this last statement as though it were a question. Looking at the expressions on their faces, however, it was pretty obvious. They'd done that hit and now they knew the evidence she was talking about was tying them to murder as well as kidnapping.

She went over and turned on the TV. "Let me show you what I've prepared so far. And. I'll let Tony tell you in his own words." Hitting the play button, she walked away and sat down. On the screen, she appeared wearing her full gi uniform with her hair cascading down over her shoulders. She looked very sweet and innocent. In the background was a view of the bed with the handcuffs and chains. After a brief introduction where she explained who she and Tony were, followed by a short description of what Tony had planned, she moved off camera and shifted over to where Tony was seated. For several minutes, she interviewed Tony who answered all her questions without hesitation, but not always in a clear voice. He looked as though he'd experienced something pretty terrible and every once in a while, his answer would become somewhat garbled. Missy would quietly insist he repeat his answer and, from the look of abject fear in his eyes as he hastened to do whatever she asked, it was very clear. She was in total control and he wasn't holding back on anything. Tony was terrified.

He talked all about his buddy Frank McCarthy. How Frank needed him to launder their money and, when Tony needed anything, how Frank would arrange it. Frank knew someone in the New York organization. So, for those hits on his wife and daughter, all Tony had to do was have a folder waiting at a specified motel for some guys coming up from New York. Everything was taken care of, per Tony's instructions. Tony's payment afterward was made so it wouldn't trace back to Tony.

Then Tony talked about making a similar arrangement to have Missy grabbed. Frank called the same boss in New York. A folder was left at the same motel. Tony got a phone call when Missy could be picked up. Why Missy? Because she'd interfered, forcing him to sign over his home in Salem to his wife. And, he was now paying for everything so his wife had no financial problems. Why? So Missy wouldn't turn him in. Have him arrested. For what? For being a pedophile. For raping his step daughter, starting when she was thirteen. Just like with his own daughter years earlier. Tony's shocking confession was delivered in a voice showing no emotion. Dead. Matter of fact. Whatever Missy wanted to know, he would calmly babble away, freely talking about these things as though nothing mattered.

What were his plans for Missy? Oh, she was going to be tortured. Raped and ravaged. Over several days. Then murdered. She'd never be found.

As Tony's voice droned on and on, both Billy and Donny kept looking over at Missy. She knew they were trying to understand how she'd managed it. Why was Tony babbling away like this? What went wrong? How had she escaped? A gradual change in their attitude was taking place. They began showing her some respect. And, they were worried. No sign of any fear yet, but they were definitely worried. They were also now experiencing severe bladder control issues due to their being restrained for such a prolonged time period.

The scene abruptly changed and now it was the two of them, unconscious on the bed. And there was Missy, looking rather spectacular with her hair tied back and her well defined muscles rippling as she strutted back and forth, looking now a lot like in those photos from that martial arts tournament she'd won. And, with those scars on her shoulder and back, she no longer was looking sweet and innocent. Not at all. They had to be wondering about her, and indeed they were.

The information she provided in the video, about them being the ones sent up from New York and about their grabbing her, was all very clear. She positively identified them and there was no doubt. The two folders tied everything together. Kidnapping and murder. They watched as the taped portion came to an end. Missy hit the stop button, having gone over to the recorder during the last minute the tape was playing. She turned to them and asked, "Okay, are you guys clear about my Plan A yet? I call the FBI and you both go to prison. For a long, long time. Maybe forever. I wonder how your boss in New York will want to deal with that situation."

She let them think that over for a bit, knowing there was only one logical conclusion. Their boss wouldn't wait for them to strike some deal with the FBI in exchange for reduced sentencing. Some deal involving his being named. No, he'd have the two of them taken care of immediately. And, if he could arrange it, in order to make an example of their deaths? There would be quite a bit of pain involved with those deaths. And, yeah … he could arrange that. No problem.

"Risk versus reward, right?" Missy asked. "Tony tells me his buddy Frank has this whole risk-reward thing. So, you have to be asking yourselves, what's the risk here? Your New York boss, right? You ready to risk he'll be just fine about the two of you? I don't know … I'm just a sixteen year old girl, here. Tell me. Will you be able to serve your time, however many zillions of years they give you for these crimes? Or, will something *really* bad happen?" Missy emphasized the word *really* as she looked into each of their eyes. She could see they were straining to talk, but couldn't say a word because of the tape over their mouths.

"Now, let's talk about Plan B. You see, as much as I would enjoy seeing you both locked up in prison, or maybe even something worse if that boss in New York can get to you, I don't want the risk to my family which Plan A represents. No, even if the two of you aren't able to reach out from prison to get some sort of revenge for my turning you in? Maybe that boss of yours in New York might decide to do something. To me or to my family. Maybe he'll be worried you told me something, you know?" She studied them both, carefully, to see if they were getting all this.

"No, I much prefer Plan B. Plan A exposes me and my family. In Plan B, you guys agree to two simple little things. And then? You can go home to New York and I can go home to my life. Almost like nothing ever happened here. You see, I want to be able to live with no worry that anything will ever happen to my family. Or to me. And, that's one of my two simple little things. You guys are going to go home, stay home and never ever say, do or even think about anything which would cause a problem for me or my family." Looking at the confused, yet hopeful expressions they now had, Missy knew they were listening. Trying to understand. Trying to figure things out.

"I can see you both are considering this. That's good. Your life can go on. Free to just keep on doing whatever it is you do, down there in New York. Everyone will be happy. And, if you should ever forget? If anything bad ever happens to me or my family? Well, then you'll have picked Plan A after all. Because, several copies of this little video you've just watched, along with these folders, will suddenly be sent to the FBI." From the way they were now studying her, she knew they were seeing it. This was their way out and it was only because she was so concerned about her family's safety. She might actually go through with an offer like this. Yes, they were beginning to see the whole thing. And, she was right. If they were arrested, their boss would most likely go after her. She had no way to prevent that. It would all come out that she was the government's key witness. And, that would be enough. She would indeed be a target. Suddenly, they were a lot less worried and a lot more relaxed.

"Revenge," said Missy, looking very sad and tired. "Look how that bastard Tony has caused me all this trouble. Just for my not letting him continue to rape my friend. I probably should have handled him with Plan C, and maybe none of this would ever have happened. Roseanne would still be alive. I'm feeling really guilty about that." She stood up and walked around for a bit, letting them understand by the severe glances she was giving them, that she was not at all happy about them being the ones who'd killed Roseanne. "Have I explained about Plan C, yet? No?"

Missy stopped pacing and faced them squarely. "Plan C is that I kill you both. Here and now. And walk away, free and clear. No one knows I was your target, except for Tony. He never told Frank and until you got here, you didn't know. I doubt you bothered calling your boss after seeing Tony's folder, did you?" She could tell immediately they hadn't thought of that, but Billy looked like he sure wished he had. Oh, well!

"Maybe you don't think I'm capable of Plan C. That I wouldn't really kill the two of you? Me being just a sixteen year old girl, right? Well, I can understand how you might think that. Even after seeing how Tony appears in that video." She walked over to study the TV, even though it was now off. She knew they'd been affected by watching Tony. His terror was obvious. Their thoughts were definitely all about what she might be capable of. They'd stopped all the lustful, lascivious looks quite awhile back and their eyes no longer lingered on her boobs. Now they just wanted to find a way out.

Turning around, she said, "But, if you're not worried about Plan C then you just don't get how important the safety of my family is and what desperate measures I'll go to. I'll do *anything* to make sure they're completely safe from the likes of you and your organization in New York." She had really emphasized *anything*. Now she paused, letting them think about that. "Back to my Plan B, guys. That's the one you'll want. I'm sure you'll both agree. Anything I say right now is just fine so long as you guys get to go free, right?" She could see they really wanted Plan B. Almost as badly as they wanted to go take a leak and relieve their aching bladders.

"Only, here's the thing," Missy continued. "My Plan B video tape? It's not quite finished yet. No, no. I want zero risk that either of you will ever think of coming after me or my family. Or, that your boss ever will either. So, I need more on this video. Yes, I need you both saying you admit to everything, just as I've explained it all. That will help. But, the clincher? You're also going to name your boss. The one who sent you up here. I want him named right on this tape. My insurance tape. My safety tape. My family's safety tape." She could see they both now thought she was crazy.

"So, who's ready for me to remove the tape over your mouth so you can point the finger at your boss? Come on, guys! No one's ever going to see this tape, right? What's the problem?" Neither Billy nor Donny was looking very cooperative, but she went over and ripped the tape off both of them. Now they could finally talk. She'd had her say and had explained everything well enough.

Donny yelled, "Enough about the A-B-C's already! Let me up, you bitch! I gotta go pee!"

Billy said, "Shut up, Donny!" He turned to Missy and snarled, "Look, we can't give up our boss. No way. Not gonna happen. We want Plan B and you've already got plenty on us, so you don't need any more. And, you're so right about Plan A being a problem for you. Our boss will make you wish Tony had been successful. And Plan C? I don't think so. So, just let us go."

Missy looked at the two of them, and slowly shook her head. "Well, Billy, you've listened to everything I've explained and still you're not convinced. I was afraid of that. So, let's not waste any more time. Donny's going to wet the bed any minute."

She walked over to where she'd put the ice bucket. "Let's see what's in the freezer." She opened the mini-fridge and pulled out the ice tray. After dumping more ice cubes into the bucket she went back to where she'd been sitting earlier. From a box on the floor, she picked up a pair of shears. Stainless steel bone cutting shears. "Look what Tony was going to use on me, guys! He really thought of everything, didn't he?"

She came over to the bed, carrying the shears in one hand and the ice bucket in the other. She put the bucket on the bed, reached out and grabbed Billy's right hand, which she positioned over the bucket. Before he could say or do anything, she brought up the shears and cut off his little finger. Plop! It dropped into the bucket. She quickly placed the strip of duct tape she'd removed earlier back across his mouth, muffling his scream. Then she looked at Donny. "I'm ready for some cooperation from you guys and unless I hear who your boss is, I'm going to keep cutting things off. My Plan C is going to be slow and painful. For you guys. And, Donny? You're next."

They both were completely shocked, as this was so unexpected. Not waiting for them to over think it, she let a predatory yellow glow appear in her eyes, showing through from her cat form. "I think they can sew Billy's finger back on, if he maybe gets to the hospital in time. That's why it's on ice. I hear they can even sew your penis back on. Shall we test that theory? Oh, right. Somebody already did that. I read about it on the internet. Good to know."

Donny was done. He'd seen enough. He also couldn't hold it any longer and the sudden strong scent of his urine made that very obvious. "Okay, okay. His name is Salvatore D'Amato. I'm dead if he ever finds out I gave him up, so I'm gonna trust that freaking video will never be seen again, right? Not until I'm dead already, so Sal can't ever get me." His fear about his boss was very clear, but Missy's little demonstration had convinced him. He was "all in" for her Plan B, now.

She looked at Billy, who had his hand wrapped in a portion of the sheet he'd managed to pull loose. There now was a resigned expression on his face, so she pulled away the tape. "What about you? Can I set up the recorder now?"

Fifteen minutes later, she had her video, complete with comments from the two of them each naming Salvatore D'Amato as the one who'd sent them up there, first to kill Roseanne and then for this mission, which ended up being to kidnap her. The evidence contained on this video was now very complete. They assured her they'd never breathe a word to anyone about any of this. They couldn't survive Sal ever finding out.

She told them, "See? Wasn't that a simple little thing? I told you my Plan B only required two simple little things. That's one of them." They stared at her, bug eyed, and Billy asked, "What else? I wanna get to the hospital!" They were still restrained by the handcuffs and chains keeping them on the bed. Frustration darkened their expressions as they looked around wildly. Enough was enough, right?

Missy said, "My other thing? You're going to take care of Tony for me. Then, you'll tell your boss there wasn't any folder. So, no hit this time. Tony's buddy Frank will know Tony somehow messed up, because his body will show up in a day or two. But, since Frank doesn't know who the target was, he can't complain very much to Salvatore, can he? Even if he does, your story is still solid. There's nothing which connects you to Tony, right?"

While at first they seemed confused, Billy quickly sorted through all this and figured it out. "Yes, that works. We'll be sure nothing connects us to Tony." He stared at Missy and shook his head. "You really are one cold little bitch, aren't you? Too bad Tony messed up. Where is he, anyway? You already killed him, right?" He no longer doubted she was very capable of having done that. When she'd started cutting off fingers, they'd both been thoroughly convinced her Plan C threat was very real.

"Oh, no, he's still alive. I saved him for the two of you. His death has to look like an *accident*. You two are good at that, right? He's wrapped up in that blanket, out in the trunk of his car. That's his Honda parked out there." She walked over to the window and pulled the curtain open. "Donny's going to drive me back to my car in that, while you're getting your finger sewn back on. Then you'll both have to figure out how to take care of Tony. Just make sure his *accident* doesn't look like his wife or step daughter are involved. They'll probably inherit his businesses and I don't want anything to interfere with that. You don't want to mess this up or it's back to Plan A. Got it?"

They did. Twenty minutes later, Missy was back at her car. She had Donny pop open the Honda's trunk and wait while she checked on Tony. She unraveled the blanket so she could look at his face one last time. His expression showed resignation and despair. He knew there was no hope since she'd already informed him earlier of exactly what she had planned for him. These guys wouldn't listen to anything he might say and they needed to silence him, in order to save themselves.

Missy was feeling her "loss of innocence" very deeply. But, just as she'd had to accept becoming a wild predatory animal in order to survive, killing prey for those two years in the mountains, she now fully accepted what she was doing with Tony. She knew there was no other choice. Her only regret was not having understood things more clearly earlier. Earlier, when she'd wanted to protect Alice and her mother. Yes, she'd succeeded with that, forcing Tony to move out and sign those agreements. She knew what Tony's exposure would have cost Alice and she still strongly believed in what she'd done. But staying silent and not exposing him? It had cost Roseanne her life. She knew she'd always feel somewhat guilty about that.

After slamming the trunk closed and nodding to Donny, she watched the Honda drive off. She continued to watch long afterwards, standing there next to her car, all alone in the parking lot. Thinking. Then her tummy rumbled, bringing her back to face reality. She'd Shifted twice since yesterday's lunch and still hadn't eaten a thing. She was so starved! She drove to the state forest and Changed. Then she feasted on a deer which she easily was able to locate and chase down. Afterwards, she crawled into a small cave she'd located weeks earlier and went to sleep. She was far more comfortable with just being a cat for a while.

When she woke up hours later, she feasted on what remained of that deer and then ran free, experiencing great joy in her cat form. She wasn't in any big rush to return to her far more complicated life as a girl. Later that Saturday afternoon, just about twenty four hours after being grabbed, she finally drove up to her house. Inside, her mom told her she was just in time for dinner. "Oh, thanks, Mom! I'm really hungry. You're the best!"

Chapter Twenty-Nine
Apr 2017

"Hey, Alice. Can you do something for me?" Missy asked. They were at one of Tony's restaurants and Missy had just finished going through the computer in his office, just like she'd done at all his other places, both at work and at home. This was her last stop. Alice didn't know why Missy had insisted on doing this but Missy had been such a great help with things, she couldn't say no.

Missy had now accessed all of Tony's files and online accounts using his passwords and had uploaded copies of everything she'd wanted to her storage site on the internet. She didn't bother deleting things since, without his passwords, no one else would be seeing any of this stuff. She did delete one file, however, where he'd listed some additional passwords along with the special code needed for accessing his safety deposit box. This code would be required in addition to the key he'd given her. She was the only one having all these now.

Next, she wanted everything from Tony's safety deposit box. Pulling out the key and handing it to Alice, she said, "I have this key that Tony gave me. Can you tell your mom you found it in some of Tony's things? Since she's still his wife, and is going to inherit everything, she can use it to open his safety deposit box at the bank, right?"

Although Tony had moved out, neither he nor Alice's mom had bothered filing any divorce paperwork.

He'd signed over the house and made all the payments required by those agreements Missy had insisted on, so there really hadn't been any reason for divorce. Now that he was dead, after that unfortunate "accident" in his car, the lawyers were saying Alice's mom would get everything. Tony had no other family and had never made any will, so she was the "heir at law" per the state of Massachusetts. So, once things cleared probate, she was getting everything: the three restaurants, all his real estate properties and all his investments. There was no insurance but as it turned out, Tony was worth a couple of million dollars. Who knew?

Things had been happening so fast over the past few weeks. Alice's mom was still somewhat in shock. Shock at suddenly becoming a millionaire. She'd quit her job at Walmart and had been very busy meeting with various people every day. Thomas Mooney, the lawyer Missy's father had recommended and who had taken care of all those earlier agreements with Tony, was now handling all her affairs for her. She was overwhelmed but, with Alice's help, she was coping. Alice, of course, was continuing to rely heavily on her best friend, Missy. Missy, who knew everything about her. Whom she could share things with. Things she didn't even tell her psychologist, whom she now was only seeing every other week.

Alice was still with Mark and she believed that never would have been possible but for Missy. Mark really loved her and she was returning his love more and more every day. For the past few months, she and Missy had talked about the way her relationship with Mark had evolved and how, sometime soon, she would have to reveal what Tony had done; how he'd abused her. Mark was her soulmate and this secret was now a huge roadblock. They were getting very physical with each other and both wanted to go to the next level. Alice had some emotional scars but her sexual healing had made it possible to now thoroughly enjoy all the sex with Mark. But, before going "all the way", she wanted to tell him everything. She wasn't worried that he'd judge her in any way or that this would interfere with their fully enjoying each other. But, she had been concerned that Mark would want to confront Tony.

Suddenly, that problem had been solved. Alice couldn't believe it. After agonizing for so many months about being completely open with Mark, sharing all her secrets, she finally could do that and not worry. Missy was so supportive and reassuring. Although she was still keeping all her own many secrets, Alice had learned to just accept that. Missy was Missy. And, while she was a far more complicated person than anyone else Alice had ever met, Missy was her savior. The unconditional love which Missy always gave her was so special and so powerful. Alice knew it was Missy's love and understanding which had made possible her relationship with Mark. And, with Tony gone, she now felt comfortable going forward with Mark. In every possible way.

"I'm sure my mom will do whatever I ask her to, Missy." Alice accepted the key Missy handed her. "What's in there? And, do I want to know why you have that key?"

"No, you don't want to know what's in there. And, no, you don't want to know why I have this key. Please trust me, Alice. This is very important. You need to have your mom empty out everything she finds in there and turn it all over to you. And, neither of you can look at any of this stuff. I promise I'll give you back everything which is okay. And, there are a lot of important documents you'll need. Deeds, more bank accounts, key documents for the restaurants. But, there are some things in there you really never want to know about. For your own safety, okay?"

"Wow! Okay. I guess I can explain to Mom that she needs to just get all that stuff for me and not look. She knows how much you're helping me, Missy. And, that lawyer your dad set her up with? He's taking care of everything and she couldn't be happier. I'll explain you and I just need to go through the stuff first and then we'll be giving it all to Tom Mooney. She doesn't really want to figure anything out on her own and really appreciates all the help."

Two days later, Missy was giving Alice back many of Tony's documents. These could all go to Tom Mooney who would see to the proper disposition of everything. And, when Tony's estate finally cleared probate? It now would include a few more million dollars. Alice asked her, "How did you know, Missy? Without that key and that special code you explained using, these documents might not have showed up for years. Mom said the way Tony's safety deposit box was set up … it was all done in a very unusual manner."

"I'm glad I was able to help, then. You and your mom are pretty well set for life, financially, right? Free and clear. And, the stuff I didn't return? Please just forget about that stuff. Be sure to tell your mom that if anyone ever asks her about it, she should just say she turned everything over to her lawyer, Tom. Everything. Without looking. It's important." Missy could see Alice was a little concerned but she trusted Missy.

Alice had known about Missy going to see Tony on her own. And, Missy was Missy! "Sure. Your story seems simple and logical so I'll explain it that way to Mom. She doesn't really know it's not exactly what happened, anyway. I happened to find the key. She got the stuff and gave it to her lawyer. More millions. Lucky us!" Alice laughed. Then she changed the subject. "By the way, will you be going to the school prom this year? I've invited Mark to our senior prom, of course. And, Claire's going with that football player, Ralph Beahner".

Claire and Missy's brother had stopped seeing each other when John had gone off to college. Claire had been dating several guys since then, but wasn't really getting serious with anyone. Jeff and Missy had also parted ways when he went away. His college was in Pennsylvania and their relationship wouldn't have gone much further anyway. Jeff just wasn't the one and Missy was able to break up with him easily enough. Alice thought she knew all the guys Missy had dated since then. There had only been three and she didn't think Missy was seeing any of them now.

"Well, I haven't had a chance to tell you about this guy I met at the gym, Alice." Missy actually blushed a little. "He only joined the gym last summer. He goes to the Prep and was on their swim team and water polo team. He's invited me to their senior prom and I'm probably taking him to our junior prom the week after.

We'll see. So, I won't be going out with anyone else right now and won't be at the senior prom with you and Claire."

"Oh, really? And, just exactly when did you start dating this guy, Missy! I know you like keeping secrets from me, but really? Come on. Give. Details, details!"

Missy giggled. "We only just started dating, because I've been ignoring him all year. He always watches me at the gym, but you know me. I don't actually work out with anyone else as a partner. But, lately he's been coming to watch me spar at my martial arts club. He definitely has a 'thing' for me. Won't take no. And, I finally let him buy me an ice cream. He really is kind of a hunk. Six three, dark hair, blue eyes, big shoulders, very fit. Great smile. Smart too. He's going to a really prestigious university next year, over in Medford."

"Wait 'til I tell Claire! She's been saying you're just way too picky, but maybe you finally are finding Mr. Right? Maybe, huh, maybe?" Laughing out loud, Alice pulled out her cell phone and pretended she was calling Claire.

"Stop being silly, Alice. Otherwise, I won't let you guys meet my Mr. Right Now. I don't think I'll even tell you who he is yet. You're not ready. Either one of you." Now Missy was laughing. She was really going to miss her two best friends when they graduated next month. Yes, they'd have the summer but then in September, Claire was going to a college in New York and Alice was going to a university in Boston, to be where Mark was.

The next day, Missy placed a call to Robert Ulrey. "Robert, I'd like you to set up a meeting for me. With your organized crime guys. I have some very interesting documents, all about this guy Frank McCarthy in East Boston. But, I'm only going to trade this information. I need to protect myself and my family. So, I'll only give you guys this stuff in exchange for everything you FBI guys can tell me about a guy named Salvatore D'Amato in New York.

Chapter Thirty
Apr 2017

"Robert, why would we want to meet with some sixteen year old girl? You said, this was to *trade* information? What the hell? If she knows anything about McCarthy, anything at all, she has to just tell us. Or else!" Armando Sanchez was not happy. He was a large, heavy set man with a bald patch at the rear of his head, surrounded by bristly grey hair. He stared across his desk at Robert and asked, "Salvatore D'Amato? Really?"

"First, there is no *forcing* anything from Missy. There isn't any *or else*. Didn't you read the background report I gave you? What can you threaten her with? Unless you think you can make trouble for her *family*. That, she'll go to just about any lengths to prevent. Which brings up my second thing. She says she needs the info on D'Amato to protect herself and her family. Who is he, anyway?" Robert Ulrey looked at Armando with both frustration and annoyance. Yes, the FBI's Organized Crime Division probably was more important than the Kidnapping Section. It certainly had more manpower and resources. But, that didn't mean Armando could ignore the report he'd provided.

"Salvatore D'Amato is maybe heading one of the mob families in New York. Get it? New York. And, he stays away from Boston. So, what the hell? This kid Missy lives in Salem, right? If she somehow ran across something about Frank McCarthy, I can believe that. But how's that going to be related in any way to New

York? Frank's strictly here in the Boston area. He stepped up after that whole fiasco with those mob bosses who were FBI informants and what was left of the old gang in East Boston … but you know all that."

Robert said, "Yes, sure. We didn't come out looking very well after the black eye our guy gave us. *FBI handler protects murderers.* After everything with our guy and those bosses, no one here wants anything to do with FBI informants. I get that. So, everything's been squeaky clean ever since. No informants, right?"

"Well, you can see why I'm not interested in any *trade of information*, then. Sounds *tainted* somehow. We don't do things that way." Armando opened the report on his desk which Robert had sent over earlier and quickly glanced over it. Then, he stopped and went back to read it more slowly. "Your girl maybe *killed* some guy a year ago? Hey, I remember hearing about her. Girl goes missing from soccer camp … that was three years ago. That story got a lot of publicity at the time. You handled that, huh?"

Missy arrived at the FBI office in Boston and met Robert Ulrey in the lobby. He escorted her up to a conference room on the twelfth floor. She was introduced to Armando Sanchez and several others on his team. There were three men and two women, all seated to his left. They eyed her with a great deal of skepticism, which Robert had warned her to be prepared for. But, they'd agreed to this meeting.

She glanced around the room and looked out the windows at the great view. She remained standing, even though Robert had brought her over to a chair at the head of the large table. He sat to her right, opposite to Armando sitting on her left. She deposited her folders and computer disks and passed out copies of a single summary page which she'd put together.

"Thank you so much for this opportunity," she said. She looked at each person and then stared directly at Armando. "As you will see, I have gathered some information which should be useful for your case against Frank McCarthy. While most of this is probably not usable in court, it should give you what you need to go get evidence which can be used in court. The person who was holding all this evidence was killed in a car accident six weeks ago. Tony Gonzales. I want to point out, right up front here, that his wife and stepdaughter do not know anything about this. I will be providing you with documents and computer files showing how Tony was laundering money for his childhood buddy Frank McCarthy. Millions and millions of dollars over the past twenty-five years."

Several in the room were now shifting in their seats, looking up from the paper she'd handed out to stare at her and then quickly look back down to read what she had summarized for them. Armando said, "This is very interesting, Miss McCrea. And, how did you happen to get this? You say the wife knows nothing?"

Missy replied, "Correct. She was working at Walmart until Tony's accident and never was involved in any of this. They were only married for about four years and had been separated since Tony moved out last

November. She only knew he owned three restaurants. She cannot testify to anything whatsoever. She just never knew. She's actually in shock right now, since it seems she will inherit everything. That'll be almost five million once she liquidates the restaurants and various other assets. As for how I happen to have all this?" Missy smiled and once again looked at each person in the room. Looking back to Armando, she explained, "I do not intend to share that. The documents and data will speak for themselves. You don't need any testimony from me."

"Wait just a minute, young lady!" sputtered Armando. "If you think you can waltz in here ..."

"That's exactly what I think, sir! And, you're free to investigate me and my family. There is not a single shred of evidence which could possibly tie any of us to Tony or what Tony was doing. I'm here to trade this information. I'm not here to provide any explanations." Missy was dressed in black slacks with a sporty green blazer jacket over a white blouse. She had her hair up in a bun. She removed the jacket and placed that on the seat behind her. The blouse was sleeveless and when she turned around to face everyone, some of the scars on her shoulder were visible. She was purposely distracting them, since it served her purpose.

While everyone had read the report Robert had provided, along with the additional file he'd sent them before the meeting, the scars -- a stark reminder that she'd been missing in the mountains for two years -- were sobering. While many in the room had obviously been noting what a beautiful, attractive, sexy young female she was, the reality of what she'd experienced had not fully registered on them. Now, it did. Somehow, that made her statements about what she would and would not provide a lot more credible.

"I am giving you information which you might never have put together. Some of this would maybe have come out during the lengthy process for Tony's estate going through probate. Maybe. But most of this, where I've connected the dots? No way. It would all have died with Tony. Once you've reviewed it all, I think you'll agree." Missy then looked at Robert. "Our deal was they get all this, look it over for two weeks, check stuff, and if ... if they agree that it's valuable information for their case against McCarthy ... then I'll get what I've asked for. I'm putting my faith in the FBI. I'm counting on you guys to come through for me."

Armando said, "Okay, okay, we'll certainly look at everything. Millions of dollars all laundered by this Tony Gonzales over the past twenty-five years?"

"According to Tony ... allegedly ... it's what allowed Frank to get to where he is in the organization. He was able to launder their money and each year, as he moved up higher and higher, there was more and more money which Tony took care of. His three restaurants were just for the beginning years. As you'll see, those weren't really needed in recent years because of all the other holdings. Deeds, documents, computer files, bank accounts, it's all there. You'll note there are several million dollars which anyone can claim, provided they have the right passwords and codes. This is an FBI freebie, guys!" She laughed and several around the table began chuckling along with her.

Others suddenly sat up and showed even greater interest than before. The man sitting next to Armando, whose name she'd already forgotten, spoke up. "You mean, there's money … but, what about the wife? Doesn't this go to her, after probate?"

Missy smiled. "She's got enough. She doesn't need to get dragged into this, does she? Trust me, guys. Hey, if you can't trust the girl who just handed you over ten million dollars, free and clear? Who can you trust?"

"So, I can give Missy all this information on D'Amato now? Just like she asked for?" Two weeks had gone by since the meeting with Missy and Robert was once again sitting across from Armando. "And, you want me to continue being the one who stays in contact with her?"

Armando looked at Robert and nodded his head. "That girl gets any damn thing she wants, any time she wants it. And, yeah, we all think it's best that you be her contact. You worked her case for years and so it's quite normal for you to continue staying in touch. Looks good. Proper."

"No problem. I'm happy to help. And, I definitely am very interested in her. Most of my other cases don't end that well, as you know. Hers is special." Robert smiled. "And, she really is a sweetheart, isn't she?"

"Oh, she's adorable all right, I'll give you that. But there's something …" Armando let that thought hang there. Then he added, "One of my guys did investigate her, you know. Just in case. She's squeaky clean, along with her whole family. At least, on the surface. There's absolutely nothing connecting her with that Tony Gonzales, other than Missy being a close friend with the stepdaughter. You know where she was when Tony had his accident? Autopsy confirmed his time of death was between two and four in the afternoon. A dozen witnesses all saw her that day at the local gym where she works out. Pumping iron. Nowhere near the location of the accident."

"Why were you checking that?"

"Hey, it's in your report, Robert. How maybe she killed her kidnapper, right? We wanted to be sure all this stuff she brought us from Tony wasn't going to be fruit from some forbidden tree. We don't need a scandal. But, the accident was either an accident or the guy committed suicide. Either way, there's nothing tying him to Missy. Well, almost nothing." Armando looked down at his file and said, "She made a phone call on Friday night, just a quick call home, but it was from Plum Island. And, no one saw her that night or most of the next day, Saturday. Then, Tony dies on Sunday."

"I'm not seeing the connection ..."

"Well, it turns out that Tony owns a cottage out there on Plum Island. But, our guys went through the place. Nothing. And, no one saw anything out there. It's just that no one saw Tony at all after he left his restaurant Friday night."

"You're thinking Missy saw Tony on Friday? At his place on Plum Island?" asked Robert.

"Well, it's possible. And, maybe Saturday. And, well … it's just that she brought us all this stuff she couldn't possibly ever have access to. My guys are telling me if they didn't have the passwords and codes which she provided? They'd never be able to get into the files she gave us. Or, those bank accounts and investment holdings. Tony had it all set up with several dummy corporations, each with only electronic codes to control transfer of titles and currency, so no one but he could manage things. There's no way he would just give her all that stuff. No way. My guess? She met with him, all right. We'll just never know what she did to get this stuff. But, she's covered her tracks. She's clean."

Robert asked, "And, did she really give us all that money? Free and clear?"

"More than ten million, just like she said. It took my team three days to sift and sort through it all, even with the document she put together for us. Her *connect the dots* document." Armando laughed out loud. "She actually called it that, you know. It's a Word document titled *Connect-The-Dots*. Amazing."

"Can you use the stuff she provided about McCarthy? If he had Tony launder millions, like she said, can't you somehow get him on something?"

"Not right away. This stuff isn't what we can take to court. But, we'll be able to get what we need, soon enough. Now that we have all this information, our team will be able to build a solid case and get all the evidence we need to support that case, no problem. Give us a few months and we'll be arresting Frank and several others. While not for murder or any of the violent crimes we know they're all guilty of, they'll still be locked away for years. I doubt they'll ever get out. This is going to be very big for us, Robert. It's probably good that Missy can't be tied to this in any way. I've already made sure my team won't ever leak she was our source."

"Great. I'll mention that to Missy," said Robert. "Do your guys have anything showing links to this D'Amato in New York? She won't tell me anything but insists it's important. I'm worried. If she's really in danger, she should let us protect her and her family but she absolutely refuses to discuss the subject."

"Well, there are some phone calls between Frank and Salvatore. Not very often, but they do know each other. Apparently they're friends. It wouldn't surprise me to learn they do favors for one another, but we don't have any real evidence of that." Armando handed Robert a thick folder. "Here's everything we have on D'Amato and his organization. If it helps keep her safe, she's more than welcome to it. Just so she doesn't give any of this out, but I guess that's not very likely, is it? She really did buy our trust. And, that girl knew exactly what she was doing. She played us. And, we loved it!"

Robert took the folder. "I was just as shocked as the rest of you. Ten million dollars. Wow."

"She could have just kept all that money, you know. Our guys claim she didn't take one dime. All the other funds and properties will be going to Tony's wife.

You can tell Missy we're going to keep watch over the wife and stepdaughter for a while. Just in case any of McCarthy's guys come looking for anything Tony might have left, you know?"

Missy thanked Robert for all the information on D'Amato and was happy to know he was going to continue as her contact person. Just in case. They were sitting at a coffee shop in Salem, not far from her home. She didn't want her family to know any of this and had asked to meet him there. "I do have one more little favor to ask," she told him. "I'm hoping the FBI can provide me with some special software."

Robert laughed and said, "I guess I'm not surprised." He looked around to be sure no one was listening to their conversation. "Ten million does give you a rather large line of credit with us. So, no reasonable requests will be denied. As long as it's legal, of course."

"Oh, I think the software is legal," Missy told him. "Let me give you a possible scenario. Let's say that I had this homework assignment for school. My teacher wants me to watch some movies. Video tapes, actually. And, whenever someone says *Mickey Mouse* my teacher wants me to write down how many of Mickey's friends are with him. So, I could sit and watch all these movies, which would take me hours and hours. But, if I had your software which could do that for me? Software which could process these video tapes and recognize whenever the words *Mickey Mouse* are spoken? And, maybe send me a text message which identified where on the tape this happened? Each time? Then, I could be out with my friends or playing softball or working out at the gym and check the tapes when I got home later. I'd be able to quickly find each of those sections on the tape and check for Mickey's friends. I could complete my assignment in no time at all. You can see how handy that would be, right? Perfectly legal."

Robert stared at her as he considered all the other possible scenarios. He realized she wouldn't be looking at any Mickey Mouse movies. "I suppose you'll want to program the software to recognize various words. In case your next assignment was for *Donald Duck* or *Elmer Fudd*?"

"Oh, yes! That would be so helpful, Robert." Missy's smile lit up her face and her eyes sparkled with warmth. "My sister has this friend in college who studies computers. She read how the government searches news reports and stuff on TV with software which can find key phrases. Maybe even monitors phone calls? Finding those terrorist cells?"

"And you thought this would be handy to have? For saving you some time on your homework? So you can go play soft ball?" Robert sighed and looked up at the ceiling, then back at Missy. "I sure wish you'd let me help you, Missy. With what I'm guessing you're really doing? There's some very real danger, isn't there? Can't you let us help with that?"

Missy sighed and looked at Robert with her green eyes suddenly growing serious and concerned. "You guys have rules and I respect that, Robert. I really do. So, while I appreciate your offer, I'm not ready to accept any help except for these little favors I've asked for. Information. Software. Maybe I'll call you again. We'll see." She thought about Roseanne and Tony. Then, about Alice. Should she have handled things any differently?

"Hey, Drew?" A young woman named Marsha Goodding was standing at the doorway to Drew Martinson's office. She was one of the research technicians on his team. Her husband was another "P" Branch team member. Both were sworn to secrecy about all their activities and it helped a lot that they didn't have to keep secrets from each other. When he looked up and raised his eyebrows, she continued. "That girl Missy you have us keeping tabs on? The one who was missing for two years and then reappeared when she rescued that family up in the mountains? Got them out of their car right before it exploded?"

Drew said, "Sure, I remember. She's in high school now, right? I saw something last year on her when she won that Amateur Women's Middleweight trophy in mixed martial arts. I knew we'd be seeing more examples of her physical prowess. I don't think she can stay hidden. Special abilities, right? What's she done now?"

"Well, yeah, she's got special abilities and physical prowess all right. But, you're not going to believe what I just learned from our links into the FBI database."

"Oh, oh! What's she done? One of my worries, as I've briefed all of you about many times, is that these individuals might either self destruct or else go off the deep end, causing all kinds of problems. That's why we're monitoring them. In case we need to step in to contain things and deal with …"

"Relax, Drew, you don't have to kill this kid, yet." She was laughing at her joke, which she was hoping was merely a joke. They'd never actually terminated anyone that she was aware of. "She gave the Organized Crime Division up in the Boston office a little gift. She even called it an FBI *freebie*. Along with lots of information about money laundering, which they think will help in taking down several local mobsters up there."

"Information about money laundering and mobsters?" He smiled as he sat back and reflected on that for a moment. "What was the FBI freebie?"

"Oh, not much. Just some cash and investment holdings which are now theirs to claim, free and clear. But, she actually traded all this, so maybe it's not really a freebie. She insisted they give her some information about Salvatore D'Amato, in New York. Along with some pretty advanced surveillance software." Marsha was enjoying this. "They apparently gave her everything they had about D'Amato and his organization. And, the software of course."

"Did they, now? Why would they …? Wait! How much was that cash and everything worth, anyway?" Drew realized she was setting him up.

"Ten million dollars." Marsha laughed. "Special abilities, you said, right?" More laughter as she watched the shocked expression on his face get slowly replaced by an incredulous smile. She couldn't wait to tell her husband Lester.

Chapter Thirty-One
May 2017

"There she is!" Mike Ryan pointed out Missy, which was hardly necessary since she was the only girl surrounded by more than a dozen guys. His twin sister Michelle was seated next to him in the stands and her boyfriend Aaron Brooks was next to her.

Michelle was the same height as Missy with a very nice figure. They could probably wear the same clothes. She and Mike both had dark hair, thick and wavy. There were other similarities they shared as twins, such as their amazing blue eyes and nice smiles. But, there were some differences also. Michelle was quite pretty and very feminine looking while her brother was a big handsome hunk, very masculine with a strong jaw. She had no athletic ability but Mike was very physical and had played well on various sports teams.

Aaron was six one, a couple of inches shorter than Mike. He had dirty blond hair and, like Mike, was athletic and good looking. Aaron and Mike both went to the Prep in Danvers but since that was for boys only, Michele attended a different school. She was Aaron's date to the Prep's senior prom and now that Missy had agreed to go as her brother's prom date, Michelle had insisted on finally meeting her. Mike had said that watching Missy spar would be a special experience and would help her understand why he was so crazy about this girl. So, now they were all watching from the spectator seats at Missy's mixed martial arts club.

They weren't alone. These seats were usually pretty full, especially after Missy had won that trophy last November. Membership at the club had doubled yet again since then and there was a lot of interest in watching activities and events by both nonmembers as well as members. On the one day each week that Missy came in to spar, there was always a big crowd in the stands and ripples of excitement were obvious whenever she finally made an appearance. Missy was definitely fun to watch.

"Why is she the only girl out there? You told me she won a trophy competing against other girls." Michelle was looking all around. She'd never been to anything like this before and had not watched any of the video clips showing Missy on YouTube, although she had heard about them. She had heard a lot of things about Missy McCrea from several people, long before her brother had ever mentioned her. According to some, she was big trouble. Michelle went to the same school as Marcia Newton, the leader for one of the more popular girl cliques. Although she was not that friendly with Marcia and her group, she couldn't ignore all the negative things she'd heard. But, there were some other girls who really seemed to like Missy and insisted that everyone who really knew her would only say good things about her.

Aaron now explained, "She's the only girl in this club, Michelle. That trophy was when she represented the club at the World Expo in New York. All the best mixed martial arts fighters went to that. She beat the best of the best. Of course, that was against girls. Girls only compete against girls." Mike had been talking to Aaron about Missy for months, so Aaron had learned many things like this. He'd seen her from a distance a few times but today would be his first time actually getting to meet her.

"But ... Mike told me he watches her spar. He's been coming here for weeks." Michelle had been very surprised at seeing the two full size photos of Missy when they first walked in. She had never seen Missy but had heard that she was very pretty. While she could see how sexy Missy was, with that killer body, she didn't think pretty was the right adjective. Attractive? She could understand her brother going for that. Sure. But she thought intimidating was more appropriate than pretty. And those scars? What was that all about?

Mike spoke up, "Missy spars with the guys. It's not a competition. She does it for the training and exercise. Other girls just don't provide her with ... well, just wait. You'll see." He had discussed all this with Missy several times, after finally approaching her at the gym. It had taken him a long time to get Missy to really start talking to him and explaining herself. He could still remember last summer when he'd walked into the gym to sign up and had seen Missy in the lobby. When he had asked them at the desk who she was, they'd laughed. "That's Missy McCrea. She's in here all the time." He hadn't looked at another girl since.

"Wait a minute, wait a minute." Michelle had been staring at Missy who was wearing her gi uniform, as usual. She could see Missy was smaller than in those photos. She looked at her brother and said, "Those pictures hanging up out front? They're photo shopped or something, right? Now that I can see her better, she doesn't really even look like that. And, when she smiles,

I can see maybe why you're interested. She seems nice. Not anything like in those photos."

Mike only laughed. He had actually watched Missy bulk up for that World Expo competition, when she had switched to lifting much heavier weights. Instead of the usual twenty to twenty-five reps she normally would do as she went through her circuit training routine at the gym, she had used weights she could only lift six or eight reps. And, she'd gone crazy with her eating. He later learned she'd increased from her usual intake of about 4,000 calories per day to between 8,000 and 10,000 calories. Everyone at the gym had been amazed at how much she'd bulked up. Back then, she was always covered up in her gi uniform but her voluptuous body was still very obvious. Then she went to New York. He had no idea how she'd lost so much body fat, getting ripped and shredded the way she was in the photos. But, he'd stopped being surprised about anything Missy did.

Once she'd won that trophy and the gym had put her picture up, she'd started working out in much more revealing gear rather than always being covered up in her gi uniform all the time. Like in the photo, she often wore shorts and a sports bra, only not as skimpy. The shorts covered the scar on her thigh, which Mike didn't even know about. The scars on her shoulder were obvious but Missy never discussed those. He often found himself mesmerized just watching her. The play of those incredible muscles under those scars and under her silky smooth skin everywhere else was just so amazing. She had quickly slimmed back down and now merely looked fit and athletic rather than being so pumped up. But, he knew her looks were deceiving.

She was not a normal girl. And, she still had the strength to handle those heavy weights, if she wanted to. Those and maybe a lot more.

He had eventually decided he just had to come watch her spar. There was so much controversy about her, not only at the gym but amongst all the guys at school. He'd watched the video clips and studied the photos on the internet. Then, he'd started watching her here at the club. She really was a different person when she stepped into that ring and faced off against an opponent. He'd talked with many of them and they all said the same thing. If they thought about her as a girl, even for a fraction of a second, she'd have them on their ass. Nobody was as fast as she was and she had such tremendous power in each of the blows she'd use. They had to totally focus on her being an opponent and give it their all. They'd all stopped worrying long ago about hurting her. If they held anything back? Once again, they'd be on their ass.

Mike had actually worried about her getting hurt. At first. But, after watching her week after week, bouncing back up from whatever was done to her, even when the guy was twice her size, his worries subsided. Missy never seemed affected in any way. She'd smile, acknowledge the guy had gotten her good, and come right back at him in a blur. In the ring, she wasn't a girl. She was just something else. So, today he'd brought Michelle and Aaron, so they could see for themselves. He had no words to describe her.

Two hours later, the four of them walked into Missy's favorite ice cream shop, two blocks from her club. She always wanted to eat something after working out and didn't want to wait until she got home. Mike knew, from talking to her brother Patrick, that she still ate every meal at home like it was her last and like she'd not had any food in a week. It was his persistence in chasing her, finally winning her over with these ice cream dates, which had led to her agreeing to be his prom date. Since Missy still waited until she got home to shower and change, she'd resisted at first. But when he'd told her it was a huge turn on for him to sit next to her while she was all sweaty from her sparring, that had made her laugh and so she'd finally give in. As long as they'd pick a booth in the back which was away from everyone else.

He'd made the introductions and they went back and settled into a booth in the far corner. He slid into the booth next to her while Michelle seated herself opposite from Missy and Aaron slid in next to her. Mike knew his sister would have some questions to ask. And, she did.

"Missy, my brother has been telling me how athletic you are, but … what you did back there? That was too amazing! And that one time? When Big-and-Ugly threw you up against the wall so hard? That had to hurt. Tell me the truth." Michelle was laughing, but she was also really curious. She would have sworn Missy must have gotten some broken bones from that. But, after watching it actually happen, before she could turn in horror to say anything to Mike, she'd seen Missy quickly leap back up and somehow manage kicking the guy back so hard he actually raised his hand to stop for a minute. The guy was huge and had to weigh at least two hundred and fifty pounds.

Missy chuckled and said, "You mean Jimmy? Jimmy, the Pipefitter? Don't let Jimmy hear you call him ugly, Michelle! He thinks he's God's gift to women." She could see that Michelle and Mike were really close and shared a lot. They seemed to interact very well together. She wondered if that might be one of the reasons she'd grown to really like Mike. He just seemed able to interact with *her* so much better than any of the other guys she knew.

"Really, stop kidding around. That had to hurt." Michelle wasn't going to give up and she was having a hard time seeing Missy now, sitting there like she'd maybe only been bicycle riding, rather than tossing huge guys around and having them smash her up against the wall or bounce her off the floor a dozen times. "Surely you have bruises! You must be black and blue all over!"

"Okay, okay, you have me! My secret is out. I probably even have some ugly yellow green splotches. Wanna see?" With that, Missy actually opened up her gi uniform jacket and started to take it off. Because they were sitting in the back booth, they didn't have any audience. She was wearing her sports bra, of course, but her upper torso was otherwise exposed. And, she indeed did have several dark bruises with some of them looking a very sickly yellow. This variety of colors was due to her rapid healing and the bruises would be gone by the time she went to bed. She always waited until getting home to change, just to avoid anyone seeing her body looking like this. But, there was something about

Michelle. She knew this was a test. And, she really liked Mike.

"Oh, my God!" gasped Michelle. She was now also noticing those scars which Missy had on her shoulder. Obviously, there had not been any photo shopping for those pictures of Missy. She looked at Mike and Aaron and could see they also were shocked. "Why aren't you asking us to take you to the hospital? Those are terrible!"

Missy broke out laughing. She felt a bit giddy and wondered if it was because of the way Mike was looking at her. She really liked him. A lot. She knew he was getting very aroused and that was turning her on. "Don't worry, guys! Really! I'll be all healed up before bedtime. I have that big softball game tomorrow and then I'll be hitting the gym, same as always. Mike, I'll see you then, right?"

"Don't even try to change the subject, Missy! Those look awful." Michelle was not about to let go of this. The two guys just sat there, mouths hanging open. She figured she'd push harder, so she demanded, "And, those scars? What happened?"

Missy started out with a snappy reply, saying "I'd tell ya, but then I'd have to kill ya," Then, she smiled. She didn't really know why she was willing to share some of her secrets but she found herself just blurting things out. "It was when I was up in the mountains. I don't explain about that time in my life to most people, so please don't ask me for any details. I was forced to live up there and some of my experiences were pretty difficult for me. Getting all clawed up by a black bear was one of those." She looked at Mike and added, "If you get lucky, maybe I'll show you my other scar, high up on my thigh. My shorts at the gym keep that pretty well covered up. Since that's on my right side, it doesn't show in very many of the photos out there, which all seem to be showing my left side." As she thought about Mike getting lucky, she suddenly blushed. Damn! What was happening to her today!

Now all three were staring at her in shock. They had heard so many rumors about Missy. But, this was the first time they'd heard anything about a bear. And, they didn't really know about her being in the mountains or just where she'd been. Mike had heard she'd disappeared from soccer camp up in New Hampshire maybe four years ago. There hadn't really been that much of a story about her return. Just a lot of rumors.

Before any of them could voice it, Missy addressed what most rumors would eventually get around to saying. "Just to set the record straight? Those two years that I was gone and forced to live in the mountains? I am *not* damaged goods. Okay, guys? But, I'm not going to talk about it. I just don't discuss this. And, I trust you're not going to tell everyone about the bear which mauled me. Or, the bullet wound on my thigh?" Now she was getting a bit excited. She suddenly realized she'd not actually said anything earlier about any bullet. Why was she so flustered? What had happened to all that control she always had?

The other three all rushed to assure her they'd never think of her as damaged goods. Or, allow anyone else to suggest that. How terrible! And, no one would ever be hearing any of her secrets from them. They each felt deeply moved that Missy had opened up to them about something so personal. They recognized this was indeed very rare for her. Mike, most of all, felt something very deep inside. While this incredible creature was certainly capable of holding her own, sparring with guys twice her size, she actually was vulnerable. He reached over and touched her hand. Then, he wrapped her jacket around her and pulled her close against his side, letting his arm slide around her back so he could pull her tight.

Missy suddenly felt so wonderful, having this big strong guy hold her so protectively. She let herself relax, pressing up against Mike's side and going limp. She wanted to be held. Her body craved it and instead of her control wrenching her away from what her body wanted, she allowed herself to just freely experience the moment. For the past three years, she always had fought against any physical desires or compulsions. She'd resisted what her instincts were demanding: first, as a cat, going into heat time and time again without relief; then, being human and getting overwhelmed by all the sensations and feelings. She was so very, very physical. It was much more than just teenage hormones for Missy. But, she had always been able to compartmentalize her thoughts and control all her emotions. Today? She wanted to forget all about being a cat. Today, she just wanted to be a girl.

Michelle sat quietly in the passenger seat while Aaron drove. She had come in Aaron's car while Mike had brought Missy. Suddenly, she turned and asked him, "What just happened back there?" They'd finished up without anyone really starting any new conversations. They had somehow just run out of things to talk about and then had quietly said their goodbyes and mumbled other pleasantries as they'd all walked out. She and Aaron had gone over to his car and had let Missy and Mike go off together. "Did my brother just have a special moment with her?"

Aaron looked at her and said, "You know Mike better than anyone, Michelle. You tell me. All I know is all of a sudden, it was the two of them and the two of us, but those two were so deep inside their own world ... we didn't exist."

"Exactly, Aaron," said Michelle. "It's funny. I was so sure I'd be making a list for Mike. The ten reasons why he shouldn't be dating Missy McCrea. Nobody will ever be good enough for him, you know?" She sighed. "Instead, I find myself making a list of the ten things I like best about Missy McCrea. How does she do that? I really ended up liking her."

"Yeah, me too," said Aaron. "He's been brainwashing me all year, but at the end of the day? None of that mattered. Just as you say. I ended up just really liking her." He and Mike had first met their freshman year at the Prep and they'd become best friends right away. Then, not long after that, he'd started dating Michelle. For the past two years, they'd been pretty exclusive. No one said "going steady" any more, but they were definitely not interested in anyone else. So, Aaron really liking Missy was not at all threatening for Michelle. They'd both been trying to fix Mike up with various girls for the past couple of years.

But, since last summer, he wouldn't even consider anyone else, even though it took months before Missy would even let him buy her an ice cream.

Chapter Thirty-Two
May 2017

"Oh, Mom! I'm so nervous! What's different this year? Last year, going to prom was no big deal. This year? I'm so worried my hair doesn't look right, my dress doesn't fit, my shoes will make me fall and break my ankle, my boobs ..." Missy stopped babbling. Her boobs were probably not going to fall out even though the low cut of her gown had them prominently on display. She knew her bright yellow dress with the high sleeves covering her shoulders was making her once again look spectacular. Yes, her breasts were showing some great cleavage, but those were her breasts. Why not show them off? And her hair? Rather than being up in any fancy arrangement, she'd instead let her hair cascade down straight, all around, going well past her shoulders. It reached halfway down her back and she knew she was going to stand out tonight. She wanted to be looking really great for Mike, and in spite of all these sudden jitters, she knew she would be. Even her shoes with their four inch heels would not fail her. It only made her hips sway in an especially sexy manner as she walked -- or, to be more accurate -- as she strutted and glided her way along any path or walkway.

Julia sighed and told her, for the umpteenth time, to relax and stop worrying. This was a special night and she should just try to enjoy it. Mike was already on his way. No limo this time. Mike was picking her up in his car, a sporty Acura, and would drive them to the hotel in Peabody. They'd meet up with Aaron and

Michelle and several other couples who were all good friends. Since she had now finally met Michelle, along with Aaron, she didn't need to feel like a total outsider. The evening was going to be a great success. Wait and see!

Missy grew even more excited, thinking about Mike. On his way. For her. She'd pushed him away for so many weeks. Months actually. At first, it had just been her normal shyness and reluctance to get involved with any guy. Then, she'd been focused on winning that mixed martial arts trophy, which indeed had been fun. That had, of course, exposed her once again to the public and while her video clips on YouTube had not quite gone viral, she certainly had stirred up plenty of interest. She'd pulled back from most of that, and had kept to her routine. School, sports, karate, sparring, being with her family. There'd been no time for any relationships. After Christmas, her sister had needed help with tracking down Jonathan Baxter. That little adventure, at least, had worked out quite nicely, with Lisa and Marie now making that bastard suffer the death of a thousand paper cuts with everything they'd been doing, messing up his life. He still hadn't figured out Marie was inside his computer every day. And, for him, the worst was yet to come.

Getting kidnapped in March? Dealing with Tony, then those two hit men up from New York? While she thought she'd handled that well enough, it had resulted in a ton of work afterward. Helping Alice and her mom. Sorting out what was free and clear for their inheritance from what she'd given to the FBI. She still had some concerns, as it would be a few more months before Frank McCarthy was arrested and put away. If he or his organization ever went after Alice and her mom? She didn't know if the FBI was really able to protect them.

And, it was only last weekend that she'd finally managed getting all her surveillance stuff installed and set up in New York. Marie had really helped and, of course, they had all that equipment from Jonathan Baxter. They'd added to that and with the software the FBI had given her, she now had video and voice surveillance all set up. She was becoming an expert on breaking and entering. But now, if her name came up at either Billy's place or Donny's place? Or if any of the other key phrases and trigger words she'd selected was spoken? She'd get a text message and could download the tapes and review what was being said. She'd have some warning if her Plan B wasn't working out with those guys.

She figured she had very minimal risk but these added steps for mitigation were helping her feel much more secure. Safety for her friends and family. Adding all that to her other activities had left her no time for guys. But Mike? He'd snuck up on her anyway. He was always there at the gym, then he'd been watching her spar, and finally she'd let him buy her ice cream. She was going for the ice cream anyway, so how could that be any big deal? But, she now recognized it somehow had become a very big deal. She really cared about Mike and the fact that he had feelings for her was making her feel weak at the knees.

Those feelings of his weren't just sexual attraction. Lots of guys were all lusting after her and she ignored that. No, it was that he really cared about her as a person. What she felt inside was important to

Mike. He made her aware of just how much that mattered to him, how much *she* mattered to him and that awareness had awakened things inside her. Things she wasn't sure she could control. When he was able to make her feel all "thrilly and glowy" inside, so any resistance she might feel towards being in a relationship would just completely melt away? Just be gone? That made her feel exposed and weak at the knees. Not having her normal controls when around him was definitely making her nervous.

Mike drove his Acura into the hotel parking lot and Missy felt her excitement begin to build all over again. She thought her controls had returned while driving there. Apparently, she had only just begun the emotional roller coaster ride. When Mike came around, opened her door and helped her step out, her heart raced and her pulse quickened. Without even thinking about it, she moved up against him, pressing her breasts against his solid chest, lifting her face and staring into his deep blue eyes. His arms went around her and he lowered his head, bringing his lips down to hers, and he kissed her. This was actually their first kiss and she felt it all the way down to her toes. She parted her lips and quickly thrust her tongue out, only to feel his tongue pressing its way into her mouth. She groaned, sliding her arms around him and then she pushed her pelvis forward. When she felt his hard erection pressing against her abdomen, she gasped.

They both pulled away and, each too embarrassed to acknowledge what had just happened, they turned towards the entrance. Mike closed the car door and she heard the door locks click as he pressed the button on his key fob. Pocketing his keys, he led her with one arm entwined with hers, his hand squeezing her hand. Together they walked into the hotel lobby, then down the hallway to the grand ballroom. They were met by some of his classmates, standing around just outside the room. They greeted Mike warmly and complemented Missy with great enthusiasm. Then she and Mike were quickly inside. Party time. The music was playing and several couples were already dancing.

Mike spotted his sister and Aaron right away, seated with two other couples. They joined them and she was introduced to the four people at the table whom she didn't know. Missy forgot their names immediately. She was surrounded by sights and sounds and scents, all bombarding her enhanced senses, and she was oblivious. Her controls were not just slipping. They were gone.

Mike was ready to burst and this feeling had been growing since he'd first watched her come down the stairs to meet him back at her house. They'd somehow survived all the photos Missy's family had insisted on taking and had managed to finally get away in his car. She hadn't said a word but his awareness of how excited Missy was didn't seem to need any words. He just knew how she felt and it was making him crazy. He had never experienced anything like this before with anyone. He knew it had really been building for weeks now. She was the most beautiful girl in the world and she was actually there with him. She was his date tonight and this time, it wasn't just for ice cream.

Her emotions were sending him all these signals and, once again, he felt this connection with her. Ever since she'd opened up that day, just a couple of weeks ago, when his sister had rudely asked all those questions. Did it hurt? Were there bruises? What about those scars? He didn't know why Missy had responded the way she had. He was guessing she didn't know either. But, *something* had happened. They'd both felt it then and they were feeling it even more now. Her green eyes were glowing and ... damn! Did she suddenly have lots of golden yellow speckles shining in there! Her eyes were wild. He'd never seen anything like it.

Missy wanted to move. She couldn't sit still and she pulled Mike with her out onto the dance floor. It was a fast song which suited her just fine. She had so much energy! She needed to burn that off and so she let herself go, moving with the music. She kicked off her shoes and Mike reached down and scooped them up. She spun and undulated, letting the movements of her body express some of what she was feeling inside. Mike was right there, mesmerized, and she wanted him to know it was all for him. She wasn't even aware of anyone else in the room. Her excitement and her arousal were driving her crazy. And, they'd only just arrived.

The music changed, and it was a slow dance. She moved forward, melding herself against Mike's body, and let him take over. Wherever he led, she followed. She flowed, always touching him, but giving him free rein. His arms encircled her and she pressed her face into his neck, her head lying on his shoulder. She breathed in deeply and the scents were almost overwhelming. She knew her enhanced senses were experiencing things way too strongly and that she'd better slow down. She could tell that her emotional overdrive was affecting Mike as though he were an Empath. While she loved having that connection with him, it was all happening too fast. She needed to dampen things down.

She dragged him off the dance floor, went back to their table and sat down. He gave her back her shoes. Then, she sent him off to bring her something to drink. Poor Mike! They both needed to come up for air. Gradually, her heart stopped racing and the crazy thrumming all through her body which she'd been feeling finally slowed down. Her pulse returned to normal. She looked around and saw Michelle watching her very closely. She could practically read her mind and decided maybe they should try some girl bonding. "Will you go with me to the ladies room, Michelle?"

"Of course, Missy! I was just about to suggest that … great minds think alike, right?" Michelle laughed and got up and walked around to meet her.

Missy joined her, saying, "Maybe it's just our bladders! I don't know about your great mind but mine is telling me that I suddenly gotta go pee really badly!" With that, they both burst out laughing.

Michelle said, "Stop! If I laugh any harder, I'm gonna pee in my panties!" That, of course, had them both in hysterics and they scampered off to the ladies room.

After relieving themselves, they washed up and stood in front of the mirrors, checking themselves out. Michelle, feeling bold all of a sudden, managed to ask, "So, now that you and Mike have started dating, does that mean you'll be sparring with him as well? I'm not sure that I … well, I'm not sure about something. Whatever!"

Missy looked at her and, without blocking any of her real thoughts and feelings, she began blurting them all out. Stuff she'd never even thought about and didn't realize was how she actually felt. "No, not with Mike. Never. When I look at his hands … well, the only thing I can think about is how his hands will feel. Touching me. All over." She sighed and then began to blush like crazy. "I can't ever be with Mike the way I am in the ring, sparring with those guys the way you saw me, Michelle. I mean … is it only me? Or, do a guy's hands sometimes make you have thoughts, make you get all tingly … make you think about what each part of your body might experience? You know? From his doing things with those hands?" She actually moaned softly.

Now it was Michelle who started to blush like crazy. "Oh, god, Missy!" she groaned. "You've got me going now! And, no! It's not only you! Just thinking about Aaron's hands can get me so wet sometimes …" She stopped and looked at Missy with an incredulous expression. "You and my brother haven't already … you know … been having sex have you?"

Suddenly feeling very embarrassed, Missy said, "No, no! We only just kissed for the first time. Earlier. When we first got here. Out in the parking lot. Aggghhhhh!" She could see Michelle looking at her with raised eyebrows. "You wanted to know about me maybe sparring with Mike. Well, now you at least can understand why that's never going to happen, right? It's not the same, for me ... not with someone that might actually ... that I might actually let ... this isn't coming out right, is it?"

Michelle started laughing. "Oh, it's clear, Missy. Relax. I guess I did sort of ask ... only, I didn't quite expect ... never mind. Thanks for sharing!" She came up and gave Missy a hug. "Let's go back and enjoy the evening. I think by now our guys are probably about ready to call out the National Guard to search for us."

The rest of the evening went great and they all had a wonderful time. Missy's little trip to the ladies room accomplished two things. She and Michelle were somehow closer and by the end of the night, a real friendship was forming. They actually had a lot in common and found it very easy to talk to each other about just about everything. And, she had regained enough control that she could be with Mike and really enjoy his company without her emotions spiraling out and away causing complete overload. They danced and they laughed and they had some quiet moments. Some really special moments. Missy realized by the end of the night that she was truly in a relationship.

This was very different from when she had dated Jeff and the other guys. This was so meaningful that she didn't want to think about it or analyze it or speculate as to where it might be going. She just wanted to experience it. So, she accepted it at that. And was happy.

When Mike brought her back home, she kissed him again before going inside. The kiss was very nice and lasted a long time. She was once again pressed up against him, with her arms circling around to hug him close and his arms squeezing tight around hers. Each time their lips would part, rather than break away from him, she would shift and press herself up against him all the harder. His lips would immediately claim hers all over again and when his tongue would enter her mouth and move against hers, she'd feel such delicious quivers of excitement go suddenly racing through her body that she'd thought she might faint. At last she pulled back, pushed his chest away with both hands, and said, "Mike, this has been the best night. Truly, the best night in my whole life and I can't thank you enough. Please, just let me go in."

Mike groaned and said, "Missy, you're making me crazy, you know that, right?"

She laughed, reached to open her front door, and looked back at him over her shoulder. Lowering her eyes in what she hoped was a seductive look, she whispered in a hoarse voice, "Save it for next week when you bring me to *my* prom!" She opened her door, went inside and added, "Good night, Mike, and thanks so much for tonight!" Then she closed the door behind her.

Chapter Thirty-Three
Jun 2017

"So, tonight will be your final class? Will you get your certificate right away?" Alice was asking Missy about the First Aid and CPR courses she'd been taking to get certified by the Red Cross as a lifeguard. They were sitting on the porch glider, looking out over Missy's back yard.

"Yes it is and yes I will. Just in time, too," Missy told her. "I'm going to be working over at Revere Beach starting on Monday." Laughing, she added, "We can't all be millionaires like you, you know."

Alice laughed. "Mom's the millionaire, not me. Or, she will be when Tony's estate finally goes through probate. But, Tom Mooney has already arranged a big line of credit for her at the bank, so we're basically all set. He really has been a huge help."

"I know, I know. Just kidding. But, you certainly don't need to work, which is probably a good thing. I know how busy you've been helping your mom with everything. Who knew becoming a millionaire was so much harder than working at Walmart? All those meetings and stuff." Missy laughed. "Will she be able to manage when you're away at college in September?"

"Well, yeah, she'll be fine. She knows she can trust Tom's advice and she can call me. I'm only going to be in Boston. And, you're still right here. You know she actually trusts your advice more than anyone else's, right?" Alice had watched her mother slowly adapt over the past three months. There had been a lot of adjustments and a lot of decisions for her to make. It had all been good, of course.

"If she needs me for anything, anything at all, I'm only too happy to help. And, you both know to call me immediately if anyone starts asking any strange questions about Tony's money or anything else related to Tony, right?" Missy was still worried someone from Frank McCarthy's organization might decide to drop by. She knew her FBI buddies were keeping an eye out, which was comforting, but even so.

"Don't worry, I've made sure she understands about that." Alice looked at Missy closely. "You know, Missy, it's bad enough you keep all those secrets about yourself. Why all the mystery about Tony? I know you're hiding a lot of stuff about him as well."

"Alice, trust me. Please. You truly do not want to know any of the crap which Tony was mixed up in, okay?" Missy believed Tony had done enough damage to Alice already. "By the way. Did you ever explain about Tony? To Mark?" She knew this was huge for Alice and hadn't seen her for a few weeks. Alice had stopped coming to the gym and had been very busy with her graduation and all the end of high school stuff.

"Oh, but you want to know all *my* secrets, huh?" Alice laughed. "Actually, yes. And, I can't say enough about how wonderful Mark has been. He was upset, but only because he loves me so much, you know? We have had several long talks." Suddenly, she blushed. "And, I may as well admit it, since you know how we … how I …"

Missy broke out laughing. "You mean, about you and Mark sleeping together now? I don't want to pry ..." Now she wiggled her eyebrows up and down. She'd known right away, of course, as soon as Alice had come over. Mark's scent on Alice was very obvious to her.

"Oh, damn! You know already? I have been bursting inside with this and you're the only one that I can really talk to. I've not even told Doctor Thomas, yet." Alice put on her best pouty face. Then, with a huge grin, she said, "Mark was so worried, at first. But, I was able to convince him and ... well ... you know. Once he saw that I was really, *really* happy to have sex with him." She blushed deeply as she emphasized the word *really*.

Missy picked up on that, of course, and asked her, "By *really* happy, I'm going to guess he could see you truly *enjoyed the experience*, right? Not just that you were willing to let him ...?" Pausing there and leaving the rest of her question hanging so she could watch Alice's reaction, she got her answer. She'd noticed how Alice had really glowed when she'd emphasized the words *enjoyed the experience*. And, yes -- from the way she was acting now, Alice had definitely enjoyed sex with Mark.

"Each time has just been better and better," Alice explained, with excitement in her voice. "And last night? Well, that's why I rushed over here today, if you want the whole truth. I mean, you really are the one who made it all possible for me, you know that." Now her voice got serious. "Tony had me in such a bad place. If you hadn't saved me, I know I never would have been able to ... you know."

"Enjoy sex?" asked Missy, with a big smile and a raised eyebrow.

Alice couldn't contain herself any longer and just blurted it out. "Have an orgasm! Oh, Missy, it was so wonderful ..." There, she'd said it. She'd been dying to tell Missy all about it, as this was one thing she really had not been sure about. She had come a long way with Doctor Thomas but had just no way of knowing. "I wasn't sure if I ever would be able to. I even faked having them so Mark wouldn't know. But, last night, he was so ..."

Missy laughed and said, "Congratulations! I couldn't be happier! For *both* of you, of course." She was truly thrilled since she certainly had no way of knowing about this. After what Alice had been through, orgasms might not have been possible for her, regardless of how much sexual healing she'd managed once Tony had stopped abusing her a year and a half earlier. "My best friend just had an orgasm! Do we celebrate with pizza and ice cream?"

"Sure," said Alice. Then, she began laughing. "I'll be having three scoops of that ice cream, too. One for each orgasm!" She stopped for a moment but then, since she could always tell Missy anything, she had to continue. "You see ... when Mark realized what he was doing ... the way his tongue was making me act like a bucking bronco? He figured out all those other orgasms were faked. So, once he knew how ... well, he just kept doing it! I'm so sore, today! But, a really *good* soreness, you know?" Hilarious laughter which Missy joined in on.

Missy suddenly groaned, saying, "Oh, Alice! You realize from now on, we will never be able to talk about ice cream again. All that I'll ever be able to think about when you mention scoops of ice cream, will be how many orgasms you're talking about." Hysterical, hilarious laughter from them both.

Missy was driving home through Lynn, after going off duty at Revere Beach. As she passed the jet engine factory where Heather was once again working, her thoughts were happy ones. Her sister was thrilled with her latest co-op assignment and already talking about this great guy she'd met in there. Her parents were excited about the summer and having everyone home again for the next three months. John was back after his first year at college, which had gone well. He, Mark and Jeff would be painting houses again, same as they'd done last year. And, her little brother Patrick was excited to have finished grammar school; he'd be joining her next fall at high school.

She was looking forward to next fall as well, when she'd be a senior. Wow. So much had happened during these past four years. Her seventeenth birthday was a week away and was probably the reason she was having all these thoughts. Thoughts about what she'd accomplished since her return. And, surprisingly, thoughts about those two years in the mountains. Her dual nature was something she now embraced. She was a werecat, both human and cat, and while that certainly posed many challenges for her, she was grateful.

Her special abilities enabled her to do things. She wanted to continue developing those abilities and doing good things with them. Her instincts guided her but she knew she needed to control those instincts. Dampening the wild predator instincts was often necessary. She was not a perfect person but she was trying to do her best. She had probably made many mistakes. She hoped the good which she'd managed doing was making up for those.

There was no guidebook. No "*Werecats for Dummies*" which she could read. She was still figuring things out as she went along. She not only had special abilities, she had special needs. That made her laugh, thinking of herself as a *special needs* person. But, it was true. She *needed* to be very physical. All the sports activities, karate and martial arts, working out at the gym and even being a lifeguard. Extreme activities were necessary for her and helped with dampening down many of her other driving needs. Like her insatiable sex drive. Having enhanced senses was indeed making it quite a challenge to keep that under control.

She didn't really care about winning competitions. She only competed when it served some other purpose. Like, last weekend, she had won yet another trophy. She had recently passed her second degree black belt test and her Sensei had wanted her to compete. Just as her winning a big trophy last year had helped her mixed martial arts club, her winning this trophy for her Sensei would do likewise for her karate school. Of course, she did enjoy it. Competing not only helped her build confidence but it was fun. Sometimes, a girl just wants to have fun. Especially when she won't allow herself to have sex.

Daydreaming like this was only driving her crazy! Now she was getting aroused as thoughts of her recent date with Mike began crowding in. Her junior prom had been another wonderful evening. This time, she had worn her hair up and had slipped into an exquisite blue dress. Everyone at her school had pretty much accepted her now and so she'd worn a sleeveless gown with spaghetti straps. She didn't care anymore about hiding her scars. They were just a part of her and she didn't explain them or apologize for showing them. Yes, she'd noticed a few stares but there'd been a lot more staring going on at her boobs. With her hearing, she'd noted this was true about all the various comments as well.

Her scars, as it turned out, had not even come close when it came to all the comments she'd heard. Sure, her breasts had definitely won first place, thanks to yet another revealing prom dress style. That probably had a lot more to do with her pushup bra than anything else. While the front of the dress was somewhat low cut, it was her lovely cleavage on display which had mattered more than how much of her flesh was exposed.

But her ass had not been far behind and she smiled at that thought, with pun intended. Her curves had been especially noticeable from how the gown's gossamer material had hugged her hips and when she'd walked by on her four inch heels, that often had stopped all the talking in mid sentence. The talk had quickly started up again, only the subject had then been about her and how she looked. The descriptions had been too numerous to count and the categories had varied from highly complementary to extremely vulgar.

Oh, well, she figured those comments -- all of them -- were well deserved. She had plumped herself up just enough and, by not Changing for two weeks, had kept her shape on the voluptuous side. With her wide, curvy hips and her narrow waist, her figure had indeed been quite spectacular.

Mike had been going crazy all night but she'd managed controlling herself and that had helped maintain the necessary balance for him as well. He was always so sensitive to her emotional state that she could truly do this. She'd known it was totally up to her. He'd never force her to do anything she didn't truly want. Of course, since she would have loved having him ravish her right there on the dance floor, it had required extra effort to keep things platonic all night.

His musky scent alone had been more than enough to show her how aroused he'd actually been. She really hadn't needed all that brushing up against his constant erection, feeling how hard he was, to heighten her own awareness. Oh, but that had been such delicious fun! Poor Mike! Being on edge all night had been very difficult for them both. The heat she'd felt between her thighs, with things getting all slick and slippery, had been a rather new experience but one she then couldn't resist. Each time, as those waves of desire would wash through her, making things pulse and throb down there, she'd pull back and force her libido to calm down. She'd be good for a while and find things to distract them both. But only for a little while. Being naughty was just so irresistible and that kept winning out. She'd lost track of how many times she'd relaxed and allowed herself to indulge. Again and again. And again.

Recalling all this now, driving along slowly in the stop and go traffic, was making her horny as hell. Yet another indulgence. She sighed and tried to clear her thoughts. She was still wearing her one piece lifeguard bathing suit after being at the beach all day. When she'd hopped into her car, she'd removed the matching jacket, which came down to mid thigh. The day had been warm and glorious with a nice breeze off the ocean. She didn't need the jacket now that she was away from that wind. She had the windows down and breathed in deeply, to help with clearing her head.

She smelled smoke. From somewhere up above there was a fire. Probably a house in the hilly section of Lynn located just before she'd be crossing over to Salem. Damn! She couldn't simply ignore this. Someone might need help. She turned off at the next street and headed her car towards the fire.

Chapter Thirty-Four
Jun 2017

She arrived at the burning two story house just as sirens could be heard off in the distance. This was not an affluent part of the city and there were some homes which had been abandoned. This was one of them. The windows had been boarded up but the bank had not been able to dispose of the property for more than a year; it had been broken into and invaded by the city's homeless. These were the street people who often were either selling or using drugs. Or, manufacturing them. From the scent coming right at her, she knew this fire was a meth lab which had exploded. And, she could smell human bodies inside. Crap!

There was a crowd gathering in the street and she hopped out of her car and ran towards them. When she approached, running barefoot and wearing only a swimsuit, she realized how ridiculous her appearance must be. But, once she began hearing what one woman was yelling in an excited voice, she didn't care about herself.

The woman was crying, "My little boy is in there! My little boy is in there!" She kept trying to push her way past two men but they were holding her back. The flames had engulfed the entire second floor on the front and half the roof. They were spreading very quickly. The men were trying to convince the woman to wait for the fire department.

From what the neighbors were saying, Missy learned there were at least a half dozen people who had been staying there, off and on. This woman's boyfriend was one of them. He was supposedly watching her nine year old son while she'd been gone to the local grocery store. No one could say who was now in the house but apparently no one had seen either her boyfriend or the nine year old. Missy ran up to the woman and asked, "Where inside the house was your son?"

"In the back, but on the second floor. I don't see him out here anywhere. I have to go in there and find him!" The woman was very distraught and the two men holding her looked at Missy and shook their heads. It was obvious they considered it suicide for anyone to attempt going in there. From their expressions, they were not really very optimistic that the fire department would be able to save anyone. The place looked too far gone from the explosion and how the flames were now spreading.

Missy didn't waste any more time. She quickly slipped past everyone and broke free from the crowd, running up to the house. She ignored all the warning yells and ran around to the back. The explosion had been in the front apartment but smoke was pouring out from all the windows out back and from the rear door, in spite of everything being mostly covered up. She found a downspout and began climbing up the side of the house. When she was high enough she leaped over and grabbed the bottom ledge of a second floor window, several feet away. She was drawing on her cat as this was not a leap which any human could do. With the added strength from her cat, she tore the plywood away from the window and then smashed in the glass.

Smoke came pouring out but the sudden flow of air into the room did not result in any backdraft or flashover or any further explosions. Missy scrambled inside, getting several cuts from broken glass as she did this. She was using all her enhanced senses, but the smoke was so bad she really couldn't use her nose any more. There had definitely been the smell of human bodies when she'd been out there on the street but inside, she couldn't smell anything very clearly. There was just too much thick smoke.

Moving very quickly, she crawled along the floor and searched the room. No one was there and she could only hear the roar of the flames, so enhanced hearing wasn't helping her much now either. But she could still see clearly enough. She reached the doorway and crawled through into the hallway. The fire was spreading all around her but she crawled forward, over to another doorway. She went into that room, which also faced the rear. She found the boy lying on the floor, already passed out from smoke inhalation. No sign of the boyfriend. After a quick search, there was no one else in the room and she grabbed the boy and went back out. Dragging him behind her, she went back into the first room. When she reached the window she had entered, she picked him up and leaped straight through while holding him in her arms. She dropped about twenty-five feet to the ground below, still holding onto the boy.

It was a hard landing on rough ground and she definitely felt something break in her left leg. But, she'd been able to protect the boy. She immediately began CPR and, after about thirty seconds, the boy began coughing. She helped him sit up and checked him over for any injuries or burns. Then, because the house was in danger of crumbling on top of them, she picked him up and moved further away. Ouch! Yep, she'd broken something in her left leg. She was bleeding from several cuts but only one of them seemed very deep. This was from her right forearm, halfway down, and blood was pumping out from an artery. She tore up a shirt she found hanging on a clothes line and managed to use that as a tourniquet along with a wooden stick she found lying on the ground.

She then kept asking the boy if he was okay but he seemed too groggy to really respond. He was still breathing on his own, however, which she knew was a good thing. Looking up, she saw the house collapse with the second floor and roof caving in onto the first floor below. The fire trucks had arrived out on the street and she heard police sirens as well. Water was suddenly being sprayed from several fire hoses and a few minutes later, she saw a couple firemen walk around to the back. When they spotted her and the boy sitting there, one of them began yelling into his headset and raced over. She stood, picked up the boy and handed him to the fireman. She asked that the boy be given some oxygen immediately.

Twenty minutes later, she was out in front of the house, watching the ambulance leave with the little boy. His mother had shrieked wildly when she'd seen the fireman carrying her son out from behind the house. She'd raced up and when her boy had looked up at her and smiled, she'd gone to pieces. The EMT's had finally managed to pry her away and administer oxygen to the boy, whom they'd strapped onto a gurney. Then, he and his mother had been loaded into the ambulance, which had left for the hospital soon afterwards.

The fire was now under control and the firemen had avoided having it spread to any of the other homes. The house, however, was not yet safe for entry. It wouldn't be until the next day before they'd find and identify the bodies of those inside. There would be four, including the boyfriend. All had been in the front apartment when the explosion had occurred. Not much else would ever be learned. The boy would recover just fine but would have no clear memory of what had happened. He'd not remember Missy very well or know how she'd managed getting him out. One minute he'd been sitting on the couch, watching TV, and the next there'd been an explosion. There'd been the noise and then all the smoke. Then waking up in the back yard, but that was just a blur.

Missy was being given first aid by EMT's from a second ambulance which had arrived right after the first one. She was wearing an oxygen mask while they bandaged up all her cuts. She'd let the firemen bring her out on a stretcher, due to her leg injury. She'd then been transferred onto a gurney but had not been loaded into the ambulance yet. The crowd was trying to gather around her but there was a policeman who insisted everyone stand back. One of the firemen who'd carried her out had stayed there and was asking the EMT's if it was possible to get any statement. A photographer from the local news was taking all sorts of pictures from every angle he could manage.

Missy removed her oxygen mask and told the closest EMT that her left leg was broken, somewhere below the knee. There was now a lot of swelling and a very dark area all black and blue. She said, "I'm hoping it's only a fracture but maybe an x-ray will show if it needs to be set or anything, right?" His nametag showed his name was Murray and he assured her they'd be checking that out at the hospital, first thing.

When the fireman heard Missy talking, he came forward and asked, "Miss, are you okay? Can you tell us anything? What happened back there?" He was looking at her injuries and could see from all the smudges that she'd been inside the building. She definitely reeked from all the smoke. He was wearing a head set and she could actually hear the voice on his headset speaking to him. Someone had interviewed the people out on the street and several bystanders had reported how she'd raced off and disappeared around the back of the house. He was getting briefed about that and was being directed to get her story, if possible.

Since she had the broken leg, she realized they'd know she'd jumped out the window, so she may as well explain that part of it. "I'm okay, now. Thanks! I went inside and found the boy passed out on the floor in one of the rooms upstairs. I jumped out the window with him and got these cuts ... and ... I guess my leg's broken." With that, she put the oxygen mask back on and laid back on the gurney. Murray figured that was more than enough and with the other EMT, they picked up the gurney and pushed it inside the ambulance. She again pulled off her mask, sat back up and called to the fireman, "Hey, can you call my mom? That's my Toyota over there and maybe she can have someone drive it home for me. My name's Missy McCrea." She gave him her phone number and he assured her he'd take care of things for her.

At the hospital, she refused any pain medication and insisted they x-ray her leg as soon as possible. The nurses had examined her, making her strip down and then put on one of those hospital johnny gowns. She wanted to know if her bones needed to be set. She knew how quickly she always healed up and didn't want them to have to break anything later in order to set the leg properly. She'd been cracking bones all the time, mostly her ribs or sometimes a clavicle, only no one else really knew about that. Fractures, like those she kept getting during her sparring bouts, would heal in just a day or two. This time, something had really snapped inside and she wanted some medical help.

Doctor Harold Lisiewski was staring at Missy and trying to understand what the EMT's had explained. This girl had jumped through a second story window, carrying that boy whom he'd seen brought in. She reeked of smoke, had numerous bandages for cuts she'd received and he could see her lower left leg looked pretty bad. She was barefoot and he wondered whether her feet might also have damage since, according to the girl herself, she'd landed on them.

She came in wearing only her lifeguard bathing suit and from what the nurses told him, there were no other apparent injuries beyond the numerous cuts. But he was worried. She wouldn't take medication and didn't seem bothered by the pain which by now was probably excruciating. If she was going into shock, she might not be feeling things all that much. Or, the pain in her leg might be masking other pains. Either way, if there were any internal injuries, she simply might not be noticing. The more he considered her situation, the more concerned he became. While they were all focused on her leg, she might bleed out from some internal injury. Going out a second floor window, with a child in her arms … she'd managed to protect that kid well enough. But, who knew what damage to herself that may have resulted in. That boy had looked like he might weigh eighty or ninety pounds.

He made a quick decision and ordered a complete CT scan. That would show everything and provide assurance there really was no other injury to worry about. Her broken leg would show up clearly, so if they needed to set any break, they could do that easily enough afterwards. But, if any more serious injury showed up, they could rush her into surgery. He wasn't all that worried about her leg. Better to be safe and make sure there wasn't some life threatening situation to deal with.

So, Missy had her second CT scan, this time at the hospital in Lynn. While the one at the hospital in Virginia had not shown any internal injuries or broken bones, this one was different. There were no internal injuries, which was certainly very good and a big relief for Doctor Lisiewski. And, sure enough, Missy's fibula was broken and needed to be set. Her tibia was fractured as well, but did not need to be set. Her feet were okay, which was somewhat surprising as they had really absorbed a significant impact.

But, what had the doctor and his team all staring in amazement were the numerous other fractures which showed up. These had all healed, and the bone was denser at each location. Bone grows and strengthens under pressure but weakens when barely put to use. While breaks and fractures might temporarily become stronger due to the healing process, the surrounding areas become weaker due to not being used during that healing process. Typically, therefore, the strength of the bones will end up being about the same.

Missy's bones, however, showed evidence that during the healing process, the bones were still being fully used throughout and thus where these fractures had occurred, she really had ended up with stronger bones. "How can that be possible?" asked one of the interns. "I realize she probably wasn't wearing any cast, but wouldn't the pain have prevented her from putting any pressure on these bones?"

Doctor Lisiewski said, "Normally, yes. So, perhaps this girl doesn't feel pain and can ignore any discomfort during the healing process. That might explain how these fractured areas have now become stronger. But, how the hell did she manage to get so many fractures? If they'd happened all at once, there's no way she could have ignored them. But, if at different times, she'd have to be cracking a rib or something else at a very unusual rate. Surely she'd know … I suppose we'll just have to ask her. Let's see if she has any explanation."

When the doctor and his team came into her room, Missy asked them about her leg. Did it need to be set? She was relieved at what they explained were her injuries. A fracture and a break, and only the break needed to be set. She was quite happy they would now be setting her broken fibula, which they said was the smaller of the two bones going from her knee to her foot. Then they explained they'd be putting her leg in a cast.

"Oh, no! Please don't do that," Missy said. "Just set the bone and wrap my leg in an Ace bandage, okay?" She knew she'd be fully healed once she returned home and Shifted a few times. Changing to her cat form and back again would always heal things for her and she wanted to be good as new by Monday. She may need to do that at least a couple of times but she could call in sick for one day, and then she had the weekend off. Plenty of time.

She'd learned those energy bursts whenever she Changed were definitely quite healing. That had been why she'd recovered so quickly that first time, down in Virginia. Walking out of the hospital only three days after being brought in on a stretcher had been her first experience with rapid healing from Shifting. Thinking how those Changes also helped burn away any body fat, she began smiling to herself. Her metabolism was indeed special. She could bulk up in shorter and shorter periods of time. Muscle memory. She only needed to increase her exercise routine and add more calories. Good thing she really loved to eat!

Then, of course, she could make a few Changes, back and forth, and strip away all the body fat. She'd now learned how to balance things very, very well. How much to eat. How much to exercise. How much to rest. And, she'd noticed something else very interesting lately. Unlike two years ago, she could now Shift forms and the time required before she could Change back was only two and a half hours. She'd then have to wait three and a half hours, or about six hours total, before Shifting again. Her body apparently needed six hours or so for recuperation, before Shifting that *third* time. But perhaps she could continue reducing how long she waited in between only *two* Changes.

Realizing she'd been daydreaming, she looked back at the doctor. "My not having a cast isn't going to be a problem, is it?"

Doctor Lisiewski was watching the way Missy just sat there, actually smiling to herself. Daydreaming. He didn't quite know what to think about her. He said, "Young woman, please don't argue. You need to keep that leg immobilized for the next six weeks. Now, we'd like to put you under when we set this leg for you. Do you know if you have any allergy to anesthetics?"

Missy laughed. "Oh, I don't have any allergies, doctor. I'm not allergic to anything. But, you're not going to give me any anesthetic. Please, just hurry and set my leg, okay? Then we'll discuss that Ace bandage. Just hurry. We don't want to have it heal before you can set it, right?"

The doctor looked at her with a somewhat incredulous expression. "Are you one of those people who don't feel pain, Missy? We saw some things on the CT scan which suggest you may have fractured some bones before, but somehow ignored that. We, ah … we were wondering if you knew. I mean, do you have any idea how many times you've fractured your ribs?"

Now, Missy smiled and shrugged her shoulders. "Those showed up on that CT scan, huh? Oh, well. I hope my secrets will be safe with everyone here, doctor. Please don't make a big deal about this, okay?" Although this conversation had been only with the doctor, there were several others in the room with them, listening to all this. She now looked at all of them for several seconds and then continued, "About the pain? Actually, I do feel the pain. I probably experience pain even more than most folks. I have this heightened sensitivity thing going on. But, I choose to ignore it. Since I heal so quickly, it really doesn't matter because then the pain goes away. So, it's only for a little while. That makes up for my heightened sensitivity thing, see?"

Doctor Lisiewski said, "But, that doesn't make any sense. You can't just *ignore* pain like that." He stopped to consider all those fractured places which were evident on the CT scan. Maybe she didn't realize her own condition. Perhaps she had no idea how many times ... and, what was she doing, anyway, that it kept happening? "Do you even know when you crack a rib, Missy?"

"Sure!" Missy laughed. "Every time. But, it's only been these past two years. Since I came home and began sparring. Before that, I don't think I ever broke anything." She could see he was not getting this yet and she didn't want to delay things any longer. She wanted her leg set. "Look. Please just set my leg for me, okay? I break bones almost every week. It happens when I let those guys throw me around so much at my martial arts club. Sparring. What doesn't kill you makes you stronger, right? So, my leg? Please?"

Now, an intern spoke up. He suddenly remembered why her name meant something to him. "You're that girl who was missing from soccer camp. Then, you came back two years ago. Right?" He remembered what else he'd read about her. "You won that mixed martial arts title last year." He blushed suddenly, remembering the photo he'd downloaded. "Ah, you were bigger then, I think, so I didn't recognize you." Her hospital gown covered her scars, which he definitely would have recognized, since he'd stared at that photo several times, fantasizing.

"Martial arts? Sparring?" The doctor was looking at her like she had two heads. He went on to say, "Let's see about the leg. We'll continue this discussion later." Then, with help from his team, they went ahead and set her fibula. She insisted on having no medication whatsoever. They kept checking to see if she was reacting, but she merely grinned at them. She did, however, break out in a sweat which was very obvious and the intensity of her facial expression made it very clear. She was not oblivious to what was happening. She was indeed experiencing something. Possibly, as she had stated, she really was able to just ignore it.

Missy's ability to compartmentalize things in her mind had indeed allowed her to ignore it. Just as she had that "quiet place" in her mind where she'd go when she Shifted, she had learned how to go to various other places in her mind. She could ignore pain until her rapid healing made the pain go away. Or, until she Shifted. That burst of energy from within which her body used each time she Changed would always heal things well enough that she always felt pretty good afterwards.

Drained and starved, yes, but she'd no longer be in any pain.

Once the leg was set, they wrapped it in an Ace bandage. Then, they wanted to discuss the need for a cast. Missy realized they really weren't getting it. "Guys, guys!" Missy figured she may as well just tell them. They weren't going to ever understand anyway. "I'm going to be back at work on Monday. I'm a lifeguard at Revere Beach, okay? And, my leg will be completely healed up. If it will make you happy, I'll stop in here first thing that morning for an x-ray, just so you can check up on me. Will that satisfy you? I'm really starved now and this has definitely been a long day. So, I just want to go home now and get something to eat. Okay?"

Chapter Thirty-Five
Aug 2017

Missy and Mike were driving up to Senator Maxwell's vacation home on Ossipee Lake in New Hampshire. They were in Mike's Acura and this was the first time they'd ever gone away together for an overnight. They'd be there for two nights actually, along with the Stratton family. And, since Senator Maxwell was now engaged, his fiancé would be there as well. He'd invited Missy so she could reunite with the Strattons and had assured her it was okay to bring a friend.

Missy had already explained to Mike about the Strattons and Senator Maxwell. When she'd accepted the invitation a month ago, she'd told him about meeting them when she'd first come down from the mountains. In Virginia. And, yeah. She'd helped a little, rescuing them from their car. She'd known he'd go research what he could learn about her being down there, just as he'd done concerning everything else pertaining to her. She'd continue letting him just figure things out on his own. So far, that had worked okay. He'd been pretty good about not asking her to explain things. He'd learned just about everything about her which was available from the many newspaper articles and the internet. And, he'd accepted that she just wasn't ready to provide him details about all sorts of things. The fact that he was willing to accept her on those terms meant the world to Missy.

On the way up, he started telling her what he'd managed to piece together once she'd shared this latest info. "So, now I know you came down from the Blue Ridge Mountains in Virginia. That's a long way from Keene, New Hampshire, where you went missing." He looked at her but she only nodded her head and smiled. "Okay, then. Two years in the mountains. That's what you told me. I guess it didn't occur to me that your escapades up in those mountains would take you quite that far down the East Coast ..." Again, he looked at her and again she only smiled.

Missy knew it was killing him, not knowing, but she really couldn't share anything with Mike about those two years. Maybe someday. She was still waiting to explain to her little brother about being a werecat. She'd been really tempted, too. That weekend after she broke her leg, rescuing the boy from the fire? She'd locked herself in her room and Shifted that first night. Then, when she could, she'd Changed back. The next day, she was actually able to walk on her leg but didn't do that in front of Patrick. She'd eaten double rations for herself the whole weekend and had Shifted back and forth again on Saturday. That had been enough and Sunday she was back to normal. Her leg was completely healed. And, her brother was completely baffled.

Of course, baffled didn't begin to describe the way others reacted. Showing up that Monday morning at the hospital? Before returning to work? The expressions on those faces? Doctor Lisiewski had his whole team there, waiting for her. She waltzed in there, again barefoot and only wearing her bathing suit, and twirled around in front of them. She'd announced she was ready for her x-ray and it felt like she'd won a prize. She'd almost asked them for a lollipop.

That intern had done some research. He had included all sorts of stories he'd managed to find. Not only about the mixed martial arts and karate trophies. She'd played on four different teams during her junior year and, for each one of them, her name had managed getting into the papers for one reason or another. And, he'd blown up some of those World Expo photos -- guys really seemed to like that one with the fierce expression on her face. That one kept showing up. She insisted they take a new photo of her, right there in the hospital.

By now, a crowd had gathered around. There'd been a big write-up in the news and the story had even been mentioned on TV. *LIFEGUARD SAVES BOY FROM FIRE!* When she'd mentioned posing for them, the cameras and smart phones all appeared like magic. She'd laughed and then said, "Wait, wait! I have to untie my braids!" She was wearing two braids, one on each side, with these then tied together on top of her head. It was how she liked putting up all her long hair, both at the beach and also for sparring or working out.

Pulling her braids out straight on each side, she'd said "This is my Pippi Longstocking look!" Several onlookers had all gotten the joke right away, comparing herself to the super-strong redheaded girl in Sweden whose various adventures had been a children's classic for more than fifty years. Her dark red hair and the two braids sticking out were just right. A lot of photos were taken that morning and she'd enjoyed being the celebrity. Of course, the fact that she'd looked especially great parading around in front of them like some model for the Sports Illustrated Swimsuit Edition had certainly added to everyone's interest.

Mike glanced at her once again and finally asked, "Okay, tell me what's so funny! I see you sitting over there, barely able to contain your giggles." As always, he was picking up on her mood. Today, she was really happy.

Missy laughed and told him, "Pippi Longstocking! I was remembering how much fun it was watching those old movies. My dad rented them one year and we watched them together. I was maybe eight?" She saw he was not getting this at all. "Didn't you ever watch those? I'm sure Michelle did. They were great!"

Mike laughed. "Oh, I'm sure she probably did. The way the two of you always manage liking the same things, I'd bet on that. But, no. Not me! Sorry!" Glancing her way he added, "Of course, if you'd like, I'd be happy to rent them for you. Anytime. Just as long as I get to snuggle up next to you while we're watching them."

"Ha, ha! You'd agree to let me watch just about anything, under those conditions, wouldn't you?" She felt a warm glow inside, the way she always did when bantering with Mike. Then she sighed. Time to put her shields up. Or, was it down? Whatever. Time for those controls she needed. Besides, they were almost there. She was really excited about seeing the Strattons again. Especially Emily, all grown up at seven years old. Hey, she wondered to herself. Maybe Emily would enjoy watching Pippi Longstocking.

They were welcomed with great enthusiasm and Mike was really impressed with how highly regarded his girlfriend Missy was. By the senator. How cool was that? And, he'd read up on Bill Stratton, who was an impressive businessman. Real estate and luxury hotels. A millionaire several times over. Even Jennifer Chesworth, the senator's fiancée. She was a well known lawyer and lobbyist, especially for women's rights issues. She lived in Washington D.C., like the Strattons, but lately was spending more and more time in Massachusetts because of the senator.

Senator Maxwell's first wife had divorced him after only three years and he'd been dating various women for the past five years. He'd only started dating Jennifer a few months ago, but had proposed soon after. Something had obviously clicked for them. She'd been married before also but had lost her husband to cancer two years earlier. She was very attractive, with dark hair and intelligent brown eyes. She was only five-two and rather slim but she exuded such a positive energy about things that she somehow seemed much bigger. When she walked into a room, people noticed.

Emily and Missy were immediately drawn together and it was obvious they somehow had a real connection. They were like secret conspirators, already off plotting and planning things. Mike tried to not feel overwhelmed, but it was difficult. He and Missy were among some very important company who were all doing big things out in the world. He had only just graduated from high school.

He was glad they had arrived just before dinner. Somehow, he felt sure he'd be able to relax a bit and get to know these people better during the meal. Lobsters, steamed clams and corn on the cob. Food you used your fingers to eat with and you'd wear a bib and have plenty of napkins. No way could anyone be formal during a meal like that. He was already looking forward to watching Missy eat. She enjoyed it so much! She'd already pointed at two of the lobsters, both good size, and claimed those for herself.

Now she was insisting he join her out back. There was a private dock and she wanted to walk out to the end of it and experience the lake and the surrounding mountains off in the distance. Mike suddenly could feel her emotions. He realized immediately that those mountains were affecting her. He really had no idea what she'd gone through but she'd spent two years living up in them, somewhere. He went out and joined her right away. "How long has it been, Missy? Do you miss those mountains?"

Missy replied, "Yes, I miss them and it's been two years. Things have just been so crazy and so busy! But, I really am going to keep coming back. I have to. Just seeing them again is really such a rush, you know?" She sighed and then took some deep breaths. "Ummmm, I can smell them!" Her eyes closed and the expression on her face was pure bliss.

"I know you won't say much about those two years." Mike looked at her. "But, did you spend time up in the White Mountains? Or, were you only over in the Keene area until you went south?"

Missy kept her eyes closed and continued inhaling the air. She had her mouth open and seemed to be drawing air through her mouth as well as her nose. "Oh, yes! I was all over up there. Mount Washington … looking out over everything from those peaks up there. That first winter … so, so beautiful! But cold! Oh, it was cold!" She actually shivered and began to laugh. Then she opened her eyes and looked at him.

He wanted to pull her into his arms and kiss her. He knew she really wanted that, badly, and he was about to move forward when he heard the senator calling everyone to dinner. Right away, Missy's face changed. Her whole mood changed and it made him laugh. No, he was not about to get in Missy's way once she knew food was ready. Romance would just have to wait. And, worse yet? She really loved lobsters and clams. He grabbed her hand and raced back, trying to keep up with her.

An hour later, they were still sitting around the table. All the food had been cleared away along with the clam shells and lobster shells plus the tools and utensils needed for cracking open those lobsters. Watching Missy show Emily how to get all the lobster meat out had been fun. She'd put on a real show and made everyone laugh. Very messy, which she'd explained was the best part. Now, everyone seemed content to just stay right there. The view out the window was gorgeous, with the sun setting over the lake.

Jennifer said, "Missy, it's a real pleasure to have you here. Back when I first started dating Ed, he right away brought me over to meet Bill and Mary. And Emily, of course. And, I've heard them all make such nice comments about you. I know you've stayed in touch and Emily even has a scrapbook she showed me." She looked around and everyone seemed relaxed, so she continued. "Ed told me how you saved his friends. He even explained how it was decided to keep your secret. Not giving the media your name back then. Well, I won't go on and on about all the things Ed told me. I just wanted to let you know that I was really impressed and now that I've met you, I'm even more impressed. So, again, thank you for coming up this weekend."

Right away, the senator and Bill both jumped up and said, in unison, "Hear, hear!" Mike looked over at Missy and it was obvious she was quite overwhelmed by this. She even had tears in her eyes.

Mike wanted to help, so once they sat down he said, "Mrs. Chesworth, that's such a nice thing to say about Missy. Look, you've got her sitting there speechless, which is something I never get to see." Everyone laughed, which is what he'd hoped would happen. "Yep, she has tears in her eyes. But, I know how much she's been looking forward to coming up here. This trip is very special, getting reunited with you folks again. I can only say, as her chauffeur, how honored I am to be included in all this. And, did I mention how delicious those lobsters were? Speaking for Missy -- still speechless, I see -- since I know how much she loves lobsters and clams, we both can't thank you enough!"

Everyone laughed at that. And, in unison once again, the senator and Bill stood up and said, "Hear, hear!" More laughter.

But, Missy now was able to find her voice. "My heart is bursting here, everyone," she said, waving for them to sit down again as she stood up. "You're all way too sweet. And, as for my *chauffeur* ..." She paused to look around, after emphasizing *chauffeur*, and of course everyone was chuckling. She continued, "I just may have a promotion for him." She turned and looked at Mike. "Now, don't go changing your Facebook relationship status or anything. But, maybe *Boyfriend-in-Training* might be an appropriate step up for you. Of course, you still have to drive me around to wherever I want to go." More laughter, all around. Missy felt a really warm glow inside and sat back down.

The weekend was going by much too quickly and Missy was amazed at how well all their activities had gone. She didn't play golf but Mike did. The guys had all gone golfing that morning and were now bragging about how well Mike had done off the tee. His drives were consistently several yards longer than anyone else's and usually straight down the fairway. She and Emily had gone swimming while Mary and Jennifer had run some errands. The weather had been perfect.

In the afternoon, they'd all gone fishing in three separate boats which the senator had rented. She and Mike had Emily in their boat and when Emily caught an eighteen inch bass, which turned out to be the biggest fish anyone caught that day, everyone was thrilled.

Mike scooped it up in the net after several minutes of pretty exciting action during which Emily would scream each time the fish jumped out of the water. It weighed well over two pounds and the photo they took with her holding it up was special. She was so proud of herself.

Missy and Mike didn't catch any fish, but both Bill and the senator each caught a bass and Bill caught a large lake trout. They grilled all four fish that night, along with some shrimp, and agreed that life didn't get any better than that.

Mary and Jennifer were really funny together and Missy could see they were becoming close friends. She felt honored they were treating her like such a grown up, including her in their conversations and sharing all sorts of interesting gossip about the goings on down in Washington. Some of the behind the scenes escapades were indeed unbelievable. But, the hilarious comments the two women kept making, filling her in on things, were what made her feel accepted and a true member of their inner circle. Each comment was more outrageous than the one before it. She finally had to excuse herself and go find Mike.

She and Mike did get some private time together also, which was special. They went and sat on the edge of the dock and just talked for over an hour, watching the sun go down and staying there long after as the moon slowly climbed higher and higher. Mike was going to live on campus at his university in Medford and she wouldn't be able to see him as often, even though it was less than a half hour away. College would be very busy for him and she had so many activities planned for her senior year at high school, they'd be lucky to manage dating all that often. When she asked him about his maybe wanting to date other girls, since after all, she was still only in high school, he laughed.

"Missy, I'm so crazy about you, I can't think straight. There won't be any other girls. Not as long as you're willing to put up with me. That's my only worry, you know. That you'll move on and leave me behind." He already had one arm around her and when she turned to look up at him, he bent down and kissed her. Her response left no doubt that, at least for now, she wasn't moving on. He wanted more, lots more, but she pushed him back after only a minute.

Missy was breathless and pushing Mike away was difficult. Kissing him was so great but she knew she needed to restrain herself. She was thrilled that he seemed so completely into her but she also wanted to be honest. It was time she made him aware of her plans. "Mike, I'm not exactly going to be leaving you behind. It means everything to me that you feel this way. But, I am looking ahead to when I go to college."

He knew she'd scored well over 600 on both Math and English for her SAT scores, and these would probably go even higher when she took them again next spring. With her lettering in four sports each year, not to mention all those trophies in karate … well, she could probably go to any college she wanted. She just hadn't actually mentioned anything about college plans. Until now. "I'm almost afraid to ask. Okay, Missy. Where are you hoping to go to college?" After asking her that, he sat back and studied her.

Missy looked at him and said, "West Point. I plan to ask Senator Maxwell to help with that. While I'm up here. Maybe even tonight." She'd been planning this for quite a while but now was actually the first time she'd mentioned it to anyone. Hearing herself verbalize it, she knew she wanted to ask the senator right away. She hoped it wasn't already too late as many candidates started the whole admission process early in their junior year. "I hope you can be okay about this, Mike. It's what I really want to do."

Mike was initially shocked. He had no idea why she would want her life to go in that direction and couldn't help being surprised. Then he recalled how she always talked about her Granddad McCrea and his serving in Vietnam. Now he was scrambling to recall whatever he'd ever heard about West Point. He realized women had been going there for forty years or so, but still. Missy at West Point? Of course, she was so physical about everything and she did all that sparring. Maybe he should have known. Then, a thought crept in which made him look at her more closely. "Does that mean … umm … you're not supposed to get married or anything, huh?"

She laughed. "Nope. Not until after graduation. No getting pregnant until then either." Missy kissed him on the cheek and stood up. "But, Boyfriends-in-Training are okay. If they're willing to wait around and stuff." Giggling, she walked off to go find Senator Maxwell.

Chapter Thirty-Six
Oct 2017

Missy looked at her cell phone as she walked into her house after driving home from that week's soccer game. Having won four to three, after helping make that happen with a goal and two assists, she was feeling rather euphoric. Playoffs were coming soon and she hoped they'd go on again this year. Coming in second last year when they'd made it all the way to the state championship finals was still rankling.

She could see from the caller ID that it must be Alice's mother calling from the house phone. She knew Alice was in Boston, doing something with Mark this weekend. "Hi, Mrs. Gonzales," she answered. "It's me, Missy."

"Oh, thank God! Missy, you have to help me! I just don't know what to do!" Her voice was frantic and desperate. "It's about Alice. But, you can't tell anyone. Missy, please, I beg you to just listen. I got this call. They said ... no cops. If I tell the police, they'll kill her. Missy, she's been kidnapped. They took my little girl. And, if I don't tell them where Tony stashed their money, they'll kill her!"

"Okay, slow down, start from the beginning. You know you can trust me. How can I help? What do they want? Tell me everything. I'm walking out the door and coming right over." Missy quickly ran outside and got into her car.

"They called me just now and put Alice on but only for a few seconds. Then they got back on and told me how I better come up with three million dollars or Alice will die. If I call the police, Alice will die. If I don't cooperate, Alice will die. Oh, Missy!" Alice's mother started crying and she couldn't continue. Only incoherent sobbing could be heard.

Missy said, "Just hold on, I'm almost there. We'll figure this out, I promise!" It only took another minute for her to pull up in front of Alice's house. She hopped out and raced inside, where she found Alice's mother rocking back and forth, sitting by the living room phone.

Seeing Missy, she burst into tears. "What can I do, what can I do?"

Missy had her explain everything, from the beginning, and soon she understood. The kidnappers knew Alice's mom didn't yet have any inheritance. That wasn't the issue. They had decided she must know where Tony had hidden some money. The three million they were demanding was what they figured she'd be able to come up with on short notice. When she'd tried to explain she didn't know anything about Tony having money hidden away, they'd told her to find it or Alice would die. They'd somehow known she'd been able to get into Tony's safety deposit box. They apparently had been investigating for months, trying to find where Tony could have hidden money. They'd finally decided grabbing Alice was the only way they'd ever find out. They'd be calling back later that night with instructions on where to deliver the three million.

After calming Alice's mother down and assuring her she'd find a way to help, Missy finally managed to leave. She didn't want to call Robert Ulrey, because there was just too much risk in that, for Alice. She knew her FBI friends were still building their case and it would be a few more weeks before they arrested Frank McCarthy and several others in his organization. She decided there was no time to plan anything complicated. A direct approach was the only way. She knew where McCarthy could usually be found, over at a nightclub in East Boston. She went home to change her clothes.

An hour later, she pulled up outside Frank's favorite nightclub. Then, she drove down two more streets and found a parking space. She was wearing a brown and white checkered dress with a beige cardigan sweater which made her look like a school girl. Her shoes were Mary Janes, plain and sturdy with one inch heels. She was not going for any hooker look and wasn't sure she even knew what that might be anyway. Jeans and a sweatshirt didn't seem right either. She was a seventeen year old high school girl and she wanted to look exactly like that.

She walked inside the place and looked around. It was a nice place and didn't seem to have any obvious bouncer for the front door but she spotted a couple of men who obviously were there to prevent anyone they didn't want in there from coming inside. She walked up to the first guy, who was built like a linebacker, and said, "Hi, is Mr. Frank McCarthy here?" She was not wearing any makeup and her fresh face was obviously very young. She had arranged her hair in a high pony tail on top of her head with her long hair then hanging down loosely in back, going well past her shoulders.

The man stared at her for several seconds and then asked, "Who are you? Does Mr. McCarthy know you?" He was checking her out and, after all, she was a very attractive girl. He wasn't going to ignore her completely or ask her to leave without finding out a little more information. He glanced over at the other guy who was not as big but looked like he'd been a boxer at one time with a nose which had been broken more than once. The two of them seemed to be enjoying this and made no effort to hide the way they were undressing her with their eyes.

"Oh, just tell him it's about his friend, Tony Gonzales. Tony passed away a few months back, but they were really close friends and I just know Mr. McCarthy will want to see me." She smiled and looked around for a place to sit, saw a booth nearby and went over and sat down. She was not carrying any purse and had left her car key in a magnetic holder attached to the inside of her rear fender.

The linebacker guy studied her for a few moments but then walked into the back and disappeared. There were about two dozen patrons scattered around inside, some at the bar and the others all sitting in booths. No one was seated at any of the tables. The night was still early. Missy could see she was being stared at by a few of the people in there but most simply ignored her.

When the linebacker guy returned he told the boxer guy that Frank had agreed to see the little lady and to hold the fort. He'd be taking her back there. The boxer guy seemed a little disappointed, saying, "Okay, Ramon. If you say so. But next time? I want to be the one who gets to bring them back there." His eyes were watching Missy while he said this and he chuckled, in a nasty sounding way.

Ramon said, "Perks of the job, Marco, perks of the job." Then he directed Missy to walk in front of him to a doorway over on the far side, where he had gone earlier. Once Missy was through that, they were in a hallway with a couple doors along the way and a door at the end. She walked towards the door at the end and then Ramon said, "Wait. I have to check you don't have any weapons and aren't wearing a wire. Frank says you should be expecting this, since you're asking about Tony."

Missy stopped and looked at him. "Do you have one of those wand things like at airport security?" Looking around, she didn't see any, but she did notice a video camera overhead.

He walked up and said, "No, we do things the old fashioned way. Spread your legs and hold your arms out to the side and don't move. I'm gonna pat you down." With that, he started running his hands all along her body, feeling her everywhere that she could hide anything, including along her rear and in between her legs. Standing behind her, he continued his exploration. When he got to her breasts, he made a point of cupping them with his hands and thoroughly feeling them all over. Then, finally giving them a firm squeeze and pinching her nipples, he said, "Nice tits, little lady, nice tits." He apparently thought this was funny and laughed quietly to himself.

Missy had endured all of this and now said, "Can I go in now?" She was furious but kept her control firmly in place.

Ramon ushered her into a large room which evidently was Frank's office. She had seen photos of Frank and recognized him. He was sitting behind his desk staring at a computer monitor and from the expression on his face, he had been watching every bit of Ramon's patting her down. He was a large man, six two, perhaps two hundred and fifty pounds. He was not as big and muscular as Ramon but he looked fit. He probably worked out at the gym. That thought made her smile.

"Frank, I won't say that I'm happy to see you. But, I am happy to see you have that monitor there. Do you have internet access?" Missy waited to see what sort of reaction she'd get.

"Young lady, who the hell are you and why are you here talking about Tony?" Frank was clearly suspicious having anyone show up right after he'd arranged for Alice to be held as ransom. Ransom for Tony's money. He didn't think this was a coincidence which was the only reason he'd even agreed to seeing her.

Missy said, "Who I am doesn't really matter but I do have something which Tony left behind. I'll be glad to show you what that is, but I didn't bring it. I can show you if you can get to the internet, though. It's actually a little video which Tony made. You might even say these were practically his last words." She looked around the office and noticed there was another door behind Frank, which probably went to the outside. Ramon was standing guard in front of the door they'd come in at, which he had closed. It was a good size office and Frank was about twenty feet away. She walked forward a few steps and stopped, waiting.

Frank stared at her for a moment and then said, "Yeah, I can get on the internet." He was really curious about her but wasn't going to commit to anything. Maybe Ramon had missed some wire she was wearing in spite of how thorough he'd been when patting her down. "What's this about? I don't have time for any videos. Why would I care? Are you trying to shake me down?"

"Oh, this won't be the usual video for Tony. I realize you are quite familiar with his proclivities, of course. Raping young girls. Like his stepdaughter Alice. No, this is more of an interview. About money, amongst other things." She looked behind her to see where Ramon was and then looked back at Frank, raising one eyebrow. "You don't mind having Ramon listen in? Hearing all about those *other* things?" She emphasized the word *other*.

At her mention of Alice's name, he definitely had reacted. Now he was certain about her purpose in being there but how she'd connected him with Alice being kidnapped was still a mystery. He figured he'd better watch the video. He now wanted to find out exactly what she knew. "What's the website? You'd better not be trying to shake me down."

Missy gave him the website address where she'd stored the video file and then the user name and password so he could log in. She'd edited the tape she'd made with Tony, Billy and Donny. There wasn't any discussion about her being kidnapped but the arrangements for killing Tony's first wife and his daughter Roseanne were there, with clear mention of how both Frank and Salvatore D'Amato had been involved. She waited until he'd logged in and then she said, "Oh, wait, Frank! I know you definitely won't want Ramon to hear any of this. Hold on." Her voice had been very calm throughout all of this, from the time she'd first walked in. Frank now merely glanced up at her.

Drawing on her cat, she spun with speed beyond what any human might be capable of and taking a couple of steps toward Ramon she quickly kicked upward, catching him right between the legs. He was caught completely off guard and the incredible pain made him lean forward, bringing both hands down towards his groin. Missy spun again and planted a solid kick smashing his chin upward with tremendous force. Ramon dropped with a huge thud, out cold. He was going to need his jaw wired up and would be eating through a straw for the next few weeks. Once he eventually came to.

She spun back around, taking a couple of steps to return to where she'd been standing just a moment earlier, and calmly said, "Now, Frank. Now you can watch that video and listen to what Tony has to say.

You'll see a couple of other guys on there, too. They work for yet another one of your close friends. A Mr. Salvatore D'Amato."

Frank was staring at her in total shock, as everything had been so fast he'd not had a chance to move. When she mentioned D'Amato's name, he became even more concerned. "Who the hell are you?" he yelled. He pulled open his desk drawer and pulled out a revolver, which he pointed right at her.

She hadn't moved while he'd pulled out the gun. Now she said, "Frank, you don't want to shoot me. You *really* want to watch that video." She emphasized the word *really* and her voice now had a very hard edge to it. "There's a copy going to Sal if anything happens to me. Or to Alice Morris. Or to her mother." Now she walked slowly forward until she was standing right in front of his desk, with the gun still pointed directly at her.

Frank suddenly wanted to see the damn video in the worst way. He didn't even insist she back away, but switched the gun to his left hand so he could use his right hand to click his mouse and start the video. As the video began playing on his monitor, his eyes kept moving back and forth going from her to the video. As he watched, the full weight of her warning slowly registered with him. She hadn't said anything about the cops. No, she'd said this video was going to Salvatore. When Billy and Donny each named Sal, Frank lowered the gun and put it back in the drawer. Without waiting for the video to end, he started it over from the beginning. This time, he didn't look at Missy at all. He watched the entire video until it ended. Then he looked at her. Then he looked at Ramon.

"It was *you*, wasn't it? *You* were the one Tony wanted taken care of." He was staring at her now as though she were an alien from outer space. "Sal told me his guys came back empty handed. That Tony must have had his accident before … oh, shit. Tony didn't have any accident, did he?" Frank was rapidly connecting the dots. "You probably have all of Tony's money, too. We couldn't figure out how his wife could have managed … she's just not that bright. So, we figured the daughter, maybe."

"Glad you brought that up, Frank." Missy walked around the desk so she was standing right next to him. "Where's Alice?"

He paled visibly as he thought about what he'd already arranged and what the possible consequences might be. If Salvatore ever saw that video, he was going to die a very slow and painful death. There wasn't anywhere he could hide. Certainly not in prison. Even witness protection wasn't going to save him. "She's okay, nothing's happened yet."

"Really? That's good to hear, Frank. Let's just call and check, okay?"

Frank sat back and looked at Missy. The shock of everything he'd just seen, both her taking down Ramon and what he'd watched on the video, was slowly ebbing away and the reality of what he'd seen began to sink in. He'd definitely noted how terrified Tony had been. And, he knew those other guys wouldn't have talked about

Sal that way. Not in a million years. What the hell had this girl done? How had she done it? She looked about sixteen years old. Except when she was talking. Then, she seemed like something else entirely. This was no little girl.

Missy asked him, "Is there a problem, Frank?"

Frank realized that, indeed, there was a problem. The two guys he'd used to kidnap Alice were only supposed to keep her alive until he gave the word. He'd wanted to see if the mother would come up with any money. If she couldn't, then he'd figured maybe the daughter might know. Either way, there was never going to be any letting Alice go. And, these guys knew that. They were really looking forward to taking care of Alice. And, he had insisted that it all be on tape. No way was he going to let them find out where the money was and not tell him.

"She should be okay …" he began. Then he realized he still had no idea who Missy was. Unbelievable. He didn't even know what to call her. *Young lady* no longer seemed appropriate. He started again. "Nothing's supposed to happen to Alice. She needs to convince her mother to cooperate. So, ah … she should still be good."

Missy had picked up on the fact that things for Alice were precarious. "I want you to call your guys and explain that nothing is to happen to Alice. Tell them you're coming out there a few hours from now and you need her to be safe and happy. So she can convince her mother for you. Right? Can you make that call? Right now, Frank?" She didn't trust any part of this entire situation and could see that asking Frank to tell his guys to release Alice, unharmed, was probably not going to work. If they were already planning to get rid of her, any change of plans like that would be a red flag. They'd realize something was up and probably assume Frank had been arrested. If so, they'd take off with Alice and no one would ever see them or her again.

Frank made the call and then Missy had him go with her, out the back way. No one saw them leaving and she walked with him to her car. He was no longer looking to make any problems for her, as he believed what she'd said about Sal getting that video. She had obviously prepared all this long ago and probably would have been shaking him down anyway. His grabbing Alice was now looking like a really bad idea. Obviously, it had pissed her off and he wasn't at all clear just where all this was going. But, he knew if those guys had already been messing with Alice, he was in trouble. And, since they knew they would be killing her eventually, there really wasn't much reason for them not to have already started. They didn't sound too happy about his now coming out there, insisting they leave her unharmed until he got there.

Missy had Frank sit in the passenger seat and give directions to where Alice was being held. She had him spell out in detail all the plans. She also was concerned as to who else knew anything. The more he talked, the more she realized that Alice's fate had been sealed. As she'd suspected, the two guys were definitely counting on the fact they'd be getting rid of her. Eventually. Once they'd finished with her. If Frank ended up getting any money, either from the mother or from Alice, that was just an added benefit. They'd made a clean grab and were confident they'd never get caught. So, they were in this more for the fun of having her. Any money they might get paid was secondary.

The drive out to Boxford took almost an hour, since there was traffic. Once there, Frank directed her to a large cabin in a somewhat remote section, surrounded by woods. Evidently, these guys had not wanted any neighbors close by. Missy drove past and down the road another quarter mile, then pulled over. She told Frank to get out and walk around to the rear of the car. He looked at her and said, "You'll never get away with killing me, you know. My guys all saw you come into my place." But, he was worried. He'd seen how easily she'd knocked out Ramon and was still wondering how she'd managed everything she'd obviously done already.

"Relax, Frank," said Missy. "As much as you probably deserve killing, I actually need you to be my alibi. You're going to swear the two of us just went for a ride, to talk about old times. About you and your buddy Tony, who you grew up with, right? I'm just a local kid from the neighborhood who knew Tony, so we merely talked. That's our story and if you ever decide to tell it any differently, then Sal gets that video. Clear?"

"Sure, sure. Whatever you say. But, what about the guys holding Alice? I can't control what they will say." Frank was feeling a little relieved, since being her alibi meant he'd be okay. Maybe. He still couldn't see how all this was going to play out.

"Let me worry about that, Frank. Now, since you're going to have to wait a few hours and I don't want any accidents in the trunk of my car, how about you maybe try taking a leak to relieve yourself over by that bush?"

Missy opened her trunk and took out a set of handcuffs. Funny how handy it was to have these. First Billy and Donny and now Frank. When Frank had finished pissing and zipped back up, she handcuffed his hands behind his back and then placed duct tape over his mouth. Then she made him climb into the trunk of her Toyota. It was a tight fit, but she'd made room and once he was settled inside, she slammed the lid closed.

"Don't go anywhere, Frank. And, just keep thinking about how we're only riding around tonight, talking about Tony. And, when I take you back later tonight to your place? You're going to make sure Ramon doesn't get any ideas about me, right? Keep thinking how you're going to control that situation. Otherwise, Sal gets the video."

Chapter Thirty-Seven
Oct 2017

Alice was terrified. She'd been sitting there for hours, listening to the two guys who'd grabbed her. They'd pulled her into their van just as she was walking past it, after coming out of her dorm. It had all happened so fast. They'd held a towel with something in it against her face and it had made her black out. Ether, maybe. She knew they were planning to kill her. That and a lot of other horrible things as well. Things even worse than what Tony had done to her. She kept thinking of Mark and how worried he had to be. And, her mom. She knew they'd both be devastated by her death. That only made everything she was experiencing now just that much more agony to go though.

"Hey, Luis, where the hell is Frank? It's been more than three hours. Call him again, okay?" Jose was getting very impatient and looked at Luis with a very exasperated expression on his face. Things had gone great up until now and he wanted to get going. Just sitting around like this wasn't what he'd signed up for. The blond bitch they'd grabbed was totally hot. He couldn't wait until they got the go ahead to interrogate her. He hoped her mother really didn't know about any money and that it was something they'd be able to get her to talk about. On tape, no less. He and Luis were going to enjoy watching that tape long afterwards.

Luis said, "I already called twice. There's no answer at his office and his cell just goes to voice mail." He knew his buddy Jose was getting pretty antsy. He also knew he didn't want to mess with Frank. If Frank wanted the girl left alone until he got there, then they'd leave her alone. And, Frank had been very clear about their not talking to anyone else in his organization. This whole deal had been engineered so Frank didn't have anyone else he needed to worry about. Minimal risk. As Frank liked to say, everything's a risk but then there's the risk-reward part. This girl Alice they'd grabbed? She was the reward part this time. They could wait. She wasn't going anywhere.

He looked over at her, sitting there on the bed, just waiting. Trembling. She knew what was going to happen. That actually made it better. More exciting. He said, "Hey, Alice? You think Jose can keep it in his pants much longer? I'll bet that's why Frank's on his way. He wants to watch in person, rather than just seeing the tape. Anticipation is everything, right?"

They were in a large one room cabin, with two beds set up against one wall and a sliding glass door out to a deck on the opposite wall. Room dividers normally kept the beds hidden away but had been removed. A kitchen and pantry were along one side, along with a dining table and four chairs. The bathroom and utility room were along the opposite side along with a large flat screen TV mounted on the wall. There were no couches or love seats. Just a couple of large recliners around a low center table made out of marble. The view out back off the deck was clear for a hundred yards of open space and then the tree line began, with deep woods beyond.

The front door was next to one of the beds, but there was a divider so when someone came in, they wouldn't actually see anyone in the beds. He and Jose had used this place before. Lots of privacy. And, they'd wired the outside with plenty of security lights and alarms, so no one would be surprising them.

Jose liked the way Alice had reacted to what Luis had just said and decided he'd go over and check on her again. Frank had said "unharmed" but that didn't mean he couldn't examine the girl. Maybe even touch her some more. Touching wasn't harming, was it?

Suddenly the outside floodlights all came on and alarms began sounding. What the hell? Before either Jose or Luis could do anything, there was a loud crash as the sliding glass door was smashed in with glass flying everywhere. By a mountain lion. The animal didn't stop but came straight at Luis and leaped on top of him, with claws raking and jaws snapping. Missy had Changed and then had waited outside for two and half hours, during which she'd been able to watch from the woods. She hadn't wanted to wait any longer, once she saw one of the guys go over to where Alice was sitting.

Jose was paralyzed with shock at first. He watched as the big cat attacked Luis, who went down under the onslaught and didn't move. The animal had snapped his neck with its jaws; then … it looked up at him. With an ear piercing scream, the animal came straight at him. He tried to run but there was nowhere to go and nowhere to hide. His revolver was on the kitchen table and he headed in that direction but he never made it. The cat jumped onto his back and its jaws grabbed his neck. Then it was over.

Missy looked at the two men, checking they were both dead. Then she looked over at Alice who was screaming. Poor Alice. But, this couldn't be helped. She stepped carefully and slowly and walked over to the bed. Alice stopped screaming and stared at her, helpless. She was bound to the headboard and couldn't run. All she could do was stare at Missy and wait. Missy turned around and went over to the center of the room, hoping Alice would relax just a little. Then she Changed.

Alice was watching this wild animal and, after seeing it kill the two men, she had no idea why it suddenly stopped and walked away from her. Then, she saw a shimmer of light and felt the burst of energy. Suddenly, instead of the mountain lion, there was her friend Missy. Naked. The cat was gone and she'd appeared instead. How was that possible?

Missy spoke to her and said, "Well, Alice, you finally are learning all my secrets. I hope I can trust you to please keep them to yourself, okay?" She walked over and hugged Alice, then looked at how her bindings were attached to the bed. Before Alice could find any words at all, Missy freed her. Then she stepped back two steps and smiled. "Alice, I hope you can forgive me. I truly never expected anything like this would happen. Please believe me. My FBI buddies have been watching, just in case. I don't know how these guys managed getting you, but obviously they did. This has to have been such an ordeal for you." Missy was waiting for Alice to say something. Anything. "Alice, please. Please forgive me, okay?"

Alice managed to finally say, "It's you? Missy? You're a mountain lion? Or ... something?" She looked around and then stared back at her friend; finally, she ran forward and grabbed her. "Oh, Missy, you saved me! Of course, I forgive you, there's nothing to forgive, you silly girl! But, how …?" She didn't know how to continue.

Laughing, Missy answered, "Or something. Yes. I'm a werecat, Alice. That's why I disappeared four years ago. And, it took me two years before I was able to Change back. Other than my family, you're the only one who knows. I still haven't even told Patrick but I'll probably have to finally do that soon."

Alice looked around once more. Two dead bodies on the floor. Missy had really killed those guys. As a cat. This was a lot to process. She backed up and sat on the bed. Then she looked at Missy again and said, "You know you're naked, right? Totally bare ass? You do this much?" Suddenly, she broke out laughing.

Missy draped her long hair over her breasts and said, "It's my Lady Godiva look. Like it?" Then she too began laughing. After a few moments, however, she got serious again. "Look, Alice, we're going to cover this up. I have no intention for anyone to find out about me. I am not going to end up some lab specimen buried in the U.S. Government's secret whatever-place, you know?"

Alice stood up and said, "Of course not. I get that. What do we do here?"

Missy explained how fire should be good. There'd be no DNA left behind and all that would be determined about the two guys would be an attack by some wild animal. She'd even left plenty of her cat footprints outside and back in those woods where she'd waited. That would not be anything which would lead back to her. Especially since she was going to have an alibi. She explained briefly about Frank who was in her trunk.

"Alice, let's torch this place and then I'll drive you home. Once I drop you off, you have to find a way to keep your mom quiet. And, Mark too. I'll be taking Frank back to his nightclub and none of this will have ever happened. Frank's not going to tell anyone, believe me. And, nothing will connect you or me with these two dead guys. Or the fire. Let's get going.

A half hour later, Missy was back standing beside her car. Fully dressed once again. She'd explained to Alice about not saying a word since she wanted to just drive her home and didn't want Frank, in the trunk, to have any clue about any of this. They both got in and she started the car up and drove away. Back at the cabin, the fire was going nicely. They'd found some lighter fluid and had worked to make it look like something had spilled in the kitchen, caught fire, and had spread from there. Hopefully, it would just look like an accident and the wild animal would be blamed for everything.

Once she dropped Alice off and drove back to East Boston, she pulled over and let Frank climb out of her trunk. He was pretty upset but before she pulled the tape off his mouth and released his handcuffs, she explained how the whole thing with Alice being kidnapped had never happened. No one else knew, right?

When she then ripped the tape off his mouth, Frank swore a few times. Then he asked, "What about Luis and Jose? They might talk. I told you I can't control them."

Missy said, "And I told you I'd take care of that. Those guys are dead. Okay? Their cabin has hopefully burned to the ground about now. So, no kidnapping. And, if anyone asks about me, you're my alibi, right? We still clear?" She removed the handcuffs and handed him back his phone. She could still feel her cat inside, in spite of having Changed back.

Frank stared at her. Then he slowly shook his head, thinking about his two guys. Who was this girl? Then, as he realized she'd asked him a question, he quickly began nodding his head. "Oh, yeah! We're clear. You and I, just driving around Boston, having a great time talking about poor Tony. Right. Got it. Oh ... and, I'll make sure Ramon doesn't get any ideas." Then he looked at her closely, noticing all the yellow speckles in her wild green eyes. "Who the hell are you, anyway? If I'm your alibi, I need to know your name."

Missy looked at him and nodded her head. She'd known from the beginning there would be plenty of witnesses and all she could do was stick to this bullshit story she'd come up with. Her FBI buddies would be skeptical, of course. She figured they already had this nightclub under surveillance and would know when she'd arrived and also when she'd left with Frank. But, she had turned off her cell phone and Frank's cell phone, taking out the batteries, so there'd be no GPS record of where they'd gone after that. She hoped it was enough. Since no one would know about the kidnapping and there wasn't anything connecting her to the cabin in Boxford, all anyone could do was guess as to what really had gone down.

"My name is Missy McCrea. I know you'll be checking *me* out. Just make sure I never have any further reason to check *you* out." She looked at him and let even more of her cat come into her eyes. "I won't be using you for my alibi if there's a next time." She got back in her car and drove away.

Chapter Thirty-Eight
Nov 2017

Missy was pretty happy with how well things had been going lately. This year, they'd finally won the high school girls soccer state championship. The euphoria and camaraderie she shared with her teammates was so wonderful and fulfilling. Achieving something like this was so satisfying after all the hard work the team had put in, striving for it year after year. She was really thrilled she'd been a part of it. Participating on a team, contributing to its success, was just so special. She knew opportunities like this were fleeting. This was her senior year. Life would surely change in many ways next year. So, for now? She was happy.

Things with Alice were also special. They'd had many long talks since the kidnapping last month. First and most important was that Alice really was okay and had not been traumatized by what she'd experienced. Or, by what she'd witnessed. She had managed getting through all that and her emotional state was now stronger than ever. Surviving the evil things which others had done to her had helped her fully understand who she herself really was. Being a victim had not meant she was diminished in any way. She now valued her own self worth very highly. Having loved ones who constantly showed how much they valued her was really helping. And, she wanted to give back in return. Especially to Missy.

Missy was so happy that Alice was in her life. She could share things now, without hiding anything, and it was such a relief. Since she'd always kept Alice's secrets, she'd not shared anything with her family about Tony. So, in spite of her family knowing all about her being a werecat, there still had been many things she'd had to carry alone. Now, being completely open with Alice was making a huge difference. Explaining things to Alice had helped her understand many of those things so much better than before. Life was good.

Thanksgiving had been wonderful so far, with everyone home for the long holiday weekend. Mike had come over after the big Thanksgiving Day feast her family had enjoyed. They'd all sat around talking for an hour and now she'd brought him up to her room. She selected one of her playlists on her iTouch and her music started playing through the speakers in her room. Mike was looking around while she did this and when he saw the two mountain lion photos she'd hung on her wall, he went over and studied them. "You know? I think I see why you have these. This animal is really beautiful. In this one, it's showing how fierce it can be, with those fangs ready to tear into something but in this other one, it has such an intelligent expression on its face. Look at those eyes. How did the photographer manage getting such great shots? These weren't taken in any zoo, were they?"

Missy laughed. "No, they were not. And, my mom took those. I had them blown up and framed special. I'm really glad you like them, Mike." She sat down on her bed and arranged some pillows to sit back against. Mike pulled the chair away from her desk and seated himself backwards, with the back of the chair pulled up against his chest, so he could look at her. She said, "My eyes can sometimes look like that, according to what I've been told." Smiling, she relaxed her controls just a bit and allowed herself to get sexually aroused. She knew that was one way to bring her cat into her eyes and make those gold sparkles appear. Breathing in, she could scent how turned on Mike was, just being up in her room. Looking at her on a bed. She smiled.

Mike stared at her and said, "It's true! I think I can see the resemblance right now … damn! Are you doing that on purpose, Missy?" He had seen her eyes glow like that on occasion, and usually when she was feeling amorous. He was sensing her mood right now was indeed very romantic and he wished he was over there on the bed with her, holding her, instead of sitting here. He didn't want to break the mood by moving, so he continued with discussing her lovely eyes. "You are being naughty over there, aren't you? Making those eyes at me? With me helpless, unable to ravish you since your entire family is all around. Bet you feel pretty safe over there, huh?" He laughed and she laughed back at him.

"Ravish me? Gosh, what an idea, Mike! Ummmm!" Missy stretched slowly and enjoyed the way Mike's eyes showed his appreciation. She was wearing blue jeans and a soft cashmere sweater, in a lovely shade of green which matched her eyes and went really well with her red hair, which was loose and cascading all around her. She felt sexy and from the way Mike was studying her curves she knew he was getting excited by just watching her. Of course, his scent was also telling her how aroused he was and the fact she was turning him on sent delicious tingles zinging through her from head to toe.

She slowly got up from the bed, came around and seated herself behind him, pressing her breasts against his back and circling her arms around his chest. Squeezing herself up against him, she whispered in his ear, "Maybe we should go somewhere else ... give this ravishing plan of yours ... or, should I say, this plan of yours for ravishing ...?" Closing her eyes and holding onto Mike was so intoxicating. Or, was it that huge turkey dinner, perhaps, that was affecting her like this?

Mike groaned and said, "Hey, we can drive over to my room at school, you know. With everyone gone for the holiday weekend, that should be private enough." Wow. He couldn't believe he'd actually said that, but she was driving him crazy. His pants were feeling very tight and the blood racing through his veins was pounding so loudly, she had to be hearing his heart beat.

She actually was hearing his heart beat and more good feelings washed through her, making her consider his suggestion. The temptation was so strong and her needs began fighting with her controls. She had finally bared her soul with Alice, sharing everything, and that had been so cathartic. Now her feelings were no longer contained and she didn't really want to bottle them back up. She wanted to experience *more*. "That actually sounds great, Mike. Just the two of us. Let's get out of here for a while." She could feel the tremendous excitement he felt at her response. "Only, we're going to set some boundaries. This ravishing thing? Sorry, but that's really not going to happen."

"Boundaries?" His voice actually squeaked a bit as he said this. "Where will those boundaries be, exactly?"

Laughing, she told him, "Oh, you'll know where they are. I'll be letting you know when you reach them." Jumping up she scampered out of the room and he could hear her going down the stairs. He got up slowly, adjusting things so his pants didn't feel so tight, and started after her.

They walked into his dorm room and Mike turned on the lights. As he'd said, the place was rather deserted and there weren't very many other rooms showing any lights. Missy could hear that no one was anywhere near where they were and a guilty thrill went right through her. This was really the first time they'd ever been alone like this. She walked over to the light on his desk, turned that on but angled it so it faced the wall. Then she went back to the light switch near the door and turned off the overhead light. "We don't need bright lights. How about some nice music, though?"

Mike was already selecting some music and it started playing just a moment later. He turned around, removing his jacket, and helped her off with hers. She had visited him here at school twice before but there had been others all around back then. Now, there was only the soft music playing and she moved closer to him. They had talked on the way over, both trying to distract themselves more than make any real conversation. Now, they didn't feel like talking at all. Mike pulled her into his arms and kissed her.

She kissed him back. She loved the way his body felt, hard up against her body, and she wrapped her arms around him. His tongue was doing incredible things inside her mouth and she pushed back with her tongue and moaned softly. He moaned loudly, which made her laugh. She pulled back and smiled up at him. "Wow. Is this how a girl gets ravished? Where do I sign up?"

Mike laughed and pulled her towards the bed. "Right here, of course. Let me help you … ahh … sign up." He sat down on the bed and pulled her down next to him. "Now, where's my pen?" He began fumbling with one hand searching his shirt pockets, which of course were empty. He stopped and looked into her eyes, which he could see were again showing those yellow specks. How did she do that?

She pushed him back so he was lying down and she crawled on top of him. Wiggling against him felt so wonderful and, when she felt his hard erection pressing against her abdomen, her blood raced that much harder. Delicious tingles were causing a warm glow to spread throughout her body and she moved up and kissed him, with her hands on each side of his head. Her breasts felt really full and her nipples were getting extra sensitive. Almost as though he was reading her mind, Mike moved his hand up to caress her left breast and she gasped.

"Does this feel good, Missy?" Mike asked. He was massaging her breast through her sweater and she closed her eyes. Her obvious pleasure made him roll her onto her right side, with his left arm trapped underneath her but with his right arm free and his hand able to continue fondling. He was now on his left side and pulled her toward him, rubbing his left hand along her rear. His right hand slid down her side, then over to briefly pull her rear so she was hard against him. She ground her hips right back at him and he groaned.

Missy was thoroughly enjoying this whole experience. Why hadn't she been letting him ravish her until now? Giggling, as she continued to grind her pelvis up against him, she sighed into his ear. "Oh, Mike! I'm beginning to feel as though I'm on fire." She was moving her hands all around, touching him and hugging him. She didn't want to stop and she knew he was now completely into pleasing her. She felt his right hand slide under her sweater and slide up her bare skin until reaching her bra. His fingers probed under her bra cup and began working their way along her breast, slowly moving the bra higher and higher and exposing more and more of her tender flesh. That combination of his hand doing things to her and her breast being exposed made her get so wet all of a sudden! Damn, that was exciting!

Mike finally reached the area around her left nipple and he began circling it with his finger, pushing her bra even higher and completely off that breast. As his fingers then lightly touched the nipple itself, which hardened to his touch, he felt Missy's body shudder. She had her face buried against his neck and somehow her left leg had wrapped itself around his right leg, pulling them together in a way which clearly showed she was enjoying this. He closed his hand over her breast and captured her nipple between two fingers. As he began massaging her breast, his fingers worked on her nipple, flicking it back and forth.

Missy wanted to tell him how fantastic this felt but held back saying anything. At least, saying anything with words. Her body, however, was definitely talking to Mike and telling him how good everything was. Telling him to continue. She wriggled and arched her back and let those sensations he was causing her breast to experience just wash through her in wave after wave of pleasure. Her right breast was definitely feeling neglected and she began pressing that up against him, trying to rub his hard chest but not quite managing to get the sensation she wanted. Suddenly, he twisted and she was lying on her back with him above her. He lifted her sweater up, sliding it all the way to her neck and he slid his hand down to grab the bra cup still covering her right breast. He pushed that up and both her breasts were now completely exposed, bare and needy. Oh, so needy!

Mike was supporting his weight on his elbows and lowered his mouth so he could trace her right breast with his tongue. He continued working her left nipple with his fingers but focused all his attention now on that right breast. His tongue began licking and by the way Missy's whole body was reacting, squirming and wriggling below him, he was sure this was indeed making her feel good. After several minutes of playful licking and lapping he finally reached her erect nipple, standing there at attention. When he licked her nipple with his tongue she gasped and her body bucked underneath, with her arms suddenly going around him. She pushed her breast hard upward, forcing her nipple into his mouth. He began to suck on her breast and she once again spasmed. He was amazed at how sensitive Missy seemed to be with every little thing he would do. She was moving as though each of his actions was causing something involuntary to happen to her body, completely out of her control. Yet, she was certainly volunteering for more and more, so he continued. She had such perfect breasts and nipples and he was ready to explode from how inflamed he was getting, just playing with them.

Missy had her eyes closed and was just letting her body have its way. There was now so much wetness between her thighs! The throbbing she could feel down there was almost too much. Her heightened awareness of each little movement Mike would make with his hands and fingers, with his mouth and tongue, with his hard body pressing down on hers, caused an excitement to start building which she'd never felt before. This was a truly new and unique experience and her entire being wanted nothing else but more and more. As his hands began doing more things she realized she had lost all control. And, she didn't care. All she cared about was that he continue touching her, fondling her, pleasuring her.

Mike could sense how very aroused Missy was getting and how her body was moving constantly, making his own body ache with desire. Her wild and uninhibited enjoyment of this was going way beyond anything he'd ever imagined. As he continued to play with her lovely breasts, licking her nipples and teasing her sensitive areolas, sucking and even gently nibbling with his teeth, she was writhing and moaning and began grinding her pelvis against his hip and thigh, crushing his throbbing erection. He pushed her away and twisted to the side, just to make a bit of room for himself. As she swiveled her hips toward him he brought his hand down across her abdomen, firmly pressing her away. This somehow only seemed to trigger even stronger reactions.

Missy felt Mike shift back and away and the excitement which had been building within her suddenly wanted to explode. No, don't stop! She tried to press herself against him but felt his hand pushing her away. Agggghhh, that hand felt so good on her tummy. She cried out, "Touch me, Mike, touch me, please. Anywhere, everywhere. Again. Again and again. That feels soooo good. Please, please!"

Mike let his hand slip inside the waistband of her jeans and moved down to cup her pubic mound. Her panties were soaked and she immediately thrust her hips forward, pushing up against his hand. He began to play, moving his fingers over the slick folds underneath and inside those wet panties, and she opened her legs spreading her thighs apart. She clearly wanted more movement down there and he pressed harder.

Missy was now going crazy, the throbbing pulsations from where Mike's hand was touching her making her entire body want to explode. Then, as he pressed down harder she began splintering apart, shattering as convulsion after convulsion completely overwhelmed her. He seemed to understand she wanted him to keep moving his hand right there, and his fingers just kept squeezing her, exactly the way she wanted them to. She bucked and she bucked harder, screaming her pleasure at the tremendous release this was giving her. Each convulsion was accompanied by an even greater wave of pleasure and this went on and on and on. She was sobbing when, finally, after what had seemed like an eternity but had probably only lasted a minute or so, her sensations gradually subsided. Her panties and inside her jeans were completely flooded with fluids she'd released in what had certainly been an orgasm.

She sighed, allowing her sobs to stop as she hugged Mike tightly against herself. Wow! Her first orgasm. That had been great! Then ... she began experiencing aftershocks. Oh, those were so delicious! Mike had slowly withdrawn his hand but it didn't matter. Her body continued to quiver as more waves of pleasure washed through her. She didn't want to be selfish but the lassitude which now replaced what those driving, pounding, overwhelmingly intense sensations had done to every nerve ending in her body could not be ignored. She was limp. Exhausted. All her bones seemed to have melted. Oh, that had been nice!

Mike was shocked and amazed at the extreme melt down he'd helped make happen. Missy was now cooing, making little mewling sounds and it was very obvious she was oblivious to just about everything. His heart went out to her, and in spite of the way his own desire was still raging and his throbbing erection was aching, he was even more affected by what had just happened for her. The spasms of pleasure she'd so obviously enjoyed as her orgasm wracked her entire body were so beautiful to see. So unbelievable to have not just witnessed but to have truly been the one who made that happen.

Her emotions had been so overpowering during the entire build up and her blissful contentment now that her sexual energies had so thoroughly been spent was more than special. It filled him with such warmth and love for her that he now didn't want to move at all. His passion subsided as he felt the much deeper flush of satisfaction in just holding her. In just having her body, so completely limp and spent, resting solidly on his after such extraordinary and passionate moments had been shared with her. He knew this was her first time and that she probably had never intended for things to happen this way. Where were those boundaries she'd mentioned, anyway? Smiling to himself, he relaxed and just let her lie there. She owned him, whether or not she realized that, and it was his greatest thrill to be able to just hold her like this.

Missy woke up and realized she had actually fallen asleep in Mike's arms. Poor Mike! She groaned as she sat up and stared at him. He was actually awake and smiling at her. She tugged her bra back down and then her sweater.

"Do you feel ravished yet, Missy?" he asked, and his laughter was contagious.

"Oh, yes!" She was still trying to get her bearings back. But, she certainly knew she'd been ravished all right. That part was clear. "Mike, I can't begin to say how wonderful that was. And, how sorry I am as well. I never meant for anything like that to happen. I certainly never meant to get you all worked up and ... and, just leave you hanging like that. You must think I'm an awful tease, coming on to you, using you ..."

"Missy, please. Don't even try to apologize for anything. I enjoyed this more than you'll ever know, really. I never expected things to … well, you know. I don't regret any of it. I'll treasure tonight for as long as I live, I truly will. So, please don't say anything more. Giving you that orgasm was more than enough for me." He pulled her down and kissed her but then sat up. "We really should get you back home, Missy."

They got up and put on their coats, turned off the music and the lights, and left. They didn't talk much at all during the drive back to Salem, but they didn't feel the need. What they'd shared had been special for both of them and they knew it. Words just weren't necessary. When Mike pulled into her driveway, she leaned over and kissed him on the lips. She sat back and stared into his eyes. This was yet another moment and Missy was feeling more emotions than she'd ever felt before. She kissed him once again, hard, and then hopped out of the car without saying a word. She ran up to her door, turned to wave briefly and went inside.

Mike drove away and felt his entire life had somehow changed. Of course, moments with Missy kept making him feel that way, so he continued driving. While his brain focused on his surroundings so he could drive home safely, his heart began daydreaming about more moments with Missy yet to come.

Chapter Thirty-Nine
Nov 2017

Missy walked into the coffee shop and saw Robert Ulrey sitting at a booth way in the back. She was wearing jeans, but not the pair she'd worn on Thanksgiving, two days ago. Thinking about that pair, which had been washed yesterday, brought a smile to her face. When she saw Robert look up, she widened her smile and said, "Hey, Robert. I trust you enjoyed turkey day." As she removed her coat she looked around and lowered her voice. "Is this meeting to tell me about you guys taking Frank down?"

Robert smiled and nodded his head. "Partly. That will be making headlines later this week. Armando sends his regards and now wants me to recruit you. He says you can attend any college you want and the FBI will take care of the tuition. Just agree to join his team afterwards." They both laughed. He was studying her and realized she'd grown up an awful lot in the past two years. She was now a young adult and really looked it, in spite of those long pigtails she was wearing today. A very attractive young adult with an extremely confident and self assured manner.

"What's the other part then?" she asked. She actually had been waiting for this, since she figured they'd watched her go out that night with Frank. She also wondered what they knew, if anything, about Alice being grabbed. They were supposed to have been watching, after all. "Is this about my date with Frank the other night?"

"Yeah, I'm sure you know we saw that. Armando's team got pretty excited, afraid you might be interfering somehow just as things were going to go down. But, whatever you discussed with Frank, it hasn't caused any ripples and their case against him is solid. Obviously, you didn't warn him. So, what did you two talk about?" Robert had gotten a very excited phone call, insisting he bring her in right away. He had reminded them what Missy had said about trusting her. The ten million reasons she'd given them for doing that. So, they'd held off and had waited to see how things played out.

They had investigated, of course, trying to determine what might have happened. They knew she'd mentioned Tony Gonzales; saying that had worked in her getting in to see Frank. And, since one of their experts had actually hacked into Frank's surveillance system, they'd watched how Ramon had patted her down out in the hallway. But they didn't have any surveillance in Frank's office, since he had that swept for bugs every day. When she drove off with Frank, they'd lost her. No one had expected anything like that would happen since he never went anywhere unless he was in one of his own cars with at least two of his guys with him.

Missy said, "Oh, I'm sure Frank will tell you all about it. We just drove around and talked about his good friend Tony Gonzales. We talked all night, in fact. He'll tell you I'm just a kid from the neighborhood who knew Tony. Chit chat. I'm quite sure that's what Frank will be telling you." She watched as Robert processed this information. When he smiled a little, shaking his head, she asked, "Since by now you know I didn't say or do anything to compromise your case, why are you asking me about this?"

"Well, there have been a few little questions which have come up." Robert looked at her, sitting there so prim and proper. "We know what you did to Ramon. The hospital records showed extensive surgery was required to repair his jaw. He also complained about damage to his groin area. Lucky for him, nothing permanent was damaged down there. The guy has definitely been in a lot of pain and still hasn't returned to any normal duties. He'll be included in next week's round up, by the way."

Missy nodded and smiled. "Good. If you happen to interview him about stuff, I understand he likes things done the *old fashioned way*." When she saw the way Robert broke out laughing at the way she emphasized *old fashioned way*, she knew. They had watched the tape. "Did you guys get to see what happened in Frank's office, too?"

"No, no we didn't. But, we know how skilled you are at karate and martial arts. What we can't figure out, though, is why Frank has obviously put the word out. You're completely off limits. Untouchable." Since the FBI team knew all about that surveillance software they'd provided her with, they were all taking bets as to just what she was blackmailing Frank about. "I don't suppose you have any additional evidence we can use against Frank?" She obviously had something.

"Sorry, but I don't have anything for the FBI or the police. Not really. Of course, you understand Frank has his friend Sal to be worried about, right?" She figured she may as well admit that much. She'd asked them for all that information about Sal. "You mentioned there are questions which have come up. Anything else?"

Robert stared at her and processed what she'd said. She was blackmailing Frank with something she could show or tell Sal. Something she wasn't ready to share with the FBI. Maybe she did know what she was doing since that would explain Frank and his organization leaving her alone. She indeed had said the FBI's info on Sal was important for her safety. He knew he probably wasn't going to get anything further from her about any of this.

In answer to her question he went on to say, "Well, actually, yes. There was a strange mishap. Probably not related. But, the same night when you and Frank were out riding around? Two guys who are known associates of his were found dead. Their house burned down with them inside. Over in Boxford." Robert had only recently seen the complete report. It had taken several days for the autopsy findings and it was only because of the connection to Frank that the case had even been noticed by Armando's team. "There apparently are wild animals running around in those Boxford woods. It appears these two known associates were both killed when some animal broke into their place. Broken necks. Very strange. The fire was accidental and the theory is that it got started somehow by the same wild animal."

"Broken necks, huh?" Missy asked. "Why do they think it was an animal?"

"Well, there were very clear footprints outside. And, in the woods. Some sort of puma or panther. Or, maybe a mountain lion. I think those actually are all the same thing, just different names. But, they're not known to be around here. At least, not that anyone had noticed before now. Apparently there's also some evidence over at the state forest in Andover. Some deer remains have been reported by a park ranger over there. He insists the kills were by a large cat and not by any dogs or wolves." Robert had been surprised about that but the database search had turned up that info once the Boxford police had reported and identified those tracks. "The autopsy results show bite marks on the necks of both victims, consistent with the kind of animal which could make those footprints."

"Well, that's interesting but it does sound unrelated. Just a coincidence, obviously." Missy was surprised about the park ranger finding some of her deer kills. She'd have to avoid using that area for a while.

"Yes, there doesn't seem to be any way those guys … well … there was this one aspect which made me wonder." Robert stared at Missy. He realized she was really good at hiding her emotions. He was never able to guess what was going on inside her head. She would just calmly sit there, with those incredible green eyes of hers, giving nothing away. "Those two guys have actually been on my suspect list a couple of times. For kidnapping young women. The bodies of those girls were eventually found but there was just no evidence to prove anything. I wish I didn't have so many open cases like that. As you know, your case was one of my very few with any sort of happy ending."

"And, the fact that these guys may have been kidnappers is making you wonder what, exactly?" Missy was getting a sense she might not like where this was going.

"Well, it's because you had us looking out for Mrs. Gonzales. And, her daughter Alice. Did you know Alice disappeared that same day?" Robert was not seeing any reaction. "At least, we think she did. But, someone dropped her off at home late that night, so maybe not. We couldn't put anyone on watching the two of them full time, but … you get why it made me wonder, right?"

"Hmmm. Let me see if I understand this." Missy knew she could trust Robert. "Maybe Alice was kidnapped, but only for a little while, by two known associates of Frank's who somehow were attacked and killed by a wild animal. And, since Frank might have some interest in Alice, since Tony had all that money which disappeared, you're wondering. Trying to connect some dots. And, coincidently, all this happened on the one night when Frank and I had our mysterious chit chat. Hmmmm." Missy just stared at Robert. Then, she let her cat do that thing she'd learned she could do with her eyes. Gold speckles began glowing as she continued to gaze at Robert. She saw him suddenly sit back.

Watching those eyes change like that was what convinced him. Robert had absolutely no idea how she'd managed getting those guys killed or in getting Alice safely dropped off at her home, but he was certain she had somehow done exactly that. Just like he suddenly remembered how Armando had mentioned checking her alibi for the time when Tony had his accident. "Well, I guess we're done here, Missy. By the way, what can I tell Armando about his offer? Have you decided about college yet?"

Missy laughed. "Well, yes, I've actually got my heart set on going to West Point. Senator Maxwell thinks I have a really good chance. After graduation, there's a five year commitment to serve in the Army, so I don't think I'll be joining the FBI any time soon."

"Really? Wow, that's wonderful, Missy. I don't suppose you're planning which branch you'll choose. The Army Military Police, which was the branch I was in, would be a good choice, *considering*." He looked at her and could already see by the humor in her eyes that she was *considering* something else entirely.

"Why, Robert, that probably would be a good choice, *considering*." She emphasized *considering* just the way he had. She realized she'd basically admitted being responsible for several things, but these were things no one could possibly prove and things which Robert had no intention of telling anyone about. He only knew she was responsible but had no clue whatsoever as to how. "But no. I plan to be in either the Special Forces or else become an airborne Ranger. Basically the infantry, you know? They finally are allowing women to do this but that's only been for the past couple of years. I intend to complete all the training for both and then see which makes the most sense when the time comes."

Later that day Missy went over to see Alice. They'd planned a girls' night out since Mike and Mark were both busy, each with family events which had been scheduled for quite a while. They were invited, of course, but had decided they'd rather take this rare opportunity to get away. Who knew when they'd get another chance?

Missy had lots she wanted to share and when Alice's mom went out to run some errands, they sat down and began talking about things. Missy explained about the conversation with Robert that morning, including those few little questions which he'd brought up. She ended that by saying, "So, even though I didn't admit to anything in actual words, he knows. He knows but he really doesn't know. And, I know he's okay with that. Make sense?"

"Sure, I get it." Alice smiled at her friend, her friend the cat. She was still adjusting to that. "He knows you're working some crazy mojo but has no clue you can get all furry with fangs and claws." Giggling, she added another thought. "When you gave them that ten million dollars from Tony, were you already thinking this far ahead? To perhaps someday having them turn a blind eye to all the crazy shenanigans you'd be pulling?"

"No, not at all! I had no idea that things would ever get this crazy. I suppose I am concerned about that D'Amato guy in New York. But, so far, my surveillance stuff is working great. I'll maybe have to break in and change some batteries over Christmas vacation, but otherwise nothing to worry about."

"Have you gotten very many text messages? To go check which trigger words they used and what they're talking about?" Alice had been really impressed with what Missy had explained. She'd laughed herself silly listening to Missy's description of herself as a *cat burglar*, breaking into their apartments in order to set up all her equipment. Hanging from a rope outside after rappelling down the side of the building from the roof. Getting in through windows without anyone catching her. Being really creative with her various hiding places. Too much!

"Sure, I get lots of them. It's then a tedious task to go download the tapes and check. Boring stuff. Usually, they're just bitching to each other and my name comes up. I've had to tweak that software to add some new trigger words. They really don't like me very much and keep inventing new references for who and what I am. They are so pissed off that I got the drop on them like that. But, they are being careful enough."

"When Frank gets arrested, do you think he'll do anything bad? You know, to get back at you somehow?" Alice was worried now that Frank knew who Missy was. "What if he decides to get revenge? Things change and maybe he'll think of a way to explain things to Sal. Get Sal to go after you? Then, if that tape you've got comes out later, he'll hope for Sal's forgiveness? Or, maybe just someone from his organization will do something? I don't know. But, I do worry about you, Missy!"

"You mean, if maybe Ramon can find the balls to do something? Once his balls stop hurting, of course." Missy started laughing and Alice had to join her. "Actually, that brings up something I really wanted to talk to you about. You know how guys complain how we can tease them, getting them all aroused and then … you know … they get blue balls, right? Very painful, supposedly."

"Sure, it's true. Prolonged arousal will have them doubled over. The aching can last for hours." Alice blushed and said, "Mark explained how I used to cause that for him all the time." She smiled as she realized that wasn't a problem anymore. Sex with Mark was just getting better and better.

"Okay. Well, that sounds exactly like what Mike was describing. Poor guy, I feel so bad. I mean, I really don't …" Missy looked at Alice and suddenly giggled. "Did I mention how we're going for pizza tonight? And, then ice cream. Only, I'll be ordering this really, really *huge* scoop." She blushed like crazy as she emphasized *huge*.

"Oh, my god! You had sex with Mike? Missy, you have to tell me everything. Details, details. Come on!"

Missy laughed and said, "Well, not exactly. At least … well, that's why I'm telling you about poor Mike. About his balls." Now she was getting flustered. "About his blue balls. Oh, I think you know what I mean!"

Laughing like crazy, Alice said, "Oh, I know what you mean alright! But, forget about Mike's balls and tell me all about your orgasm. Stop *pussy* footing around, Missy!" As all the various meanings for *pussy* occurred to the two of them, their laughter almost got hysterical.

Alice couldn't resist and asked, "Did I really just tell a cat to stop being a *pussy*?" More laughter.

Finally, Missy calmed down and managed to explain some things. "Well, you know how I told you all about my sensitivity to pain? How it's probably much more than what you normal humans experience, because of my heightened awareness to everything? But, since I can go places in my mind, I can block it off? I still feel the pain but I can ignore it, right?"

"Like last summer when you broke your leg? Then, drove your doctor crazy by not letting him give you any medication?" Alice had listened to the story a couple of times now and even had obtained one of the photos taken the day Missy went back and posed for them. Missy had called it her Pippi Longstocking look. "Sure, I get that. All part of you being a werecat. Or something. You said you're still trying to figure it all out yourself."

"Right. Exactly. Fortunately, since I heal up so fast, I don't have to ignore it for very long. Sort of a tradeoff, I guess. Much greater pain but for much shorter duration." Missy blushed. "Two nights ago? I found out it's not just pain. The same is true for pleasure. Well, almost the same. My body experiences pleasure in a much greater way. At least, it sure seemed extra, extra, you know? I truly had no idea. Only ... the part about the shorter duration? That part wasn't true. I mean ... Alice, it seemed to go on and on forever!"

"You really had an orgasm, then? I'm so happy for you. It sounds as though whatever you and Mike were doing, you really let go. Lost all control. Maybe you really needed that after everything you'd just been through. Saving me. Those guys. Frank. Your crazy metabolism. Just blame it all on that, right?" Alice started laughing.

"But, I feel so guilty now," Missy told her. "I was feeling frisky and playful and, well … yeah, horny. I admit it. But, I always have been able to control myself whenever that happens. I rely on that. It's my built in self defense mechanism. I mean, you do realize that I fully matured, sexually, when I was in cat form, right? Up there in the mountains? I have been controlling these urges of mine for four years. That never was a problem until two nights ago."

Alice was now getting really interested. "Details, girl. You haven't exactly explained anything, really. Not yet. What were you and Mike doing? Are you still even a virgin? Can virgins have orgasms? Help me out here, Missy!"

"Of course virgins can have orgasms! And, yes, I'm still one. A virgin. It was mostly what I felt when he was … well, he did probably every imaginable thing to my breasts, so I suppose this isn't such a big deal. You probably have sensitive nipples too, right?" Missy could see that while Alice was agreeing, she wasn't really understanding. "I let him play and he was so wonderful. I'd read about orgasms and breast stimulation isn't what the books say will trigger them. I thought I'd be able to stop. Set some boundaries. I'd never had anyone do anything like that. The more he kept touching me the more excited I got. I can see that now. My body wanted more and more and those boundaries I was supposed to set? I wasn't even thinking about those."

Alice was actually enjoying the way Missy was trying to explain things. "It took me awhile to get so Mark could do it for me. Give me orgasms. But, once I experienced that first time? Those three scoops we laugh about so much?" Alice sighed. "Now, after things get really going? I think Mark still believes I require extra measures of foreplay because of the abuse I endured from Tony. So, he's so really wonderful about it and I admit my breasts do love all the attention. I probably don't even need as much foreplay now but I don't mind it at all."

"You were saying ... about when things get really going?" Missy laughed. The two of them had been so open and sharing about everything, but this conversation was going places they'd never been before.

"Well, you've had an orgasm now, Missy. And, if you really feel things more intensely, then so much the better. I don't need to tell you. When things really get going? Then, all of a sudden, things will *really* get going and forget about controls and boundaries. All you can think about is wanting to come. Once I get to that point, it suddenly becomes that place where *I-don't-care-if-I-die-as-long-as-I-get-to-come-first!*" She closed her eyes and enjoyed thinking about how wonderful it was with Mark.

"Exactly!" exclaimed Missy. "I was enjoying everything so much and then things began racing faster and faster. I think Mike actually was trying to pull back but I kept asking him to touch me. I just got so wet and when he finally touched me down there, I exploded. My jeans weren't even unzipped. He slid his hand inside them and when I felt his fingers touching me, I went a little crazy. My panties were soaked so badly I wasn't even sure about trying to wash them out. I almost just threw them away."

"So, you let him explore inside your panties? That set you off?"

"Actually, no. He never even got that far. Just having his hand cupping me, even though it was over my panties, made me come so hard I ended up a complete zombie. A basket case. I actually laid there on top of him and couldn't move. I wanted to try … since Mike … you know … poor Mike! But, after things finally slowed down and all the little explosions which kept going off even after … well, I just couldn't move. I fell asleep and he just held me the whole time."

They ended up finally going out for pizza and actually did go for ice cream afterwards. It was one of the nicest times either of them had ever had.

Chapter Forty

Dec 2017

The headlines in the Boston newspapers were all about the big arrests made by the FBI. Frank McCarthy and eight of his associates were arraigned for various money laundering and tax evasion charges. The case against them was very solid and the story ran for days. Armando Sanchez was quoted in several of the articles and appeared in a few press conferences as well. The stories and TV broadcasts went nationwide. This was one of the biggest victories against organized crime in years and helped restore the FBI's reputation which had been tarnished rather than enhanced by many of the other events which had played out in recent years.

Drew Martinson came into Robert Ulrey's office and introduced himself. He'd made an appointment after his staff had fully vetted Robert. They chatted briefly for a few minutes and then he finally brought up the reason for this visit. "Robert, I'm here to ask if you'll join my team. This shouldn't interfere with your present duties here at the FBI but, from time to time, it will require your going on special assignment for us. Not really any conflict of interest but you do need to be sworn in. I can't even discuss anything further until you can agree to that. Everything we talk about from now on must be kept secret."

Robert was not prepared for this but was intrigued. He'd tried to look into who Drew Martinson was and what his mysterious "P" Branch was all about when he'd agreed to this meeting. He hadn't been able to learn much other than how highly classified everything to do with this "P" Branch was. Apparently, it was highly regarded, very important and had almost unlimited resources but was also one of the U.S. Government's agencies about which very little else was known.

"Okay, I think I can accept that," said Robert. "I'll probably agree to being sworn in but can you at least tell me why? Why me?"

"Well, I can tell you that, I suppose. But, you must keep this confidential. Even if you don't get sworn in and join up with us, you have to keep this to yourself." Drew studied Robert and then went on to say, "It's because you have a special relationship with Missy McCrea. She seems to trust you and I'm pretty sure you care about her. You're already acting as liaison with her for your Organized Crime Division, right?"

Robert was shocked and surprised. At first. Shocked this had anything to do with Missy and surprised Drew knew anything about her involvement with the Organized Crime Division and his being their contact person for her. But, as he thought about how this mysterious "P" Branch had unlimited resources, his surprise quickly faded. His shock, however, took a little longer to get over. "Why Missy?"

"Can you accept our terms? If so, let's get you sworn in. Then I can explain everything." Drew saw that Robert was in agreement and they went ahead with all the formalities. Then, he said, "Welcome to "P" Branch,

Robert. Now that you've come on board, I can tell you about the pay increase you're getting. Thirty percent on top of your present salary. There are other benefits but we'll get to those later."

Robert smiled and said, "First, just explain what the hell "P" Branch even stands for, Drew. What is your mysterious group and why are you interested in Missy?"

Drew said, "That's two questions but I'll see if I can answer them both. "P" Branch is the Paranormal Branch for the U.S. Government. We monitor -- and handle -- a lot of various matters. And certain individuals. Ones who, like Missy, have special abilities. You know about her rapid healing, right?"

Robert tried to process this. He still wasn't sure he was getting it. "Well, she did make a rather miraculous recovery after that head injury. I assume you know about everything which happened when she showed up down there in Virginia?"

"Oh, we have all that, yes. It's what first caught my attention. That rescue, which required superior strength. Superhuman strength. We've been following her ever since. That's why we know all about her activities up here, including that little freebie she gave your guys in Organized Crime. Ten million dollars. My team really enjoyed that, Robert." He smiled. "Did you know about her broken leg this past June?"

"Actually, no. Missy didn't have a broken leg that I know of. She worked all summer as a lifeguard at Revere Beach. They commended her several times, in fact, for rescues she made. There are several young kids and even a couple of adults who owe their lives to her quick actions, apparently. I know those were dramatic, even heroic, but I didn't think any of those involved anything superhuman."

Drew nodded his head. "She actually holds back on the superhuman stuff, most of the time. Superstrength and superspeed aren't always perceived as such, since people only notice what they believe is possible. But, she broke her leg that first week on the job. That boy she saved from the fire in Lynn?"

"I did read about that. But, she was at the beach the very next week. She even saved a kid. I remember hearing about the commendation and thinking back to how she'd saved that family in Virginia and how here she was now saving two kids in two weeks. Amazing and heroic, but still. She is a very gifted athlete and I wasn't all that surprised."

"Exactly my point, Robert. She does all these incredible things in plain sight and everyone just figures she's normal. But, she broke her leg when she rescued that kid from the fire. She jumped out a second floor window with him in her arms. He didn't get hurt -- thanks to her -- but she fractured her tibia and actually broke her fibula; the break in her fibula needed to be set. The doctors can't explain how she healed up in four days. Completely healed. Can you?"

Robert was surprised at this news. Missy had never mentioned any injury and the newspaper story hadn't really said anything about that. Only that she'd gone to the hospital in the ambulance. "They actually had to set her bone? And, are you maybe saying her head injury down In Virginia was as serious as that first MRI showed? That wasn't just some glitch like everyone figured?"

Drew said, "Take a look at these two CT scans. The first one shows not a single broken bone or fracture. That was the one that hospital in Virginia took. Now, look at this one taken two years later. Not only can you see the damage to her left leg, but look at all the other fractures. Notice anything unusual about them?"

Robert wasn't a doctor and asked Drew to explain it to him. After hearing the lengthy explanation of how bones normally heal and how Missy's bones were all healed up with added strength, due to her continued use of them while ignoring pain, he asked, "She ignores pain? You're not saying she doesn't feel pain, you're saying she feels it but then ignores it?"

"Robert, this girl feels everything with much greater intensity. Enhanced senses for sight, sound, smell and taste as well. Superhuman. That's why we're monitoring her. And, why we want you to handle her for us."

"Well, she has very definite plans for herself. I'm not sure what you mean by my handling her. She also keeps a lot of secrets but I'm seeing you already know that about her."

"Oh, yes. We do know all about her plans and we're very pleased. She's been training herself and educating herself even better than anything we could ever have done for her. Team sports, individual trophies in karate and martial arts, accelerated learning while home schooled, combined SAT scores of 1280, and she wants to get all the military training any female can possibly get? West Point? Infantry branch, with Special Forces and Ranger qualifications? Read your own reports, Robert. We did." Drew laughed.

"Okay, I guess she is pretty special. And, when you combine the rapid healing with all the other stuff, maybe she is some sort of supergirl. But, why me? Can't you recruit her, if that's what you want?" Robert was staring at Drew, trying to understand the big picture which he still couldn't see.

"Oh, we're not trying to recruit her. Let her finish high school. Let her go to West Point. We're excited about that. But, if we approach her, there's apt to be trust issues. You already have a relationship with her and she trusts you. I explained that. We accessed your file on her, Robert. The one on your computer? Not the file you've uploaded for the FBI but that private file. Where you describe the way she acknowledged her responsibility for those two deaths in Boxford? Obviously, she trusts you. And, it's those deaths which are forcing us to get a bit more involved. We believe your assessment is probably correct and that her actions were justified. We're hoping you can help her stay on the right side and not get too carried away. Being a vigilante is not what we want for this girl."

Robert was very surprised to learn they had accessed his private file. He didn't really want to think about that. He was still trying to catch up on what Drew was explaining about Missy. "You know those guys were supposedly killed by a mountain lion or some sort of large cat, right? The autopsy evidence is very clear and there were those footprints. I'm only guessing she somehow was responsible but only because of that look she gave me."

Nodding his head, Drew said, "Yes, we know. And, she actually did that to those guys herself. There are others like her, you know. We're monitoring all of them. But, your Missy is very special. She's also the only female in recent times. And, by that, I mean going back for at least two hundred years. We don't really know that much about these cases before that."

Robert asked, "When you say she did that ... and, there are others like her ... what exactly are you saying, Drew?"

"I'm saying she did that to those guys in her other form, Robert. Those were Missy's tracks and Missy's bite marks on their necks. She's a wild predator in her other form. When Missy came down from those mountains after disappearing for two years? She finally had figured it out. How to Change back. Missy is a werecat."

Epilogue
Dec 2017

"Hey, Patrick? Promise not to tell?" Missy laughed. It was fun to tease her brother and she was in a great mood. Christmas vacation and everyone was home. Heather and John. Alice and Mark. Mike. She felt a delicious thrill go zinging through her body as she thought of Mike. And, she'd just returned from New York. Alice and Heather had gone with her which had made the trip lots of fun. The cat burglar jokes were getting so lame and outrageous! She loved the fact they could all talk freely about this now. It made the whole experience much less nerve wracking. Missy didn't really like taking risks if she could avoid them.

As far as her actually breaking in, however, everything had gone just great. The replacement batteries would last for months and Billy and Donny still had no clue she was monitoring their places and was able to hear every word. Her early warning system should continue working just fine.

Patrick looked at her with a very pained expression on his face. His sister was always baiting him like this. "Only if I like what you tell me. If I don't like it, then nothing doing. I'll rat you out."

Missy laughed and picked up on his choice of words. "Rat me out? But, that's not much of a threat, once you hear my secret. You see ... cats kill rats. You know that, right?"

"So?" Patrick looked around and the fact that his entire family was sitting there, already smiling at what Missy had just said, made him very suspicious. Obviously, they knew something and he was the only one in the dark about her secret.

"So, I'm a cat." Missy laughed. "That's my secret."

"Very funny, very funny!" Patrick looked at the others and wondered why they were now laughing at him so hard. Missy could be such a pain sometimes.

"Sorry, but I'm not joking. Mom and Dad said it's okay for me to tell you now. They think you're old enough. Not to tell anyone on me. You won't, right?"

"Riiiight, you can be quite sure I'm not going to go around telling anyone that my crazy sister is a cat." Patrick looked at her like she had two heads. "You don't think I want everyone thinking that I'm crazy, do you?"

Missy said, "I knew that I'd have to show you. But, everyone agrees I can do that right here. I don't need to bring you out to the state forest like I did for them. You don't mind if I spend the next few hours lying around in here, watching TV and stuff with you guys, while I'm being a cat do you?"

Patrick was getting a little concerned, mainly because no one else was acting like she was crazy. Why not humor her, since that's what everyone else was doing. "Sure, sure. No problem. Be a cat if you want. I won't mind."

"Actually, I have to warn you. Prepare you. So, you won't get nervous. You know those pictures in my bedroom? The mountain lion pictures? That's me. Mom took those. I'm a werecat."

Patrick suddenly realized she was being serious and that everyone else was going right along with this. Seriously!

Missy stood up and so did his mother and Heather, who suddenly were holding up a blanket. Missy said, "I have to get naked now, so I can Change. You understand. Okay?" She walked over and stood behind the blanket.

Patrick could see she was taking off her clothes but only her head was showing above the blanket. He looked at his dad and John but they were just calmly sitting there like this was no big deal. "Isn't anyone else going to say anything?"

John said, "Missy's a werecat, Patrick. It's in our genes, so you really need to know this. That's why she disappeared for those two years. She stayed in the mountains until she figured out how to Change back. She's been Shifting back and forth ever since, but we haven't been letting her out of her room when she does that at home. Until now." Looking at Missy and laughing, he said, "Okay, Missy. You can stay out here tonight. No more hiding out in your room as long as you promise to be good."

His dad got up and said, with a big sigh, "I better go get those raw steaks out for her. You know how hungry she gets whenever she does this." Chuckling, he walked into the kitchen.

Patrick looked over at Missy who seemed to have finished undressing. She smiled at him and said, "I'll be back in a *flash!*" Then, she ducked down and for a few seconds, nothing happened. Suddenly, there actually was a flash, a great shimmer of light behind the blanket and he could feel a mysterious burst of energy in the room. Heather pulled the blanket away and there stood his sister. Missy the werecat.

From the Author

Thank you for reading *Missy the Werecat*, my first book about Missy. I hope you enjoy reading about Missy and her friends as much as I enjoy writing about her. I've always loved stories about female characters with special powers along with stories about witches and werewolves. Future books in this series are planned and can be found using any internet search.

I hope you will consider leaving a review for *Missy the Werecat* on whichever website you used to download my book, letting others know what you think about this book and this series. Word-of-mouth is crucial for any author to succeed. Your kind words, even if only a line or two, will help others decide to read about Missy and inspire me to keep this series going for many more books. That would make all the difference and be hugely appreciated. Thanks in advance!

To be notified when P. G. Allison's next novel is released, go to: http://eepurl.com/bCtlh5 and sign up for the Missy the Werecat Newsletter. Your email address will never be shared and you may unsubscribe at any time.

Made in the USA
Las Vegas, NV
05 July 2023